THE LIFEBLOOD OF ILL-FATED WOMEN

THE LIFEBLOOD OF ILL-FATED WOMEN

Kevin James Breaux

ISBN-13: 9781537260457
ISBN-10: 1537260456
Library of Congress Control Number: 2016918266
CreateSpace Independent Publishing Platform
North Charleston, South Carolina

Editor: Gretchen Stelter of Cogitate Studios

Cover Artwork: *Soufiane Idrassi*

Cover Design: Kevin James Breaux

This book is dedicated to all the gamers out there.

Gretchen,
Thank you for challenging me to let go and not hold back with my
writing.

CHAPTER 1

812 AD, Scandinavia

"ASTRID, YOU MUST WAKE."

The young woman ignored the softly spoken command and rolled to her side, the crackle of the dry hay beneath her louder than her sister's hushed voice.

"Now, you lazy cow!" Astrid's sister spit, shoving her with both hands.

"What is it, Yrsa?" Astrid peeked with one eye out of the wolf furs she was wrapped snugly in.

"We're being attacked!"

Astrid's ears were suddenly overwhelmed with noise, a rush of sound that moved like the cold water that swelled the rivers that flanked the city of Birka. Dire combat could be heard from all sides of the small, stone home. The clang of swords and axes vibrated across her skin, while the screams of her kinsmen echoed, making her stomach feel hollow.

Astrid tore the wolf furs from her tall, naked body. She jumped to her feet, but panic gripped her when she gazed down at the empty beds of her sibling's two children.

"Where are the others, Yrsa, the young ones?" Astrid's mouth grew drier with each syllable.

Yrsa, her only sister, cracked the door just enough to peer out. A gust of wind blew in, scattering Yrsa's straggly, blonde hair across her face. The smell of burnt wood laid atop the cool damp air, so strong both women could taste it.

"Father ordered us all to the fortress. We must go now." Yrsa gazed back at the empty beds. "Gyrd took the little ones and left me to rouse you, the hibernating bear."

Astrid moved once she heard that her niece and nephew were safe in the hands of Yrsa's husband, a seaside guard. A trained soldier herself, she dashed to her armor where it hung on its old, wooden stand.

"Your husband moves too slow," Astrid said, repeating a statement she had made many times in the past. "He'll need my help."

"Bite your tongue! There's no time for your ego."

Astrid found her arm suddenly restrained by her sister's trembling fingers.

"We must go now, Sister." Yrsa's words were punctuated by the sound of something slamming against the roof.

Astrid pounded her chest above the hang of her full breasts, her long blade and wooden shield, both beloved heirlooms, held tight in her hands. "Then I will fight naked like my ancestors' ancestors," she boasted proudly. "Father's blood in my veins, Thor's strength in my limbs, and Odin's blessing on my soul are all I need."

"Here." Yrsa handed Astrid a long cloak. "Gyrd will be glad to see you draped in his favorite bearskin, instead of unclad for all the children to gawk at."

Although she suspected it would hamper her ability to fight, Astrid donned the heavy fur.

"Ready?"

Astrid gave her sister a nod, and Yrsa swung the heavy wooden door open.

"Death to the enemies of Birka!" Astrid let loose as she launched herself out into the town over a pair of dead bodies like a deer vaulting over a felled tree. As loud as her scream was, it was overwhelmed by the hiss and crackle of flames. Birka, her home, the city she loved, burned all around her.

"Astrid, to the fortress!" Yrsa tried her best to scream over the sounds of battle.

"I will be right behind you, Yrsa."

Astrid felt the shifting wind as it caressed the tops of her shoulders but not her back. *There must be someone behind me. Only a sellsword, thief, or assassin would sneak in from behind in hope of a quick kill, cowards one and all.*

Astrid turned, expecting, wanting to find her first opponent. *Whoever dares to challenge me today will go to the afterlife knowing the families of Birka are not so easily defeated.* Shield up, Astrid swung her long sword, yet her blade found no target.

"Do not run from me. Come out and fight, coward!"

Astrid crept forward, her eyes panning the town. Smoke and fire filled her vision. She spotted a man whose legs had been severed at the knee. When she looked closer, she realized the back of his head was caved in and charred black, still sizzling with white vapor. Sadly, the man was not alone; he was holding hands with a boy, most likely his son, who was nearly hidden in the shadows of their damaged home. Blood spilled from a gaping wound that resembled a large claw in the boy's back. The sight made her shiver.

Astrid heard her sister call out again but could not see her through the fog. Sensing movement, she jerked her gaze back to the man. She could have sworn she saw his arm twitch.

"Yrsa! Where are you?"

As she warily turned from the man, a jolt from the ground made her lose her balance and threw dirt into her eyes. She drew in a deep breath and blinked…and her eyes opened onto a new scene, a world awash in the brightest golden light she had ever seen, a light so powerful everything else was eclipsed by it. Unable to move or even feel the ground beneath her feet, she panicked.

What's happening to me? I need to go. I need to fight. I need to protect my sister, my family, my city.

But she was suddenly filled with a potent sense of peace, and her heart and thoughts slowed. *I must be dead; this light the great golden hall of the gods: Valhalla.*

Astrid exhaled slowly, closed her eyes, and accepted her fate.

Nothing was left.

CHAPTER 2

Astrid's eyes fluttered open, and she took in the clear night sky, a black canvas sparkling with bright white diamonds. The world was calm and quiet—it felt wrong. The recent violence flashed through her mind and she saw dying men—hundreds, maybe thousands of them—all reaching and calling to her for help. Every nerve in her body screamed to flee; her reflexes told her to seek shelter, yet her body did not move. She looked down her body and saw she was lying in a deep cradle of fresh snow.

As Astrid sat up, she felt the weight of her thick armor trying to shove her back down. *I am clad for combat—but how...*

Her eyes took in the wolf-skin leg wrappings she wore and where they ended at her thighs and her bare flesh began. Soft snow had crept under the pleats of her heavy, leather skirt and numbed her mound. Astrid scooped a handful of snow from between her legs and raised the quickly melting powder to her face, so she could examine its color— pure white, no blood. She breathed a sigh of relief; her fears of being raped after bested in combat were quickly put to rest. Astrid sifted the snow through her fingers—she saw no sign of urine either. *I haven't been lying in the snow for very long...*

"What happened?" Astrid said to herself.

She rose to her knees and brushed the snow off her bare arms while she examined her surroundings. Nothing was familiar—not a tree or hill on the horizon. There was only pale snow as far as she could see.

Astrid stood slowly and found her legs as strong as ever. "The mightiest of oaks carry my daughter from plunder to plunder," Astrid's father always boasted. His hearty voice echoed in her mind, pulling at the corners of her mouth until a smile formed.

"Was the battle all a dream? Or was it you, Father? Another test?" Astrid yelled into the darkness. "Did you see me drunk before you abandoned me here in the wilds? Has your daughter not proven herself to you time and time again?"

Her father's voice did not answer; instead, the shrill howls of a pair of wolves replied. The two large, grey wolves snarled as they cut a path toward her.

Instinctively, Astrid reached for her longbow, yet her fingers found only splintered wood and a limp, lifeless twine. This may have panicked someone else, but not her. Astrid had fought wolves up close before, armed with only sticks and rocks; all members of her family had.

"So be it."

At her waist hung a long, two-handed sword she called Ugla, and in her right boot was a silver dagger, but it was the largest weapon, strapped to her back, she intended to use. Right hand over her left shoulder, Astrid untied her battle-axe.

The weapon's weight swung it free of its harness and down to her side as she watched the wolves approach; the smaller of the two would attack first, she guessed—a dire mistake for him.

Astrid took a defensive stance and waited for the beast to lunge, the three-foot battle-axe hefted in both of her hands. Frothy slobber spilled from the wolf's mouth as it snapped at the air between them. *The beast is touched, diseased.* She could see it now; the marks of mange were much clearer at this distance. Rabid or not, the wolf roused her blood no more than sparring with her sister's husband.

When it finally lunged, Astrid sidestepped it and positioned herself to drop the axe on the animal before it landed.

Crunch.

The sound of the wolf's spine being severed was both wet and dry—the brittle *snap* of bone, the moist *thunk* of meat and gore.

Astrid cheered as she withdrew her bloodied axe. *Too easy.* When the other wolf growled, she growled back, her teeth bared as fiercely as the beast's. The wolf immediately cowered, submissive. Astrid advanced, slamming a hand into her breastplate, and shouted, "Face me! Face Astrid the White!"

The wolf circled her twice, never removing its eyes from the tall warrior woman. At the start of its third turn, it dashed off, following the tracks it had made when it had approached moments before.

"Great Allfather, I pray this test was for the wolf and not me," Astrid called to Odin in Asgard.

As she slowed her breath, she took her first long, careful look around. The murky night had stolen away any details. *Where am I?* she wondered. *Which direction is home?*

Axe returned to her back, Astrid thought about the fire. *Birka must have been razed. Could that be what happened? Was I laid wounded upon a dead cart and rolled from the town?*

The thought stirred her blood more than the attacking wolves had. Had she been on top of the pile, she could have slipped off and fell to the snow without a sound, left to die in the cold. A good enough explanation, even if the thought enraged her. Yet, as Astrid gazed at her long limbs, she found no wounds.

The bright light. What was it? Was I burned? Could I be so eager to serve the gods that I mistook the flames that surrounded me for the golden glimmer of Valhalla? Wait…I was not dressed to fight. Who… She paused to consider the possibilities. *I thought I was dead. Others must have thought I was dead too. It's the only fitting answer…one of my siblings found me, and must have dressed me for the pyre.*

Again, Astrid looked at her arms and legs. What bare flesh there was, was unmarked by fire. Her mind was full of questions, but she quieted them. Her father always taught that a good warrior did not allow her weak mind to overcome her strong body. These mysteries would have to wait until after she found her way home.

Tilting her head up, to look the stars, Astrid felt her long braids slide down her back; wet and cold, they weighed the same as thick ropes. *I should ask Yrsa to trim my hair before it ends up as long as hers.* Astrid's concerns shifted to her sister, unarmed when they had left the house, a mere milkmaid not known for her skill with any weapon. *Yrsa...* A tremor ran down Astrid's body when she thought of her name. *I failed you, Sister, and now you're no doubt dead...or worse.*

"Yrsa, I pray your death was quick and noble." Astrid forced a smile. "I pray you find peace in Freyja's meadow."

With her eyes shut tight, Astrid held back her tears. When she reopened them, her only thought was of vengeance.

The stars were bright in the sky, there was not a cloud to disguise their design, yet they appeared misaligned. Astrid traced constellations with her eyes until she found what she was looking for: the North Star.

The dark that lay north of her position held many possibilities. Her father had trained her extensively in map reading. Astrid knew that north of Birka stood the frozen wastelands, a stretch of desolate territory that went on and on, seemingly with no end, but no man in her lands had ever ventured far enough to create a map. Such a trip would be deadly if one attempted it unprepared for the deep winter snow and Hel's icy grip.

To travel far south of Birka meant to cross paths with dozens of small, poverty—and disease-stricken villages. Rumored to have suffered the plague for a dozen or more years, there was no end to what horrors would be found.

Astrid's sense of ambivalence gave way to one of frustration, and deep concern for her family crawled back into her heart. When a tremble of remorse ran through her chest, Astrid stomped in anger.

"No!"

She yanked the dagger hidden in her boot free, drew a shallow line across the meat of her forearm, and let the blood dribble down her elbow and onto the stark white snow.

"Gods, I call upon you with a gift of blood, an offering to protect the blood of my kin. See that the young ones are safe, and I promise to present to you more blood, that of our mutual enemies."

A brisk wind blew through the valley, and Astrid knew it was her gods' acknowledgment. She also felt that the answer to what direction she should travel was but one more offer away.

Astrid trudged back through the deep snow to the wolf carcass several feet behind her, grabbed the wolf's tail, and lifted the beast from the ground until its nose was the only thing that remained in the powder. She cut through the thin bone with her sharp dagger, and with a thud, the carcass fell to the ground.

"I welcome your wind, my gods. Now I beg of you: clear this haze and reveal to me the direction of my fate."

With the tail pinched between her index finger and thumb, Astrid raised her hand high above her head. Instantly, the wind whipped it about, and Astrid released it, the current carrying it several feet before dropping it to the snow.

"So be it. I shall travel south."

CHAPTER 3

ASTRID WALKED FOR FOUR LONG days before the snow cleared and wet, green grass replaced it under her boots. Her eyes blurred from fatigue, she did not realize she had wandered into a field of wildflowers. When the stem of one of the larger plants snapped under foot, Astrid stopped and forced her eyes to open wider. Beneath her was a large patch of Reinrose. *Never have I seen such an abundance of them; it's so beautiful. And now… It's too early for these to bloom.*

Two years ago, days before her twentieth birthday, Astrid had marched a longer trek than this, her brothers at her side. They had sung, joked, and jeered, without so much as a groan or moan. It was during that trip that Astrid's brothers had showed her another side of their father's teachings about the mind and body: the advantages of a strong willpower. From that moment on, when Astrid's body told her to stop, to complain, to give up, she thought, *Lift, step, lift, step. March on. March on.*

Now, her eyes and shoulders forward, Astrid had not looked up from the ground in ages. Her mind and body were in total conflict; hunger had bested nearly all that she had learned. Her stomach growled, a reminder to eat the last small chunk of wolf meat she had. Astrid patted her stomach over the thick armor. The hollow sound the metal made when struck by her thick leather glove made her frown. It seemed she had grown skinnier in the past days, her breastplate looser now than ever.

She shuffled forward another few feet, her teeth gritted. The voice inside her head mocked her again. She had repressed it for much of the day, but it would not go unheard any longer. *This is not the direction of Birka. This is not the direction of Birka. This is not the direction—*

An unfamiliar voice rang out to her left. Her eyes suddenly heavy—nearly impossible to lift—but still she looked. A tall, middle-aged man adorned in peasant garb waved as he led a fat cow out of the dense forest. Astrid sized him up and quickly noticed his lack of metal armor, furs, and visible weapons.

He was calling out to her in a language she was unfamiliar with. Astrid sneered at its twang and jittery sound as she tried to decipher it.

The man's handsome face wore a smile that was so large it made her uneasy. She never felt comfortable under the steady gaze of men outside her family; a smile always seemed to lead to a lustful remark or advance, and each of her brother's friends had suffered a black eye or broken rib at one point as a result.

As she watched him, the smiling man called out to a shorter portly man, who jogged up to his side and immediately began to speak in the same language.

Astrid did not move. She simply watched them. When the smiling man took two steps forward, her combat training overcame all else. In no time, she had examined his every detail for weakness. *His stance, strong and steady, does not match his overly friendly expressions. His muscles, large and well-sculpted, they belong to a man who has swung a heavy sword, not a shovel. He is no farmer.* After another few steps forward, the smiling man spoke again.

"Stop," she commanded in a voice so deep and stern it made both of the men's seem girlish.

She withdrew her sword, and both men raised their hands, palms out; they were unarmed. His hands up, the closest man continued to speak. Astrid marveled at the flash of his pearlescent teeth; men where she came from rarely had a mouthful, let alone ones so bright. She could not break her focus from his smile… He meant to hurt her—she could sense it, but unless he had more friends hidden in the forest, she knew he would not take her so easily.

"Do you seek a fight, odd man?"

The smiling man peered over his shoulder; the portly one shook his head in response. Astrid assumed it was some sort of signal between the two—a clash was imminent. "I have faced the Stone Giants of Halostadt and the Dwarven Iron Raiders of the Endless Isles in daylong combat. I have hunted and killed the Great Red Wolf of the Black Forest. You two and your cow are no match for me!" Astrid shouted.

The taller man hushed the shorter one before he knelt slowly. He picked up a small, broken branch, deliberately turned it over, and pressed its tip into the muddy ground.

Astrid followed the man's motions with the tip of her sword, the lines forming symbols, but then suddenly blurring and overlapping. Astrid's eyelids felt like they were weighted with anvils, and the sword in her hand grew heavier with each shallow breath.

What's wrong with me? I have never suffered as such before, not even as a child. The meat... she thought. *Was the wolf I killed so greatly diseased that its meat was tainted?*

Astrid blinked and realized she had let go of her weapon, that it was lying in the mud beside her. Bending to retrieve it, the downward motion of her head could not be stopped. Tumbling to the ground with a heavy, moist thud, Astrid's world went pitch-black.

CHAPTER 4

WARREN AND HIS YOUNGER BROTHER, Hammond, stood in silence a moment. Neither man wanted to move, and neither was sure how to proceed. After studying the way the woman dressed, Warren was only sure of one thing—she was ready for combat. *Barbarians have not been seen in our region for many years. I should know...*

"H-her voice... So strong. It carries her stern language well. Have you encountered its kind before in your travels, Warren?" Hammond asked.

"There must be several dozen different barbarian languages, Brother. You don't seriously expect me to remember them all, do you?"

"Well, what do you think happened to her?" Hammond asked.

"She looks ill. Hurry, run back to my farm. Retrieve my mule and wagon."

"To move her? You plan to bring her back to your home? Are you mad, Warren?"

"Look at her, Hammond. She's unwell. She needs our help."

"Sure, then. If she wasn't quite the beauty, maybe covered in boils and missing teeth—oh, like old Miss Miller—would you still be so quick to help?"

"Hush and do as I ask."

"Right, right."

After Hammond dashed back through the forest, toward town, Warren knelt at the warrior woman's side. Hammond was, in part, right. She was even more beautiful than Warren had allowed himself to realize.

Her face was free of scars, her nose straight. He placed a hand on her skin; it was surprisingly hot to the touch. On the inside of her left arm were faded marks from old wounds and a fresh bruise. Near her wrist, there were signs of a callus. *Produced by the straps of a shield,* he thought with a quick peek at his own arm, where he had similar marks.

"Let us see what all you have stashed."

It had been seven years since he had stepped foot on a battlefield, but it felt like a mere week suddenly. He knew that, just because she had collapsed, it did not mean she was no longer a combatant, and although he meant her no harm, he could not say for sure the sentiment was mutual.

Warren turned his gaze from the old leather band that wrapped around her forehead and kept the broken strands of her long hair out of her eyes, to the thick fur boots she wore. The shiny handle of a large dagger sparkled in the sun.

"Well…" After he carefully pulled it free of the sheath tied tightly to her calf, he tossed the blade to the side, near her sword. "Do not worry. I will see your weapons cleaned and carefully stowed. If you are a soldier, like I was, I know their importance to you."

His attention shifted to her armor. He had seen female barbarians before, even faced women on the battlefield, yet none wore such heavy plate. With his knuckles, Warren tapped it gently. Polished to a bright shine, a spiral design weaved up and around the armor corset and circled the two large cups her breasts filled. *Distracting,* he thought, unable to take his eyes off it even after he told himself to.

"Thankfully, I never faced an opponent with your armor," Warren whispered to her as she lay unconscious.

Back on his feet, he gazed at the tall, exotic warrior head to toe. Her cloak, which was split down the back so that her battle-axe could be reached, splayed out to the sides like the large, brown wings of an eagle. The sight, Warren thought, was oddly angelic.

"Who are you? Where did you come from?"

Moments later, Hammond returned with the mule cart. He seemed more anxious now than when he'd left, and Warren thought he knew why.

"You told Helen, didn't you, Brother?"

"She asked me if we found your cow. I may have let slip that my older brother found a new set of teats to milk."

"Your vile humor is wasted on me."

"It was wasted on her too. Regardless, Helen doesn't want me to touch any strange women."

"Have you told her about Anabel yet?"

Hammond chuckled as he dismounted the mule cart. "Look who jokes now," he stated.

"Well, if Anabel is a joke, then many of the men in our town have told it."

Hammond thumped his brother's arm with his fist, a clear signal he was done being teased. "Bastard."

"Help me lift her up." Warren pointed to Astrid, who had not stirred the entire time. "I'll take her shoulders. Her top looks much heavier than her bottom."

"You think I am not strong enough to lift your woman?"

"Yes."

Hammond laughed. "Perhaps we should arm wrestle later today. Winner gets a boot of ale."

Warren grunted and grumbled through his clenched teeth as he lifted. "Be sure to bring enough coin. I'm very thirsty."

Hammond did, in fact, strain to get the woman's legs up and into the cart. "Look, we best move," He said over the creak and moan of the old wood of the cart. "The wheels are sinking! Lords, she's much heavier than she appears, Warren."

"It's her plate armor—very thick and quite the fine craftsmanship."

"Her armor? That old thing? Are you sure?" Hammond motioned to her belt. "Perhaps those pouches are full of gold coin."

"I doubt it. Anyway, that pouch there." Warren pointed to the leather bag on her right side. "See the bloodstain? That one holds raw meat."

"Ah, at least that explains the smell."

CHAPTER 5

ASTRID DREAMED OF HER FAMILY. Her father was the most important man in her life, and for the past twenty-two years, she had loved and worshiped him like a god. She had seen him at his best, fearless against two dozen men on the battlefield, like Týr himself, and at his worst, humbled at the bedside of her mother as she died.

The youngest of his children, Astrid was unmarried. With more adeptness in combat than farming or household chores, she fit in well with her four brothers—at times, they even called her their fifth brother. Ulf, Vignir, Hak, Jokul: the sons of Kol, the Ruler of Birka.

Astrid dreamed of a day they had all spent together, a great deer hunt in the dense forest outside of Birka. It had been a contest to see who could provide the most meat for the town, and Astrid was determined to win. She had already felled her third deer, a large buck that would make a great trophy, when her youngest brother, Jokul, had marched to her spot in the forest with a deer over his shoulders. Without a word, her brother dropped the dead animal into her pile. With a smirk, he withdrew the arrow he had fired into the deer's neck, snapped it in two, and tossed its pieces into the thick brush.

Astrid had asked Jokul to explain himself, but he ignored her. Her brother had simply walked past her, grabbed one of her arrows from her half-full quiver, and returned to her pile of kills. He plunged her arrow into the deer he had killed, marking it as hers.

"Why?" she had asked.

"You deserve this, Sister," he replied, as he combed dry leaves from his waist-long, blonde hair. "You deserve this."

CHAPTER 6

ASTRID AWOKE FEELING AS WELL rested as she ever had. The scent of freshly baked bread reached her nose before her eyes opened, making her mouth water. *Yrsa has outdone herself; her baked goods never smell this delicious.*

Astrid peeled one eye open to spy on her sibling's children, a habit that formed when she had first moved into Yrsa's home. The wee ones were always up to some sort of naughtiness.

But on this day, Astrid realized she was not in Birka at all. Wherever she was—a modest family home by the looks of it—was built unlike the steadfast stone homes in Birka. This dwelling, smaller than her sister's, was built of old wooden logs with a large, fireless stone hearth in the center.

Astrid could hear the rustle of animals outside: cows mooing, hogs snorted—this was a farm. She knew that much.

As Astrid rolled off the small hay bed, she finally realized what she was wearing: not leather, not fur, but something else, something soft. It was wrapped around her from breast to groin. White as the snow she had walked for days in, the garment did not fit her right. Tight and short, its length barely covered her fine, sandy curls nestled beneath it.

She pinched the fabric between her thumb and index finger. *Soft.* This wrap, whatever it was made of, was so smooth it tickled her flesh as she moved. *This fabric—Yrsa would love it. Yrsa...* Astrid groaned—her heart ached like it was being crushed between two stones. *I must get back home...*

The sound of footsteps alerted her to possible danger, and she dropped into a crouch, her muscles taut, ready to be harnessed.

The rickety door of the home opened with a loud creak as the smiling man stepped in. Astrid dashed across the small room and was upon the man before he knew it, slamming him against the now-closed door with such might that pots, jars, and plates spilled to the floor, their clatter so loud, she was sure anyone else nearby must have heard. Yet there was no response from the man save for the huff of breath that escaped him.

Astrid's left forearm pressed into his neck as her right hand held him against the door. Only an inch or so shorter than the smiling man, she figured she was his equal in strength.

"Who are you? Where am I?" Astrid shouted, her entire body on fire, burning for a fight. "Answer me now, and I will give you a moment to pray to your gods before I crush your throat."

The man coughed, then replied softly, though it wouldn't have mattered, as it was only gibberish to her. Astrid had heard many threats in her life, and just as many times, her ears had welcomed the voices of her defeated opponents as they pleaded for mercy. This man's expression read as neither a confrontation nor surrender. Astrid pressed her forehead to his, an act that pinned his head back to the door. His clothing was soft, like what she wore. Around his waist was a belt, but no weapons were attached to it.

"You dare to confront me unarmed, jailer?" she growled in his face still pressed forehead to forehead.

The man responded, and as he did, Astrid's ears filled with a deep buzz. She winced and shook her head. Suddenly, she realized the man, who had been drowned out by the noise in her head, had spoken words that made sense.

"…please listen to me…"

"What?" Astrid said, brow furrowed, unable to fathom why she now understood this odd man's language.

"I am not your enemy."

Her warrior's intuition told her it was over; she had won, regardless of there being no bloodshed. She sensed herself calming, but her will to fight was bottomless. Astrid took a small step back, easing away from the smiling man, but before she moved farther away, she shoved him hard into the door again. The look in his eyes—*there it is.* Astrid saw it; she had finally agitated him. *Now what? Now will you fight?* she wondered.

"I spent the entire morning in search of a woman in town who matched your build...one who would have clothing that fit you proper, and this is how you treat me?" Warren rubbed his sore neck.

"B-build?"

"Wait, what did you just say?"

Astrid was sure, by the way his mouth moved, that he did not speak in her tongue—and, although she understood him now, she did not know how or why.

Maybe the sickness that plagued me has affected my memory, my thoughts, my ability to speak...

"Do you understand me?"

Astrid nodded and frowned. She found little comfort in this new ability.

"I...mostly...understand." Astrid concentrated on each word. This language would require much patience.

"Good then," he answered as he brushed his tightly cropped hair back with his hand. "I brought you gifts. You understand...gifts?"

The man reached for a pile of clothing he had dropped when she attacked him. Astrid wanted him to know she still paid close attention to his every move, so she stomped her foot hard on the floor the moment his hands wrapped around the garments.

Startled, he yelled out. "What?"

Astrid shrugged.

"Fine." He lifted the clothing.

"Fine."

"Right. Well, you are wearing my wife's bed dress, bless her departed soul. Seeing it on you reminds me of happier days." His ever-present smile shined bright. "It was all I had. Clearly, it doesn't fit you, such a… tall and strong lass."

"Lass?" Astrid did not know this word.

"Girl. Woman." The smiling man pointed at her. "You."

"My name is Astrid."

"Forgive me, Astrid, but we need to cover you up. I can see your… I can see more than I should." Warren's observation trailed off as his eyes drank her in.

Astrid saw his gaze turn lustful, but with his hands full of clothing and no weapons on his belt, he posed no immediate threat. Lust or violence in his eyes, it mattered little; she was taught to show him no weakness. Although he appeared brawny, with arms and legs that displayed large muscles, she was sure she could best him in a fight. She was strong and fast; she had fought and beaten many a man twice his size with just her fists. Yet the more she looked at him, the more she began to think there would be no confrontation with him at all.

Odd, I sense a great deal of kindness in you, smiling man. Your eyes tell a mysterious story—one I wish I had time to indulge myself with, but I don't. Astrid's gaze turned to the door. *I must get home.*

"You are not keeping me here?"

"Keeping you here? No. I mean you no harm. I only wanted to help you."

Astrid relaxed a bit more. "And you have brought me better garments?"

"Yes, I have."

"Better than these useless, soft, farmer's clothes, I hope. They are far too thin and would do nothing to protect one in a fight."

"I found what I could."

Astrid gripped the dress she wore by the bottom and yanked it over her head, making Warren jump and raise his hands in defense. She reached for the clothes the smiling man carried, but he did not readily give them to her, so she yanked them free of his grip.

"You should know, Astrid, my brother's wife dressed you. I did not touch you," he said as he spun around on his heels to give her privacy.

No opponent has ever turned their backs to me, not unless they were fleeing. She smiled as she thought it. *Such an action shows further weakness— or perhaps—*it occurred to Astrid—*could this man be a slave, property treated no better than livestock, castrated by his owner, the true man behind my capture?*

Counting the numerous ties on the dress as she tied them, she lost her patience, snatched the fur rug from the middle of the room, wrapped it around her body, and pushed by him and out the door.

"No, wait!"

Astrid found a troublesome sight outside. She was on a farm, as she'd guessed, but it was not the only one. The smiling man's home sat in a scattered collection of houses, and as far as she could see, a series of farms stretched through the land. Green grass, yellow wheat, pink hogs—she even spotted what looked like a patch of purple flowers. Such color was almost overwhelming. To the south was a low hill and several dozen more homes.

A town, but which one? Astrid thought of her maps. *No villages south of Birka are this large or developed.*

Upon first glance, Astrid assumed there must have been a hundred small log cabins there, two small stables, a well-sized mill, and two large granaries. This place had been established many years ago—not only was it obvious by the place's size, but also by the moss and ivy that grew on the roofs of many of the homes.

"Where am I?"

She thought back to a time when she was much younger and her father and brothers had taken a long journey aboard her father's largest longboat. The destination was a farming village like this one; unprotected and unprepared, it had been ripe for plunder. *This is impossible.* Astrid began to breathe heavily. *I cannot be there again.*

"Please, would you come back inside?" the man begged.

"That trip was long," she whispered to herself. "This is not that place. It just cannot be."

"Astrid, do you hear me?"

The way she looked at the man must have worried him, as he nervously moved side to side. *I understand your words, strange man. It's everything else that makes little sense to me.* With no desire to respond, Astrid stared at the town as she gathered her thoughts.

A loud noise in the distance grabbed her attention, but not long enough that she missed the man retreating back into his home.

"Wait," she called out. *I need my arms and armor. I need to get home.*

The smiling man returned a moment later carrying bread.

"My brother's wife, Helen, made bread early this morning." He broke off a piece and placed it in his mouth. "Food."

Astrid nodded at him. The bread looked good.

"Please, come sit with me and eat." He pointed to a table and pair of benches that sat a few feet away, under a tall tree.

Astrid snatched the rest of the loaf of bread from his hands. "I'm starved."

"Well, Helen's going to be thrilled someone likes her bread. I've always found it a little dry to be honest, eaten better on march actually, but I do not complain," he stated.

Astrid proceeded to devour the bread as she walked, only pausing to nod briefly. It was the most delicious bread she had ever tasted. No enemy of hers had ever fed her so well. Perhaps, she thought, these people were her allies.

"Birka," she announced hopefully. "You know of it, right?"

"Birka?" he repeated.

"My home."

"I can't say I know of the place."

"Everyone knows of Birka." Astrid slammed her bread filled fist into her chest as she again proclaimed her homeland.

"Please, sit."

Astrid stared intently at the smiling man as he guided her to the bench and waited for her to sit. *What odd custom is this,* she thought, *that a man will not sit first to dine.* After she was seated, he sat down across from her and pushed a metal goblet across the table. Astrid did not drink; instead, she nibbled on the bread gripped tightly in her hands, filled with suspicion.

"I need to get home to Birka. I need to know which direction to travel from here."

"Birka… Why does that name hold a distant familiarity?" Warren pondered as he drank. "I cannot recall where your home is. However, a trip to our elder council, once you are properly attired, should aid us."

Astrid shook her head with frustration. "Mead?" she asked, with a peek into the goblet.

"Ha!" He laughed. "Any soldier would understand that one."

There was that word again; she smirked when he spoke it. Soldiers were fighters, and Astrid understood fighting. *If he is a soldier—a warrior—then why is he dressed so and not armed? Armies have soldiers*, she thought. *Did an army attack Birka? Was that army from here?*

After he dashed in and out of his home again, the man poured a new mug full of drink for her.

"Ale," he declared.

Astrid gave him a faint smile before she introduced herself again. "Astrid."

"Warren." He smiled. "Now we understand each other."

"Aye."

When Warren took his mug in hand, she mirrored him, and raised hers at an equal pace. Looking over the rim of the metal, she waited for him to drink first before she opened her lips.

"Good?" Warren asked before another, much longer drink.

"You are a warrior, Warren?"

"Hmm? No, I *was* a soldier. I tend a farm now."

"You are no farmer." Astrid stood, her elbows tucked in to hold up the fur rug she had wrapped around her body.

Astrid watched as Warren lost his pleasant look, and it was replaced with one of deep concern. She had seen that look on an opponent's face before. *Will the truth finally be revealed? Will you fight me now?*

Warren stood up slowly and said, "What's wrong, Astrid?"

"Was it your army that laid siege to Birka? Was it you who took my weapons and my armor?" Astrid slammed her mug down on the wooden table, its contents splashing over the rim. "Did you kill my sister, my family?"

"Easy. I thought we understood each other."

"You are a soldier. I am a warrior. Soldiers and warriors fight. Capturers and captives fight. Understand, he-goat?"

"No!" he shouted. "No fighting! If your home was attacked, I am truly sorry, but I had nothing to do with that. *We* had nothing to do with that."

"Do not lie to me."

"You were sick and needed rest, Astrid. I wanted to help you. I *want* to help you. Now, please, sit down and eat your meal."

When Astrid did not comply, the man's face turned red and the veins in his thick neck protruded. "Listen to me: sit down! Do not force me to knock you down!"

Astrid had learned long ago that there was honesty in anger. Birka men spoke their thoughts and took what they wanted—there was no place in their lives for lies or trickery. Her father taught that an assassin's blade could be easily draped in kindness and smiles.

This man's tone might have been aggressive, but she trusted him more now.

Only an ally would turn away from so many challenges.

"Know this, Warren"—Astrid nodded slightly—"I do not fear you. Why should I? All you have succeeded in is earning my patience...for now."

Once again content to eat the tasty bread and drink the sour ale, she sat.

"Fine." Warren exhaled the breath he had been holding.

Some time passed in silence. Astrid enjoyed the view, if nothing else. She could see for miles: homes, farms, trees, a forest, children at play, livestock milling about. It all seemed so peaceful. Awash in contentedness, Astrid allowed her concerns for her family and her arms and armor to fade a bit.

In the clear blue sky, she saw the moon; its appearance during the day was a good omen to her people. The gods were happy. Perhaps, she considered, Birka repelled its invaders; the gods had always showed her home their favor in the past.

"Possibly we can be friends?" Warren asked.

Astrid ignored him, her eyes on a pair of goats eating grass near-by. *A goat would make a perfect gift to the gods. A perfect symbol of my thanks.* It was settled; she would slaughter one of Warren's goats and offer up its blood and horns to Odin.

Finished with her meal, she stood back up, slowly this time, so as to not worry her companion.

"You really need to get dressed, Astrid. There are children about, not to mention men who would get an earful from their wives if they saw you free of clothes."

"Where is my armor?"

"I cleaned it and your weapons. They are stowed safely inside. You may have them when you are ready."

His words relaxed her further. Head tilted back, she identified the north, then the east, the south, and finally the west, but what she did not find were the snow-capped mountains that stretched high above the clouds.

Her eyes frantically searched for the holy mountain. This place had just begun to feel comfortable, and now she felt sick to her stomach; she suddenly feared she knew exactly where she was. The elders of her home spoke of a land like this, one where Asgard was missing, and that place was called Helheim.

"Helgafjell."

"What?" Warren replied.

"The mountain."

"Mountains? They are east of here." He pointed. "Many weeks' journey."

"Where have they gone?" Astrid pointed to the sky. "Where?"

"Oh, right, I understand. Well, the region around the town of Grømstad is a deep gully; we cannot see the mountains from here. A little under a week's march north or east, and you will see them begin to crest over the horizon."

"No." She shook her head repeatedly. "This is all wrong."

Astrid began to feel light-headed. Something was amiss inside her, but before she could identify it, she blacked out and crumpled to the ground like a rag doll.

"Astrid?"

"What…" She trailed off as she opened her eyes.

Warren scooped up her head and lifted her gently onto his lap while he searched through her thick, greasy, blonde hair in search of wounds.

"Astrid, are you well?" he asked as the muscles in her neck strained to turn her head.

"What happened to me?"

She looked into the sky, at the brightness of the sun. In Birka, the sun rarely peeked from behind the clouds this time of year, and throughout the other months, when it was plentiful, its warmth was still no greater than the chill of the Ice Mountains. *Where is this place?*

"Astrid, I fear you are still weak from your travels. The meat you carried, it smelled rancid. I pray you did not eat it unprepared."

"A little."

"I think you should return to bed," Warren stated with a grimace. "More rest will do you well."

Astrid pushed her body to its limits just to stand, she did not enjoy being cradled in this strange man's lap like a baby. "Rest…in your bed?" she asked.

"Yes, in my bed, but I will sleep elsewhere. Consider all that is mine to be yours until you are well."

That smell—what is it? Warren raised his hands to his face and sniffed his fingers.

"You gave me your clothes—"

"Not mine. My wife's."

Whatever the stench was had transferred itself from the woman's hair to his fingertips, and it reeked of death and was as sour as rancid milk. Warren's smile vanished when he inhaled it again.

"You gave me your food, now your bed, and I did not even need to raise my weapon."

"No, Astrid, you did not, but you do not require steel in your hands to be dangerous. Am I right?"

She nodded and bowed deeply, a motion that caused her long braids to fall around to her chest. "By the looks of you people, I could conquer this town barefisted. Do not forget this."

With a sigh, Warren nodded. He meant her beauty was a weapon, but she had taken his comment in a different way. Even now, as she flexed her muscles and was wrapped in the old rug, he could not help but be drawn to curves of her body. She could have any man she wanted, even a king.

"Do yourself a favor and rest today. I promise to take you to the elders tonight."

"That…that would be acceptable."

"One other thing." Unsure how Astrid would respond, Warren carefully considered his next statement; he did not want to ruin the progress he had made. "I need you to bathe."

Astrid's response to his remark was to tilt her nose down to her shoulder and inhale deeply. After a slow stroll to the entrance to his home, Astrid replied, "We shall see," over her shoulder.

CHAPTER 7

WITH HER ARMOR ON AND her weapons at her side, Astrid rested more soundly. She even succumbed to sleep for a bit between tired glances around the empty house. In some ways, Astrid found her ability to drift off so easily there troublesome. She had not had much luck in the past when she tried to sleep away from the safety of home, especially on raids.

Later that evening, Astrid stretched as her senses came alive. The room was dark, but she had taken a visual survey of it before she had closed her eyes, and there were no changes. Everything was where it was earlier, even the footprints that smeared the dust and dirt on the floor. No one had come near her while she rested; the thought brought her the most comfort she had had all day.

Astrid knew there was no one inside the small house, and as best as she could tell, there were no guards anywhere near its perimeter. To be sure though, she listened for a sign of soldiers posted at the door, but the loudest sounds she discovered were the hoot of an owl and the chirps and buzzes of nocturnal insects unfamiliar to her.

This land, it is much more alive than my home, where all that is heard at night is the howl of Njord's winds and the cry of hungry wolves. Even the livestock hold their voices at night in Birka, to stay hidden from the cold, cruel gods. Here, everything seems so different. As she listened, she swore the night held a tune. *This place, it hums.*

Footfalls interrupted the melody of the night, and before she knew it, there was a knock on the door.

"Warren, ho, it's me."

Hammond opened the door slowly as he called out louder, "I came to make sure you're still breathing, Brother. Where have you been all day?"

Before Hammond's eyes could adjust to the dimly lit room, he was struck squarely on the nose. He stumbled backward, tripped over his feet, and fell to the ground several feet from his brother's door.

"Blessed fury!" he screamed, his right hand gingerly pinching his nose. "What was that for?"

He tried to look for his brother, but a flood of tears made him barely able to distinguish shapes. Through the threshold, there was movement, a body leaner than his brother. Hammond's heart sank. It was the warrior woman.

Astrid massaged the knuckles of her right hand as she stared down at the man she had just struck.

"Father of the old gods, you broke my nose," he said.

"Consider yourself lucky I decided to repel you with my fist instead of my steel. Had I drawn my sword first, your hands would be filled with your own guts."

Astrid spotted Warren as he ran up a path from the center of town to his home.

"Astrid, ho, please stop!" He waved his hands in the air.

"She broke my nose." Hammond held out his hands to display the copious amounts of blood coating them.

"You know this sad, little man, Warren?" Astrid called out.

"Yes, stand down."

"The thief attempted to enter your home—"

"He's no thief. He's my brother."

"Does he live here with you?" she asked.

"No."

"One man cannot enter another man's household without the head of the family present, brother or not."

"What?" Warren shook his head at Astrid before he knelt beside his brother. "Are you okay, Hammond?"

"Broke my nose."

"Let me see the damage."

"The head of the house must be home to invite another man in. Our laws, Warren, they are very simple."

"We are not governed by the same laws here, Astrid."

"You broke my nose." Hammond spit blood onto the grass.

Warren's recoil gave away the severity of the damage—his brother's nose was clearly broken, as it now sat crooked on his wide face.

"What did you strike him with, a cudgel?"

"My fist."

"Truly?"

Astrid showed Warren the redness on her knuckles.

Warren chuckled. "All those years growing up, fist-fighting, neither of us ever broke the other's nose."

"Perhaps you were not making a proper fist," Astrid replied, withdrawing her hand from Warren's.

"Can you help me up?" Hammond interrupted. "Great, now I will not be able to smell anything for a month."

Warren clasped his brother's forearm in his hand, and with a quick tug, Hammond was back on his feet.

"In a day or two, you will boast how you no longer suffer the scent of stale ale and rancid piss in the tavern."

"No," Hammond replied, "Helen plans to make a rabbit and potato stew tomorrow, and you know—"

"How awful it smells?" Warren interrupted.

"Yes, and now I will not have to pinch my nose with each swallow."

Astrid looked back and forth between the two men as they shared a chuckle. Their relationship was not unlike the relationship her brothers had and their interaction made her miss her family all the more.

"I only wanted to make sure she had not killed you," Hammond explained as he pointed at Astrid.

"I nearly killed *you*," Astrid interjected.

"See? I told you she is dangerous!"

Astrid could smell the alcohol on Warren's brother's breath as he spoke. "Well drunk, are you?"

"Ah, so you rushed right over after a few rounds, that right?" Warren teased.

"A good thing too or this might *really* hurt."

"Go. The healers will straighten your nose. They will wash you up and pack that bloody mess with herbs. You will no doubt feel worse in the morning, but regardless, you will live."

"Very well. I guess I will need some of that special grog you have been storing, Brother...to help me sleep tonight."

"Yes, I bet you will." Warren sighed, then pointed to a key that hung off a nail on the wall just inside his door. "You know where it is. Take what you need and get going."

Astrid watched Hammond, key in hand, rush off around the back of Warren's home and disappear into the darkness. Once he was gone, she spoke.

"I must apologize to you, Warren. I did not recognize your brother before I struck him, and for that I am sorry. It is a sad day when one's brothers are gone." Astrid held her breath a moment and eased her nerves before she continued. "I would not want to take yours from you."

"Thank you," Warren replied. "But what would you have done differently if you had recognized him?"

"Nothing."

CHAPTER 8

WARREN DREW IN A DEEP breath and exhaled slowly.

Is it the light breeze on this clear night that makes me shiver? Or is it the woman at my side that gives me the chills? Astrid acts more civilized now, but how long will that last? Her mood, like my brother's dealings, I wager cannot always be trusted.

"My brother is a lucky man."

"Oh?"

Astrid had been staring off into the night sky.

Does she enjoy the night as I do, or does she simply seek to read the stars—search for the direction of the mountains like she did earlier in the day? Warren could not tell.

"He's a merchant, and well, I always say, if his lingering eyes don't get him killed, the slippery tongue in his mouth will." Warren smiled. "You know, you might have done his family a favor. With his nose broken he might spend more time at home."

Warren finally allowed himself to take a long look at Astrid; she was dressed for combat. Now that Warren had cleaned up her weapons, he knew their sum. Five daggers, in various sizes and shapes, were strapped to and hidden inside her attire. At her back she wore a battle-axe. Strapped to her side was a long sword, by far the most impressive weapon in her possession. It was clear to Warren, when he had polished it earlier, that this was a family weapon, one that, like her armor, spoke of her status and lineage. Wherever she came from, she was highly respected.

"I see you have all your possessions."

"Thank you for taking such fine care of my arms and armor."

"No problem at all." Warren smiled, happy to hear both an apology and a thank you in the last few moments. "The elders await us. We should be going."

His head bowed slightly, Warren pointed in the direction they needed to go and paused for her to go first. Unfamiliar with his gallantry, Astrid simply stood her ground.

"Warren!" his brother shouted from the darkness of his fields.

"Heavens above, now what?" Warren sighed.

When Warren saw the warrior woman whip her head around and lower her stance, the annoyance at his brother's shout transformed into a cold lump in his throat. It had been a while since he felt such a strong sense of dread and watching Astrid's hands move to the hilt of her long sword only made it worse.

"Trouble," she whispered.

"Warren!" Hammond yelled. "Thieves! Thieves!"

"Thieves," Warren shook his head as he grumbled. "The scum keep raiding our supply cellars—"

Before his sentence was finished, Astrid was off.

"Wait!" he shouted, but she did not listen.

The sound of Hammond's screams led them both behind Warren's house. At the edge of the fence, where Warren penned in his cows, stood six armed bandits—Hammond was cornered. Four other men dashed off into the darkness, away from the small tree that sat above Warren's hidden storage cellar. Satchels full of stolen pots and jars, and arms filled with stolen food supplies, the men rattled as they fled.

"Halt!" Astrid commanded as she drew her sword.

"Look at 'er, all big and dressed to play," one of the bandits said to the leader, a man who stood tall and skinny with a pair of thin swords pointed at Hammond.

"Just when I thought we found the last of the treasures here, boys, look at this golden goddess." The leader pointed one of his swords at her.

Warren stepped up beside Astrid, surprised to see that the bandits had not scuttled off yet; in all the reports and rumors of thievery, the culprits had never once been seen by the guards.

"Careful, Astrid," Warren warned.

"The husband comes unarmed, yet his wife is ready for the fray. I told you boys, this hamlet is full of cowards and weaklings."

"Run, Hammond! Find the guards! Now!" Warren shouted.

"No!" the leader of the bandits yelled. "None of you are leaving this spot alive."

"Brave words for a dead man," Astrid spit.

The mouthy bandit stepped forward and squealed with excitement. "Let me kill 'er. I never stabbed a woman before."

"Very well, make it quick. There's much more work to be done tonight." The boss lowered his swords.

"Come, try and pierce me with your blade, little man." Astrid pounded the hand gripping her sword against her armor-plated chest as she spoke. "Astrid the White, daughter of Kol, fears no man."

The bandit's eyes gleamed. Astrid determined the man had killed before when she sized up his attack stance, but the way he held his weapons suggested he lacked skill. When he chuckled and lunged in with a pair of dirks, he missed her entirely. Astrid had quickly sidestepped and parried both blades with her sword.

He wants to kill me so badly he's telling his moves—a fatal mistake. Astrid tightened her two-handed grip on her sword as she stepped back with her right foot.

"Gonna spill your pretty blood!"

The bandit lunged again, his movement a mere flash of metal. Astrid took several steps back as he pressed forward, to plunge both his weapons into her belly.

Clang! Thump!

Astrid flinched when she heard the impact—a wet thud as the little man's left arm fell to the ground. Stunned by the loss of his limb, the bandit froze a moment and in that split second, Astrid detached the man's head from his body with a swing of her large sword.

"Hartwig!" one of the other bandits yelled as he watched his friend die.

"For Hartwig, kill them all!"

Astrid squared up and challenged her next opponent. She felt her battle-axe being lifted from her back harness, and spun her head to see Warren with the weapon in his hands.

"I need to borrow your axe, Astrid."

She nodded as the bandit leader gave orders to his men and stepped back—an act of cowardice so obvious to Astrid, it made her want to kill him even more.

"I'll see you dead!" she shouted to the bandit leader.

As one bandit approached Astrid with sword and wooden shield, another with a long spear stood back and jabbed at her stomach with the tip of his weapon.

His spear is crudely made and will not pierce my armor, but it could puncture my skin if the bandit were smart enough to poke at my bare thighs.

More threatened by the spearman than the man with the sword—who swung it as if it was the first night he had used it—she changed her target. Astrid unsheathed a dagger, feigned a strike with her sword, and shoved her weight into the swordsman's shield. The swordsman stumbled backward long enough for her to lift and aim her dagger at the bandit with the spear. Astrid watched the moonlight flicker off the blade as the heavy dagger sailed through the night sky to its mark.

"Wench, you missed me!" the bandit with the sword and shield yelled.

Did I? Astrid replied with a gesture of her sword at the man's feet where his partner lay. The spearman pawed wildly at his throat—gurgled and groaned in panic-filled pain.

"Wendel! You bloody killed Wendel!" the other man cried as he stared down at his friend.

Astrid's sword slid easily into the swordsman's ribcage as he lowered his shield in shock. With a twist of the handle, the bandit's ribs cracked, the vibration dancing up her weapon. Now, eye to eye with her enemy, Astrid pushed the sword deeper before finally withdrawing it.

Leaping over the bodies of the two men in search of new opponents, she saw two of the three remaining fought Warren while the other, the leader, stood back and watched.

"Fight me." Astrid commanded the leader as she approached him.

"No, my beautiful warrior, not tonight, but I promise you very soon."

Behind her, she heard the familiar sound of her axe cleaving bone. Warren had dispatched one of the bandits and was about to finish the other.

"Karl, flee now!" the leader yelled, backing further away from Astrid.

His focus split, the bandit stumbled when he turned to run, a misfortune that awarded Warren ample time to change his attack. He dropped the weapon down on the thief, the sharp blade slicing him open from shoulder to leg. Nearly cut in two, the bandit's blood sprayed in every direction, a fine mist coating Warren from head to toe.

"Are you hurt, Astrid?" Warren asked as he approached her.

"Not at all." Astrid grunted with frustration.

"What's wrong then?"

"If my bow were not broken, I would place an arrow in that coward's spine."

"Don't worry. With his men killed, he'll flee into the forests never to be seen again."

Astrid finally peeled her eyes from the bandit who was just now being swallowed by the darkness. "Were you hurt? Where did your brother disappear to?"

"I'm fine." Warren smiled. "Did you not see my brother slip off during the fight?"

"I *saw* you nearly cleave a man in two. My brothers would be proud. They have a long-running wager on who will cut a man in half first."

Warren raised an eyebrow in response.

"Tyr would be proud of you, Warren. You wear the blood of your enemies and have not shed a drop of your own. Tonight we should celebrate with ale and song."

"Ale and song, you say?"

Warren sounded apprehensive. Astrid asked, "Don't you celebrate battles won here?"

"Astrid, the guards will be here soon. They will have many questions for both of us. Not only that, but—"

"Why would they waste their time on words when they should be hunting the bandit who escaped?"

"As I said, no petty thief would return now, not after witnessing his friends dead at the end of our steel."

Astrid smiled. *Warren sounds more like my brothers now,* she thought, *perhaps he's not all that bad…*

"At any rate, I wonder, Warren…where are your guard towers? I did not see them today."

"Grømstad has no towers."

As she cleaned her sword with a swatch of fabric she had cut off the spearmen's leg, she continued, "No towers, and no army, but you have a sizeable force of guards, right? How many?"

"Thirty men, but we are a day's fast ride from the kingdom that governs us. They can have their fastest cavalry here in half that time."

Astrid retrieved and cleaned her dagger. "Thirty men. No towers. No fortress." Astrid could not help herself. Her mind had already begun to catalogue it all and she was sure she and her brothers could best this place in a nighttime assault. The plan would be simple; *Jokul and I would burn the fields and then launch flaming arrows into the center of town at the larger structures. Hak and Ulf would assault the barracks first, kill the guards while they slept. Vignir would steal one of their horses and ride the perimeter, and kill any soldiers that went to douse the fires. Such easy prey,* she thought. There was just one thing absent.

This place, where is its wealth. What secret treasures lay hidden here? She smiled. *Vignir would have known. It was his job to gather such knowledge.*

Astrid's smile quickly faded. *I pray...I truly hope with all my heart that my brothers are still alive.*

"We have a stronghold," Warren added when Astrid went silent.

"Oh, a stronghold?" Astrid repeated with raised eyebrows. "Where is that? What does it keep?"

"To be honest—"

They heard Warren's brother and several guards in the distance. Hammond's voice, loud and clear, was easy to discern as he repeated a grandiose tale of how his nose was broken during a conflict with one of the bandits.

"Well, at least now I don't owe him any grog."

"His lies will not find favor in the afterlife."

"Afterlife? No, I fear my brother does not think that far ahead," Warren replied. "Regardless, what were you getting at, Astrid? Why are you so interested in Grømstad's defenses?"

"I fear your nice, little farming town is ripe for plunder."

"That's foolishness!" Warren exclaimed. "With the exception of a few bandits, our lands are safe. I fought in the last wars. We expelled the barbarians from the greater north and those who invaded from the southern seas. Our king has allied himself with the lands of the west and north. We are at peace."

"Peace," Astrid huffed. "What have these thieves been stealing from you?"

"For the past few months, mostly foodstuff, water, furs..." Warren's voice fell off. "Supplies."

"Supplies."

Astrid watched Warren's blank face turn to one of deep concern and realization.

"You...you don't think—"

"That out there, in the dimness of the forest sits an army of bandits waiting to strike? No, that would be foolishness," she said sarcastically.

"Ho there! What happened here?" the largest of the five guards asked as he approached. His shoulders heaved between laborious breaths. "We have reports of bandits not just here but on the opposite end of town as well."

Of the five men in heavy leather armor, only the lead guard did not stare at Astrid. Being the oldest of the group, he seemed more focused on the gore. *At least the senior guard is doing his job. At least he is concerned with what happened here.*

"Who are you?" the youngest guard interrupted her thoughts.

"I've never seen her before," a second guard added, his face flustered, and covered with a grin that spread from ear to ear.

Astrid, who stood tall, could look over their cone-shaped helmets—this town, she would call it the home of smiling dwarf-men when she returned to Birka.

"I am Astrid, daughter of—"

"She's my guest. I was just about to escort her to the elder council when we came upon these thieves," Warren interrupted.

The lead guard took in the splatters of blood that coated her forearms and legs, and pooled in the seams of her thick plate armor.

"You fought? You did this?" He pointed at one of the felled bandits.

"I killed these three."

"Did you? Warren, might I speak with you privately?" The senior guard took Warren by the arm and led him a few steps away.

"What is it, Gathon?"

Warren's voice was full of exasperation. *Is this one of his superiors?* Astrid wondered. *Has Warren broken orders?* When Gathon scratched his thick, grey beard roughly, it reminded Astrid of her brother Ulf. Ulf only scratched like that when he was in deep contemplation.

"Warren, who is she? She looks like those barbarian raiders we fought some dozen or more years ago. Do you recall those first battles after you joined my division?"

"Yes, Gathon, I recall all my fights and I agree, she holds a certain resemblance, but the armor and arms are all wrong. When I cleaned them, I examined them closely. The way they are constructed, they seem—"

"Guard master, you said there were other bandits?" Astrid interrupted.

"On the opposite side of town. They tried to pilfer one of the granaries."

Astrid turned her eyes to Warren who nodded. She knew she was right.

"I have a suspicion that these raids may be to support a larger force… a rogue army that gathers and prepares to attack," Warren offered.

Gathon laughed.

"Why would a group of miserable marauders attack us?"

"Why not?" Warren asked.

"You know as well as I do these kinds of bandits do not band together in groups larger than twenty or so."

"Then perhaps these are not bandits at all," Astrid stated.

With a deep breath and a solemn gaze at both Warren and Astrid, Gathon continued, "You said you had dealings with the elders. I suggest you go take care of that now. Leave the bandit problem to me, Warren. Remember, you are no longer enlisted."

"Gathon, don't be petty."

"When you are done with the elders perhaps you will come to the barracks and explain where you got that battle-axe. You know the laws state no citizen can own a two-handed weapon."

"Who are you to say what—" Astrid began, but she was interrupted by Warren.

"He's right, Astrid, we should go now. Let us seek out your answers."

CHAPTER 9

THE TOWN HALL WAS THE largest building in Grømstad, and stood over two stories high with a steeple-like peak that stretched past a third. Its construction, like the other homes of Grømstad, was entirely of wood, yet sturdy enough to survive a crudely-built siege engine. Seated at the center of town, yet recessed from the main path where the shops and merchants stood, the town hall was lit up with many torches and candles. Now Astrid knew what it was that glowed like a collection of campfires from the distance of Warren's home.

Warren escorted her inside the building but told her to holdfast in the vestibule while he entered the main chambers to announce their arrival. Astrid stood still. She may not have liked being told what to do, or so closely watched by the four town guardsmen that surrounded her—their judgmental eyes a match to frowned faces—but she forced herself to stay calm and silent. In Birka, it was against the law to speak when in the company of honored elders unless spoken to first, and she preferred not to disgrace herself in the eyes of the gods, as she knew they no doubt watched her after such a glorious victory.

When Astrid crossed her arms over her chest, she noted the lack of chill on her breastplate. *It is late winter; it should be colder and the sun should have fully set already. This is all wrong.*

Even the water that Warren brought her from the stream earlier was, at best, mildly cold. Astrid sighed, *I've never found unheated water to be so… so pleasant to wash with.*

When I return to Birka, I will tell everyone of this place, yet perhaps not for plunder—for possible occupation. Worse places could be called home.

"Astrid?" Warren beckoned her from the doorway to the inner chamber. "They are ready to speak with you."

The room the elder council sat in was much darker than the entryway, and two tall candelabra flanked the double doors to the room to fight the shadows. With her first step inside, Astrid could sense she was under the careful scrutiny of the elders.

"Hold there," one of the guards ordered. "Hold or relinquish your weapons."

The flicker of light masked the elders. At times it was hard for Astrid to tell if there were three or four of them. The way the light danced made the room feel as if it swayed side to side like a longboat. The sensation, sans the crisp ocean air, nearly made her ill, so she closed her eyes to clear her vision.

"Please tell us your name, shieldmaiden," a raspy old voice requested from the shadows.

"Yes, your name," another dry voice entreated.

"I am Astrid the White, daughter of Kol."

"Kol," the dry voice mimicked hers.

She squinted and tried to deduce who spoke, but all she could see were robed figures in the deepest black shadows.

"Warren tells us you came from another land. What is your home called?"

"My home is the fortress city of Birka," Astrid stated, full of pride.

"Birka," the dry voice again repeated her answer. "Birka."

"I am acquainted with this name." A new, sharp voice emerged from the darkness.

"You know of Birka? Tell me, was it razed? Does the great, dark, stone keep still stand?"

"Too long ago…too long ago," the sharp-voiced male said.

"Too long ago?" Astrid replied, not sure what the elder meant.

"We have come to the conclusion that the city of Birka cannot be your home, shieldmaiden."

"Birka *is* my home. My father is—"

"Birka belongs to the dead," the sharp voice firmly stated.

"What?" Astrid had feared this. "No."

"Its ruins are twice covered in moss and ivy. This is how it has been since long before I was born," the sharp voice said. "I know this as fact, as my family and I are from those lands."

"I was there no more than eight, maybe ten days ago. We were invaded." Astrid shook as she swallowed her pride and said, "I fought yet was quickly injured. When I woke I was in the snowfields north of here. Tell them, Warren, I walked here—"

"All wrong."

Astrid could not catch her breath. *Their words make no sense. Birka cannot be in ruins.* Astrid turned to Warren for support, but he kept his eyes forward on the elders.

"Child, you could not have walked here from the ruined city of Birka."

It was an old woman's voice and it surprised her. In her home, such an honor as town elder had never been bestowed upon a woman; it was against the law. Only a royal woman could speak as equal to the men, and Birka's queen was long dead.

"Then perhaps I was carted here."

"No, no, child. Birka is not here. The city you speak of belongs to another mass of land, one my brother and I were born on while our parents traveled."

With a sudden flurry of motion, the female elder clapped, a gesture that made an attendant spring into action. The young servant boy rushed to the long table that separated Astrid from the remainder of the room. Once there the young boy laid out two scrolled maps and pinned them to the table with palm-sized stones.

"Gaze upon these maps, Astrid the White." It was the first elder's aged voice again. "Will you aid her in reading these, Warren?"

Warren nodded slightly at the map. Only moments ago, he had stared at Astrid while she was engaged with the elder council, and even before that he had fought to keep his eyes off her. Warren did not want to reveal his desire for her to the elders, as they would surely disagree. *No...not enough time has passed*, he told himself. *My wife and child, I should mourn their loss longer, not set my sights on a new woman.*

Astrid examined the map closely, and as she did, Warren could see her hands begin to shake.

"This is the most detailed map I have ever laid eyes upon, yet the shapes do not match what I know." Her voice quivered. "What am I looking at?"

"You are in Grømstad." Warren placed a smaller stone that sat on the table over the drawing.

"Where—"

"Here are the lands of Agdar, in the southernmost tip of Noregr," Warren quickly interrupted. He circled with his index finger.

"Agdar be praised."

"My blood for Agdar."

The two nearest guards spoke out their axiom, one after the other.

"This cannot be," Astrid whispered. "I cannot be here. How—"

"How did you reach our lands? By sea—"

"I did not travel the sea," Astrid interrupted the elder.

"We are not in the practice of accepting lies, shieldmaiden."

"Remember, she is our guest," the sharp-voiced male reminded.

A long silence fell upon the room, and all Astrid could hear was her own breathing. It was fast, matching the steady pounding of her heart. She stared at the map hoping something would make sense to her, but nothing changed her initial conclusion. *This is all wrong.*

"All that matters is that you are here now," the first elder replied in his raspy voice.

"Yes, here now."

"Should you decide to stay, to make this your home, come see us again, child," the elder woman added.

"Do you have any further questions for us, Astrid the White?"

Bewildered by it all, Astrid did not answer at first; she could only continue to stare at the strange shapes on the map. With a nudge, Warren prompted her response.

"I...h-have none."

"Then you may be excused."

"My elders, may I stay? I have another concern I wish to bring forward," Warren quickly added.

Only raspy whispers could be heard, like the rattle of dry Autumn leaves.

Finally, the elder woman replied, "Your concerns over the bandit attack are as fresh as the blood that stains your clothes, Warren. Yes, you may share them."

"Thank you."

Warren pressed his palm against the small of her back, and Astrid looked at his face.

"Come, Astrid, let me walk you out."

"Warren—"

"Please, you need to leave now."

Astrid held her composure a moment longer as she marched out of the town hall.

"Wait for me here...and try not to get into any fights, understood?"

After Warren walked away, Astrid's stomach flipped.

All wrong. Lies, all lies. Lies fashioned by Birka's enemies. Astrid rapidly returned to her original assumption. *I must have been captured during the invasion,* her blood heated as she thought, *and now my father's rivals hope to get secrets from me with an elaborate deception.*

Over her shoulder, she counted only two guards, the ones that stood watch outside the town hall door.

"Dirty liars."

She imagined attacking them. She would use her sword, a sweeping blow against the right man's leg to fell him into his partner on the left. This would allow her to slice her sword across the second man's face before he could even withdraw his weapon.

So easy, she thought, *no guards in Birka would dare keep their weapons sheathed while on duty.*

Hand on the hilt of her long sword, Astrid followed her own footprints back to the two guards; she would make an example of these men before she fled to the forest.

The young men's eyes had been attached to the swing of her hips since she'd left the building moments ago, and Astrid accentuated her movements to keep him occupied.

Apparently in this land, these parts of my body are effective enough distractions, she thought—and combined with the sword in her hand, they were lethal.

"Astrid!" Warren's voice boomed as he exited the town hall. "Do not boast of the fine craftsmanship of your sword with these men. They will no doubt wish to seize it from you."

"Our laws do not allow citizens to carry two-handed weapons."

"She's my guest."

"So you say." One guard shook his head in disapproval.

"Understood," the young guard answered. "The very fact why we did not disarm her earlier."

"Disarm me?" Astrid snarled. "Disarm me? You dare—"

"Come now, Astrid, we should go."

Warren grasped the inside of her arm and tugged at her so hard, she had no choice but to turn on her bootheels and shuffle in the direction he was pulling her. Astrid's rage burned—it told her to fight, but her newfound respect for Warren cooled her emotions briefly.

"Where are you taking me now?"

"Home. It's late and the guards are already suspicious enough."

"So, you wish to imprison me longer, when I only desire to return to *my home.* You may be larger than most of the men here, Warren, but I can still best you—"

Stopping suddenly, Warren grumbled, "I thought you understood the elders. I thought you understood their maps."

"Their maps are meaningless!"

"What?" He shook his head.

Astrid yanked her arm free—the words and anger caged inside her swelling up.

"This. Is. All. Lies." Astrid lunged forward at Warren with each syllable—she snapped like a snake—and her long braids, like that of its tail, rattled.

"What are you saying, woman? Have you gone mad?" Warren tried to hush her.

"Your elders, their maps, this town…" Astrid walked a circle around Warren as she went on. "Even your pretty smile. All lies."

"Did you fall and hit your head when I went back inside to speak? Are you still sick from that rancid meat you ate? Tell me there's a reason for the madness that slides from your tongue."

"My tongue? Yours is the slippery one!"

"Me? What? You frustrate me, woman."

"Did my father repel your invasion, is that it? Do the spires still stand tall like gods above you, the walls as thick as Odin's skin?"

"Astrid, I don't understand."

She gazed deep into Warren's eyes and spoke the truth that weighed heavily on her heart. "My father will not pay a ransom. He would rather see his daughter fight her way out of his enemies' clutches…or die trying."

To Astrid's surprise, her comment did not produce anger, only a heavy sigh from Warren.

"You truly believe this all to be lies?"

"Yes. Lies crafted so well the Trickster himself would be proud."

"Fine," Warren said with a stunned look on his face.

Astrid sheathed her sword with such force it clanged loudly. "Fine," she repeated.

"Tomorrow we leave town and together we will march north."

Astrid mirrored Warren's former look of shock. *Is this yet another sly deception?*

"Why would you wish to join me on such a long journey?"

"For the simple reason that I want to see your face the moment you realize I am not a liar."

"Very well. Tomorrow we march."

CHAPTER 10

ASTRID WAITED FOR THE SUN to rise. She had sat outside the door of the smiling man's house for most of the night, her mind full of questions. *Why have I not killed him? Why not escape, run to the forest the moment he went to sleep?*

Astrid watched the sun as it peeked over the distant trees. Her home, the mountains—even at a month's march south, she would have been able to see them. *Where is this place?* she asked herself for the thousandth time since she sat down the night before. Once more she considered the unfavorable thought that she was no longer on Midgard.

Perhaps I am dead; perhaps this is Helheim. No, that cannot be. Odin would never punish a loyal warrior to live in a realm as oddly quaint as this one.

"Morn, Astrid. Would you like some bread?" Warren asked as he approached.

"Bread would be good."

"You sound different today, Astrid. Are you feeling well?" Warren asked.

"Well enough to best any man here in a fight."

Warren laughed. "There's your fire."

Astrid did not notice how long Warren had been gone, her attention still on the sun as it rose, but when he returned, it was with a heavy sack that clanged and rattled as he placed it on the ground at her feet.

"I stored this."

Astrid knew the sound of arms and armor. With the slender dagger she hid in her boot in hand, she sliced the rope that bound the sack until its contents spilled out.

"This is all my gear from my many years of soldiering."

Astrid lifted up the chest plate, her gaze on the two crisscrossed cuts that scored the stomach.

"Either your armor is stronger than it feels or your enemies' weapons were dull."

"Barbarians," Warren chuckled. "Dull weapons. Both of those were done with spears."

"Stone?"

"Yes."

"Pathetic."

Astrid retrieved his small, round, iron shield next, its weight and craftsmanship clearly evident. "Warren, your shield is quite impressive." Astrid ran her fingertips over the nail heads.

"It protected me for many years. I owe it my life."

"Only our leaders carry shields made with metal plates."

"Mine is made of solid iron. It was awarded to me after a long battle."

"Such a thing should be paid better respect, Warren," Astrid said crossly. "A warrior's shield such as this should be hung upon the wall with the rest of your war trophies, not cast aside to rust."

"I have never kept war trophies."

"What?" Astrid's mind went blank with shock. "Bring the shield with you. Perhaps I will keep it as a trophy when we reach Birka."

"If we reach Birka, it is yours."

"Good then, it is settled."

Astrid opened her arms to Warren and quickly wrapped them around him in a firm hug. Released before he could embrace her back, Warren looked stunned, so she followed her hug with a light tap to his arm and a smirk.

"Very well." Warren nodded. "Let me dress in my armor while you eat. Afterwards, we will set off."

"Agreed. We should not waste another moment of this clear day."

"Today *is* a beautiful one," Warren said as he gazed up at the sky.

"Another oddly warm day for winter," Astrid commented, curious at the height of the sun in the sky.

"Winter has passed here, Astrid. My lands are blessed with an early spring," he answered as he drug his equipment bag off.

"Too early..."

"Oh, I will bring my bow with us too. This way I can prove myself as a first-rate hunter."

Astrid suddenly remembered the days her sister was being pursued—*an odd time for such a vivid memory,* yet when the image of Gyrd bringing Yrsa a pair of rabbits he had killed entered her mind, she understood what the thought was borne of. Although he lacked Warren's finesse, Gyrd's actions during his attempt to win her sister held a similarity, and like Warren, Gyrd made himself available for her sister's every need.

Such a dangerous pastime, courting a daughter of Kol, Astrid thought. *Gyrd was lucky my father showed him leniency and still awarded him Yrsa. Perhaps that is why father calls him Gyrd the Brave.*

"Astrid?" Warren called from inside.

"Aye?"

"Did you own a helmet?"

"I did."

Astrid hated that she had lost her helmet, though at the same time, she had never enjoyed wearing it. The way it often slipped over her eyes angered her and put her at risk during a fight. Astrid brushed the broken strands of blonde hair that floated into her face up and over her head and grumbled. *Without Yrsa, how will I ever re-braid my hair?*

"I detest helmets. They ruin my hair. There are more bald soldiers in our army than I can count. I am glad I left the service before I lost my hair," Warren joked.

Astrid shook her head. She wanted to feel superior to the smiling man, to think her concerns outweighed his, yet in this topic they were in agreement.

"I hate helmets too."

Moments later, Warren stepped outside, fully suited for the journey. Adorned in his chest plate and plated shin and armguards, he looked like a warrior, yet this was not the attire of a man who fought in the cold climates, like the soldiers of Birka. Regardless, Astrid saw Warren differently. He was quiet pleasing to the eye, especially now that he was dressed for combat. Astrid could not remember a time she had owned such a thought about a man. As she stared, in attempt to make sense of her thoughts, Warren strapped his shield to his left arm. When his muscles flexed and turned rock hard, she felt herself suddenly overcome with warmth.

"All set?"

"I…" Astrid paused to set her mind straight. "No, you will need furs. The temperature drops much lower where we are going."

"I wager the snow you woke in several days ago has already melted. The air grows warmer with each breath we take. Don't you feel it? Summer is on its way."

"Summer," she said with a puff of air through her front teeth. "You speak of it so grandly."

"Some of my favorite memories are of the summer. Do you not like the summer, Astrid?"

"I'd rather not talk about it."

Astrid no longer wished to talk to him like they were friends. She may not have seen him as a true enemy, but she was not ready to call him a proper ally either. *This smiling handsome man,* she thought, *would he still want to help me if I told him the story of the last summer I enjoyed.*

"Hail, Astrid, have you seen these people's leader?" her brother Hak called out as he flicked the blood from his thick-bladed long sword.

Astrid watched the arrow she fired find its mark in the throat of a watchtower archer before she answered, "No."

Schhwaff. Thunk.

An arrow pierced the dusty, red dirt at the mining settlement's entrance where Astrid stood, drawing Hak's full attention.

"By Thor's Hammer, Astrid, you were nearly hit. Have you nay moved since we began this assault?"

"I thought it would be a bold challenge to stand still," Astrid said after she launched another arrow into the bright sky.

Hak watched as it hit the last watchtower guard in the chest, the man knocked over the wall by its force. Hak's gaze followed the man as he fell to his death.

"I will need to know the number of arrows that could have killed you, Astrid, in order to praise your courage properly in song when we return home."

"I have not counted."

Hak turned to look at the arrows cluttered on the ground at his sister's feet. "They missed you twelve times?"

"Thirteen. One arrow struck the side of my armor and all but shattered. These things might as well be made of green reed and seashells. They are no match for Birka iron."

"Indeed!" Hak cheered. "You should see the weapons these miners carry, nothing more than sticks and stones."

After Astrid returned her bow to its place at her back, she pulled her sword free of its scabbard.

"Where are the others?"

"Ulf and Vignir cleared the settlement's interior as planned." Hak pointed.

"As planned. The sons of Kol do not follow the plans of other men. Tell me why we heed the commands of Delk and his brothers again?"

"As a favor to Father."

They walked away from the main gate, toward the closest watchtower, as they spoke.

"Such a long journey, to such a faraway place, it seems dangerous to leave Father for so long."

"He's safe, Astrid. Yrsa will keep him from trouble." Hak waved to one of the men in Delk's force, who was pulling the boots off a dead guardsman.

"The time for looting has yet to be called! Check the perimeter, full around."

"Who say?" the man yelled back.

"Hak, son of Kol."

"Kol? Oh-oh, aye. Fine."

Hak shook his head in frustration as Astrid approached one of the first men she had shot off the watchtowers. He was younger than her and wore little armor past a leather chest piece and a helmet made of hide and bone.

Such an odd place—its people so small, their skin so dark.

The boy lay still, but in the shivering movements of his eyes, Astrid could tell he was still alive.

"He yet lives?" Hak asked.

Astrid quickly positioned her two-handed long sword and, with a loud grunt, plunged it into the belly of the young man.

"No, he's dead."

"My mistake," Hak answered as he looked away from the boy to the river, where their longboats where anchored.

"Yrsa will fill his belly until it bursts."

"What?"

"Father," Astrid grunted. "Yrsa overfeeds him when we are gone."

Hak laughed loudly, his entire body quaked with amusement.

"You worry too much, Sister. Remember wrong begets wrong."

Astrid turned sideways, raised her sword, and tightened her grasp.

"Raise arms, Brother. Looks like your boot thief found more combat for us."

From the trees rushed at least ten men. They appeared to be no more than farmers, covered in rags and dirt.

"Too bad Jokul is not here with us, aye, Astrid?"

"I like the odds as they are." Astrid smirked. "Fight well, Brother."

"Die brave, Sister."

Astrid lunged into the mass, her long sword swinging from shoulder to waist, halting two of her attackers before they could reach her. She had only a heartbeat to look into their eyes, but she saw it—the glimmer from their souls as it exited their body on the way to the afterlife.

She squared off and deflected the blows of the next two men —one with a crude wooden mallet and the other a wooden pitchfork. When Astrid parried the mallet, the man who swung it fell to his hands and knees behind her.

"Get up!"

Astrid wanted to scream at the bite of the pitchfork in her thigh, not from pain but from embarrassment, yet to do so in front of her brother Hak would be shameful. Instead, she grunted and dashed forward so that the pitchfork—wielding man would not have enough space to strike her again. At this distance, she could use her body as a weapon instead of sword. She slammed her elbow into the farmer's gut, doubling him over as her leg rose up. The impact of her knee shattered the man's jaw and his teeth sprayed out like a gambler's dice. The man's weapon dropped to the ground as he staggered backward. Astrid did not wait for him to recover, she plunged her sword forward, directly through her opponent with a loud growl.

"Leave me some!" Jokul rushed from the shade of the thick forest, his hands fumbling at his sword belt.

"Leave you some? Have you ever left me any?" Hak replied, while he severed the arm from a man who held a crude hammer.

"Aye, these farmers make the prettiest dark-haired daughters. There's a whole load of women in the passageway under the—"

"Under?" Astrid deflected a spear strike. The last of the farmers were better armed than the first.

"Aye, you should see the splendor these dirt farmers hide in their tunnels."

A horn sounded from the opposite direction, from within the crude wooden walls. It was Ulf's horn—they all knew its sound. Their eldest brother was announcing the battle was won and the time to loot had come.

"You think Ulf found their leader?"

"I did," Jokul laughed as he sidestepped an attack and then plunged his two swords into this enemy's back.

"You, Jokul?"

"Caught him trying to slip out after we slipped in, Sister. What, you thought I abandoned you for the short, stout women of this town?"

"You have chased things far less pink and much more hairy."

Hak laughed, and when he did, his foe landed a lucky blow with his mace.

"Hak?" Astrid called out, not sure if he was hurt.

"This cold stone hits as hard as Ulf's knuckles when we fight for jest."

"Then you must be fine," Jokul laughed. "Astrid hits harder than Ulf."

"Aye. Let us finish this fight, my time is better spent elsewhere."

"Odin will still be pleased," Astrid announced.

"Ha! Hel grows tired of opening her home to these sad men. If we do not face some worthy opponents soon, she will lose respect for us."

"Jokul!" Hak yelled after he killed the last of the attackers with a slice of his blade that nearly halved the man. "How many times must we tell you to not speak her name, especially on the battlefield?"

"Sorry."

"You almost won." Astrid pointed to the body of the man Hak had just killed.

"Aye, I did, didn't I?"

"Never mind Her. Odin would praise us for another victory. Now let us find some treasure in this miserable fortress of stick and mud that would befit Him," Astrid announced.

"Can you do that alone, Astrid? I would like to see these brown-haired beauties Jokul boasts of."

"When they see you, Hak the Huge, they may all run away," Jokul teased. "Better yet, they may all run into my arms."

"Go, Hak." Astrid nodded. "I will be fine."

Astrid watched her brothers jog off as the setting sun warmed her skin. The place, its people—she had never seen their likes. Eyes on the field of bodies, she saw one move. Odin did not honor failure, and it was her belief that if defeated in combat, death was the only recourse.

Astrid trudged through the corpses and found the man who struggled with life. Right away, Astrid saw his wound; he had been gored with a spear, one of the roughly made things that the other men here carried, not the metal ones her people carried. The man, closer in age to her father than her brothers, tried desperately to remove the thin, carved wood that was still in his belly, but his hands, which were covered in deep-red lifeblood, just slipped off, smeared the shaft, and turned it almost black. His dark eyes shifted up to her, and he stopped and just stared.

Astrid listened to him whisper one word over and over, but she did not know his language. Still the word did not seem a threat to her— more of an honor.

"Astrid!" Ulf yelled from the main gates, his arms and legs coated in blood.

"Ulf."

"You fared well?"

Ulf was a compassionate man; Astrid knew he would find her, and make sure she was safe before he began to loot.

"I am fine. You, Brother?"

"Good. Is that one still alive?"

"He's staring at me and muttering something over and over."

Astrid relocked gazes with the older man. She did not wound him, but suddenly felt responsible for his fate. *I-I am sorry.*

"Perhaps he thinks you are a Valkyrie."

Ulf's statement snapped her attention back to him. There was no room for pity on the battlefield, her father taught her that at a young age. So why did she feel so?

"A Valkyrie? In this savage land?"

"Even savages need passage to their afterlife."

Astrid raised her boot over the man's head, took aim at his throat, and dropped it.

"Come, little Sister, I found you one of those large red gems you enjoy so much."

"Really?" Astrid perked up.

"As fat as your fist."

Her heart racing, Astrid dashed back to the gates, the wounds in her leg all but forgotten. "Who do I have to fight for it?"

"Ha! Father would be proud of you, Astrid the White."

"I hope so."

CHAPTER 11

ASTRID HAD NOT SPOKEN MORE than a dozen words to Warren in three days. She refused to give him the pleasure of her voice until she reached the spot where she had awoken in the snow. The elders had lied to her, she was sure of it. However, she desired to prove her claims to Warren, and that made her angry.

Still, she found it hard to stay mad at him, often forced to remind herself to grimace at him from time to time. He was a skilled hunter, much better than she; he easily found them a good dinner for each night. Astrid could not remember a time when she ate so well away from her family. Even now, as they marched, she wished she had more of the rabbit she had eaten last night; it was that tasty.

Although she had not spoken, Warren himself had not stopped. He told her stories about his past, like the tales her brothers would sing at the taverns, though Warren's were different; in fact, most of the battles he had fought were in defense of his lands, not for conquest or profitable gain.

Battle had always been glorious for her and her ilk, yet the images Warren painted made war a much less attractive thing. *What would the gods think?* she often pondered. Such horrors and still this man found himself smiling. He was quite the mystery, to Astrid. After years of combat in the service of this land's ruler, the gods must have given him their good fortune.

Upon reaching the open field that led to the spot where she had awoken, Astrid finally broke her silence. "We are here."

"Here?"

Snow remained in the area, but more as a muddy veneer over grass than the thick bed she had described.

"Aye, this is the field where I woke after Birka was invaded."

"You truly walked all the way from here to Grømstad?"

Astrid nodded.

"No wonder you were exhausted."

"Not so much exhausted." Astrid's tone made it clear she did not like that word being used to describe her. "I was sick from the rancid meat, remember."

"I remember."

"Stay still," Astrid said sternly as she held out her arm, a signal that could have been misunderstood as a more serious caution.

"What is it?"

"I see my tracks."

Her tracks were no more than shallow marks in the snow, windows to the muddy grass beneath, yet Astrid retraced the path, and stepped carefully in each spot she claimed was one of her former footprints.

"What are you doing?" Warren asked.

Astrid crept forward a moment before she called back to him. "See, I was resting here, atop a soft bed of snow."

Warren followed her finger. "I see nothing more than a puddle of melted snow and bent grass. Are you sure?"

"Don't you see my outline? That is me."

Astrid drew a shape in the air with her finger, but Warren shook his head and shrugged. Astrid released a frustrated grunt as she lowered herself into the spot, and placed her limbs out to her sides.

"You see it now?"

Warren nodded his head. Astrid was a sight, that was for sure, and when Warren looked upon her, sprawled out against the melting snow, his mind drifted to a moment long ago while he courted his wife. They had raced out of town early one morning before the elders awoke and the town guard sobered up. They had run across the snow until they found a secluded spot to make love. After all this time, it was still hard to accept she was gone.

"Do you believe me now? Do you see that your elders are wrong?"

Warren breathed deeply and smiled, while he stored the memory of his wife.

"What was the first thing you remember?"

Eyes closed, Astrid put her hand between her thighs and then up under her leather-strap skirt, an action that stole Warren's breath.

"First thing, I checked to see if I was violated. There was no blood."

Warren huffed a deep breath in and out then forced his mind back on the track of a soldier. *This is not the time to desire her,* he told himself, *this is not the time. Remember the task at hand.*

"Was there urine?"

"None."

"Then you were not unconscious for very long."

"We share the same thoughts."

Astrid attempted to stand quick, but her boot slid in the wet grass, and she dropped to her seat with a loud thud. Astrid cursed from embarrassment, slammed her hands down, and then tried to stand again. Almost up, her other foot slipped and again she fell backward.

"Let me help you up, Astrid."

Warren reached to her with both hands and a friendly smile. With a swift and sturdy pull, Warren lifted the warrior woman, from the muddy ground to her feet, but he did not dig in—and his own feet slipped out from under him. They fell in a loud rattle and clang of metal on metal which broke the tension of the moment.

"I guess *you* will have to help *me* up now."

Astrid smiled, and if only for a moment, Warren sensed warmth where coldness normally clung to her.

There are more layers to be discovered beneath this warrior woman's shell of anger and frustration, he was sure of it now.

"We have words for men like you in Birka," Astrid stated as she hovered above him.

"Kind? Charming? Handsome?"

As she knelt to answer him, something stole her attention. Before Warren could ask what, she placed a gloved hand over his mouth.

"Something moves," Astrid whispered before she dashed off.

Warren had never seen a man, let alone woman, with such heavy armor move so lithely. Her motions were so fluid and easy, he found himself jealous when his knees screamed and his back ached as he stood. *I feel no glory in my age—none received for a veteran soldier.*

Warren held still and watched her go. Astrid had drawn her long sword and raced off across the field toward the tree line north of them.

Warren wanted to call out to her, to tell her to wait, but doing so would spoil any element of surprise she had, and he was unsure what she sought. All of a sudden afraid he might lose track of her, he rushed to follow, sword in hand, careful to muffle the noise his armor made as he moved.

Warren ducked behind a large tree when he heard a sound in the distance, but when he peered around it, Astrid was gone.

She's vanished. No, I bet she stalks her prey. This is a hunt; she is the hunter.

In time, Warren spotted her long, golden braids, a beacon in the otherwise drab setting. She was not alone. Warren watched as she flanked a man draped in the shadows. All Warren could tell of the man was that he moved slowly, staggered like he was tired or wounded.

"Ho there!" Astrid yelled at the man from her position beside a thick tree.

When the man stepped in Astrid's direction, he became easier for Warren to see. On his chest was what appeared to be thick plate metal. Crudely shaped and bulky, Warren had seen its likes before, but he could not remember where.

"Speak your intentions and make them true." Astrid sounded impatient.

Warren found the man's leg pieces were gone and so were his bracers. All that remained upon his legs were a pair of heavily stained padded leather pants.

"Who's there?" The man seemed dazed.

"Astrid the White, daughter of Kol."

"W-who?"

Sunlight sparkled on a streak of moist blood that streamed down the man's arm.

"Astrid, he's wounded. Stand down."

"I know he's wounded. And dripping like that," Astrid pointed. "Warren, he's lucky I found him before the bears and wolves did. *I* do not devour my adversaries. Not anymore."

When Warren closed the distance, he finally spotted the man's sigils, a clear indication of what army he belonged to.

"Morn, soldier! I am Warren of Grømstad," he said, as he stepped into full view of the man.

"Grømstad, yes, finally an ally?" The wounded man looked up from the dirt. "I'm Sven, scout of the fifth light cavalry division of Baldelag."

"Baldelag? Are you from the great river outpost?" Warren paused to imagine the elder's maps. "Northeast of here?"

Warren watched as Astrid crept up behind the wounded man and held her sword to his back.

"I've never heard of Baldelag." She sneered. "Can we trust him?"

"I survived…" the man mumbled.

"Baldelag is far, far north of here," Warren answered, then looked back to the soldier who seemed to be regaining his clarity, although slowly. "I hear it's a just land, filled with honorable men. He's not our enemy, Astrid. Lower your sword."

"North you say? Then you must know of the glorious fortress city of Birka?" Astrid asked, but he did not answer.

The man shuffled toward Warren a few more steps, and the short sword he carried loosely in the hand of his wounded arm dropped, its clang swallowed up by the dense forest.

"What are you doing so far from your home?"

Astrid's voice was flat and she looked set for a fight, she had not lowered her sword as he had asked. Warren could see how pale the man was and when the wind gusted, he finally caught a whiff of the foul odor rising off him. He was in poor shape, his arm covered in both dried and fresh blood.

"Are your wounds severe, Sven?" He asked.

"I-I…we were attacked. My outpost was attacked in the middle of the night. The enemy was fast and fought with a fierceness I've only seen in the worst barbarian tribes."

"Where is your outpost, my friend?"

Warren looked past the man to Astrid, who had not moved or removed her eyes from Sven.

"Gone! Did you not hear me? It's gone! My wife, my child, my friends, my home: all gone."

The soldier collapsed only a few feet from Warren.

"What do you mean gone?" Warren asked as he slowly knelt. "What happened there, man?"

"Everything was on fire. It burned to the ground," he sobbed.

"And yet here you survived?" Astrid circled the man. "Did you flee?"

"Astrid!" Warren chastised. They needed to hear what the man had to say and accusing him of cowardice may quiet him.

"Flee?" Sven finally responded, and when he did, he looked at Astrid with angry eyes. "The night was filled with chaos, woman. Yellow fires burned so bright I could not see! There was thunder and smoke. I tried to save my family, but we were separated. I fell wounded and was dragged out by a guard. He—and the other men who escaped, we rallied in the forest and when dawn came, we tried to counterattack, yet by then the outpost was nothing but blackened timber."

"Where are the other men?" Astrid asked unsympathetically. "Are they near?"

Although Warren understood why she asked and knew the dangers inherent with a group of wounded and desperate men, he still reprimanded her.

"Astrid, stop interrogating him," Warren demanded.

"Fine."

"My apologies, Sven. My friend…she's not from our lands and does not apply herself to our customs. Here, take this water." Warren handed the man his waterskin then unpacked his rations.

"Warren, his blood spills everywhere!" Astrid pointed to his wound.

"The very reason I intend to give him aid."

"Listen to me. It may be your custom to aid injured strangers, but it is not my custom to allow—"

"No, you listen to me." Warren stood suddenly and stepped up to Astrid in a way that made her flinch. "I am here now, helping you. Your quest to find your home can wait a moment."

Astrid backed off, and retraced her path to the spot she had awoken days ago. Warren watched her walk away, unsure how she would react when given a moment to reflect on the situation; regardless his soldier's intuition shouted not to give Astrid his back.

"I have never seen a woman of her likes before," Sven stated after he took a large bite of the fruit Warren had handed him. "You might find me odd to say it, yet she reminds me of the seafaring marauders my father used to tell tale of. That was long ago."

"Yes," Warren agreed. "Yet she is here now."

"I must thank you…for your hospitality, my new friend." Sven's eyes fluttered as he spoke, his head bobbed back and forth mid-drink.

"You rest now, Sven. Worry not. I will set up camp."

CHAPTER 12

WARREN BUILT A SMALL CAMPFIRE just inside the forest in a clearing not far from where they had first spotted the wounded man, a space between a downed, rotten tree and a large, moss-covered rock. It provided shelter from the wind and gave them some protection in case bandits were about.

Having soldiered for over twenty years, Warren knew how to tend to a wound, but Sven's was unlike any he had seen before. The puncture in his arm looked like that of an arrow or spear strike, but when he pushed the torn sleeve up, the red, splotchy marks he found appeared more like a burn. The flesh closest to the hole had bubbled up and turned black; the sight was nearly as off-putting as the smell.

Warren packed the wound, applied fresh herbs, and wrapped it tight, but none of his efforts stopped the bleeding. This was a quandary best left for the healers back home. Warren knew Astrid would disagree with his plan to head back in the morning, but he would have to press the issue, and if she did not like it, he feared he might be forced to part ways with her.

Astrid returned to Warren and Sven after spending much time in the field alone. She had studied the area once more. This night was much clearer, as if her eyes had been veiled before. More lucid, she realized nothing was where it should be. When she had awoke that dark night, the fog had claimed the horizon and had masked the forest and remote mountains. Now Astrid could see them all better; nevertheless she was even less comforted. The mountain range was not where it belonged; it was to the east of her when it should have been to the south. More troublesome, the cloud-piercing peaks of the holy mountain were still undetected. Had she truthfully been near her home, they would have been visible.

More and more, Astrid began to comprehend, and accept, that she was further from home than she had originally believed. Where she was, she was still unsure, and how she got to this place seemed too impossible to fathom.

"Warren," she called and nodded to him as she approached.

"Good evening, Astrid."

"I have mulled over a few things."

"Me too."

"First, answer me this: why would a northern ruler need an outpost here?"

"No doubt to keep in contact with the southern kingdoms."

"You mean to keep watch on them. This man, he is a spy, Warren," Astrid deduced.

"Doubtful. Anyway, it matters not." Warren waved off her comment. "Look at the gauntness of his face, the way his wound seeps. He's too injured to do either of us any damage."

"You would be surprised," Astrid said, as she gazed around them and sat down. "When my father was a mere boy he was caught and held for ransom. He was beaten and kept barely alive, but when conscious, he counted all the guards, noting them each by the way they walked. When his brothers came to rescue him, he was able to give them details that allowed them to overcome the great numbers. Two men and a boy escaped that day, having killed twenty guards."

With a groan, Sven awoke.

"I thought I heard my wife speaking."

"That was me," Astrid nodded.

"Nothing like her, you are."

The man took in his surroundings as he sat up slowly.

"How do you feel, Sven?" Warren asked.

"Much improved. Once more, you have my thanks."

"Can you tell us again what happened to you?" Warren asked kindly.

"My outpost was attacked unexpectedly. It was night, and our enemy came at us so fast that the place was burning down before many of us had even arisen from our beds."

His words hit Astrid like a punch in the face.

"Those of us who survived the initial attack regrouped in the forest..." Sven's words dropped off. "My family—there was nothing left."

"Your family could have escaped as you did."

Sven nodded to Warren's comment.

"It was...maybe two days later...that we faced our enemy again, a brigand army."

"Brigand army?" Astrid repeated.

"A large, motley force of bandits. They seemed frustrated with the results of their siege. There was little to nothing left to plunder. When they left...I followed."

"Wait, you were following the bandits?" Astrid asked.

"For three days, I think."

"Three days?" Warren was surprised. "Sven, when was your outpost attacked?"

"Seven...no, eight days ago."

"If that were true, your wounds should have sealed. To bleed that many days; you should be dead, Sven." Astrid stated.

"Truly, Sven, I've never seen a burn that bleeds. Or known a man to spill as much blood for as long as you have."

"I do not know." Sven gazed down at his arm. "It stopped bleeding yet started again."

"Do you recall what kind of blade pierced you? Was it sword or spear?" Astrid's tone was that of an interrogator again.

"To be honest, I am not sure, I was trying to get my wife past the walls when something hit me. I smelled the burn. Initially, I thought it was a flaming arrow."

"But you no longer think it was?" Warren grimaced as he asked.

"He never found the arrow."

Sven looked at Astrid, a flicker of surprise on his face. He nodded in agreement.

"Wait, Sven, you say you were following the brigands. Which direction was this army traveling?" Warren asked.

"South—"

Astrid heard the rustle of leaves and the snap of a dry twig in the distance. She jumped to her feet and unfastened the strap that held her battle-axe. *This is what I feared.*

"What did you hear?" Warren whispered.

"Something large and heavy."

"Where's my sword?" Sven stood wobbly.

"I tried to warn you of this." Astrid sniffed the air. "Predators have tracked the trail of blood."

"Predators? You mean wolves?"

"We should be so lucky."

Astrid turned as the repeated clump of four heavy feet grew louder. Her ears knew the direction the attacker came from, but her eyes did not see it until it was too late. Out of the shadows lunged a large bear. The bear, nearly three times the mass of Astrid, slammed hard into her. Thrown to the ground, the shock jarred the battle-axe from her hands.

"Astrid, no!"

Warren pulled his sword and ascended the boulder rapidly. Atop the rock, he could see the bear as it straddled Astrid. Astrid's head was pinned against the stone, her body motionless. He feared she may already be dead. The very thought gave birth to a fire inside him, he had thought long gone.

Warren released a war cry as he dove at the bear. Both hands squeezed tight around the handle of his sword, he landed a downward strike that plunged the metal deep into the beast's wide shoulders. The bear reeled back in pain and jolted onto its back feet, throwing Warren from its hide.

"It's my blood you smell, beast!" Sven yelled as he approached from around the boulder. "Come have a taste!"

The bear dropped back to his front paws and sprang into Sven. When the beast bared its teeth; a mouthful of ivory daggers, Warren was sure they would all die. Astrid was already down. She was lying still, her arms bloodied by the bear's claws, her face untouched, angelic—

"Help!" Sven screamed as the bear sank its teeth into his shoulder.

Sven had dropped his sword, and Warren grabbed it as he rushed to the man's aid. With it in hand, Warren sliced the bear's thick hide just under where his own sword was still lodged in its deep back muscle.

"Let go of him, damn you!"

Warren shouted as he hacked away at the bear's back, its slavering jaws finally dropping Sven after a fifth slice carved a chunk of flesh free. The bear set its red-eyed sights on Warren as it pivoted slowly.

Warren mounted the mossy boulder again; he felt safer on higher ground. From his vantage, he could see how badly Sven was hurt—blood spurted from his neck in amounts that would surely lead to his death if the wound was not treated fast.

"Off him!"

The bear snorted at Warren but turned to Sven again.

"No!"

Warren leapt down to the campsite, reached into the fire, and yanked out a piece of timber. As the heat seared his hand, he heaved the wood at the bear.

"Back off! Find your meal elsewhere!"

When the fiery wood struck the ground next to the bear's head, the bear swung around. Warren swallowed hard and made a fist, *I have your attention now.* No sooner did the massive animal spring forward than Warren dashed away, around the boulder to where Astrid's battle-axe lay. The thunderous footfalls drummed into his mind and rattled his teeth. Warren knew it was right behind him as he hefted the axe.

With a lumberjack's swing, Warren pivoted, fully expecting to find the bear's large mouth about to close on him, but the beast had moved much slower than he had thought, and his attack was right on target.

The blade struck the bear's head, shattered its skull, and popped both its eyes free with a burst of wetness. The follow through nearly took him off his own feet.

"Damn you," Warren exhaled his rage. "Damn you!"

"Warren?"

Astrid had come to and was leaning up against the boulder.

"That thing ran me over like an unbroken horse."

Warren began to chuckle.

"Look at my arms…" she marveled.

"You will need to wrap—"

"These will leave worthy scars," she stated.

As he examined her arms, he noticed how fast her breath was and how it nearly matched the accelerated beat of his heart.

"These cuts are deep." Warren took a closer look. "You are bleeding fast. I have more wraps in my equipment. You must tie these off now."

"Had I bested the beast too, these marks would have made for an excellent display during the tale. You are a most fortunate man, Warren."

"Fortunate," he exhaled. "Go wrap those."

"I will live…unlike Sven." She nodded in the direction of the man.

In his concern for Astrid, Warren had almost forgotten Sven. He rushed to Sven's side but the man was long gone, his neck torn open, pools of his blood staining the ground red.

Astrid spoke over her shoulder as she retrieved the bandage wraps. "His soul has passed to—"

"I know!" Warren snapped. "He died protecting us both."

Warren snatched up a rock that sat near the dead man's foot and threw it off into the darkness.

"We can't stay here any longer, Warren…" Astrid began, interrupted by the hoot of an owl. "Other predators will come. The owl will lead them here. We must first mask that trail of blood and then burn this body."

"Sven will be buried before we leave."

"Buried?"

"Stay here. Rest. I will veil the blood trail."

"Warren, curse you, I'm fine," Astrid snapped as she tied a wrap around her left arm. "I can—"

"Stay here, Astrid."

CHAPTER 13

IF SHE HADN'T BEEN LIGHTHEADED, Astrid might have contested Warren. Then again, her respect for the normally passive, smiling man had grown. He acted more and more like a resident of Birka with each trial they faced.

"I pray you find the path to Valhalla, Sven of the northlands."

When Astrid touched the man's left arm, his body began to glow a deep gold, the light growing so that Astrid had to shield her eyes. As the bright light began to stretch out toward her, she shrunk back in fear. Without a sound, the light abruptly shot into the sky like an arrow fired from Jötunn's bow.

Startled, Astrid fell backward and stared up at the golden light as it ascended into the heavens. Witness to this miracle, Astrid felt as if she had been touched by the gods, and safe in their hands, she lay still.

How long had passed before Warren returned, she was unsure, but the look on his face when he gazed down at her was as full of confusion as her mind.

"Astrid, what happened here?"

When she did not answer, he dropped the small pile of wood he had cradled in his arms and yelled her name.

"Quiet, Warren. You should lower your voice, unless you wish to slay another bear."

"What are you doing?"

Astrid moved, finally tearing her eyes off the sky above. She was numb from head to toe. As she stood, she discovered new power in her legs. Her bloodline had always been rich with strength—a golden blessing from Odin himself, her father always boasted—but at this moment, Astrid felt as if she could move mountains.

"The gods gift me, Warren. I feel reborn."

"With such short rest?" Warren finally smiled. "You are the fortunate one. The old gods must love you."

"You jest, but it is true." Astrid paced a bit. "When you left, I witnessed something grand. The Allfather bestowed a gift upon my eyes."

"What did you see?"

Astrid smiled and said, "I witnessed Sven's soul rise up and ascend to Valhalla."

Warren did not respond.

"Did you hear me, Warren?"

"Astrid, to declare yourself witness to the first steps of a man's afterlife—this is fool's talk. No one believes—"

"Fool's talk?"

"Did you eat more rancid meat while I was gone?"

"Damn you!" Astrid shouted. "I saw this miracle."

"Astrid, you were attacked." He pointed at the bear's body. "You struck your head."

"Your meaning?"

"I think you are ill. Once, when I was younger, Hammond punched me, and my eyes filled with strange sparkles of light—"

"Are you calling me a liar?" Astrid's hand moved to the handle of her sword.

"What you are saying does not make sense."

Astrid drew a deep breath and held it a moment. "Sven died in combat. He died bravely. He died protecting us."

"Wait...do think you saw a Valkyrie?" Warren tilted his head back and gazed up into the blackness of the sky. "I see only the twinkling of stars above."

"I...no..." Astrid closed her eyes a moment to gather her thoughts. "I mean, I do not think so."

"I have fought many battles, seen many brave men die in combat, Astrid. Never has a Valkyrie come down to collect a soul for Valhalla. Those are the legends of old."

"Now who is ill? Because it must be an illness that is making you speak out against our gods."

"I don't speak out against them." Warren sighed. "I'm just the owner of a much diminished faith in them is all."

"That is *all*?"

Astrid marched straight to the boulder and placed her hands on its moss-covered side, shoving it with all her might until it dislodged from its home in the frost-covered earth and rolled toward Warren.

"Who are you, woman?" Warren stepped back in alarm.

"I—"

While she spoke, Warren pushed at the boulder but the thing did not move, not even a bit. Astrid walked to his side and placed her hands directly where his had once been. To both their surprise, it did not budge. Angered, Astrid rocked back on her heels and slammed herself against the stone, the impact of her left arm against a sharp corner sliced the bloodied wrapping right off.

"Astrid, your arm!"

Where the bear's claws had carved deep into the flesh of her arm no longer bled; all that remained of the wound was five splotchy red scratches.

"Warren, what is happening to me?" Astrid watched Warren's hand move to his sword.

"I would have sworn you were cut deeper than this."

"I-I was. Wasn't I? Is this all a dream? Am I dreaming, Warren? Did I fall asleep in the field as you bandaged Sven? Or am I still asleep in your home; still delusional from the rancid meat I ate?"

"You are not dreaming," Warren said as he took hold of her shoulder. "This is real."

"And Sven," Astrid's voice cracked when she said his name. "He's real too?"

"He was. He's dead now," Warren stated bluntly.

"Then I beg to know what the meaning of all this is?" Astrid stated with a false sense of calm.

"Perhaps we were meant to come out here, just to find Sven."

"And then what? What do the gods want me to do now?"

"I am not sure what the old gods want you to do, but *I* want you to answer this one question, one last time: do you truly still expect to find Birka north of here, Astrid?"

Astrid was silent a moment as she watched Warren's patience fade. She added the facts together again and came to the same conclusion she had earlier—nothing was as it should be, *this is all wrong. This land, whether it be what Warren's elders claimed it or not, it is certainly not the place of my home.*

"Astrid?"

"The bears...the bears of my lands are coated in thick brown fur, not coarse black fur. A journey could be made for months in any direction, north, south, east, or west, and still the holy mountains could be seen. Where I come from, a warrior such as Sven would be burned atop a hero's pyre not buried to rot."

"Yes. So?"

"This place, I fear, is not Midgard at all."

"You speak like the elders at times, Astrid, do you know that? It's one of the reason why I trust you."

"Trust is hard for my people."

"A warrior's trust is earned on the battlefield."

"Agreed."

"Hear me, Astrid the White: as much as I may have prayed you wrong, I now fear that your conclusion about the bandits was accurate. Sven said the brigand force traveled south days ago and—"

"Now you believe the men who destroyed Sven's outpost are going to attack Grømstad?"

"I do."

Astrid turned her back to Warren and sighed. "Then go, return to your home. Protect your home."

"So much has happened today, Astrid." Warren rubbed his scruffy face. "I don't know what to believe at the moment, but there's one thing I know as fact. Even if we push on, travel north another day or even another week in search of your home, I promise you not a single trace of Birka will be found."

"Why do you tell me this?"

"We should turn now, run back to Grømstad, and perhaps we can stop the men who may have destroyed Sven's home and killed his family before they destroy my home as well."

"You still want me to believe that these are not the same lands as mine? Then how do you explain Sven's tale, and how it echoes mine?" Astrid faced Warren again.

"I don't have all the answers, Astrid." Warren shook his head. "All I know is that I need you. Grømstad needs you...your help."

Astrid drew a deep breath and exhaled slowly. "You know we will certainly be outnumbered. Are you prepared to die, Warren?"

"If I fall, it will be protecting the women and children of Grømstad."

"A hero's death indeed," Astrid proclaimed.

Astrid paused a moment, and her gaze turned north. Her thoughts were on her family. She had not been able to defend them when enemy forces invaded her city. It disgusted her to think of her home as being destroyed and her family lost. She could not allow it to happen again, not now, not to Warren and his kin. This was her chance for revenge albeit against a different enemy.

After another deep breath, she had made her decision. "We should hurry, Warren. We have a town to defend."

CHAPTER 14

AFTER THEY RAN FOR ALMOST three days with little rest and less food, Astrid and Warren came upon a yellow-orange glow in the distance. Fire. They both knew it, the way it flickered up filtered by the abundant evergreens and changed the night sky from black to blue.

Though moments before the pair had discussed setting camp, they now pushed their bodies further and raced across the forest floor toward the light.

As they drew closer, the sounds of combat became apparent. A large battle was being waged inside the forest not a full day's march from Warren's home. Dreadful, high-pitched screams pierced the night sky and echoed through Astrid's hollow stomach. All they could see was violence blurred by the firelight and thick vaporous smoke that surrounded them. With her hand over her mouth, Astrid tried in vain to catch her breath.

"The bandits?" Warren huffed as he caught up to her.

"My guess as well. Hard to tell who they are fighting."

"Perhaps the army was dispatched on mere merit of my report to the elders."

A breeze cleared the smoke and the scene shifted drastically. This was not a battle; this was a slaughter. The screams were not battle cries; they were howls of terror.

"Whoever has engaged them, they are wiping them out speedily. I must go and get my revenge before I miss this opportunity!"

Astrid stood up from behind her cover and drew her long sword, a family heirloom decorated in symbols which were hand carved by her great-grandfather. She treasured the weapon; it was a symbol of her kin, and she loved her family more than anything. Today she would avenge her dead with this ancestral steel called *Ugla,* her native word for owl, named after the screech her enemies made when she cut them.

As she began to move around the rock, a loud rumble was heard across the forest battlefield and the subsequent sound of heavy rain followed. When a hand, blackened by heat, its fingers still twitching, landed several feet before Astrid and Warren, the two realized it was not rainwater that had suddenly moistened the ground and their bodies; it was a splattering of blood.

"What in the heavens?" Warren called out, as he pointed to a chunk of hair-covered scalp not far from the hand.

"The very gods themselves are putting an end to these bastards!" Astrid's eyes grew wide with excitement, but as she prepared to lunge forward, Warren tackled her to the ground face first.

"Stop, Astrid."

"What are you doing?" Astrid could not move from under the weight of Warren's large body.

"You can't!" Warren yelled over another thunderous rumble.

"Let go of me! I must fight!"

A second rain of blood covered the entire place.

"No, you will die!"

"Let me go, Warren!"

Astrid struggled to free herself, but the smiling man had her pinned to the ground in such a way that she could not get leverage. His boldness and disrespect doubled her anger.

"Let me go!" she screamed again.

"You will die! I cannot let you die!"

Astrid clawed at the ground in front of her; she was only able to turn to face the battle. She watched as a bandit yelped in horror at some-thing that had him by the legs. Suddenly the bandit's body shifted and he slid on his back into a puff of smoke that billowed from a new fire. The man's screams turned into an indefinable screech then abruptly stopped. *Whichever god has him has finally put him out of his misery,* Astrid thought.

As the sounds of dying men quieted, Astrid once more witnessed the golden light. From the ground in front of her were two deep-amber lights, which began to float slowly but then raced into the sky. Less than a breath later, more of the lights popped into existence. *Two, three more, five, now seven.* One by one, the golden lights shot up to the heavens.

"Do you see it, Warren?" Astrid shook with excitement. "By the gods, do you see it?"

She had not realized Warren's forehead was pressed down into her mid back. He could not see anything.

"Astrid—"

"Warren, their souls are ascending," she shuddered. "Please, Warren…"

Another crash, that-wait, that was a true roll of thunder. But what was that other sound that shook the ground? A steady fall of rain, crystal clear and cool, began to fall. It doused the smaller fires first, then some of the larger ones.

"No!" Astrid shouted as she realized the fight was over, her need for vengeance unquenched.

"What, Astrid? What?"

"Damn you, Warren, let go of me now, or I swear I will gut you," Astrid reached for one of her daggers.

When her words met his ears, he finally released his grip, and Astrid slithered out from under him to stand.

"You," she growled. "I should kill you now."

"For saving you?"

"Saving me?"

"Yes, you stubborn fool! Those men were being ripped apart by… by I don't know what manner of beast, god, or monster! You too would have died."

"Do not!" she yelled as she pointed at him. "Do not underestimate me again, smiling man! To do so might be fatal."

Warren did not answer her; instead his eyes shifted to the sickening scene behind her.

"Astrid—"

"Do you hear me? If you test my honor again I will—"

"Astrid! Turn around."

Astrid had had enough of Warren's commands. In fact, her body steeled itself. She crossed her arms and refused to budge.

"Astrid, look."

Warren grabbed for her shoulders, and as Astrid stepped back to avoid his hands, she glanced backward. What her eyes took in was enough to make her forget about the past few days.

"Odin's breath!"

The forest, as far as she could see in the limited light of a few stubborn fires, was cluttered with body parts. The very ground appeared to be muddied with gore and blood, bones and weapons. Astrid moved toward the scene slowly, unable to understand what she was seeing. Beneath her feet, the ground was soft and wet—sticking to her boots like blood. As she neared the epicenter of the battle, she saw damaged pieces of armor, metals that she would have thought impossible to break in such a way. Melted swords and axes lay strewn about, though not at the feet of their owners as you would see on a normal battlefield. The more Astrid looked around, the more her heart sunk into her stomach; she had seen pieces of people but not a whole body.

Accustomed to the horrific sights of combat, Astrid had seen severed limbs before, but what she looked at now seemed like no more than the scattered innards of animals. She bent down to inspect a gooey, grayish pink puddle. As she stared, Warren stepped up behind her, and asked, "Have you ever seen a man's head cracked open by a mace?"

"I have."

"The insides of a man's skull"—Warren poked at the mush with his sword—"That is it."

"Then where is his skull?" Astrid asked.

"Pieces," Warren echoed her earlier thought, "there are only pieces of men here."

"Look there." Astrid pointed to a pair of legs.

"It has taken me years to erase the barbarism of war from my mind's eye, Astrid. I held hopes that I would never have to witness any of this ever again."

"There's honor in combat." Astrid shuddered. "This...this was something else. Something—"

"Wrong?" he guessed.

Astrid and Warren walked through the stickiness to the legs, still adorned in leather pants—a nice pair at that, although soaked in urine and feces. Disgusted, Astrid began to turn pale and wretched.

"Looks like someone won your bet, cut this poor man in half." Warren smiled wryly.

"I cannot even count the dead."

"A foot here"—Warren pointed—"a hand there. Who knows if they are a match?"

Astrid stepped on the spilled guts of a man—or woman, she was unsure, since when she gazed down at the slippery mess all she saw was bloody butchery. She lifted her foot from the gore, shook her boot, and tried to clear it of the tiny chunks of flesh.

"Do you still think the old gods did this?"

"I..." Astrid thought on what she saw. There was no good answer. "This is how I imagine Helheim, Warren."

"Helheim?"

"Am I dead?" she bluntly asked.

"If you are, then I am too, and I do not recall dying."

Astrid bent over and lifted a severed arm from the ground. When she showed it to Warren, she asked, "What weapon cleaves the flesh from a man's arm but leaves a burnt hand behind to grip a silver locket?"

"None that I am aware of."

"There are no heads."

"What?" Warren replied as he examined the locket.

"I see all manner of parts yet not a single head."

The rain had grown heavier as they spoke, and the scent of gore worse. Astrid covered her nose and mouth as she walked until she was no longer ankle deep in blood and viscera.

"Warren!"

"What?" Warren asked as he jogged up.

"A trail."

Astrid fanned the air to rid herself of the stench of death, while Warren knelt to study the tracks she'd found.

"Old leathers. Some of the bandits escaped," he surmised.

"Then your home is still in trouble."

"If not threatened by these bandits, it could be by whatever slaughtered these men."

"We best run."

"Are you sure you are up to this, Astrid? You look sick." Warren's voice was compassionate, like her brother Ulf's.

"The further we get from this ungodly spot the better."

"Then let's make haste."

CHAPTER 15

"THERE! LOOK!"

Warren shouted to Astrid as they dashed out from the shadowy veil of the forest that walled Grømstad on two sides. His arm extended, his finger pointed at the bandits who laid siege to the town and the men who defended it.

"Spearmen. Our Lord did deploy some men to protect the town."

"How many, you wager?"

The shouts of men turned both their heads; more brigands funneled out from the forest on the far side of town where Warren's house sat.

"Not enough."

"Good then." Astrid drew her sword. "More for us!"

Astrid dashed to cut off the dozen or more bandits who were rushing toward town. Warren gazed first at the kingdom's spearmen; their defense of the center of town seemed to be going well. Three new soldiers on horseback came into view, officers by the looks of them. They led the town's guard toward the new attackers. Warren wanted nothing more than to rush down there and fall into rank with the other soldiers and guards. He knew how they fought and could bolster their lines with ease, but with Astrid's charge off toward the other end of town alone, he had no choice but to follow.

"I hope you do not get us both killed!"

"To die here, now, would be in the purest glory. Do not worry, Warren. Odin, the Allfather, will honor you in the afterlife."

"I wish I could be so sure."

"Fight well, Warren."

"Stay safe, Astrid."

Astrid watched seven rogues break off the line that entered the rear of town, the last of whom she recognized as the leader from the other night. The man smiled as he approached her, staying safely behind his men.

"You face Astrid the White, daughter of Kol!"

Astrid boomed as she swung her long sword into the first bandit's gut. His leather armor was no match for the force and sharpness of her blade; her steel cut through it like was no more than a fat cow's belly. Shocked, the man's jaw fell open as his sticky guts spilled down to his feet.

These men, they dress in dark rags, patchwork leather, carry wooden shields; there's no way they could have defeated the men of Birka and their expertly forged arms and armor. It was this very uncertainty combined with her overconfidence that put her in danger.

Astrid deflected one and then another attack from two gritty brigands before she could readjust the grip on her sword. Pushed back, her anger began to build in her chest. *I have faced more than two men at once in combat before. What is wrong with me?*

While she blocked another blow, an opportunity presented itself. The second attacker's sword was shorter than the first; all she had to do was retreat further back on his swing.

"Cowards!" she shouted, goading them to attack.

The pair swung wildly at her, one and then the other until Astrid was able to parry the first man's blade as she hoped and then retreat a few feet. His wish to strike her caused the second man to overextend himself and subsequently stumble into his ally's strike path. Astrid did not even need to attack; the first bandit had done it for her, and lopped off his partner's hand at the wrist.

While the two bandit's were befuddled, Astrid slid forward and plunged her long sword through the side of one man and directly into the stomach of the other. Astrid laughed; *I wish my brothers could see this— two men skewered to my sword.* Using her foot, she shoved the closer man away, freeing her weapon from them both.

With her sword loose, Astrid took a look around in search of her next opponent.

Where has their leader cowered off to?

The cold, sharp blade of a dagger pierced her skin and drew a deep line across her throat. Stunned, Astrid's eyes focused on the dirty, gloved hand that held the weapon as it cut her. *No, this cannot be,* she thought as her sword fell from her grasp.

Astrid clutched her throat as she stumbled forward then back. *Mother,* she thought, *I will see you soon.* She bumped against something behind her and a new thought screamed in her head as her warrior's instincts kicked in.

Behind you. Your killer is still there behind you. You must...

Astrid fell hard to her knees, her eyes on the blood that poured to the ground before her. She would bleed out, and fast; she knew this. Astrid feared that the breath she just drew would be her last, so she held it tight in her chest.

Great Odin, I come to serve you in Valhalla, but first, grant your loyal servant one more moment in life to know her killer.

Astrid gasped for air, as her eyes darted from side to side. She could no longer see detail, only shapes and colors: dull and soft red, pink; the world around her had rapidly faded.

"I told you I would return."

That voice. It belonged to the brigand leader; she remembered the weight of arrogance in its sharp tone.

"I promised you, pretty warrior, and I always keep my promises."

"Aaggsh—" was all she could muster, her mouth overcome with the taste of the warm blood that spilled from its corners.

"So beautiful. Too bad."

Astrid felt something tap against her breast.

"We could have had fun, you and I," he said.

Astrid reached into her boot where her thin silver dagger was hidden. Just as the tops of her fingers ran over the roughness of its chiseled handle, they went numb; and the man's laugh began to fade. She squeezed her fist tightly and willed her body to move. It was a weak jab, but just as her vision went black, she struck her mark.

"My leg, you whore!"

Something hit her chest hard and she was on her back now, face to the night sky. Astrid always hated the thought of dying facedown in the dirt, Helheim in her eyes; it was a relief that would not happen now. All in all, Astrid felt fortunate enough to smile, an eternity of glory in the service of the gods awaited her.

"Astrid!" Warren screamed so loud his voice cracked and his lungs ached.

As badly as he wanted to run to her, to help her, he could not. Warren was engaged in battle with the last of the bandit soldiers who had separated from the core group. When he glimpsed Astrid, his heart dropped. *No, Astrid, please don't be dead.*

"Astrid!" he called out again.

Dread filled his chest, similar to the dark terror he had endured when his wife lay lifeless on their bed. His mind flashed red with the memory of the blood that covered her legs from her hips to her ankles. His wife had died bearing his son—his stillborn son. *Please don't be dead...*

"No!"

In a blink, Warren had killed two more men. He was unsure how he had done it, but he did not care either, he simply pressed on toward the last man that stood between him and Astrid.

"I will kill you!"

"Oh? Was this your woman?" the leader asked. "You have my deepest condolences on her passing, my friend."

Warren looked down at Astrid, her throat wound a truly gruesome sight, yet the warrior woman had not given in fully to death. Her tear-filled eyes bounced around in her head—Astrid looked alive.

"Hold strong, Astrid." Warren would have sworn by the way her fingers twitched that she motioned for her weapon, so he braced his shield and bent down slowly to take Astrid's ancestral sword himself.

"You city dwellers, you put such credence in relics."

"I only wish to bring your death with her sword."

"*No.* I will sell her sword to merchants in the capital city."

Warren hefted the two-handed sword with one; its mass meant nothing to him. He would have torn a tree from the ground and swung it like a club had that been the nearest weapon to the man who hurt Astrid.

Warren caged his raw emotions; he knew they would get him killed if he could not control them. Shield up, he waited, but it was not long before the bandit pressed his own attack.

When Warren saw the bandit leader shift his balance, he sprung forward and rammed into the man. The impact knocked his opponent to the ground.

"Get up! Get up, so I can slice you in half!"

Up to one knee, the brigand leader withdrew a wooden flute-like thing from a pocket in his leather pants and blew upon it. The action was so odd that Warren paused, but nothing happened: no sound, no attack.

"Enough!" Warren grumbled.

The swing of Astrid's long sword knocked the wooden object from the bandit leader's mouth and shattered its end. Warren had wanted more than that; he sought to cut the man's head off, so he swung again, and then again.

Armed only with the bloody dagger that had cut Astrid's throat, the bandit kept his distance.

"Damn you, fight!"

"I have no need to fight when my pets will fight for me."

Three wolves ran across the field from the trees Astrid and Warren had watched the enemy emerge from. The wolves growled and snapped at the air as they charged. As the wolves approached, the brigand leader faded off with a bow and smile, the action clearly a practiced one.

Engaged by the first angry wolf, Warren used his shield to deflect the animal and then turned his blade on it. When the tip of his sword pierced its back the wolf growled louder. Warren was unsure if he had even wounded the thing.

Warren took his eyes off the wolves to watch the man flee for only a second, and still it cost him the upper hand. A wolf with a darker coat than the others jumped up and locked its mouth around the bracer that covered Warren's sword hand, pulling his arm down. There was no way for him to swing Astrid's heavy blade now. Like it or not, he was caught, with his only option to drop the sword and try and use his shield to batter the dog off his arm.

Warren struggled to get free, but could not defend himself from the wounded dog as it punctured and tore into the flesh of his unarmored legs. As the pain spiked, Warren began to accept this might be his end too.

The third dog had abruptly vanished, and when Warren turned to look for it, he found it sniffing Astrid.

"Leave her, mutt! If you must eat, find your meal here."

CHAPTER 16

Astrid heard Warren's voice.

There's been nothing for so long—how long? Where did it all go? Air, I need air. Astrid gasped, as she reached up to her neck. The wound was all but closed, only layers of sticky blood remained as proof she should have been dead. *Such blood...the wound...how can this be?*

"Astrid, open your eyes."

She heard her father's voice. She attempted to peel open her eyes, but they would not budge. With much effort of heart and soul, her right eye opened to a flash of golden light that burned the scene around her. Her left eye, once open, brought clarity to the uncertainty.

The stars, so beautiful. It feels like years since I've gazed upon them on such a clear night in Midgard. Wait...how is this possible? How am I not awaiting Odin's praise in Asgard?

Once more, Astrid searched her neck for a wound. She smeared around the wet blood, but found only an abrasion where a deep cut should have been.

"Astrid..."

Warren's voice prompted her to sit up, a movement that finally startled the wolf that had begun to sniff at her bloodstained hair. Eye to eye, the beast did not growl at her, nor did it show fear; it simply acknowledged her with a cocked-headed stare and then turned. She felt as if the thing knew her. *Could this be one of the wolves I faced when I first awoke in this strange land?*

Astrid tried to speak, but her voice was gone. Her throat was raw, swollen; it was hard to swallow. It was a sign of weakness to be sick, and being a woman who fought shoulder to shoulder with men, there was no time for such a display.

Back on her feet, Astrid unhooked a dagger from her belt and prepared to throw it. Aiming carefully, she launched the blade at the wolf that had Warren's arm. Still a touch wobbly on her feet, the dagger did not strike the wolf's neck as she had targeted, but its hindquarters. Luckily, it was still enough to make the animal let go.

Warren brushed off both wolves and stood, ready to fight, edging forward with his front foot. The two wolves moved in a figure eight around him, one following the other as they glared and growled.

He's going to be fine, Astrid thought. *Don't worry about him. Worry about yourself.*

Bent over, hands on her knees, Astrid tried to catch her breath. She was winded and with each breath her throat still burned. She watched the wolves size Warren up and she wanted to scream at him to attack, but her voice was still stolen. As she blinked, chunks of time seemed to vanish before her. *Breathe, Astrid, breathe slowly.*

When Astrid reopened her eyes, her strength returned and the world around her began to stabilize.

"No, you don't get to bite me and then run off to your master!" Warren shouted, as the wolves turned their heads and raced off. "Come back!"

When Astrid coughed, Warren spun around and gasped. The man looked as though he might pass out.

"Astrid, you're alive!" Warren cheered with a surge of happiness.

Warren planted her sword into the ground by its blade to wrap his arms around her. Enclosed tightly in his bear hug, Astrid allowed herself a moment of respite. Going numb, she fell into his arms and let him hold her up.

As Warren separated from the hug, all he saw was blood. Crimson painted the front of her from neck to groin, so much so it stained her armor and leather skirt. Astrid did not look well; her skin was pale and the way she pawed at her neck made her seem nervous and childlike.

"What happened?"

Soft words buried inside a scratchy cough was all that he heard.

"Astrid, how badly are you hurt?" he rushed his words.

Warren could not help but notice how she had not raised her eyes to meet his after the hug. *Astrid is a proud warrior; for her to act this...this timid...there must be something very wrong.*

"Astrid?" he asked again, as he reached out to lift her chin.

As his hand was about to touch her, she jumped back and lifted her gaze. Panic filled her eyes. Warren reached for her again, but suddenly his vision went black.

Astrid had not meant to strike him in the nose, but the thought of his fingers on her neck triggered an immediate reaction. Hands up, she covered her throat; the area felt odd. It burned one moment and tickled the next.

"Don't..." she could barely say.

Warren shook his head and blinked his eyes open. "Relax, Astrid. You're safe now."

Safe now? Astrid did not know if that was true. *Will I be claimed by the Valkyrie's golden light soon? Or will I just crumple back to the earth and return to the darkness that had claimed me moments before?*

Either way, her heart fluttered and she had the impression she was living on borrowed time.

"I..." she tried to speak.

"Careful, Astrid, you suffered a neck wound...at least I—"

"I...was...cut," she said with a hand motions that showed how.

"You were cut?"

Astrid nodded.

"How deep?" Warren stepped closer as he dipped his head to look at her neck. "How deep is the cut?"

Astrid covered her throat with both hands and backed away.

"Let me see."

Astrid shook her head as she unwrapped the old bandage that was around her arm and retied the dirty, bloody thing around her neck. *I thought he saw me cut…saw me die. No, I can't do this.*

"Better." Her voice squeaked. "You?"

"I have suffered worse. I'm more worried about my brother and the rest of town."

Astrid pulled her sword from the ground and handed it to Warren.

"Your sword?"

"Take it," she whispered.

"Will you be okay here?"

"Go." She pointed off to the center of town.

Warren did not move. He just stared, and the intensity of his gaze made Astrid uncomfortable. She could almost see her pain and frustration reflected in his gaze.

"Go to my home, or better yet my storage cellar. There's a hidden space in the back, behind some crates."

Astrid nodded and pointed toward the center of town again.

"I'll be back soon, I promise."

CHAPTER 17

Astrid shuffled off toward Warren's home. She looked down at her hands; her leather gloves were coated in blood, ruined. She didn't have the luxury of asking her sister to sew her a new pair, like she did when she came home from raiding with her brothers mere months ago. It had not been her blood that time; it had been the blood of a tribe of skinny, pale men who, although living in the cold climate, danced naked at night around huge fires. Tall and thin, these men fought skillfully with their hands and feet, but were still no match for her; she was Astrid the White, after all. She was...

Something was wrong; Astrid felt strange-empty. *Has my will to fight seeped out of me along with my lifeblood? Where is my fire?*

There was no clear answer, only the need to clean the blood and grime from her body and the desire to curl up in her skins and sleep for days.

As she drew closer to Warren's home, she could see the firelights from town. Nothing seemed out of place to her—the town was undamaged. When she reached the door, she turned back and looked into town again. This time she fully expected to see the golden lights of men's souls as they rose to Valhalla, just as she had seen earlier. Part of her was scared to witness this miracle again. It did not seem right that only she would see it and not Warren. Astrid began to tremble.

Why did I die and return? Why didn't my soul light up the sky as it ascended? H-have the gods rejected me?

From her vantage point, she saw torches move about town; their pace and distance from one another seemed too organized to be bandits. The garrison forces must have been victorious and now searched the town for any further trouble.

She should have been happy—her enemies were defeated—but the only emotions she could find inside her were muddied. Astrid sighed and tested her voice. The burn was less severe now, but it was still there.

With one foot nearly across the threshold of Warren's home, Astrid realized she could not yet enter. Her boots were covered in both moist and dried gore, blood from the field in the forest and that which had spilled from her neck moments ago.

"Ruined," Astrid whispered as she examined her fur boots.

Seated at the small table outside Warren's home, she slowly removed her boots. They had been a gift from her father, made for her out of the hide of a great black bear she had killed during her most famous hunt. She loved her boots so much; they were warm and comfortable. Through their age, they had molded to her feet, like a second skin. These boots had been with her on many marches; it was a shame to lose them, but there was nothing she could do. They were ruined.

Astrid tossed them into an empty fire pit then moved up to her leather-armor skirt. It too had been soiled by her lifeblood, but it had been coated with gore before, both hers and her enemies', in fact. Astrid unhooked her sword belt and dropped it to the ground. With several pouches also attached to it, it fell with a heavy thud and rattle. With a sigh, Astrid went to work on the three straps that held her skirt up. It was so tight it left deep, red gouge marks on her waist, which she normally paid little mind, but today, as the index finger on her left hand ran under the top of the garment, she found an indent of skin that was both puffy and sore. Astrid lost herself in thought a moment as she outlined the raw marks. *Why do I allow this thing to dig so tightly into my skin? Why do I hurt myself so willingly?*

When she pushed the last strap through the many loops at the top of the skirt, it loosened. After she untied the front, the heavy leather garment dropped to the ground atop her weapon belt, and gave her skin freedom.

Astrid felt the stickiness of blood on her neck again, and the sensation shot a chill down her body. Suddenly, she could not stand to be confined by her chest armor any longer. It had to come off; this second skin, which had protected her for years, through many battles, was welcomed no longer. With a grunt, she pulled at the latches on the right side, but they would not come loose with ease.

Astrid staggered into Warren's home and dropped to her knees. Exhausted, she allowed herself to crumple to the floor. Atop the fur hearthrug, Astrid grunted with frustration as she once more pulled at the straps of her armor.

"Come...free..."

Astrid's eyes teared up when she caught the glimmer of one of her daggers' handles. She crawled out the door to the belt, grabbed the dagger, and cleaved the straps that latched her chest armor together.

Once free, she tossed the weighty piece of metal to the wooden floor inside Warren's home, the boards splintering noisily when it struck them. As loud as the sound was, she paid it little mind. Her eyes locked on a bucket that sat in the rear of the home next to a small wooden tub.

The water in the bucket appeared polluted, and by the looks of the dirty rag that hung from it, Astrid assumed it was the same one she used to wipe her weapons clean after the first skirmish with the bandits the night she broke Hammond's nose.

Astrid had seen several wells in town and knew where the nearest stream was, but she just did not care to go get fresher water. What was left in this bucket, although soiled, would have to suffice, as Astrid could not stand to be covered in her own lifeblood any longer. Its presence was a constant reminder of her failure, her defeat, her death.

Splashing the cold water on her neck dislodged some of the grime; black chunks of dried blood glided atop the drips that traced slowly down her chest to her stomach. She brushed the flakes of blood from her stomach and watched as their remnants traveled down past her navel. The water changed with each handful she splashed upon herself, and became darker red with each sob she took.

"I failed you, Father," Astrid's legs shook as she whimpered. "I failed..."

When she let go of herself, she collapsed. The fall nearly broke the tiny wooden tub. Knees to her chest, she held herself tight and buried her face.

The cold bit at her limbs when it unexpectedly crept up on her, and she welcomed it like an old friend. Tonight, the air felt as though she was home, in the snow-covered lands of her family. When the chill vanished, suddenly and as oddly as it had arrived, Astrid took it as sign from the gods.

"I *have* failed..." Astrid's sobs grew louder as she tried again to clean the blood from her neck and chest, but the rag only smeared it over her body now—the water was nearly gone and her tears, no matter how plentiful, would not fill the tub. With her head tucked down, Astrid accepted her defeat.

CHAPTER 18

"Astrid?" Warren called to her from outside his home, his voice full of concern. "Astrid, are you here?"

Only her muffled cries answered him.

"The brigands are gone, slain or caught. My lord's horse archers plan to search the forests at daybreak, hunt down any stragglers that may have taken flight."

Warren had seen her skirt and sword belt outside; they were a bloody mess and would require much care to be salvaged. When he stepped through the open door to his home, he spotted a smear of bright-red blood on the ground—Astrid was hurt worse than she admitted.

"Astrid, what's wrong? How bad are you hurt?"

His eyes, locked on the shadowy outline of Astrid's naked body in his tub, did not spot her armor on the floor, and he kicked it as he walked.

"I found your armor," Warren said, trying to make light of his clumsiness, but there was no response from the warrior woman. "Astrid?"

"I was defeated," she whispered.

"All great warriors suffer defeat at some point, Astrid." Warren took several small steps forward. "I bet even your—"

"Do all great warriors get their throats sliced by insignificant rogues?"

"What?"

"Today I died. I was killed on the battlefield, Warren. You should be burning my body right now."

"You are exaggerating. I saw…"

Warren did not remember exactly what he saw. There was chaos and blood, but his own wounds ached and interrupted his thoughts.

"The gods must hate me, Warren." Her voice quivered.

"No, they reward us both by keeping you alive."

"Alive?" As she spoke, she sounded deflated. "Why would they torture me like this? Why would they deny their loyal servant passage into the next life?"

Dark patches within her pale blonde hair caught his eye—blood stains. Warren put his manners aside a moment and stepped around to gaze more closely upon her. With her knees up and head down he could not tell what her wounds looked like. Still, Warren gasped, for what little of Astrid's bare flesh was visible was painted red with blood.

"Show me the wound." His voice was tight with seriousness.

"Warren, please."

"Show me."

Astrid lifted her head slowly. Warren saw more blood, thick and nearly black, caked upon her throat and collarbone. She had smeared it all over her chest; her fingers were tinted red to the knuckle. He could not be sure what had happened to cause this much filth, and the darkness of the room did not help his vision, but to the best of his knowledge, Astrid appeared undamaged.

"You are a real mess, and this dirty water will hardly clean you." Warren finished with a sigh of relief, "But, Astrid, I see no wound."

"I need to be clean."

"Then let me get you fresh water."

Warren turned to walk away, but Astrid called out.

"So much blood...in my mouth, over my armor, my skin...I need to be clean." Astrid ducked her head as she spoke.

"I will fetch you more water."

"Hurry."

Sensing there was something more from her scared voice, he asked again, "Is there a wound you are not sharing with me?"

"Water now...please, Warren."

"Fine. When I return, I will start a fire for you. With some warm water, an honored warrior can have a proper bath."

After another few steps toward the door, Warren heard Astrid call out again. "Wait."

Warren looked over his shoulder.

"Do not go yet."

"Very well."

"I cannot get the blood off my neck."

"Well, with some clean water—" Warren began to repeat.

"Warren," she sighed. "I cannot..."

"I understand."

Warren walked back to the tub in the corner of the room and knelt behind Astrid. He bunched up the now—crimson rag until it formed a point and then pressed it hard to the back of her neck where a few speckles of blood sat.

"We really need fresh water." Warren rubbed the cloth side to side, but the red tint did not clear from her skin.

Astrid's voice shook heavily as she sighed.

Warren looked to his bed; beside it, off a peg on the wall, his two waterskins. Warren quickly collected the waterskins and opened one before he even sat back down behind her.

"Full of crystal clean river water. This well help you clean up."

"Thank you."

Warren would have smiled and commented on her politeness had he not been so worried. "Ready yourself. The water might be cold."

"Where I come from, all water is cold."

Warren tilted the waterskin over her shoulder and poured a portion down her neck. Astrid did not flinch when the water cascaded down her back; she held still, her knees pulled tightly to her chest, her breath shallow through her nose. With the rag back in hand, Warren began to scrub at the caked-on blood, this time able to free the flakes and chunks from her neckline and collarbone.

The uncomfortable silence compelled him to speak.

"Where did all this come from?"

"I told you."

Warren was sure that if he pried any further, his questions would be answered in tears, and he did not want to see Astrid cry again.

As he moved his hand slowly around her neck, he poured a little more water over her. *This blood*, he thought, *so thick. This did not come from another or the field; it had to have come from her.* Warren shuffled around as he examined her neck further and noticed a pink line that stretched from side to side. *Could she really have been slashed?* he wondered, although he found it hard to fully believe it. *Was she cut by that bandit?*

He suddenly remembered the bear fight and looked from her left arm to her right when his thoughts returned. The bandages where gone, and with them any sign of those wounds. *How is it possible to heal so quickly?* It seemed to Warren to be the work of witchcraft.

"Your neck is all clean, Astrid, but there's still blood on your chest and arms, no doubt your stomach as well," Warren announced. "You should finish up. I will start a fire."

Warren watched Astrid run her index and middle finger around her neck slowly. With a sigh, she nodded and stood, moaning and stretching as she did so.

Out of courtesy, Warren turned around, but slowly, as he wanted to be sure she didn't have any more wounds first. He expected her to be a mess and had steeled himself, but all he saw was more blood—there was still no clear source. Smudged where her knees were pressed to her chest, the stains of moist blood seemed to cover nearly a third of the front of her body.

"Astrid, all this…" Warren did not want to say any more.

"I need more help," her whisper barely reached his ears.

"Should I go get my brother's wife?"

"No. I cannot…" she sounded as if she was about to try cry. "I cannot stand this-my blood all over…"

Warren turned, and met Astrid's gaze. In her eyes, the way she stood, the rhythm of her breaths; he could feel the heaviness of her hurt and it began to equally pain him.

"Please, Warren."

"I'll do my best."

Once Warren poured the remainder of the first waterskin over Astrid's chest and stomach, he began to scrub the dirt and gore from her body. Careful at first not to touch her in a way that might be misunderstood.

"All will be better soon, Astrid."

The longer Warren touched her, the more comfortable he became with the act. Slowly, his mind drifted back to the times when he had bathed his wife. They were good memories that brought a smile to his face.

"You are smiling."

"What?"

Astrid glared at Warren while he gently scrubbed her chest clean.

"Do you find pleasure in this?" Astrid whispered.

"No." The pleasant look fell from his face.

"You lie."

Warren paused before he answered. "Perhaps, I simply smile because I am happy you are alive."

"Why do I doubt that?"

"I don't understand."

"I have been a burden on you since I arrived here. If not for your desire for me you would have—"

"I would not have."

"I'm not blind to the way you look at me, Warren." Astrid stated surely. "The way you *are* looking at me."

"Listen to me, this...*this* isn't easy for me. The last woman I bathed was my wife. My wife is dead, Astrid. And today I thought you were too. I-I saw you fall. I thought you were killed in front of me."

"I-"

"Say no more." He nodded. "We are done here."

Warren raised the waterskin and rinsed her one last time. As the water poured slowly down her chest, he watched it trickle down past her hips to where it dripped like a spring rain shower to the floor of the tub. She was partially right; his mind filled with conflict and it was not where it should be.

"What you really need is to go take a swim in the brook."

That and some of the fancy perfume the market in the city sold, he thought as he turned his back to her. The idea reminded Warren of how he had promised his wife he would one day buy her some perfume, but he never did. *I thought there would be more time. There is never enough time...*

"I-I do feel much better now. I'm sorry, Warren. You have my thanks," Astrid whispered, bringing him back to the present.

"Good. Now, let me get the fire burning and seek out some more clothing for you. Until then, take whatever suits you from my garment chest."

When Warren opened the door, he heard Astrid stir behind him, her feet heavily slapping the wooden floor.

"Where are you going?" she quickly asked.

"Outside, to gather firewood," he said over his shoulder.

"Tell me, Warren, are we safe here?" Astrid's arms slowly wrapped around herself like two snakes.

"Yes." Warren lied, still gripped by an ominous sensation that a larger force of bandits was out there, yet to be discovered. "Yes, they are all gone-all dead."

CHAPTER 19

ASTRID DID NOT GET OUT of Warren's bed the following day. She did not shift, roll over, or even release the slightest snore. She laid still, "corpse still," as Warren described it to his brother. The pair, stood outside his home as the sun set, voices lowered like a couple of gossiping old women.

"So then what will do you with her?"

"What do you mean?"

Hammond shrugged. "Will you keep her?"

"She's not property, Brother. She's a woman lost from her home. How would you like it if your wife was gone and set upon by slavers?"

"You think we could find some?"

Warren shot his brother a look, but it did not work.

"What price do you think my wife would fetch?"

"Hammond, you donkey's ass."

Warren knew that his brother was joking, but he was not in the mood to accept it.

"Relax, Brother."

"I am trying," Warren answered with a deep sigh.

"Look, you said it yourself, she was hurt in combat. You thought she was killed."

Warren cocked his head at his brother in confusion.

"What? You told me last night, you said you saw her cut up, remember?"

"No." Warren rubbed his eyes. "I said she was cut up?"

Hammond laughed. "I think *you* need to sleep for a day, old man."

"Very funny."

"No joke. You are losing your grip like you lost your sense of humor." Hammond peeked through the door at Astrid, wrapped in furs and sleeping soundly. "Let me watch her tonight. You go back and sleep with Helen."

"Do what?" Warren's voice was laced with shock.

"I meant sleep in my home, alongside my wife," Hammond explained, his eyes still locked on the outline of Astrid's curves under the furs.

Warren pulled his stout brother out of the doorway and back to the yard as he replied, "I could not do that."

"Fine, then tell her to sleep on the floor. It matters little to me."

"I will sleep on the floor...here. Hammond, you go home to sleep with your wife."

"Blah, questing through the forests, fighting bandits, bathing goddesses, you have all the fun."

"Well then, the next beautiful, blonde, warrior woman that walks out of the forest speaking a strange language can stay at your home."

With a firm grasp of his arm, Hammond answered sharply, "Deal!"

"You are a fool."

"A thirsty one at that." Hammond patted his belly.

"Go!" Warren nodded in the direction of the tavern.

After Hammond disappeared down the darkened path into the center of town, Warren peered back in on Astrid; still no movement. He crept in slowly as he wondered, *is it because my wife tossed and turned so much at night that makes Astrid's stillness bother me so?*

"Astrid?" he called out softly. "Astrid, are you well and awake?"

Nothing. She did not answer, twitch, or even blink. Across the room on his small table, Warren stared at the pile of clothing he had purchased her. All new, freshly tailored, they might have cost him a few coins, but the act of kindness he hoped to surprise her with had already made him feel good. He had not felt such a way in months.

Next to the clothes was a fresh loaf of bread. Hammond's wife, Helen, had helped him acquire the clothing and had baked him the bread, a kind gesture Warren intended to pay back. No doubt there were some chores his brother had become lax in.

He thought back to the night before, when he had found Astrid's gear so carelessly abandoned, strewn on the ground outside where it could have been stolen. Warren did not know how he was going to break it to her that her battle-axe had vanished, most likely claimed by a town guard during the clean up. He would confront Gathon tomorrow, but could hear the man's voice in his head, his use of official words like "confiscated" to explain why it would not be returned.

Lying down on the ground beside Astrid, Warren let out a grunt. *A man my age should be raising a family.*

"Our child would have been beautiful, my love," Warren whispered as he thought of his wife.

How much time had passed, he was unsure. Warren had fallen asleep on the floor near Astrid; his home was pitch-dark and still, his only indication that it was the late hours of the night. In the distance, an owl hooted; it was the grey owl he listened to every night. Warren had named the majestic creature Lunar, as it only hooted this loudly on the nights the moon could be seen.

"You hear that, Astrid? Lunar's call is different in the moonlight. He is my night watch, and I am his day watch." Warren smiled.

Warren turned to face Astrid but the darkness was so intense he could barely see her. There were rustling noises in her direction, but he couldn't discern their cause.

"Damned darkness," Warren grumbled as he felt his way across the small room to the table where his flint and steel sat. "Astrid, are you awake?"

There was no response save what sounded to Warren like the flop of a very large pike fish upon his floor. Striking the flint against the steel, launched a spark into a dish of dry weeds. Ignited, he dipped one candle into the flame, then another, and the last.

"Astrid, I am glad you—" Warren nearly dropped the candelabrum when he saw Astrid convulsing on the floor.

He raced across the room, snatching a browned reed from a pile on the floor as he did, and pinning Astrid's shoulders to the straw, he placed the reed between her teeth as gently as he could.

"Astrid, wake up!" he screamed in her face. "Wake up!"

Under his calloused fingers, her soft flesh burned. *Such heat. Is it even possible for a man to produce this much?*

Her eyelids fluttered as a moan escaped from deep in her throat. Warren had seen men die before and was sure that any moment she would leave him.

"Damn you, woman, you cannot come here to die!"

As the tremors that shook her body began to slow, her temperature broke, but Warren's grip on her shoulders did not relax. A new sensation stole away his thoughts as he saw her skin ripple and something crawl beneath it. He would have sworn that he felt an army of ants creeping beneath his fingers.

"Astrid, wake up!"

Astrid gasped for air, her eyes suddenly open.

"Astrid!"

Her only response was to roll her glassy eyes to him and stare.

"You are going to survive this, you hear me?"

Tears formed as she drew in another series of panicked breaths.

"You will live to fight another day, Astrid. You are too great a warrior to die in bed."

"Father…"

"No, Astrid, it's Warren. You are still here in Grømstad."

"Grømstad?"

"Yes." Warren smiled at her.

"Warren?"

"Yes."

Overcome with emotion, Warren wrapped his arms around Astrid, in a firm embrace.

"What happened to me?"

CHAPTER 20

Confused and, for one of only a few times ever, truly terrified, Astrid did something she had only ever done for her father—she stayed in a man's embrace.

"What happened to me?"

"You were ill, Astrid. Do you not remember?"

A violent explosion of memory made Astrid jerk herself free of Warren's arms.

A puddle of blood spanned her entire field of vision. It was the brightest red she had ever seen, a spectacular shade of crimson. It bubbled and churned seemingly all around her, but she did not feel any heat. She heard women scream. *No*, she thought, *howl in immeasurable terror.* As soon as she could focus, a bright yellow light shined in her face and washed it all away. Yet there, between the intermittent flashes of light, she saw a young woman, strapped down to a shiny, black stone table, the poor thing looking gaunt and scared, squirming to free herself.

Astrid wanted to help her, but she could not move. When she gazed down, she realized she was nude, ankle deep in the thickest, foulest smelling mud she had ever seen. It was viscous and, like oil, it shimmered a moment before the yellow light blinded her again.

Astrid growled as she tried to lift her feet out of the muck. She pulled and pulled but sensed she actually sunk more with each movement. With a prayer to her gods, Astrid mustered all her strength.

"Thor! Give me strength!"

She groaned as she strained her right leg to the point where she thought her muscles might tear. She swore to herself, her family, her gods—she would be free. Slipping upward a tiny bit, Astrid was filled with a strong sense of victory, but the moment was quickly lost to the sound of her name being screamed.

"I-I died."

"No, you did not."

"Warren, I witnessed the house of Hel with my very eyes."

Warren squeezed her hand in his, the pressure increased until she perceived the blood pumping through his veins.

"It was only a dream, Astrid. You are alive, here. Now. Safe."

She no longer listened to him, her mind on an isolated thought.

"Now, I understand what my brother always says."

"What is that?"

"That there is no safety in this world once Hel knows your name."

CHAPTER 21

IT WAS TWO MORE DAYS before Astrid dressed and left Warren's meager home. She had not said much and had slept most of the time. Warren gave her the space she seemed to require, while he kept an eye on the house in case she needed him.

He mulled over recent events until he came to the conclusion that defeat, for her people, must outweigh life itself. He had fought enemies like that; they preferred death to defeat.

Now that Astrid was outside, she sat on one of the benches in the front of Warren's house with a scroll of parchment and a piece of charcoal in hand. The town tailor was going to make a visit soon and fix the clothes he had prepared for her. Warren could not believe they still did not fit right. *At least she's properly covered*, he told himself.

"Morn, Astrid." Warren waved from the field where he gathered his crops.

Astrid waved and smiled back. She found comfort in the way Warren doted on her—it entertained as well.

"How are you, Astrid? Are you well, Astrid? Are you warm…hot… cold…" Astrid mimicked Warren's common questions aloud.

She was beginning to like how it felt to be cared for by Warren, regardless of its ill-timing. If she was going to be stuck here, it was good to have one person she could trust. One person who she enjoyed.

No, I need to get home.

With a shake of her head, Astrid flushed out the thoughts and placed the dry charcoal pinched between her fingers to the parchment before her to draw a map of the area. To own such a thing would be handy at some point; she was sure of it. Although taught to read maps by her father, she could not remember the last time she had produced her own. It had been a long while, and was carved on a large stone.

The sudden crunch of small branches startled her, and the charcoal dropped from her hand as she abruptly stood up. She expected to see the brigand leader, his blade still dripping with her lifeblood, a smile on his face, but instead it was one of Warren's goats the thing meandering aimlessly in search of something to eat. Astrid pressed her hand to her chest, her heart pounded. She remembered a time not long ago that she and her brother Jokul hunted boar. A large one had sprung unexpectedly from the brush. She should have been scared then, but she did not even flinch.

"A goat makes you jump now, Astrid. Pray your family never sees you like this."

"Are you well?" Warren asked as he approached from behind, his voice startling her further.

"I'm fine!" she snapped. "I'm fine."

"Sorry, I saw you jump and was not sure what scared you."

"It was your goat."

"Him?" Warren pointed at the offending animal as it chewed a mouthful of grass.

"Aye."

"He *is* an evil thing. Perhaps we should slay him?"

Astrid smiled slightly. Whether she liked it or not, she found his levity amusing. As concerned for her family and home as she was, she could not help but keep wondering what happiness could be further discovered here.

"Spare him. I wager he's not as sinister as you have labeled him."

"Oh?" Warren replied.

"Earlier, I saw him eat some of his own shite."

Warren howled with laughter.

"That sounded a lot like a joke, Astrid. Be careful, I might think you are going soft." Warren patted her lightly on the shoulder before he was back to his work.

Astrid sat back down and unraveled her parchment. She wanted to work on her map, but she could not seem to make her hand mark the paper. *Runes should be carved by a strong hand, not brushed…lightly,* she thought.

Eyes on the town, she listened to the sounds of the children at play. In Birka, the children did not play; they trained, hunted, and practiced skills. When she thought of her own childhood, and the many times a practice sword struck her weak frame, a chill ran down her spine where a sense of pride once filled her chest. *Perhaps this is a better life,* she thought.

On the parchment, she saw a new set of lines; she had begun to draw and not even realized it—*no wait…that is no random scratch on the parchment. That is the beginning of a word.*

Astrid had so often rejected her father's advice to study words that he had finally given up on her. It was one of the few things she knew disappointed him, and she did not like to dwell on the thought. *How do I know this character?*

While she stared at the parchment, Astrid's mind went blank and was filled with the sensations, sounds, and tastes of her death. Astrid moved the charcoal back and forth, hoping another familiar symbol might appear, but none did. Only blackness emerged from the end of the charcoal, the parchment claimed further with each stroke.

Nervous energy made her shake, so she stomped her feet to steel herself, but could not stave off the sour memory of the blood that filled her mouth. The salty taste made her choke and she lifted the mug of ale to her lips in an attempt to wash it away.

"Odin, I remain your willing servant. You have shown me the fruits of Asgard and the horrors of Hel, yet here I remain in the living world. I call upon you all: Odin, Modr, Sif. I ask for a sign, and until one is given, I guess this soft place is where I will rest."

Eyes closed, Astrid drew a deep breath and held it in her lungs a moment. Lips pursed, she released her breath slowly, repeating it until her body finally calmed.

"Much better."

When Astrid opened her eyes, it was late in the day. Time had passed rapidly, but how, she was unsure. Astrid reached her arms over her head and then back, the dress she wore stretched to its limits over her chest. *A deep breath or a long flex could pop these stitches now; a feast Warren's eyes would not care to miss*, she thought. *The man desires me, but are those his only intentions?*

In Birka, it would be her father's decision who she would marry and no man of suitable power or prestige had been found yet. Regardless, Astrid had not wanted such a union, as it would surely result in the end of her life as a warrior and the beginning of life as a child-bearer.

Astrid cleared her mind as she searched for Warren. He was still in the fields; he had worked tirelessly all day. *He must be thirsty, I should bring him water, but where...*

"The bekk."[1]

Warren had referred to the source of fresh water a few times, and she could almost hear it rush when she shut out all the other ambient noise.

It was not in the direction of the forest they had traveled through or the hill above, nor the center of town. It was behind the farms, inside the forest beyond that, a short distance from where she had first engaged the brigands. The mere thought of the enemy caused her to freeze in fear.

What if they are still out there? What will you do now, weaponless and dressed as a...girl-child? She could not answer. She just stared off past Warren's home and the back corner of this farm, past his storage cellar to an overgrown track of weeds, the very spot the brook must have been beyond. Slowly, she focused more on the line of overgrown brush in the distance.

---

1 Stream in Old Norse.

First, all she saw were tall weeds, but then the greenness of the plants faded away and the dark space between them took dominance. The blackness sucked Astrid in, made her feel as if she were sliding toward that spot across the field. Her body felt weightless and her head light, as if it floated atop her shoulders like a feather too stubborn to drop.

Her eyes refocused on an unexpected sight. Her gaze was no longer on weeds and grass; it was on a large green mass—a monstrous head, its mouth falling slowly open. Astrid's heart dropped to her feet. The thing—whatever it was—had a dark mouth full of blood-red teeth. She was sure it would suck her in and use those crimson-coated teeth to chew her bones.

The impact of the ground was harsh; it jarred her back and rattled her head, yet it freed her confused mind from what it thought it saw. Now seated on the ground, Astrid's panicked eyes searched the horizon for the monster but only found a serene scene.

The will to stand was great, but her body said no. Before she knew it, Warren loomed over her, his hand out to help her up.

"Astrid, I saw you fall."

"I...I'm fine, just thought I saw something..."

Over Warren's shoulder, she looked again.

"Astrid, you've lost your water," Warren said frankly.

On the ground between her feet was a small puddle, the wetness of which could be traced up the bottom of her dress to its origin. Astrid squinted with befuddlement.

"I..." Astrid pinched the wet fabric around her pelvis. "I—"

"Worry not. I have other dresses for you. Let me fetch some water and—"

"Where is the sense in all this?"

"Astrid, it's nothing, probably just the fall. I cannot tell you how many times I have seen Hammond do just that after drinking ale all night and falling on his seat."

Astrid could hear no more. Embarrassed, she ran back inside snatching up her map as she passed the table.

"I do not want this! I did not ask for any of this! I should be dead! I should be in Valhalla!" she screamed a moment before she slammed the door shut.

CHAPTER 22

WARREN STOOD IN SILENCE. HER reaction mirrored that of a spoiled child. Warren did not know how to react. His wife had always been so evenly mannered, her moods a constant. For a moment he considered Hammond's help, but when he considered it, he realized that Astrid, no doubt, needed to speak with another woman, and the only other woman he knew enough to speak openly with was Helen, his sister-in-law.

Helen was a kind and good woman, too nice for his often-unfaithful brother. The daughter of a family friend, she was originally intended to be Warren's wife, in an effort to bind the two families, but Warren left for war before she was old enough to wed.

Warren had always liked Helen but, before he left, he had little desire for women at all. He was too young and focused on the glory of battle, but that all quickly changed after his first day of combat.

Warren wished he had asked Helen to pray for him and he regretted not telling her that he would be happy to start a family of his own with her when he returned. The idea of dying without having a child to carry on his name weighed heavily on him.

One day, months later, when a runner was being sent back to the kingdom, Warren had his chance to relay his message to Helen, but he did not. His comrades called it fear, but he called it fate. He told his friends, that if the old gods saw to it to reward him with a family after the war, they would do so.

To this day, Warren had never spoken a word of his plans to return to Helen after the war. The knowledge would not change the fact that she was wed to his brother when all thought Warren dead. Still, when he looked at Helen, it reminded him of what could have been. She may not have been as comely as his departed wife or Astrid, but she was a loyal, loving woman, despite Hammond's shortcomings and transgressions.

Hammond's home was larger than Warren's—in fact, nearly three times as big. It was built for Hammond and Helen by Helen's father when they married many years ago. Helen's mother had hoped her daughter would fill the place with children, but unfortunately only one child was born there, a young girl by the name of Willamina. She was almost ten years old now and shy as a flower in winter. Even at this moment, the little sandy-blonde girl sat silently at play with an old rag doll, near the hearth.

Tonight, Helen had made one of her stews, often said to be bland and sometimes sour; it had tasted fine to Warren when he sampled a spoonful.

"Very good, Helen."

"Thank you. Your brother always values my cooking, why can't you?"

Helen pointed her wooden spoon at Hammond, who sat at the long table at the center of their home with his feet propped up. His nose was still red from where Astrid had struck him, and his eyes were circled with a deep shade of purple; he was quite the sight.

"All home alone with nothing to eat, that's why he never complains." Hammond smirked.

"Not at all. It's simple: unlike you, I can still taste things."

"I bet." Hammond snickered. "Leads me to ask: what have you been tasting back home these days, Brother? Hmm?"

"Hammond!" Helen scolded and nodded at Willamina. "Not in front of the child."

"Sorry."

"Yes, sorry, Helen, but Hammond does stir up a topic I need to breach." Warren said as he paced back in forth over a small rug until his boot snagged a corner and kicked it over. "To be honest, Astrid is the main reason I am here."

"Oh, does that poor girl need more tailoring?"

Warren cracked his knuckles over and over as he answered. "Well, y-yes, but—"

Helen giggled, and when she did, both Hammond and Warren's smiles dropped.

"I have never seen you so nervous about anything, Warren."

"Helen, please," Warren begged as he fixed the rug.

"I'm sorry, do continue."

Warren cleared his throat. "Astrid needs help. The kind I cannot give her. I was hoping you, Helen, could go to my home and engage her in woman talk."

"Well, I could take her some stew." Helen stirred the pot vigorously.

"She would like that." Warren finally sat down next to his brother and knocked his feet off the table.

"Yes, honey, you and Willa should take all of the stew, in fact. Brother and I will go to the tavern and get a bite there. I hear they are having fish tonight."

Helen asked as she looked at them, "How do you always know what they are serving there?"

Warren turned his gaze to the bandages on his arm; he did not want his face to tell the truth that Hammond's hid so well.

"You know I like to share a drink with my associates from time to time. It's a merchant's life, to make business connections and spoil them with fancy ale after a good deal is shook on."

"It would have nothing to do with the large-breasted trollops who serve the food there? I hear that one girl is as filthy as a cave troll with every disease imaginable."

Warren held his breath so as not to laugh.

"We all know trolls are icky and gross, right, Willa?" Hammond said in jest.

Their daughter giggled, her smile gleaming as brightly as her father's and uncle's.

"I know your eyes like to linger, Hammond. Why, if your eyes had their own set of hands, they would be responsible for molesting every woman in this town."

"I do appreciate the beauty in things, which is why I am with you, my dear Helen."

Warren nodded to Hammond, who nodded back. "Those sloppy women of the tavern…they are not the vision of loveliness and woman-hood you are, Helen."

Helen smirked. "Well, I do appreciate that, but there's no need to lower yourself to the ranks of your brother, Warren. All you need to do is ask."

"Oh." Warren frowned, and then asked softly, "Can you speak with her then?"

"Of course. Anything for you, Warren." Helen grinned.

CHAPTER 23

HELEN KNOCKED ON WARREN'S DOOR softly, calling out Astrid's name. After Helen announced herself, she took several steps back—there was something odd about the way her husband squirmed and twitched when he warned her to tread carefully. Warren's, "trust him, he knows" made her worry even more.

"Astrid, dear, it's Helen, Hammond's wife. We have not properly met, but I have brought you something to eat. Stew," she said.

Helen stayed quiet, eyes on her daughter, who stared back up at her. Ever since Warren's wife died, his home had been dark and still, filled with melancholy. She missed the days the four of them got together, told tales, and laughed. With a gaze over her shoulder, Helen stared at her home in the distance, closer to the center of town. She often worried about Warren, his home up here on the hill, so far from the others. But she could hear his voice in her head telling her that, someday, the town would grow out past him to the brook. That day, he would be as much in the center of this place as they were.

Footfalls interrupted Helen's thoughts; someone approached.

"Astrid, I brought you some stew, please invite me in."

When the door opened, the two women locked eyes and were momentarily silent.

"Greetings," Helen finally said with a nod. "I am Hammond's wife."

She was stunned by Astrid's beauty. She had seen her before, in a full state on undress nonetheless, but the woman had been unconscious;

silent and motionless, she had seemed soft. Now, Helen marveled at her. The warrior woman was built as though she was chiseled from smooth rock, her lines so strong and her muscles so taut she almost looked unreal. With only a coarse blanket draped over her shoulders, Astrid's breasts were partially visible and Helen thought, *That such soft femininity could punctuate such a hard form. One would believe such a fine shape could only be held by one of the old gods.*

She had clearly interrupted Astrid in the middle of her trying to unbraid her hair. The left side was mostly done, but the right side was still a mess of knotted hair, broken strands adrift in the breeze.

"Is that stew?" Astrid asked.

"Yes. May I bring it in? The weight of this thing is like a boulder."

Astrid had never seen this woman before, yet had heard her name spoken many times. *So this is the woman who nursed and dressed me when I first arrived in this...place,* Astrid thought. *She's tall and skinny, not unlike my sister, and her hips are wide. She has had babies.* Astrid could see Helen's muscles flex as they balanced the weight of the large metal pot she carried.

Astrid's eyes on the stew prompted Helen to say again, "It is very heavy."

"Give it to me." Astrid hoisted the pot out of Helen's arms.

"Careful, I wrapped it in leathers so not to burn—"

"I have it."

"You *are* strong."

"You may enter..." Astrid began but caught a dash of movement behind Hammond's wife. "Who is this?"

"Who?" Helen playfully looked to the right and then left. "Oh, you mean the sneaky, little gnome hiding behind me? That's my daughter, Willamina."

Astrid placed the large pot on the ground, repositioned the blanket on her shoulders, and kneeled to say hello.

"Greet our new friend, Willa."

"Hello."

"Hello, Willamina." Astrid finally cracked a smile.

She saw her sister's children when she looked at the young girl; she missed the babes dearly, but had not allowed herself a moment to accept that she may never see them again, that they were gone.

Astrid tried to cover her tears, but this was no normal twinge of emotion; she was overwhelmed. Pot in hand, she followed the pair into the dark room. It was not long until Helen had lit every candle in the space and was even igniting the hearth.

"I swear, Warren never burns a fire. All those years soldiering...it's a god's honest miracle he does not freeze."

Astrid was uncomfortable and unsure what to say, so she elaborated on Helen's comment. "So used to living outdoors on the march, he almost certainly burns only a very small fire so not to alert scouts. Probably a habit."

Astrid flopped onto the bench at Warren's table, the motion nearly catapulting Willa off the opposite end.

"I'm sorry," she said through her onset of tears to the little girl who looked startled, but then smiled.

"Do it again."

"Willa, can't you see our new friend is sad?"

"Do not be sad," Willa chirped.

"What pains you, Astrid?"

Astrid watched Helen move the stew pot onto the table with a grunt and then gather several of Warren's old, carved wooden bowls while she composed herself enough to speak. She would not have normally answered a stranger's question like this; but today, with this woman who reminded Astrid so much of her sister, she responded.

"I miss my family."

"Do you have wee ones?" Helen asked and then stuck her tongue out at Willa.

"I do not, but my sister Yrsa does. I watch over them...or I did."

"Nothing like children is there?" Helen patted hers on the head as she passed her.

"I do not know." Astrid shrugged. "I wager not."

"There's more to your sadness, isn't there, Astrid?"

"There is more."

"Care to share with me?" Helen asked as she placed a large helping of her stew in one of the bowls.

"No."

"Fine then, let us eat."

Helen sat across from Astrid and began to eat. Something about the total silence grated Astrid's nerves. There was a child present, and in all her years, Astrid could not remember being in the same room as a noiseless child. *None of Yrsa's offspring were this quiet; ever.*

Stealing a peek at Willamina, Astrid looked for some sort of reason, but there was none; the little girl just sat eating peacefully.

"Your child is too quiet. My sister's children are as noisy as a pair of crowing roosters."

"I am thankful she did not inherit her father's love to hear himself speak."

"That would be dreadful." Astrid nodded. "This is delicious, Helen."

"Thank you."

Astrid paused a moment to form her words.

"Tell me, where are your other children?"

"Willa is my only child. I fear her birth ruined me. I cannot have another."

With a gasp, Astrid replied, "My sincerest apologies."

"It is the wish of the divine."

"If so, then dare I say the gods are mistaken; you made a beautiful child. There should be more of them here." Astrid could not stop herself now. "This home, it seems so still at times. Why doesn't Warren have a little son or daughter? Or does he?"

"He has not told you yet?" Helen asked.

"Told me what?"

"Oh my, he has not told you yet."

"I do not understand."

"Warren's wife passed several moons ago. She died while birthing a stillborn."

Helen's words stole the breath from Astrid's lungs. She put her spoon down, her hunger gone. Astrid normally tried her best not to think of it, but this was the same way her mother had died.

"When?"

"End of last summer."

"He still grieves then."

"No, I would say not. Well, perhaps he did until you arrived, but you have lifted his spirits...and more. He likes you," Helen clarified.

"I like him. He's a good fighter, not quite on par with my brothers—"

"Astrid, he likes you as a man likes a woman."

"I am no breeder." Astrid's answer was flat—emotionless.

"Breeder?"

"I am meant for more in this world than bearing children, Helen."

"Is that what you think of me?" Helen sneered.

"I meant no disrespect."

A knock at the door interrupted them. When Helen stood up and answered, she was greeted by a young guard in full armor. He held flowers in one hand and his torch in the other, a bit too closely, as both Helen and Astrid instantly smelled burned tulips.

"How may we help you, soldier?"

"I am guard Jarno. I came to ask the warrior woman if she would like to join me on my patrols this night."

A small part of Astrid wanted to stand, grab her armor, and join the young soldier, perhaps even seek out some trouble. Yet the longer she did not move, the more impossible the action became.

"The warrior woman is busy tonight. As you can see, she has not even finished her meal."

"Thank you, Jarno, some other time." Astrid nodded.

Helen forcefully shut the door in the young man's face and rolled her eyes. "The men of this town..."

"Explain," Astrid said.

"They act like frenzied animals." Helen shook her head. "See, it was after a night of 'patrol' like his that one of my young cousins found herself with child."

"He would be as bold to shame me and my family?"

"Look," Helen said. "You might be tall and strong and able to best most of the men in this town in a fight—"

"I could."

"Truly rare qualities in a woman here in this kingdom. However, a woman of your rich..." Helen tried to find the best word. "*Loveliness* will eventually become looked at as a prize."

"A prize?"

"A treasure, if that makes better sense to you," Helen explained. "Heavens, how can someone so educated in battle be so naïve in life? In your homeland, do men not lust?"

"They lust. Their lust could topple mountains."

Helen sat back down across from Astrid. "Oh, really?"

"Aye, the men of Birka lust for conquest and the plentiful spoils of victory. There is a saying where I come from: *With many travels come many fortunes.*"

"Well, in this land, a woman must guard herself or become a spoil of victory."

Helen's words began to sound like a lecture, and Astrid did not enjoy it.

"My brothers regularly seized the spoils of flesh, I know all of it."

"Do you? Then listen to me very carefully, Astrid. You need to know that the men of high station have no doubt already spread word about your beauty and power. Those commanding men have many connections within the kingdom."

"The heart hidden in all this?"

"It's only a matter of time before you find yourself in true danger. I fear some of the men who will come to court you will not be as kind as Jarno. Some will be more apt to simply claim you."

"I am no man's property."

"Which is exactly your problem," Helen agreed.

"Perhaps it is time I leave your town then." Astrid pounded her fists on the wooden table, rattling everyone's bowls.

"Willa, you may go eat by the fire if you like."

"Okay, Mother."

After Willa left the table, Helen lowered her voice and spoke again. "What happened to you today?"

"What reason do I have to tell you?" Astrid answered, while she pulled at a knot in her unbraided hair.

"Tell me and I will aid you with your hair."

"Aid me with my hair?"

"I will help you remove your braids and take the knots out. I have a porcupine quill brush; Hammond traded several sacks of seed for it at the kingdom bazaar last year."

"Porcupine quills?" Astrid perked up.

"It is exquisite."

"I have never owned a brush. I shared my sister's, but it is…it was made of wood and bone."

"Bone? It must have been ancient, did it belong to your mother?"

"No, my sister made it."

Helen smiled in response, and when she did, Astrid followed. She would trade with this woman.

"Since the battle, where I was…" She wanted to say killed but could not bring herself to admit it again. "Where I was badly hurt, I have not had the same desire within me. It is like my fighter's blood spilled out and all I am left with is the shell of a warrior."

"Warren said you were cut." With a small sniff of the air Helen continued, "I think I can smell the wound. Does it need a fresh dressing?"

Astrid touched her throat, feeling from side to side for a wound, scab, or scar, but there was no sign of the incision that nearly bled her out.

"I am fine," Astrid said but did not fully believe her own words.

Helen finally went back to eating. "Warren is worried that you are ill," she said nonchalantly.

"I am not ill."

"Then what happened to you today? He said you fell and—"

"I got scared," Astrid finally spit out. "*I got scared.* For the love of Goddess Sif, I was petrified."

"We all get scared."

"The children of Kol fear nothing!" Astrid insisted loudly.

"Not even death?"

"*Especially not death.*" Astrid pounded her fists to the table again. "To die in combat means to go proudly to Asgard and be given access to the praised halls of Valhalla."

"Then what scared you?"

"I died out there and was not rewarded with an afterlife. Instead, I was cursed to remain here. Death is supposed to come with a prize, one that outweighs the sharp pain and the taste of warm, salty blood."

"How could you have died? Look at you, you are alive and well."

"I told you. The gods punish me."

Helen finally asked, "Then what scared you so badly today?"

"Is it not obvious?"

Helen shook her head.

"I gazed out into the forest and all I saw was death. Wolves, bears, trolls, bandits...anything, all of it, it did not matter. You see, for the first time in my life, I did not see battle and glory or adventure and excitement awaiting me. I saw Hel's black, emaciated hand waiting to come and snatch me. Worst of all, I realized that death does not equal glory; it means suffering."

"Astrid..."

"I looked out across the fields into the unknown and I understood only one thing, Helen." Astrid gazed deeply into the eyes of Hammond's wife. "I *do not* want to die again."

CHAPTER 24

WARREN STAGGERED HOME. HAMMOND HAD filled him with so much cheap ale, in such a short time, that his vision had blurred and he saw four of everything. When he stopped to take a piss in the bushes along the path to his home, he started to snicker. It was something Hammond had said to the new barmaid that made him laugh. Now he remembered it; he called her breasts "Freki" and "Geri," "because only old Odin would own a pair of such majestic beasts."

Warren laughed out loud as he began to relieve himself on some shrubs. When he looked down, his vision told him there were multiple streams and when he tried to right his aim he nearly soiled his boots.

"Whoa!"

Finished, he stomped his feet on the ground a few times and tried to regain his composure as he shuffled to the door. Hammond told him Helen did not care for drunken rowdiness and would no doubt frown at him if he were obvious about it. After a light tap on the door, he gently pushed it open and peeked in.

"You awake?"

The room was dim; he could barely see Helen as she ran a brush through Astrid's hair.

"Quietly. Willa sleeps." Helen pointed to Warren's bed.

The sight of a child asleep in his bed turned his goofy mood to one of deep sadness. He had often dreamt of the day when he would have children the age of Willa. They were warm dreams, filled with laughter and kindness, but they were only dreams, ones that came to an abrupt end when he woke up alone to his own private nightmare.

"Warren?" Astrid called as she approached to show off her freshly coifed hair.

"Yes?"

Her blonde hair sparkled like silver in the firelight. No longer braided, it fell down to her waist. Warren noticed she also wore one of her finer dresses.

"What do you think?"

"It is beautiful. You are beautiful."

Helen gathered her things as the two stood and stared at one another across the tiny room.

"Thank you for entertaining me with many tales of valor, Astrid."

"Thank you for fixing my hair."

Helen passed Warren, with a sniff and a sour look, just as she often did with Hammond. He figured she knew the smell of the tavern, its ale and its women, and could probably identify them each with a single whiff. Breath held, Warren looked down and spotted droplets of urine on his boots. If they weren't proof enough, the way he swayed side to side was.

"Have a good time, did you?" Helen asked.

She's too smart, Warren thought. *I might as well not even try and hide it now.*

"Hammond bought me a drink and we sat in the corner and talked about old times."

"Sure you did."

"Willa, wake up, sweetie, we need to go home."

"She can stay," Astrid whispered.

"No, no. You two need your...privacy."

Helen lifted the child up and carried her out of Warren's home with a brief wave goodbye over her shoulder. He hardly noticed them leave, and nearly waved back at Astrid when she gestured goodbye to Helen and her sleepy bairn.

"How are you feeling?" Warren asked.

"Much better. Helen is tough."

"Hammond would agree with you there." Warren laughed.

"I like her. She is kind too."

"He may not always agree with you on that."

"She tells tale of a time when you two were to be joined."

Although neither had moved, Warren felt closer to Astrid than he had since she arrived. Something about the way she looked at him when she spoke and the softer tone of voice she was using—it was pleasant.

"She told you that?"

"She did. Do you ever wonder what it might have been like had you joined with her?"

Warren thought yes, but answered, "No."

"You look tired, Warren. Please come sit down. I will remove your boots."

"Really?" Warren asked, surprised.

The world did not spin as badly as it had been when he was outside and his vision slowly began to clear; now he only saw two of Astrid as she knelt before him to remove his boots.

"I do not make a habit of kneeling before men. You should know this about me already."

"I do."

Her lips glisten in the candlelight as she spoke. "In fact, the only man whose boots I ever removed is my father."

"I thought your father would have had slaves for that. He was the ruler or something, right?"

"We did not keep slaves in Birka." Astrid's voice rose. "My father stood against slavery, even when all the neighboring kingdoms did not. He said if a man or woman chooses to be a servant then they should be paid accordingly."

Astrid untied Warren's boots quickly and pulled at the left one. Suddenly, the scene became awkward for him. It had been months since a woman—his wife—took off his boots, and when she did, it was before bed.

Warren's hazy thoughts mixed, a jumble of now and then, fantasy and fact. As he stared at the double image of Astrid, he closed his eyes, and when he opened them for the briefest moment, he thought he saw his wife.

"You…"

Astrid freed his left boot with a force that nearly toppled her over in the process.

"You have feet like my father, Warren…too grand for your meager boots. You should have new ones made, ones that fit better."

Astrid ran her palm across the top of Warren's foot and a shiver ran up his leg. Warren shut his eyes again, as the view of Astrid's bosom had drove his mind places it should not go.

"Were there gales?"[2]

"What?" He opened one eye, to his surprise his right boot was removed.

"You and your brother were celebrating?"

Astrid sat back on her heels. She seemed content to talk, but Warren's heart screamed for more. Adjusting his groin, he sat up.

"We were not celebrating." He stared longingly.

"My brothers, they only soak themselves in ale when celebrating a victory or plunder, a birth or death. I just figured—"

"Astrid, you are so beautiful."

"Warren…"

"You are," he announced. "You are the most beautiful woman I have ever set eyes on."

"You are very kind to say that."

After some time passed, during which they stared silently at one another, Warren's head bobbed. He moved suddenly, making Astrid jump to her

---

2 Festivities in Old Norse.

feet. She was unsure what was going to happen next, so she placed her hands out in front of her chest defensively, but she watched the smiling man's eyes roll up in his head, and when he stepped forward, he collapsed into her.

"You weigh as much as the wild boar I killed on my fifteen birthday, but smell more sour," she joked. "You need rest."

"You were right."

"I know."

"You were wrong too."

Dragging him across the room, she hip-checked the man into his straw bed, where he landed with a thud.

"How was I wrong?"

"I was not drinking to celebrate my wife's passing to the afterlife; I was drinking to forget her. I need to forget her."

"You loved her deeply?"

When his eyes opened and shut again, he reached up and gently grabbed onto Astrid's shoulders and lightly tugged to pull her down into bed with him.

"Lay with me."

"I cannot."

With another pull, he repeated, "Lay with me, woman."

"No."

"Have I not proven myself to you, Cassandra?"

"Cassan—"

"We are husband and wife…"

Warren's words trailed off and while Astrid stood and stared at the man, he began to snore. *Cassandra,* she thought. *I have only heard that name spoken by his brother's wife; never him.*

"Warren, you poor, poor man."

After she extinguished the candles, Astrid slipped out of her dress and wrapped herself in one of the furs Warren kept on the straw bed. She sat down beside the man as he snored away, but she had not decided what to do—lay down next to him or not.

CHAPTER 25

WARREN AWOKE IN THE EARLY hours of the morning, his feet frozen stiff. He hated when his feet got cold; it reminded him of a battle years ago where he lost the better part of his boots to a lengthy march. Back then, his feet tingled and turned a pale shade of blue for many nights, and since then, he had to sleep with them fully covered.

When he tried to move his left arm in search of the furs, he realized it was pinned under something as heavy as it was soft. Opening his eyes, he was greeted by a mass of shiny blonde hair. Though stunned at first, he smiled. *Astrid lies in bed with me.* He wanted to laugh, to cheer even, but he did not want to wake her. Lying there, he inhaled the scent of her hair. She smelled so good he wanted to taste her, to take her in with every sense he had, yet he worried that doing so would rouse her.

Last night was full of holes, black spots in his memory. He remembered drinking with his brother and the walk home, yet as he stepped into his home, his memory went blank.

Did she and I? he wondered. He racked his brain with hopes that an errant memory from last night might fall free. Nothing. *Wait, my boots, she removed my boots. There was a look in her eyes...perhaps we did...*

Not sure how else to prove his theory, he reached down and grasped his kokkr[3]. With a squeeze at the base he yanked upward to the tip.

---

3 Cock in Old Norse.

Fingers to his nose he took a few sniffs. There was his answer; had they, surely her scent would have remained.

Content either way, Warren shut his eyes. Deep down, he wanted more, but he would have to settle for sleep—a place where he could dream of Astrid, until better memories were made.

CHAPTER 26

ASTRID WOKE FIRST, YAWNING AND stretching her arms and legs as far as they would go. She had slept the most soundly since she had arrived in this town, and she wondered why until she heard Warren rouse behind her. His yawn sounded like the snort of a yawd[4]. The sound would have made Astrid laugh if she were not somewhat embarrassed.

Astrid swung her legs over the side of the bed, quickly sat up, and pulled the furs that she was wrapped in with her.

"Morn, Astrid."

"Good morning," she said over her shoulder.

Astrid's golden locks swayed side to side as she moved, tickling her back. It was a refreshing feeling to have her hair free of braids.

"You joined me?"

"What?" She turned her head slightly.

He repeated himself more clearly.

"It was warmer in bed with you," Astrid answered.

"So much so I forgot about my chilled feet. I normally have to cover them or their frigidness will keep me awake."

"Oh, do you need your furs back?" Astrid stood.

"No, I am fine."

"Here…take them."

---

4 A horse of inferior breeding.

Astrid unwrapped herself from the warm furs and tossed them back at Warren. For the briefest moment, she stood with her bare arse to him, and his words were gone until she picked up the dress she had worn the day before and slipped it over her head.

"Astrid, you misunderstand." Warren got out of bed quickly.

"It matters not."

He was on Astrid before she could fix her dress, and he spun her around by her shoulders.

"What?" Surprised and tired, her tone sounded worse than intended.

"I enjoyed having you in bed with me."

Astrid looked him square in the eye and replied, "And why should that matter to me?"

"It should matter because tonight—"

"Tonight? Do not assume I will share your bed with you again, Warren."

"Why not?" Warren reached up to her face.

Her hands clasped his wrists to pull them away, but he had already made gentle contact with her cheek and the touch of his warm finger tips felt good.

"We have shared meals, shared stories, even shared combat. Why not share a bed?"

"I am not your wife, Warren."

Her words stole the sparkle out of his eyes, and he dropped his hands from her face. "No, you are not."

Astrid sensed she had dulled his feelings for her, but only for a moment. Soon after, his large hands gripped her waist and he once more gazed deep into her eyes.

"You are Astrid the White, daughter of Kol," he said in such a way it reminded her of home. "You are the strongest, bravest, most beautiful woman I have ever met."

His breath was warm on her lips and his words were filled with fire. *No man has ever been so bold to speak to me in such a way as he does.* Hearing him speak made her emotions come alive.

She moved closer. Warren smelled strong of sweat, but it did not turn her away; it turned her on. Her hands reached to his hips, her eyes to his lips.

"What do you want from me, Warren of Grømstad?"

"I only want you to see me for who I am: a fighter like you. A man who would give his life to protect the lives of his friends, family and home. I want you to see that you and I…we make a good pair."

Their mouths collided in unrestrained passion. The energy, the excitement; Astrid had never been this overcome with power outside of combat. She felt alive again, a sensation she feared she had lost when she died. She wanted more; she needed more. Her hands gripped Warren's hips tighter and pulled them into hers, startling him free of their kiss.

"Tell me how you feel, Astrid."

"Lost," she replied instantly to his question. "I have felt so lost, Warren. So very lost since waking in that snow-covered field."

"I know," he nodded. "But you are not alone."

"I have been so confused, so empty. What is right? What is wrong? I have allowed my thoughts to weight me down, trap me inside my head, Warren." Astrid shook her head. "A good warrior does not allow their weak mind to overcome their strong body."

"What does your strong body tell you now, Astrid?"

The words formed and sounded right inside her head. "My body hurts less when you are near. It tells me you bring it comfort and pleasure when so many others have only treated it to pain."

Warren kissed her lips briefly and she thought, *Gods, please give me a sign, unless…unless this is your sign…*

"Do it, Warren," she breathed, her forehead pressed heavily against his chest. "Do the thing that you have wanted to do since we met. Make me feel."

Astrid tore her dress off and threw it to the ground. That was all it took. Warren planted his face between her breasts, and she wrapped her arms around his head. For the briefest moment she doubted herself.

This is not the way of my people.

Her thoughts melted away as Warren's hand snaked down between her legs and his fingers glided through her wetness.

Great Freyja, Astrid's mind screamed, as her legs went weak and her chest shuddered. *Is this your gift to women, my goddess? Is this what you wanted me to feel?*

When Warren removed his hand to caress her breasts, she snatched it and shoved it back down.

"I blame *you* for this strange pressure building inside me, Warren. You owe it to me to give me release before it bursts."

"I will." Warren paused when her body stiffened. "I promise."

Warren guided her backward to his straw bed, where he pushed her down with a grunt. No stranger to roughhousing and disorderly behavior, Astrid landed on her forearms and elbows. A hard piece of straw scratched a line across her hip, but she paid it little mind. Not now, not when her heart pounded as loud as a charging horse's hooves.

"Tell me what do you want."

As Astrid leaned back, she spread her legs and lifted them up so her toes were on the edge of the bed.

"I want it all, Warren. I want to be alive and I want feel it all."

Time stopped for Warren, as Astrid presented to him a gift unlike any other. Astrid was beauty, power, and sex manifested. For a moment, how long he was unsure, he just could not take his eyes off Astrid's incredible curves.

His leather shirt off, Warren tossed it across the room, where it struck and drug a bowl across the table with a crash. Hidden under his shirt was a chest packed tight with muscle; he hoped Astrid liked it.

"You have made my lisk[5] ache and tingle with a phantom touch." Astrid placed her fingers in the very spot Warren's had been a moment before and began to trace their lines back and forth.

---

5 Groin in Old Norse.

His hands on his pants, Warren nearly forgot himself.

"With all my might, Astrid, I am going to devour you."

Warren presented himself, naked and fully ready, and waited for her acknowledgment.

Astrid examined Warren's powerful body, her eyes at rest on his large manhood. "Today you are mine, Warren of Grømstad."

Warren knelt beside the bed, took aim, and plunged himself deep into her with a grunt that overlapped her groans. Collapsing off her elbows onto her back, Astrid laid still as Warren entered, withdrew, and reentered her.

"Slowly," she said through gritted teeth.

Numb with pleasure, Warren barely registered her voice; all he could think of was how much he wished he could stay inside her forever. It was not until what appeared to be a spike of pain shot down Astrid's body from where it was joined with his, to the tips of her toes, that his attention was shifted.

"Have I hurt you?"

When he spoke, she opened her eyes and gasped, "I...don't. Don't stop."

Astrid's body trembled and Warren plunged himself deeper inside her. He wanted to pace himself—to enjoy her as long as he could—so he slowed down and when he did, she hooked her hands behind his neck and lifted herself off the straw, bringing her face toward his. All of a sudden, she sneered and snapped like the turtles that dwelled near the brook.

"Wha—"

"Move your hips faster," she commanded.

As he slid in and out of her, he watched Astrid turn bright red from the tips of her jiggling breasts to the base of her neck. With the exception of an occasional gasp between thrusts, Astrid looked like she was drowning.

"Breathe, woman," Warren teased with a smirk.

Astrid wrapped her legs around his waist. She squeezed him with vice-like pressure that built and built to a point where he thought she might harm him, but as Warren was about to ask her to ease off, she released and fell back onto the straw.

She's as red as an apple; I bet my face is just as bright. Astrid lay catching her breath as sweat from Warren's head fell on her stomach. *Such power this woman holds over me, the heat, I cannot stand it any longer.*

As Astrid reached up to his face, Warren thrust himself deeper into her, a combination of physical and emotional senses bringing him to climax, but not before he withdrew. He released with such great force that his sight grew dim.

Astrid cupped her lisk as she pushed slightly away from Warren. She watched him stroke his kokkr until it no longer emptied; then he pinched the tip and knelt on the floor.

"Are you well?" she asked after Warren filled his tiny home with a loud grunt.

He nodded and smiled, and then he pointed to her hand between her legs. "Did I hurt you there?"

"Oh, no. This feels good," she said.

A moment of silence passed between them as she watched Warren's eyes drop to his kokkr, which hung between his legs, draped in shadows.

"Did *I* hurt you, Warren?"

Warren shook his head as he held quiet a moment. The silence allowed Astrid's cluttered mind to settle on one thought.

"Yrsa, you cow," Astrid stated flatly.

A total look of confusion took over Warren's face.

"Yrsa...my sister."

"What about her?"

"She's been doing this for half her life, the lucky witch."

"And you have not..." Warren's voice trailed off.

"I have trained naked, even hunted naked, but never have I allowed myself to lack clothing in pressing proximity of a lusting man before."

Warren's gaze fell back to his kokkr.

"I never would have imagined I can feel this…alive, if not more than I do in battle," she continued. "Do you feel this delighted too, Warren?"

Warren covered himself with his shirt as he stood quickly. "Yes, I do, Astrid."

Astrid smiled. *So this is what Yrsa felt when she lay with her husband.*

Had Astrid known, she may not have teased her sister so. In fact, Astrid could hardly believe it Yrsa had not teased *her* about what Astrid had been missing. *I needed this,* she told herself. *I feel…I feel alive. I feel good.*

Her father had been right to keep her untouched by men; Astrid understood this better now. Her father's words rang in her head: *A woman who lies with men risks filling herself with babies.* He always liked to brag that the day would come when she would rule Birka, and only then would she settle with a man, if there were any worthy of her.

Astrid looked at Warren, as she applied pressure to the dull ache between her legs. She imagined his warmth still inside her, the hardness of his stomach muscles still pressed against her.

I think I have found my worthy man.

CHAPTER 27

As they had neared the dinner hour, Astrid sat outside Warren's home. The morning had been as monumental as many of the battles she had been in. Astrid wished she could have bent her sister's ear, but Yrsa, like the rest of her family, was gone—at least to her.

She sighed loudly as she thought of them. *Perhaps my family is sitting someplace this very moment, missing me as I am missing them. Could it be that they are not gone, but I am? Father, sister, brothers…I wish I could see you all once more. Just long enough to tell you, each and every one, how much I love you.*

Astrid had never loved anyone outside her family. Love to her had always been about loyalty. She had never connected love with sex. She could not be sure if even a single one of her brothers had ever loved any of the women they had known, even their wives.

She recalled a night of feasting with her brothers. They were all drunk, and argued over which women they would lie with for the night. She remembered how Vignor had teased her that she would be spending another night alone, "Astrid the White is untouched by men," he boasted. "Any who would dare lay their hands on her would see their skin turn to ice and fall off."

He is right. Astrid smirked. *Or he was right. What does this all mean?* she wondered. She pushed back from the table and spotted Warren out in the fields.

To the best of her knowledge, he had not paused in his work since he began. They had not spoken much since the act earlier, which Astrid was mostly relieved by, as for the moment, she preferred to assume his intentions. *Is his goal a union, or does he only seek pleasure? Need I remind him that I am no concubine?* Astrid absently touched her stomach. *Or could this man simply hope to make me the vessel for his children? It was never my intention to bring babies into this world. What was it Hak once said? "Sister would rather give birth to a rock to beat her enemies to death with than a child to hide from them."*

This is true. Or this was true. I do miss Yrsa's babes— What am I thinking?

Too many questions took over her thoughts. Astrid pushed the worry aside and focused on the way her body felt energized.

A flutter in her chest soon grew into a quiver in her stomach. The more she thought on the details of that morning's romp the more she wanted to go out to the field and tackle Warren and do it again. As the feeling grew, Astrid placed her charcoal down, ready to go to the field to act out her thoughts, but as she stood, she spotted Hammond crossing the field away from Warren's storage cellar; carrying a jug of Warren's ale.

"Morn, Brother!" Hammond called out.

"Morn, Hammond, you look well today."

"I have always held my drinks better than you. You may enjoy the gift of our grandfather's height, but I treasure his freedom to drink all night and not suffer the following morning."

"My head *does* pounds like a barbarian war drum," Warren admitted.

"I see you managed to get her dressed today." Hammond waved across the field at Astrid.

"What did you say?" Warren stopped what he was doing. "What do you know of it?"

"My wife told tale of her distaste for dresses. Why? Is there more I should know?"

Warren wanted to keep his mouth shut, yet at the same time he wanted to speak with someone about what he had done.

"Hammond, promise me you will not share this with anyone."

"Yes, of course, yes." Hammond wetted his mouth with a quick chug of ale.

"Days ago, when Astrid and I marched north, I thought her sick or maybe a liar. She had to be a traveling sellsword...perhaps...I just...I simply did not believe her story of being from a northern kingdom. Especially one I've never heard of." Warren shook his head. "Birka? There's no such place near here. To be honest, I figured her claims to be a king's daughter were born of a boastful imagination. But then came proof."

"What proof?"

"This morning Astrid and I—"

"No!" Hammond nearly shouted.

"Brother, hush!"

The two gazed across the field at Astrid.

"You're about to make me very jealous," Hammond explained. "Okay, tell me. How sweet was the nectar of our foreign goddess?"

"Virginal."

"Old Freyja's fine golden ass!"

Warren hushed his brother again.

"Do you know what this means, Hammond?"

"Yes, you had the most beautiful woman I have ever seen and she was untaken by any man before you, a true gift from the heavens befell your—" Hammond gave his brother a playful tap below the belt.

"Hammond, you're such a wise businessman. Must you always play the fool?" Warren grumbled. "Look at her."

"I am."

"Beautiful, strong, a skilled warrior, and yet her age...it all makes sense." Warren swallowed hard. "Her claims *were* true. Her father must have been saving her for someone special, a joining of royal families maybe, a political alliance or even a sacrifice to the old gods."

"And now you've gone and spoiled the lass."

Warren sighed.

"Hammond, do you remember my tales of the years I spent along the southern coast fighting marauding barbarian tribes?"

"Of course. Stories of might and legend they are, Brother."

"I never told you about the man we found captive in the one seaside fortress. We had defeated all of the barbarians, sparing only the women and children. These people, they were total savages, taking part in many blood sports and rituals. In a room in the chieftain's hut was a man who had been tortured and left to rot. The smell in the space was enough to make you vomit. I've smelled death before, but this was worse. The man was tied to a support beam, his arms and legs cut off, only bloody bandaged stumps remained."

"He was dead then?"

"No. Through some sort of uncultivated medicines or perhaps dark magics, I cannot say, but the man was still alive."

"No."

"One of our scouts could speak the man's language and, although touched by delirium, he told us he was being tortured because he took the chieftain's daughter's virginity without permission. Every few days the chieftain chopped off more and more of his limbs as punishment. When we found the poor bastard, it had been a month or so into the ordeal, and he had almost nothing left."

"That is most foul." Hammond grimaced.

"He begged us to kill him."

"Brother, I don't know how to respond to this."

Warren shook his head in defeat. "I do. I let my desires outweigh my intelligence."

"Father always said the men in this family had larger flesh-spears than brains."

"I know." Warren sighed again.

Hammond smirked. "So you fear our lady warrior has a father that will cut you into tiny pieces, do you?"

"I do."

Hammond chuckled. "Well, what did Astrid say afterwards?"

"Not a thing."

"What, did you take her while she was asleep?"

"No!" Warren barked. "She started talking about her sister afterwards, and I simply sat there staring at the blood. Hammond, I panicked."

"Wait, I have to ask, Brother." Hammond placed his hand on Warren's shoulder and looked him straight in the eye. "She *did* enjoy your coupling, right?"

A moment passed where neither brother spoke.

"Yes, she did, very much so."

CHAPTER 28

ONE TALL AND STRONG. ONE short and plump. To gaze at them from such distance…no obvious relation is apparent. Perhaps they are from different mothers; different mothers from different lands. Astrid considered.

What might they be speaking about? She could hear their voices but not make out what they said. Being that Hammond was present, Astrid imagined Warren bragged about his triumph; that's what her brothers would have done.

A distant howl broke Astrid's concentration. It was children crying somewhere near the stream, and when she looked at the trees that hid the water, she spotted three little ones rushing out of the shadows. With banshee-like wails, the three boys ran as though they were being chased. Astrid could feel a coldness in the pit of her stomach; there was trouble. A howl, panicked children, running—it added up to something sinister, she knew it. So why wasn't she sprinting toward the trouble?

Two guards armed with spears suddenly appeared. They had heard the cries for help too and acted when she did not.

"Astrid!" Warren yelled as he and his brother ran up. "What's happening?"

Still frozen in place, she answered, "I don't know."

"I saw guards rush to the tree line. Is it brigands?"

"Brigands?"

Astrid had not thought of the possibility, and the word itself made her weak in the knees. She felt faint and when her head began to feel warm, she reached out to steady herself against Hammond's shoulder.

"To be honest, Astrid, I half expected you to sprint off after the guards," Hammond said.

"Me too," Warren agreed.

"There was a howl. I..."

"Are you feeling well?" Warren asked.

"I think I'm just hungry."

"Right, which is why I am here," Hammond said. "I nearly forgot, due to—"

"Hammond," Warren said in a warning tone.

"I came to invite you both to dinner. Helen is cooking rabbit again."

Astrid could not take her eyes off the forest, as she waited for something to happen—anything that would give a hint as to what had occurred deep in the shadows.

"A single hunter killed six this morning. This kid has the best aim of all our archers and is half their age. He came home with two deer the other day. No hunter in Grømstad has ever returned with two."

"What say you, Astrid?" Warren asked.

"Just two?" she whispered.

"Would you like to have dinner with Hammond and his family?"

"Look." Hammond pointed at the tree line where one of the guards was stepping into the clearing.

Astrid's hand clamped down on Hammond's shoulder as she watched the first guard, armed with both his and the second guard's spear, emerge. When the second man finally appeared, he was carrying something. Astrid's hand tightened like a vice—squeezed until Hammond yelped and pulled away from her.

"Oh no," Warren gasped.

Cradled in the second guard's arms was the lifeless body of a small boy.

"No."

"I will go see what happened. Stay here with her, Brother," Warren requested as he ran off toward the guards.

Astrid's heart pounded so fast she thought she might be able to see it move underneath the thin fabric of her dress. With her hand over her breast, she counted the beats.

"What's wrong with me?" she wondered aloud.

Hammond answered as truly as he could. "Besides being a little pale"—he sniffed the air—"and perhaps in need of a bath, you seem perfect, from what I can tell."

"You base your opinions on the outward, Hammond, when it's my insides that stir oddly."

"Well perhaps my brother will help you with those stirring insides."

Astrid snatched his hand from where it rested at his side and firmly planted it above her left breast.

"Your speed is astounding." Hammond was shocked. "Oh my…"

"Do you feel it?"

"Yes…truly magnificent."

"Not my breast." Astrid pinned his hand in place until she could feel her heartbeat through it. "My heart, do you feel it race?"

"Oh-right."

"Does yours race the same?"

"What is your meaning, Astrid? I do not understand."

Astrid swiped his hand away, grumbled, and stepped back.

This man cannot give me answers. My family is nowhere to be found. Who is left for me to turn to? "Gods, have you returned me, a great warrior, to this world as no more than a coward?"

"You are no coward," Hammond replied.

"Name this trial, Great Odin, so I understand it better."

Hammond cleared his throat, "Let us go, Astrid. Helen and Willa are waiting. I promise you will feel better with some food in your belly."

"Perhaps."

Astrid gazed down her nose at the man as he squirmed. Hand out, she motioned for the jug of ale he carried. A long drink cleared her mind.

"Helen is a good woman, Hammond."

Hammond stared off into the center of town before he replied, "I know."

CHAPTER 29

THE RABBIT TASTED BETTER THAN Astrid could have imagined. For someone who was treated as if she were a poor cook, Helen prepared food very well. Perhaps Hammond was just an ass, Astrid concluded, as she caught his eyes glued to her chest for the third time since the meal began.

Seated across from her was Warren. He had been quiet through dinner and had yet to announce what had happened earlier when he marched off with the town guards. Astrid wanted to ask yet feared the answer.

"This carrot tastes as if it was pulled from the fields days ago. It's delicious." Astrid savored the carrot's freshness and the distraction it provided from her worries.

"It was pulled today," Warren answered for Helen.

"Impossible."

"Why? I planted them over two months ago, at the end of winter."

"They were never stored?" Astrid asked.

"No, they were in the satchel I arrived with. Cleaned today."

"Never mind all that. It's past time you tell us what happened today, Brother?" Hammond said.

"You mean the boys?"

"Yes, the boys."

Warren nodded as he seemingly took a moment to assemble his thoughts.

"A group of boys were gathering water at the brook when a large wolf approached. One of the boys picked up a stick and waved it at the wolf in attempts to scare it off."

"Whose child was it?" Helen asked solemnly.

"Erik and Elsa's. Their youngest, I am afraid."

"The boy was killed protecting his mates?" Astrid's heartbeat increased.

"He was."

"Was the wolf killed?"

"It ran off when the guards approached."

After another drink of ale, Astrid dribbled on the table, yet it was not Warren's homemade alcohol that she saw spots of…it was bright red blood. While she traced her lips with her fingertips, Astrid's mouth was overcome with the taste of salty blood. She began to panic. Hands grasping her neck, she expected to find a deep wound.

"Help…me…" she choked, but she barely made a noise.

Not a one of them seemed to notice her. Warren continued to tell his story, while Hammond picked meat from the bones of the rabbit he ate. Helen smiled as she put more food on Willa's plate; even the girl seemed unaware.

"Help me…"

"The boy was mauled badly. I have seen these kinds of bites before. On me, in fact." Warren pointed to his bandaged leg. "This wolf was larger, I'd wager."

"You don't think it was one of those the bandit's leader commanded?" Hammond asked.

The bandit leader. He used wolves; he also used a sharp dagger. Gods, I'm bleeding to death. Frantically pawing at her throat, Astrid searched for the wound that spouted blood onto the table before her, but she could not find it.

"Warren…help…"

"You should keep a close eye on Willa until the wolf has been found and killed."

"I will tie a rope from my leg to hers if I have to." Helen pretended to lasso her daughter, to which Willa giggled.

"We should give Erik and Elsa some of your fresh ale, Warren, don't you think?" Hammond tilted his mug at his brother.

"Yes, *we* should."

Lightheaded and weak, Astrid began to fall backward. She kicked out both legs and struck the table hard with her feet, shaking it so intensely she nearly toppled all the mugs.

"Help!" Astrid screamed as she jumped up in her seat.

Her eyes anxiously searched for blood, which she could not find on her hands, her dress, or the table. There was nothing.

"Ho there, Astrid, you scared us!"

Warren said from the other side of Hammond's large cabin, where he was seated next to the fire with a mug of ale in hand.

"The blood!" she screamed. "Modi give me strength, the blood. I was bleeding all over."

"This one ate so much she fell asleep at the table and dreamt her belly exploded," Hammond playfully said to his daughter.

Astrid pawed at the table and herself. She heard their words, but what made them any more real than what she had just seen? Crossing the room quickly, Warren came to her aid.

"You are fine, Astrid, calm yourself."

"See, Helen, I am not the only one that suffers horrible dreams after eating the food you cook," Hammond joked.

"Hammond!"

"Daddy!"

Hammond smiled at his wife and daughter as they yelled at him.

"Warren?"

Although she was still, Astrid's eyes bounced around in her head.

Warren held her chin and tilted it up. "I am here," he said as he turned her face to his.

"The blood."

"There is none. You are fine. No wounds can be seen."

"What happened?"

"We finished eating—"

"We finished?"

"And you put your head down. Fell right asleep, just like our father used to, right, Hammond?"

"At least twice a week."

Astrid's heart raced again; this time it pounded so hard she could feel it in her stomach and throat. Astrid pulled Warren's hand off her chin and placed it on her chest.

"Do you feel it?"

"Your heart?" Warren asked.

"My heart." Astrid locked eyes with him.

"It races."

"Why?" she asked softly, as she pressed her hand into his.

Warren shrugged in response.

"What's wrong with me?" Astrid whispered.

"You had a nightmare. You are just scared," Warren whispered back. "Nothing to—"

"The sons of Kol do not get frightened so easily."

"You're bravery is not in contest, Astrid."

"My heart…" Astrid began.

"It slows."

"Steadies itself," she said, closing her eyes briefly. "I owe you my gratitude."

"We should—"

Astrid leaned in to Warren, but stopped as her lips brushed his.

"Leave," she said breathily. "Return to your bed."

"You should feel my heart now."

"You two are so—" Helen began, but Hammond interrupted.

"Helen!"

Quickly, Astrid marched over to Helen and gave her a bear hug as a thank you for the meal and ale. While she did, Warren followed suit and hugged his brother.

"You know how the elder council feels," Hammond whispered into his brother's ear while they embraced.

"I know."

As they left, Helen spoke one last time. "Astrid, if you need to talk tomorrow, I am here."

Astrid nodded and then stepped out into the night air behind Warren. The sky was an eerie shade of purple as it deepened to black. A cool breeze blew from the center of town up the hill, and carried with it the smell of burnt wood and meals cooked over it. The scent would have made Astrid's stomach growl had it not already been filled.

It was nights like tonight, back in Birka, she and her brothers would have footraces through the city. She smiled and said, "Race you back."

"You expect me to outrun you, all legs and muscle?"

"No."

With that she was off, like a fawn that fled from a hunter. She easily led for much of the run, but as they hit the steepest part of the hill, Warren began to close the distance.

"Ha!" she said, leaping as she cleared the last few steps. "Victory!" Astrid cheered.

"You cheat."

"Cheat? Such an accusation would result in combat where I am from."

"Everything seems to result in combat where you are from."

"Almost everything...well, my one brother once fought a man for saying he smelled like dead fish. It mattered not to Hak that he had been fishing all day."

As she spoke, she noticed Warren's attention drift over her shoulder to something behind and well above her.

"What is it?"

"Look!" He pointed up.

Astrid turned and gazed off in the direction of his pointed finger but saw nothing.

"Did you see it, Astrid?"

"No." She scanned the treetops. "See what?"

"A falling star, I wager. Bright and yellow, it fell slow, at first. I thought it was just hanging there above the treetops."

Warren's words excited her so much so she wanted to cheer.

"The gods must want us to know they are watching." Astrid smiled as she starred at the sky. "This is what they want. They must approve of our union."

"Is that what you believe?"

"I trust the gods, Warren. Now, let us go inside so I might show you the boon of their new blessings."

Astrid watched Warren enter his home and then turned her eyes back to the sky in search of another sign.

CHAPTER 30

ASTRID WAS FREE OF HER dress before she entered, and he was left to retrieve the garment before he shut the door. Warren added another log to the fire as he watched Astrid lay down on the bed, and cover herself in the furs. When she slowly slid her legs open, he felt his face brighten.

"Hurry," Astrid commanded.

His shirt off, Warren asked, "Are you mine, Astrid, daughter of Kol?"

"No, Warren," she replied, "...*you* are mine."

When Warren joined Astrid under the furs the touch of her warm body made him smile, but it was her blank expression that made him pause before he kissed her.

"Is something wrong?"

"Hmm?" Astrid said as she furrowed her brow. "No, nothing. A memory. While outside, I started thinking of a friend. So long ago...but not."

Hands placed on her waist, he asked, "Would you like to tell me about your friend?"

"Not now," she answered with a shake of her head.

Warren nodded, happy to see her mood lighten.

"Come, Warren, join with me."

He could not make sense of Astrid, short of the fact that there was more to her than he could imagine, or might ever know, and the mere thought of that aroused him further.

While he climbed on top of her, Warren felt her balmy hands grasp his manhood and guide it into her. Her warmth combined with her wetness was so deliciously appealing, he tried to fit all of himself into her in the first slow thrust.

Astrid's eyes widened as she shimmied herself backward to better fit Warren's girth. It was not long until, Warren began to piston into her, his thrusts, a steady tempo that rattled her whole body.

"Harder," she groaned as she tore at the soft straw beneath her. "Must I remind you that I am not as fragile as your tiny women here?"

Warren used all the strength in his heavy hips to slide into her, while Astrid grasped the thick muscles of Warren's buttocks and added her own force to his thrusts.

"Kiss me," Astrid instructed.

When Warren's mouth finally made contact with hers, she moved her hands up from his backside to his neck. They kissed like the famished eat, hungry for one another.

"Lick my breasts."

He did exactly what she commanded, and lapped her right and then left breast.

"You taste like cherry mead and smell as delicious," Warren said.

He pinned her down and then inhaled her sweet scent again. Astrid's moans had grown louder and more frequent; she was quick to finish, he knew it. While she ran her hands down the hard bulges of his arm muscles, she tilted her hips and then suddenly released.

Everything about her made him throb; he could not last any longer either. Warren slid out of her just before his grunt-filled climax.

"Thank you," she huffed. "I much prefer your stickiness on me than inside me."

"Of course."

When he rolled off her, she caught his arm.

"Lay with me, Warren. We can always sneak out to the bekk before dawn and wash ourselves in its cool water. Perhaps after another go… or two."

"You continue to surprise me. You are unlike other women."

Astrid agreed. "I feel different than other women. I feel very different."

After a moment of silence Warren said, "This place may seem strange to you, Astrid, but know that you have a home here. A home here with me."

Astrid smiled before she rested her head on his wide chest. "I know."

CHAPTER 31

IN BED WITH WARREN, ASTRID could not sleep. As hard as she tried she could not stop thinking about death; her death. The bandit leader's blade was cold and sharp and she felt its phantom touch across her throat over and over.

As tired as she was, Astrid could not clear her mind. The memory of the blackness that filled her eyes and swallowed her senses whole as she lay on the ground dying was worse than any nightmare born beast. She feared its return worse than anything else; an empty void where there was no life or death, there was only nothingness.

Am I alive? Am I dead?

Astrid wanted answers, but there was no sense to any of it.

I died. I felt myself die. So why didn't I move on to the Afterlife? I died here... no, I died in Birka. Astrid trembled. *Is that it? Is that why nothing makes sense? I died in Birka.*

Yet again, Astrid's thoughts returned to the holy mountain. *It was missing; Helgafjell was gone. The landscapes, the seasons, nothing is a match.*

Is this whole world a lie? All I see and feel unreal? Could this...could this truly be Helheim? No, the gods have sent me signs. I saw the signs, I sensed the signs.

Astrid stared at Warren. *Do I love this man?* She titled her head as she looked more closely at his face. *He is handsome and seemingly brave and good in nature, but why have I given myself to him instead of any other? Why now? Why risk eternal shame for his man? Unless this is all a lie.*

She tapped his hard chest lightly; Astrid only wanted to know if he was real.

No, he has aided and protected me. He has kept me safe...but has he also kept me from my family?

Astrid felt suddenly sick to her stomach.

I-I should have escaped. I should have returned home when I had the chance. So why didn't I? Why...why do I suddenly feel like there is no escape now?

The answers she sought were absent, unclear, or empty of reason—except one. *No. No. No. I-I must have died in Birka. My...my failure to protect my family must have been seen as a great dishonor in the eyes of the gods. They did not want me...so Lady Hel took me.*

The thought made her body ache from head to toe. Astrid was flushed, and began to sweat.

If this is all a lie: this town, these people, my feelings; all of it. If this is Helheim and I have been cursed to live out my eternal afterlife in a perverted mirror of my former life, here, where there was no honor, no meaning...then there are no consequences.

Astrid retrieved one of her daggers from her belt on the floor and carefully aimed it at Warren's heart, balancing its point on his bare chest. It would not take much effort—Astrid knew she could plunge the cold metal through him, spear his heart in one thrust, but when she imagined it, she felt something she had not felt since her mother died: a deep gut-wrenching sorrow.

But why? If this is Helheim, then he is dead too—or worse, a demon in the shape of a man, one who has no doubt followed his dark mistress's commands to seduce me and keep me trapped here. I should end him now.

"Father, only you held wisdom akin to the great gods," Astrid whispered to herself. "Please send me an answer. Whether it be from life or the afterlife, I need your help."

When a tear glided down her cheek, Astrid sighed.

"Is this my sign, Father? More tears for your daughter the warrior?"

She readjusted her grip on the handle, shifted her weight, and prepared to force the dagger down.

"Odin, I give you this sacrifice so you will hear my voice and answer my prayers. Set me free of this place."

"Astrid?" Warren said hazily.

"Which god do you favor, Warren?" Astrid asked him.

"Go back to sleep."

Warren rolled his head to the side; she could tell he was already fast asleep again.

"Answer me."

Warren yawned. "What?"

"Which gods do you favor?"

"I…I don't know. With all that I have witnessed in my life…I have no reason to follow the old gods or the new one."

"Then who do you worship?"

Warren went silent a moment before he answered, "Only you, Astrid."

Astrid pitched the blade across the room while she howled in deep frustration. Warren snapped awake and sat up quickly as Astrid leapt over him.

"Where am I?" she screamed and stomped the ground, her fists thrown down in the air like a spoiled child. "Odin, hear me! Answer me!"

In a single fluid motion, Astrid lifted one of the old chairs from the table in the middle of the room, spun around, and flung it into the hearth. The crash roused the guard dogs Warren's closest neighbor owned, and their combined barks echoed loudly.

"Astrid, calm yourself!" Warren pleaded.

Astrid's hair whipped around her as she paced. "This must be Helheim, as my heart and soul both hurt while my body only burns with yearning."

On his feet, Warren tried to embrace her, but his actions only caused her to scramble to the dagger she had thrown moments before. With it in hand, she took a low defensive stance.

"Stay back," she said as she kept Warren at bay with the point of the blade.

Warren shook his head. "Did you have another nightmare, Astrid?"

"I-I just want to go home!" Astrid shifted her gaze to the door—she needed to escape.

"Astrid, wait…"

It was too late; she was already in action. She ran out the door and raced for the forest—the very spot she had feared would devour her.

Warren retrieved his pants and pulled them on as he moved. *This cannot be happening,* he told himself. He grabbed her dress and dashed out the door in pursuit. *How is this possible?* he thought as he scanned the town. She was already gone, run off and swallowed up by the night.

"Astrid!" Warren called even thought he knew his voice would only wake more people and cast more suspicion upon him. "Astrid!"

There was no response. She really was gone.

CHAPTER 32

ASTRID MOVED THROUGH THE GRASS barefoot. *What was it the elders said? "This is not the same land as your home."* Their words suddenly made sense. More and more, Astrid was convinced she was already dead, trapped in the sorrow-filled house of Hel.

Jokul had always been obsessed with this place. She tried to recall what his favorite story was. *Right, that was it: Odin used to visit Hel on his horse, Sleipnir.* Jokul used to say he wanted an eight-legged horse that could traverse the afterlife as easily as one of Birka's stags did the ice-laden ground.

If Odin could come and go as he pleased, there had to be a way out; she would just have to prove herself to the gods one more time.

No sooner had the thought entered her mind than she heard a woman's terrified scream. It came from a spot not far from her, a bit deeper in the forest, on the other side of the brook most likely.

"Is this your test, Mistress Hel?" Astrid spoke under her breath as she ran toward the sound. "I hope so."

Deeper under the forest canopy, the leaves blocked out the moon's pale light, which made it harder to see. As Astrid reached the brook, the sound of running water grew louder, and so did the frightened woman's pleas. To the right, the stream wound off like a snake; to the left, it straightened like an arrow. In either direction there might have been a narrower spot, yet Astrid did not want to waste her time in search of it.

She crossed the brook from floodplain to floodplain with a leap and landed hard, her feet stomping deep in the mud and sinking to nearly mid-calf. Halted so suddenly, she braced herself, her hands sinking to her wrists in malleable mud. Astrid tried to step out of the mud, but it was too thick and heavy on her, so she crawled on her stomach until she reached solid ground and then wiped as much of it off as she could.

Suddenly another voice could be heard in the distance, that of a man. "How fast can a pregnant woman run?"

A pregnant woman. The words echoed in Astrid's mind. What evil perversion was about to be revealed? She held her breath.

"Where…" Astrid panned the tree line. "Ah, there."

In the darkness, a grey form moved silently, ducking between trees and zigzagging across the uneven terrain. Astrid had seen this pattern before; it was something her father had taught when she was very young. He said if she was ever being pursued, to stay low, stick close to the trees, and mask your steps by going up and down on rocky paths.

As the person drew closer, Astrid could see it was a woman, her long, straggly blonde hair nearly dragging across the ground as she ran barefoot, her hands hoisting up the heavy skirt she was wearing. Astrid wanted to call out to the woman, but she feared they'd be discovered; two torches in the near distance and the male voices she heard drew nearer.

Astrid crouched and ran, cutting a diagonal path toward the woman. Still coated in mud, her skin was nearly camouflaged, a gift from Sif no doubt—perhaps she would exit this dreadful place sooner than she thought. The woman was occupied, her gaze over her opposite shoulder, so she did not notice Astrid sneak up on her.

Only feet away, Astrid ducked behind a tree and waited for the woman to pass. When she did, Astrid leapt out and wrapped one arm around the woman's head to cover her mouth and the other around her swollen waist to lead her back to the brook.

"Fear not, woman, I will save you—and myself I wager."

The woman muttered into Astrid's hand, but Astrid was too busy to listen. She pulled the woman beside her as she fled and took note of just how far along she was in her pregnancy.

"Relax, you and your baby will be fine."

As they reached the brook, unfortunately at a wider spot than where she had leapt over, Astrid released the woman and ordered her to cross.

"Go now! There's a place, a farming town not far from here. Get to it and you'll be safe."

Astrid heard the men's voices and looked back at the forest. The light from their torches was bright; they would arrive soon.

"Go!"

As the woman trudged across the waist-deep, water, she looked back at Astrid and in that moment, they both had the shock of their lives.

"Yrsa?"

Astrid could not believe her eyes: the woman she protected was none other than her sister.

"Astrid…"

"How is this possible, Sister?"

"I don't. No. Astrid! Behind you!"

As she turned, Astrid was struck by one of the men as he dove into her, wrapping his arms around her waist and pulling her down.

Astrid spotted the second man while being tackled; it was him, the bandit leader and whether it was the force to her chest or the sight of the man who had killed her, Astrid lost her breath.

The water was shallow, but she was still being held under, stunned and without a breath of air to hold.

Her sister's screams vibrated through the water. Astrid knew she had to find her footing soon or lose Yrsa again.

As she kicked and trashed about, Astrid discovered that she was free of the man's hold, yet under the dark, cloudy water, she could not see his legs. Frantic, she turned from side to side—white bubbles filled her view—her attacker could be anywhere now.

Astrid had no breath left in her lungs, so she found her footing and launched herself straight up out of the water with an explosion of force.

"Fight me!" Astrid screamed before she had even taken in the scene.

The man who had tackled Astrid was in front of her, and once again diving at her. A gap-toothed smile flashed on his face; he meant more than to harm her now.

"Astrid!" Yrsa screamed in panic.

As the bandit grasped Astrid's shoulders in an attempt to dunk her, Astrid pulled a hand from the water. She still held her dagger. With an uppercut, she sliced open the bandit's leather vest from belly to collar, but only scored his flesh lightly. She had expected a killing blow, but she had miscalculated.

Blood tinted the water as the bandit staggered back in shock and hazily drew his sword.

"Hurry up, Gerhard. Kill the whore before my pregnant bride tries to run off any further," the bandit leader ordered.

"She cut me."

"Then cut her back."

"You can't kill me!" Astrid shouted. "I'm already dead!"

She dropped into the water and kicked herself forward. Astrid darted atop the water like an eel. Swinging high, the bandit missed her—and left his gut wide open for the point of her blade. Sunk deep in the fat of his belly, she felt the man's body quiver in shock.

"Bitch!"

His left hand joined his right on his sword's hilt and together they dropped hard into Astrid's back before she could roll out of the way. The power of the blow numbed her arms and caused her to release her dagger as she sunk, face-first, into the red, murky water.

"Got her!" Gerhard cheered.

Shocked by the sight of her sister hurt and floating motionless atop the water, Yrsa cried out, "Stop this!"

The bandit leader heard her; she could see a curious look in his eye, but it faded quickly as his pause prompted the other man to speak.

"She's all mine."

"No, cut her throat, let her wash down stream," the bandit leader ordered.

"Emmerich! Stop!" Yrsa shouted.

The bandit leader looked away from Yrsa, "Do not test me, Brother. I want my pregnant bride back. The wild whore is meaningless."

"Your woman ain't going anywhere. We got plenty of time for me to enjoy this pretty piece. I'm good and ready for her too. All naked and jiggling around, she got my blood stirring."

The bandit leader drew and aimed his bow. "Damn you, Gerhard, make it quick!"

CHAPTER 33

ASTRID COULD SENSE MOTION, BUT her physical sensations were dulled. She could barely feel the bandit's cold hands gripping her hips. She had no idea he was lining her up to his groin, until he slammed her first into his large metal belt buckle.

I failed you again.

Gerhard lifted Astrid's face out of the water by a twisted knot of her hair. "You were a pretty one. Prettiest I ever seen, in fact."

Jaw open, water spilled from the corners of Astrid's mouth as she began to choke.

"Amazing."

"Are you done yet, Brother?" the bandit leader called out.

"She's still alive, man. Look at her. Can barely move but still breathing. Had I not pulled her head out just now she would've drown."

"Dead or alive, just do what you must so we can get back to camp before the sun rises."

"Gotta tell you, honey, I'm gonna enjoy this so much more, knowing you're still alive." The bandit's statement filled with excitement. "Actually…"

Astrid's face lowered back into the water.

The bastard…he wants to rape and drown me at the same time.

As the man went to free himself from his pants, Astrid felt a tingle in her limbs; the feeling was returning fast.

"Are you done?" Emmerich shouted to his brother.

169

"No. Something moved…like her backbone, I think it moved."

"You're a fool, Gerhard. Shut your mouth and hurry up."

While the bandit drew his finger down her spine, Astrid found her dagger where it laid on the smooth pebbles beneath her. She grabbed at it, her fingers pawing over the handle several times until they finally drug the weapon closer.

There, I have you. She snatched her dagger up, turned the point downward, and aimed the weapon at the bandit's legs behind her.

"Frigg, mother of the old gods!" Gerhard screamed as she stabbed him.

Back on her feet, Astrid turned to face the man, her arm lashing out across his face, lacerating him from cheek to chin. Blinded with pain, he did nothing to protect himself as Astrid stepped in and drove her weapon into his belly again.

Before she knew it, an arrow had sliced across her right arm. Emmerich had already drawn his bow and aimed it again before she could decide how to protect herself.

"You…" Emmerich, the bandit leader, finally recognized her.

Astrid shoved her attacker between herself and the bandit leader a breath before the next arrow struck. Gerhard howled in pain as the arrow drilled into the meat of his shoulder, all the way to the bone.

"Fire again and he dies!" Astrid proclaimed, her dagger pressed to the injured man's throat.

"You cannot be here. I killed you!" Emmerich screamed.

"Welcome to Helheim!"

"You are mad!"

"Brother…I'm hurt…bad."

"Throw your bow into the water, turn around, and go back into the forest."

"Never!"

Emmerich aimed his next arrow at Astrid's head but she could see his hands shake. He would not risk the life of his kin. With his arms slowly lowered, the bandit leader allowed the arrow between his fingers to fall to the ground a moment before he tossed the bow into the brook.

"Now go!" Astrid growled.

"Not without him."

"Yrsa, run to the town as I told you," Astrid ordered her sister over her shoulder.

"This cannot be happening."

"Go, Yrsa! Run!"

Yrsa haggardly stood, turned, and jogged off in the direction Astrid had pointed.

Eyes locked on the bandit leader, Astrid waited until she could feel Gerhard's body begin to give out from his wounds. "Take your brother."

Astrid shoved the wounded man forward, knowing he would not stay on his feet long. As he staggered, his head dropped low, and before he could reach the bank or his brother, Gerhard sunk into the rushing water.

"Gerhard!" Emmerich yelled.

The bandit leader jumped into the water and quickly braced his brother.

"I will see you dead!"

"Not again you will not."

With the flick of her wrist, Astrid hurled her dagger. Like the arrows the bandit leader had fired, the blade flew through the air fast and straight until it struck its target.

Thunk.

Astrid had put the dagger right where she wanted it—in the Gerhard's neck. Blood splattered out like a pierced fruit's juices, while the man gurgled in pain.

As Astrid hastily followed her sister's trail, she pondered her decision. She knew she could have just as easily aimed for the man who had sliced her throat, but in the moment, she enjoyed the thought of him suffering the death of his brother.

Why give him what the gods have not awarded me?

"Astrid!"

Warren, he found my tracks, but what of Yrsa? Has he found her too? she thought.

Astrid leapt over a felled, rotting tree and caught up to her sister just as Warren intercepted them.

"Who in the world are you?" Warren was asking Yrsa.

Yrsa was a ragged mess—muddy, wet, her clothes and hair stained, yet Astrid could see that Warren could still recognize something familiar about her.

"No, you can't..."

"Yrsa!" Astrid called out as she joined them.

She stepped up, a mixture of sweat and river water dripping from her limbs. She thought the sight would have disturbed or even aroused Warren, yet he stood speechless as he stared at her sister.

Yrsa looked just as perplexed and was equally silent, simply breathing heavily.

"Here." Warren raised his hand, her white dress still clenched tightly in it. "Cover up."

With a bit too much force, he threw the dress at Astrid, the long garment striking her chest and face like a challenge to fight.

"Back off!"

"What's wrong with you?" Warren asked in response to Astrid's grumble.

"Yrsa, are you well? Is the baby well?" Astrid questioned her sister, her back to Warren as she slipped on the dress.

"Gods above, Astrid, I knew I would find you again one day, my—"

"Sister!" Warren exclaimed unable to control himself any longer. "Unbelievable..."

Astrid and Yrsa turned in unison, both shooting a look at Warren.

"How are you here?" Warren asked.

"Truly, Yrsa, how did you get here?"

"Astrid, I..." And with that, Yrsa broke down and cried.

A moment of poignant silence was quickly interrupted by another man's old stern voice.

"Ho there, Warren!"

"Wonderful..." Warren exhaled hard.

CHAPTER 34

SENIOR GUARD GATHON AND ANOTHER young guardsman pushed their way through the brush. The sun was high enough off the horizon for the nosiest of his neighbors to be awake—*no doubt the grumpy, old pair shared a loaf of bread with the guards while they discussed all the noise that comes from my home daily.*

With no desire for this kind of attention, Warren pondered what chance a bribe had of sending away the guards, but he knew Gathon too well; the man would never accept coin or ale—not in front of the others at least.

"Warren, how did I know you would be involved in this disturbance?"

"Gathon, there's no trouble here. We simply made too much noise as we ran off to bathe."

Warren motioned for Astrid and her sister to walk away, trying to push past Gathon and his friend before the flames of any tempers were stoked.

"You have woken half the village...*running off*, Warren." Gathon placed his open hand on Warren's chest to stop him.

"For that I am sorry," Warren answered.

"Who is this now?" The young guard tipped his spear vaguely at Yrsa's chest.

Warren saw a glint in Astrid's eye and quickly responded. "A guest."

"Of course." The guard sneered.

"Another guest. Well, you are the lucky man, aren't you?" Gathon chuckled. "Warren, what would you say if I thought your guests were in fact illegal slaves and that your brother was the slave trader?"

"Madness," Warren snapped.

"Madness, Warren? I have proof." The two men faced one another nose to nose.

"You have no such thing."

Gathon pointed sharply. "Do not press me, old friend."

"What is it that you want from me, Gathon?"

Warren took a slight step back, and when he did, Gathon's face lit up.

"Only your obedience, dog."

"I no longer serve under you. Why can't you accept that?"

"You know why!"

"Damn you, Gathon, it was an accident!"

"Enough!" Astrid stomped as she shouted.

In a blur of motion, Astrid moved. Warren had seen her fight before, to kill in combat, but this felt different.

She shoved Gathon's friend back and pulled the young guard's sword from his belt. Warren shouted, but he knew it would do nothing. Frozen, he bore witness to tragedy.

Like lightning, Astrid struck, nearly spinning the soldier with its force. On the balls of her feet, Astrid pivoted as the man reeled backward and then plunged the sword into the young guard, withdrawing it to square up to Gathon.

Gathon was a veteran soldier. Astrid could see it in his eyes—a deadness that only old warriors had—one that pinpointed to the vacancy death had created inside their souls. Her father once called it the "the Helheim Stare." Astrid's father warned her to not hold that stare too long, that the soldier who was gripped by Hel would fight as if he were already dead: ruthless, unpredictable, with nothing to lose.

Her father was right.

Astrid attacked, and to her surprise, Gathon was ready. His spear parried her strike, and she instantly pulled back, her eyes on his slightest movements. He struck at her with a solid thrust—one aimed to gore her—but Astrid was ready too, so quick in her movements that she was able to grab a hold of his weapon.

Laughing, Astrid sliced through the shaft of Gathon's spear with the sword in her hand, and it shattered loudly, splinters spread far and wide.

"My spear, you filthy savage!"

It's time to end this. Astrid lunged to stab Gathon with the broken end of the spear but missed as he had leapt deftly back.

"Astrid, you must stop!" Warren shouted.

"Protect my sister."

"Killing you will make my day just right."

Gathon pulled his sword, a weapon that was twice the size of the one she had. Astrid wished that she held *Ugla* in her hands instead of what she considered a sorry excuse for a blade.

Warren began to move—*finally*, Astrid thought. She watched as he grasped Yrsa by the shoulders and pulled her away.

"Time to die, barbarian whore!" Gathon pushed his attack.

With a loud grunt of frustration, Astrid parried away his blade. "Come at me!" she boasted. "Larger, stronger men have."

"I know your kind," Gathon chuckled. "I'm surprised you can even speak."

He swung, but she managed to parry. The sound the two swords made—metal on metal, rang out against the peaceful chirp of morning birds. Astrid was sure everyone heard that—both the townsfolk and the bandits hidden in the forest.

"You heathens," Gathon huffed with another swing of his large sword. "Extremely brave or entirely mindless…hard to tell."

As much as the senior guard pressed, Astrid did not give him an inch until the tip of his sword scored across the meat of her thigh.

Suddenly hobbled, Astrid gazed at the gash, and gritted her teeth; it looked like so many she had dealt others through the years. Through the blood, she could see separated muscle and a hint of bone. She knew she should have been in agony, but she was not. Down to one knee, her will to stand was all that was on her mind. Astrid attempted to stand up but unfortunately the leg was useless, dead.

"This has long been a dream of mine. Right, Warren? Remember how badly I wanted to fight one of those half-naked barbarian women we faced in the south? I always wanted to duel one, to humble her in front of her tribe then cut her damned head off while her chieftain watched."

"Leave her be, Gathon!" Warren demanded. "Fight me instead!"

"No, Warren. Go. Take my sister and go."

Yrsa's tears had begun to taper off. She clawed at Warren's hands and spat words that would make no sense to him, but made all the sense in the world to Astrid. Yrsa called to the gods for help; Freyja first. *I hope they heed your calls, dear sister,* Astrid thought as she crawled over the tall grass.

Gathon pushed Astrid face first to the ground. Head down, her copious blonde locks spilled across the grass.

"Go!" Astrid yelled as she heard Gathon positioned himself for the killing blow.

The sensation of flames under her skin, what she had felt so powerfully in her throat when it was cut, suddenly returned, only in her leg. Gripped tightly, the wound begin to close from the inside out. As her muscles rapidly knit themselves back together, her strength returned.

Maybe this is not Hel, after all.

CHAPTER 35

"I HOPE YOU UNDERSTAND ME," Warren said as he released Yrsa. "I need you to run. Now!"

Warren launched himself across the grass at the senior guard as the man's sword began its downward arc, and the collision jarred the breath out of his lungs. Together, the two large men tumbled to the ground. Unarmed and without any armor, Warren knew he had to act quickly to stay alive. He snatched up the spearhead where Astrid had dropped it and stabbed at Gathon, but not before the guard struck him across the crown of his head with the handle of his sword so hard his teeth rattled.

Dazed, Warren crumpled to the ground beside Gathon, the spearhead in his hand still moving with phantom jabs. Eyes blurred, Warren watched Gathon rise slowly and turn to where Astrid had been on the ground, but only a puddle of blood could be found.

"Such an obvious trail. You couldn't have gone far, heathen," Gathon called out. "Even a child could track this mess."

Warren heard the senior guard laugh. His vision blurred, his head spun, yet Warren would not give up. *I will not allow him to hurt her anymore.*

"I'll be back to finish you, traitor," Gathon straightened his chest armor, and patted the spot where Warren had wounded him.

"Stop," Warren pleaded. "Please, Gathon, stop."

He didn't bother to acknowledge Warren's appeal as he continued to track the gooey marks of blood painted across the tips of the tall green grass.

"Astrid!" Warren could not see her anywhere.

Nothing will ever be the same, Warren thought. *Astrid killed a guard; her life is forfeit by kingdom laws. Gathon wants me to share her fate. How did everything fall to ruin so quickly?*

He saw Gathon pause at the forest's edge, his gaze was on something—*yes, there*—a red hand print at eye level, pressed against a tree trunk. Astrid could not have gone far; Warren knew he had to act now.

"You have made Warren weak," Gathon shouted. "There was a time when he would not have been so easy to overcome. You should have seen him then, savage. He killed many of your kind. He was a monster on the battlefield."

"I still am!" Warren shouted.

Warren's arms shook as they braced a rock the size of a wagon wheel over his head, the weight of which pulled him forward fast, and he dropped the stone on Gathon just as he turned.

"No!" Gathon shrieked.

The rough edges of the stone bent the nose guard of his helmet before it shattered his nose and cracked his skull. Teeth shot out from the side of Gathon's mouth into the thick brush. The man was dead before he hit the ground; Warren had murdered a guard now too.

Warren stumbled over Gathon and fell to the ground.

"Warren!" Astrid called out, as she limped arm in arm with her sister.

"Is he dead?" Yrsa's voice quivered.

Astrid knelt down beside Warren, her hand clutched to her leg as she moved.

"Warren?" she said tenderly.

"Astrid, your leg. I saw you cut."

"Just a scratch. You?"

"I think I need to close my eyes a moment. That shot he gave me…it made me wish I had my helmet on."

"His helmet did not save him," Astrid said as she took Warren's hand in hers and smiled.

Warren chuckled and closed his eyes, glad Astrid and her sister were alive.

"Don't touch him!" Yrsa shouted.

Warren released his grip on Astrid and nodded for her to go to her sister.

"It's okay, Yrsa," Astrid smiled. "Warren is with us."

"No…" Yrsa pointed. "Him! Do not touch him!"

"Gathon?"

"I…I am sorry, Sister." Yrsa covered her face with her hand. "So many years in *her* service, t-time is still a jumble. You understand that right?"

"I understand you need rest."

Warren took a long look at what he had done and his stomach turned. In all his years of killing, he had never murdered a man. He tried to tell himself otherwise, that this was defense, that he needed to protect Astrid and Yrsa, and those things were right, but they still equaled wrong.

"There might be more guards. I should—"

"Warren, be well-warned, I faced the bandit army's leader, just over the bekk. He and another man, they had my sister."

"Is there still an unmet force in these woods?" Warren asked Astrid's sister.

"Yes," Yrsa replied. "Emmerich commands many more men."

"Emmerich is the name of the brigand leader?"

Astrid and Yrsa nodded.

"Well then," Warren Paused. "It's obvious what happened here. Gathon and his younger just saved us from the bandits…but unfortunately they were killed in the process."

Astrid understood his meaning. "A hero's death?"

"A hero's death indeed," Warren nodded. "You two go. Speak to no one. I will sort this all out."

CHAPTER 36

ASTRID SAT STARING AT HER sister's bare, swollen stomach as she rested in the bathtub. She had seen her sister unclothed before—the two had bathed together until Yrsa was married—and this was not the first time she had seen her sister with child either. Still, Astrid found it impossible to not stare at her. There was no doubt in Astrid's mind that her sister had not been pregnant the last time she had laid eyes on her, yet here she was, far along. *This can't be*, Astrid thought. *Yrsa cannot have a baby inside her. She did not want another child; the last one nearly killed her.*

In the past few days, Astrid had accepted she would never lay eyes on her sister again. She had come to the conclusion that Yrsa, like her brothers and father, was gone to her. Seeing her now forced the one thing she wondered most to slide off her tongue.

"Yrsa, are we dead?"

"No," her sister answered quickly and confidently, her voice soft and tired. "You have not been here very long, have you, Sister? I remember my first days back too. There were times I thought I was dead, and other times I wished it true."

"First days back? I do not understand you."

Yrsa raised her eyes to meet Astrid's.

"Heroes' blood, it really must only be days for you. You have no idea, do you?"

"Yrsa, please, Sister, truth has always been your strongest trait. I need some of that now. Can you at least tell me what happened to Father? Our brothers? The wee ones?"

Yrsa nodded a moment before she answered. "Father died when Birka fell."

Astrid slid off her seat at the dining table and landed hard on her knees, as if pulled down by the weight of her heavy heart. Her lungs filled with grief and swelled until the tears that had been dammed up in her eyes were pushed out.

"Do not cry for Father. I am told he fought bravely, Astrid. He died a hero's death. No better man could serve Odin in Valhalla."

"I should have died at his side!" Astrid spit through her tears.

"You had a greater calling. We both did."

"What?"

Almost motionless in the bathtub, Yrsa tried to explain. "I saw you claimed from the battle."

"What are you saying, Yrsa?"

"What do you remember from that night?"

"I was ready to fight. I pushed out the fear and replaced it with our birth-given courage. The blood of our ancestors pumped through my veins. I could feel it." Astrid raised her clenched fist. "I exited your home expecting to confront the enemy and was quickly blinded by a flash of bright, golden light."

"Yes, then what?"

"When I reopened my eyes, I was fully armored, on my back under a star-filled sky in a field a few day's walk from here."

Yrsa cupped a handful of water and splashed her face; it washed clear her scowl.

"I saw the golden light strike you, Astrid. It blinded me too, but for only an instant. I watched a cone of glowing firelight stretch down from the heavens, embrace, and lift you."

"Yrsa…" Astrid began to tremble.

"When I looked down again, I saw the demons that invaded our home, but I did not fear them. I did not scream. You see, I too felt Odin's gentle hand reach down and pluck me up from Midgard."

"Odin…saved…us?"

Astrid looked up through her blonde hair, puffing air out through her pursed lips to push away the strands that had stuck to her face. This was why she normally wore her hair in braids; she hated the sensation of hairs tickling her face.

"We were chosen, two daughters of royalty, to serve him. Do you not remember your pledge?"

"No."

Astrid wiped her face with the skirt of her dress. If she had been graced by Odin, come face-to-face with the ruler of the gods, she wished she could remember.

"Wait, you are not feigning ignorance just to back out of our wager, are you?"

"No."

Yrsa smiled for the first time since Astrid had seen her that day. With her arms wrapped around her chest, Astrid felt no different than when they were small children and her older sister was in the midst of a tale of action and thrills.

"Well, remember this, as the days pass and your memory clears: I won, Astrid. I won."

"You won?"

"Aye, I met my quota of souls long before you did…" Yrsa looked down at herself before she finished. "Clearly."

Astrid finally began to piece her sister's comments together. She looked at her sister, her eyes wide with shock. "We are Valkyrie?"

"We…were."

Astrid's mind snapped back to the moment she had awoken in the snow-covered field and played her life rapidly forward to this moment. When this information was applied to all the unknowns, things began to finally make sense.

"This is why my wounds heal so quickly?"

"One of the many boons. We do not injure as normal men and women do."

"I thought I was dead, Yrsa, twice."

"A lasting sensation," Yrsa said nodding. "I remember it well."

"No! You don't understand," Astrid shouted before lowering her voice to a near whisper. "I thought *this* was Hel."

"Freyja warned us of the many side effects from crossing over to and from the afterlife. She said our feelings…our deepest emotions…would haunt us like bad dreams for days."

"Freyja…" Astrid's disappointment was painful; she wanted so much to remember meeting one of her most favored gods. "We shared an audience with her too?"

Instead of answering, Yrsa motioned for aid, and Astrid helped her stand up. Once on her feet, she dripped dry a moment before she responded, "Freyja was quite fond of you, Astrid. You were one of her favorites."

"Was I?"

"Don't worry, you will remember it all."

Astrid shrugged and turned away from her sister.

"You smell like the flowers Father used to give Mother. I have not smelled that scent in years," Yrsa said with a deep inhale.

With a huff, Astrid sat down; even more frustrated now.

"I do not recall that either."

"In spite of your ailing memory, I dare say you smell sweet, my warrior-sister."

"If the gods did not just grace me with your return, Yrsa, I might wish them to take you away."

"Now that is the Astrid I remember."

They both spun to look at the door as a knock stopped their conversation. Astrid hoped it was Warren but feared it was the guards. She cursed at herself for not putting on her armor since she and her sister had taken refuge.

"Warren?"

"No, Hammond."

Astrid picked up her sword before she opened the door; she was not going to take any further risks today. Warily he said, "Do not strike me."

With his hands up in surrender, Hammond looked even less of a threat than normal, if that was possible.

"Come in, Hammond."

"I cannot."

"Hammond, please come in," Astrid repeated.

"No man is allowed in the home—" he began to repeat.

"This is true. However that is not your law, and I am in your land, so please." She waved him in.

Hammond stepped into his brother's home and gasped at the sight of Yrsa—tall, naked, and many months pregnant.

"Sweet mother—"

"Careful!" Astrid shouted.

"Astrid, it's fine. I do not mind. It has been many months since I owned any modesty," Yrsa replied as she stepped from the bathtub toward the man to greet him.

"This cannot be possible. You are..." Eyes glued to Yrsa, Hammond's words trailed off.

"Yrsa, daughter of Kol."

Shoulder to shoulder with Astrid, Yrsa was a close match in height, and although a bit older; Astrid always thought her sister looked softer and kinder. *No doubt she is Hammond's kind of woman.*

"I-I was going to say—"

"Turn about, Hammond, now, before I change my mind about hitting you," Astrid said, her patience running out.

"Yes, right." Hammond turned his back to the girls quickly.

"Do you have a reason for this visit, or are you simply here to steal lust-filled looks?"

Hammond scratched his chin a moment, nodded, and then dashed out the door to retrieve the sack of clothing he had left outside. A second later, Hammond took another long look at the sisters before he presented Astrid with the gift.

"My apologies."

"What is this? Is this more clothing?"

"A collection of clothing I had stored to trade later in the season and some of my wife's old things. Helen suggested I bring them here and let you find what fits you. Please, Yrsa, keep whatever you like."

"Your kindness will be rewarded in Valhalla." Yrsa nodded. "Tell Helen she has our thanks. Now please go."

Astrid pushed Hammond out the door. Once across the threshold, he waved goodbye and smiled.

"Nice man," Yrsa said to her sister as the door shut.

"For a lusting dog..."

"Ah, no doubt you found that men treat you differently since your return to Midgard, Astrid?"

"At times."

"You will get used to it. Men, especially soldiers and warriors, can in some way sense what we are...or were."

"Valkyrie?"

Yrsa smiled. "I know it's hard to imagine, but it's true."

Astrid gazed down at her sister's belly and concluded it was time to ask the most obvious question.

"Yrsa, how is it that you are pregnant? Not enough moons have passed for you to be so close to giving birth."

"I was curious when you would inquire. Have you not asked these people the date?"

"No...not long has passed since the night Birka was invaded."

"Not long?" Yrsa smirked. "Almost two hundred years."

Astrid's legs gave and she crumpled like a rag doll. Barely over the age of twenty-two herself, she could hardly imagine the sum of two hundred years. She thought of her brother Vignir piling several rows of coins to divide among the men; he may have been able to fathom such a number of years better than her.

Two hundred years, she repeated in her mind, *everyone I know is truly gone.*

Yrsa leaned forward to help her, but Astrid swatted away her hands, content with her spot on the cold floor.

"All dead."

"Who?"

"Our brothers, their wives, their children…your children."

"A long time ago, Astrid."

"Long time…it feels like days to me, Yrsa!" Astrid shouted in frustration.

"It will pass."

Through a new flow of tears, Astrid grumbled, "You…how can you be so uncaring?"

"Me? I have had time—"

"Yrsa!" Astrid cried out. "What of the wee ones?"

Yrsa went blank a moment; her demeanor shifted. Her shoulders slumped and her eyes grew dark as she slowly slipped the first dress from the top of the sack of garments on, letting it hang loose on her body instead of tying the ties.

"Yrsa?" Astrid called out again. "What is it?"

Yrsa drew a deep breath as she sat down. "Do you recall what I told you about Gyrd and the children on that night?"

"Yes," Astrid sobbed.

"Well, years after we became Valkyrie, I found Gyrd in the halls of Valhalla. I was delivering a man who had died protecting his family from thieves. You can imagine how pleased I was to see my husband again, and the first words from his mouth were that he and the little ones escaped that night."

"What?" Astrid tried to settle herself. "They escaped?"

"Aye, Gyrd told tale of a mad dash to the fortress, only to be detoured by Jokul. Our brother was searching for you but found Gyrd instead. Jokul led Gyrd and our children out one of the tunnels to a boat. Once he saw to it they were safe, Jokul left them to seek us out."

"Of course Father would send him. No one sneaks about a town better." Astrid slammed her open hand on the ground. "I hope he did not mean for us to flee."

"Well—"

"Sister." Astrid finally stood. "Who else did you see in Valhalla?"

"The place is large and filled with many great warriors."

"Did you see our brothers? Did you see Father? Tell me you saw Father there."

"I am sorry, Astrid, I never saw our Father again."

Astrid frowned.

"Don't be sad. They were all there; Freyja told us this. They all had very important tasks in the afterlife. Father, Hak, and Ulf trained the einherjar[6] for Odin daily."

"They did?"

"Aye." She nodded. "They trained and prepared many of the men we brought to Valhalla...even the heroes."

Astrid gasped. "Yrsa, you must, please, tell me more. I have so many questions."

Yrsa laughed. "I almost forgot."

"Forgot what?"

"How curious you were."

"How could you forget me?" Astrid huffed. "It was only days ago when—"

"Not days. No, not for me. I have not seen you since...not since I watched you fly off with Kjar in your arms."

---

6 Those who died in battle, brought to Valhalla by Valkyrie, and were to serve Odin in battle.

CHAPTER 37

MAGNUS STONESKIN WAS THE LAST to fall, finally succumbing to an arrow fired by none other than the man who had sworn to kill him during the first seconds of the battle. Only moments before he fell, Magnus claimed victory atop a mountain of corpses.

Yrsa had watched it all from above—her sister at her side. There were many brave men to usher home, but Yrsa and Astrid had been given the task of bringing back the two best. Yrsa had chosen the warlord Magnus.

Magnus was the leader of the Dark Raiders, a league of giant men from the coldest reaches of the north, where the sun never sets. Men forged of ice and stone in a land where nothing grew, they thrived and drove away their enemies. Known throughout the lands for his yearly raids on the farming villages of the southern coast, Magnus killed those who stood against him, though only when forced. It was long rumored that the man did not wish to end bloodlines. Still, over the years, his desires grew from grain, wheat, and ale, to cattle and women. Stealing away the daughters of farmers earned him another title: Magnus the Hunted.

Eventually, the kingdoms came together and sought out a hero to confront him, and found Kjar the archer. Kjar was promised a hefty reward, one that a single man could not have spent alone; all he had to do was return to the south with the head of Magnus. The challenge accepted, Kjar took twenty longboats filled with soldiers and sailed north.

By the time Kjar landed on the shores outside of Magnus's home, only twelve boats remained. His numbers depleted, he no longer had an advantage, a fact he did not realize until the battle had begun.

The clash lasted the better part of a day, and when it was over, only the two warlords had survived.

Astrid pointed at the arrow logged in Magnus's chest, the one Kjar had fired as the two armies fought—she had wagered that her man would be the last to stand.

"Magnus will bleed out," Astrid announced proudly.

"Do not claim victory yet, Sister," Yrsa replied.

The two warlords met at the center of the battlefield, face to face at last. It took all the strength he had left, but Magnus managed to pierce Kjar's belly with his long sword.

The battle was finally over, and Yrsa had won the bet.

Astrid turned to Yrsa. "Damn this never-ending sun!" she said, blaming it for Kjar's failure to hit his mark and not end Magnus's life earlier.

"Quit your complaining. The contest is over. Magnus has won. I have won," Yrsa said.

"Very well."

Yrsa landed first, at Magnus's side. To her shock, the man was still breathing, his strength, for a dying man, still apparent. While she stared down at him, he smiled back. Yrsa wished him good fortune in the afterlife.

"I defeated them all."

"Aye, brave Magnus, you did."

"My people will remember me for ages."

His town was in flames but Yrsa held her tongue. "They will write songs and sing them once a year, commemorating this incredible victory."

"You honor me, Valkyrie."

"Close your eyes, Magnus Stoneskin, and when you reopen them, we will be ascending to Asgard. Once there, I will personally welcome you to your new home in Valhalla."

"Thank you..." His voice trailed off.

A moment later, Astrid appeared at Yrsa's side with Kjar in her arms, ready to leave. "I thought Magnus was dead."

"So did I."

"Seems you did chose the stronger man," Astrid conceded. "Do you think they will be shocked to see one another again?"

"Perhaps," Yrsa replied.

"Remember when the brothers Molg arrived and began fist-fighting?" Astrid grinned. "It always tends to happen when two men share a woman during a lifetime. How about we bet?"

"No more bets," Yrsa replied. "Now hurry. Freyja awaits."

"Race you back."

CHAPTER 38

ANOTHER KNOCK SOUNDED, THIS ONE more hurried than the last. Astrid knew it was Warren but huffed with frustration at his poor timing; she was caught up in the tale and did not want to stop.

"Astrid?"

Head hung low, Astrid drew a deep breath and grunted. Yrsa whispered before Warren knocked a second time, "Do not tell him about us."

"Why?" Astrid furrowed her brow.

"I made the mistake of trusting someone with the truth once. It only caused me long months of pain and suffering," Yrsa said as she rubbed her belly.

"Who?"

Warren knocked and called out her name again; Astrid had to steady her anger before she put her fist through the table. On her feet quickly, Astrid stomped her way to the door, snatched the handle in a firm grip, and swung the door open.

"Good, you *are* here." Warren walked in and began to circle her. "We need to talk."

"Yrsa and I *were* talking."

Warren reached for her hand, and his look of concern deepened when she moved away from him.

"You sweat like you have been in combat," Astrid observed. "Have more bandits come?"

"No, Astrid. When they were carting off Gathon's body, a key fell from his belt. The other guards did not claim it, and said it did not belong to the prison or stockade."

"A chest key, then?" Astrid looked back at Yrsa—she wanted to return to her sister's story.

"Astrid, listen. I followed the guards back to Gathon's supply cellar and we opened it."

"What did you discover?" Yrsa stole the words from Astrid's mouth.

"There were chests, many filled with coin, but the man had dug out his cellar so deep it took many torches to explore it. Behind a stack of crates, there was a tunnel which led to rooms with cages."

"Cages?"

"Cages filled with women."

"What?"

Yrsa stood suddenly and wobbled, trying to balance her pregnant stomach.

"He was keeping slaves?"

"Not keeping them. Apparently he was trading them. He harbored the women for a few days then delivered them. We found his ledgers. He kept a head count and a list of locations but no names."

"Slave trading is illegal here, correct?"

"It is."

"Are they in good health?" Yrsa asked.

"Well enough. Truly a blessing we found them. Had the key not fell—"

"A supply cellar full of corpses would have been found later," Astrid finished his thought.

"Caged is no way to die." Yrsa sat back down.

"It appears Gathon and Emmerich were in league, but how deeply and to what purpose? I intend to find out."

"A worthwhile endeavor," Astrid agreed, hoping to end the discussion.

"You are a first-rate guardsman, Warren. Your town should be proud of you." Yrsa bowed her head.

"Oh, I am no guard. I mean, I was for a short time when I first returned from the wars. I simply tend a farm now, Yrsa."

"A farmer?" Yrsa turned to Astrid. "Our brothers would laugh for weeks knowing you have chosen a farmer to—"

"Yrsa!" Astrid shouted. "Hold your tongue."

Yrsa shrugged in response.

"Regardless, guard or farmer, citizen or soldier, there's much to..."

Astrid stopped listening to Warren and spoke over him.

"You are right, Warren. We do need to speak a moment..." Astrid stated.

"There's much to discuss," he agreed.

She scrutinized Warren from head to toe a moment before she waved her hand toward the door.

"Join me outside."

CHAPTER 39

NERVOUSLY, WARREN REPEATED WHAT HE learned about Gathon to Astrid once they reached the fields outside the house. He emphasized his sense of shock when he found the unfortunate women caged in the man's cellar and added that none of them spoke a familiar language that allowed him or the guards any more information.

"Expect to see many more soldiers around here, Astrid. Some may be battle hardened, and…well, more aggressive."

"Will this place finally find peace?"

"It will."

"Then I think it is for the best."

Warren appeared anxious; he fumbled with his belt and looked all around.

"Are we done?"

"Astrid, I…I have few questions for you."

She knew he did. It was the reason why she had brought him out there to talk. She too had many questions, but they were best directed at her sister.

"What happened this morning? In your eyes…you looked like you were ready to kill me before you ran off."

"Warren—"

"I understand that much has changed for you, much is new, but I thought we—"

"We are," Astrid replied loudly and then lowered her voice. "We were."

"How did I lose your trust?"

"You may never understand this, Warren, I may never either. Just remember this much: This morning I was…this morning I was very tired and confused." She shook her head.

"And now?"

"Yrsa has helped me find some small bit of certainty."

Warren placed his hands on her shoulders and squeezed them gently. Astrid wanted to peel his hands off her and step away, but she did not move, though she was unsure if her steadfastness was from stubbornness or trepidation.

"Where does that leave us?"

Astrid shrugged. Warren leaned in and kissed her gently on the lips.

"I want you and your sister to stay at my home. I will go settle with Hammond and Helen. We can decide on a better arrangement later."

"Wait, now you want me to share *your* bed with my sister and not you?" Astrid was filled with disappointed, albeit sudden and strange. "Do you even know what you want?"

"I want what is best for you both."

Astrid nodded. "Fine then."

"You look sad," Warren frowned.

"I told you. A lot has happened. While I am happy to have my sister back, she has come with news most grim and unbelievable."

"Your family?" Warren caressed her face as he spoke.

His tenderness overwhelmed her, so she freed herself of his gentle grasp.

"I cannot speak of it yet."

"I understand. I will let you go rejoin your sister."

Astrid watched Warren turn and begin to walk away and when he was several feet away she stopped him.

"Wait. I will…"

"Will what, Astrid?" he said as he turned back.

"I will miss sharing a bed with you, Warren," she uneasily admitted.

Warren smiled.

"This morning, I—" Astrid began.

"This morning you figured the only way you could have all the bed furs was to kill me, am I right?"

"You are." Astrid found safety in Warren's joke. "My apologies. They are such fine furs."

"No worries. We won't talk about it again. Just know that I will trade my brother for more blankets so that we can focus on more important issues."

Astrid nodded.

"There *are* many pressing concerns." He held his hand up and ticked off his points as he spoke. "Gathon's slave trading. Emmerich and his army. The sudden discovery of your pregnant sister, Yrsa. Am I wrong to wonder if they are all connected? If they are, we may have another fight on our hands soon."

"If Emmerich wants a fight, I will gladly give him one." Astrid shifted her gaze to the forest.

"That sounds better." Warren cleared his throat. "Please, Astrid, next time you are confused or frustrated…just talk to me. There's nothing you cannot share with me, nothing I will not make every effort to understand."

"I know."

"Good."

"Good," Astrid repeated.

"So tell me, how did your sister end up in the hands of the bandit leader?"

"I have yet to ask her."

"What? Here, I thought that would have been one of your first questions."

Astrid sighed. "It was not."

She looked over her shoulder at Warren's home and stayed silent. She could not clear her head of what Yrsa said. She had not known her sister to lie, let alone spin such a fantastical tale. It explained so much of what had happened, and still, without her own memories, she was full of doubt.

Astrid felt Warren's heavy gaze on her; *the man looks tired. He's been through nearly as much as I have this day; a rest would do us both good.*

"Perhaps we should go speak with Yrsa?" he finally said.

"Only briefly."

The wind had grown steadier since they had left Warren's home, and it made Astrid shiver.

The thinness of the fabrics these people wear will take a lifetime to get used to. No. This is no good, Astrid thought, *there is no comfort, no safety to be had in these rags. I need to wear something that covers and protects better—leathers and furs, like home.*

"These garments, Warren—cheaply made, useless."

"At times Hammond has been known to trade for some poorly crafted stuff and then sell it for too much coin."

"Are there any leatherworkers around?"

"None that would supply the quality of clothing you are used to wearing I wager, but the bazaar will be here in a few days. There we can find you some better attire."

"What is the bazaar?"

"A large group of traveling merchants who move back and forth through the kingdom and the smaller surrounding towns and villages."

"Exciting."

"It is. They have all sorts of amazing things to sell. All you need is coin."

Astrid thought of the three treasure chests she had had in Birka's keep, her father's guards sworn to protect them. They were full of coin and gems. She could have bought herself a ship if she had so desired, which made her next statement hard to say.

"I have no wealth here."

"Are you sure?"

At Warren's door, Astrid paused until he motioned for her to go inside first.

"I might have filled a small pouch or two with coin I found in Gathon's storage cellar."

Astrid turned toward him, her long hair rustling over her shoulder. *Has honorable Warren stole something?*

"You surprise me."

"I figure the coin will be better spent in your hands than those whose fat purses they might have found their way to."

"You have my promise to spend it wisely."

"You sound like my brother when our father gave him a few coins to use."

To Astrid's surprise, the small home was empty. "Yrsa!" she yelled.

"Perhaps she went looking for us?"

"Yrsa!" Astrid yelled again, as she turned around in a full circle. "Yrsa!"

"I'll search the border of town, starting here at the edge of my farm and moving south. You should head into the center and see if she went that way. She could have simply wandered off in search of something to eat."

Astrid nodded in agreement, but before Warren could leave, she grabbed his arm and said, "Best take your sword."

After a nod, Warren retrieved his sword and then ran out the door.

"If you find her, Warren—"

"I will bring her back here."

"Find her alive and well."

"Don't worry, I will!"

Warren dashed off toward his fields with the sun directly above him. In order to hide, Yrsa would have had to lie down in the crops. Warren recalled a time when he chased a wolf from his freshly harvested fields after it killed one of his cows a year ago. It crept low and slow, its haunches just below the harvest lines. *It had been a sunny day just like this one,* Warren thought, his gaze up at the sky, *and still that beast was nearly*

invisible. When he panned his fields, he knew it was possible she was out there somewhere.

"Yrsa!" he yelled.

This could take all day.

CHAPTER 40

ASTRID REGRETTED NOT SUITING UP in her armor before she left Warren's home. In town, with such a serious task at hand, in a thin cloth dress made her feel weak.

How do these people live without protection? she wondered. *Can they truly feel safe here, especially after what has already happened? The people of Grømstad seem to wander around with no idea of the dangers that exist in the world. They should know fear as I have.*

After her encounter with the bandit leader that morning, Astrid was relieved to at least have a dagger carefully tucked away inside her boot. *I will be ready next time.*

As it was midday, Grømstad was abuzz with the chatter of its citizens. Men and women alike shopped the small marketplace and did their chores and business in the area that surrounded. Astrid had never seen it like this before and thought maybe it was a special day. It felt to her as if everyone in town was out—a much larger crowd to have to search through. Unlike the other days she had walked through Grømstad, all eyes were not on her. While she did catch the occasional glare and ogle of men in passing, she noticed that most people's gazes skittered over her. When Astrid reached the opposite end of town, she searched through the maze of merchant stands for her sister until a glimmer of light caught her eye.

"A woman after my own heart! See, she knows to stop and take in the finer details of the piece."

Astrid stared into the reflective surface of a bronze platter on a merchant's stand.

"I was just using its reflection," Astrid answered the shrill-voiced little salesman as she looked at herself a moment, surprised that not even the slightest hint of a wound remained on her neck. "It has been a long time—"

"Then the lass needs a mirror."

"A mirror, no, only the fat and prosperous have them," Astrid replied. "What I need is my sister. Have you seen a woman who looks like me but pregnant?"

"Sorry, I have not." The man produced a lead-handled mirror from one of his chests while he answered. "Well, it's not the most ornate construction, but with your good looks, I think the beauty in the reflection would outweigh the piece's design regardless. Don't you agree?"

Astrid looked at herself in the mirror.

"So young and attractive," the merchant chuckled. "Can you believe I cannot recall the day when I was either young or attractive?"

"There was a time and place I was called skilled, strong, and even deadly. No one except my father called me beautiful and even he used the word sparingly."

"Sad for you then."

"Sad?" she repeated.

"Yes, sad. It breaks my heart to see one as stunning as you so shrouded in gloom. I was going to offer you that fine mirror for five coins, but, I want you to have it."

"You are giving me this as a gift?"

"Yes."

Astrid wanted to laugh.

"I will see that you are properly paid, perhaps in drink?" Astrid answered. "Such strong sun today; you must be thirsty."

Astrid lifted an old, wooden goblet from his table, and turned it upside down.

"That would be kind of you. I would not refuse some wine."

"Very well, I will return with some."

Astrid headed toward the oldest building in town, one she had only laid eyes on once before now. The large structure seemed out of place, with no signs outside. If this was a tavern, as she hoped, Astrid's bet was that Hammond would be inside. *He will help me search for Yrsa.*

Not unlike the mead halls of Birka, it seemed large enough to hold a good portion of the town's populace, and when she stepped inside, it was like she was transported home. The wide building had one spacious room, filled with rows and rows of tables and benches; a sign inside the door named it Grömsala.

Why have I not come here sooner? she thought, as her ears filled with a stirring song of battle being sung by an older man in the corner. A roar of laughter echoed, passed on by drunken men from one side of the building to the other. Distracted, Astrid turned from the song just in time to watch an obese man stumble and collapse to the ground, his half-full mug of ale spilling over himself as he lay like a turtle on its back, his legs kicked out. *Like home.*

She counted four large hearths, several dozen rows of tables, and equally as many maids pouring drinks, one of whom was being aggressively manhandled by someone she instantly recognized.

She had to shove her way through the crowds of drunk, noisy men, but was able to take a seat next to Hammond, who was still preoccupied with the barmaid whose bottom he fondled under her skirt.

"Hammond."

"Yes?"

Face to her, Astrid watched Hammond struck with fright so badly, he nearly fell from the bench he sat on.

"A-Astrid, what are you doing here?" Hammond tried to slide away from Astrid, but she grabbed one of his failing arms and stopped him.

"Searching for my sister and a drink." She raised the merchant's mug. "You?"

"I-I…"

"Hammond, this place—"

"I should not be here, I know. I need to stop coming here." Hammond hid his face in his hands with a sigh. "The tavern at the center of town should—"

"I like this place."

An eruption of cheers from a group of young men drowned out Astrid. There was a celebration at hand; the people of Grømstad had prayed for a good harvest and therefore now gave thanks. She wanted to cheer too.

"What?" He peeked out from his cupped hands.

"I like this." Astrid paused as another man yelled out his name. "Reminds me of home."

"Really?"

"Very much."

"Then you will saying nothing to Helen that...wait, where did you get that mirror?" Hammond pointed to where it was tied to the belt around her waist.

"From the merchant across the way."

"Short man?"

"Very short."

"He works for me." Hammond smirked. "So how many coins did he rob your purse of?"

"Zero."

"Damned dwarf!" Hammond slammed his hand down on the table, resulting in another set of cheers from the men around him.

Astrid smiled at the joyous men who passed by and answered, "I was going to bring him some wine as payment."

"Oh, well then, at least he will not be working thirsty." His sarcasm was strong but Astrid ignored it.

"Hey, girl, fetch me more ale!" an older man said as he touched her shoulder.

"You mistake me for a mead maid," Astrid answered calmly as she brushed his hand off her shoulder.

The tall, bearded man stumbled back and scoffed. Astrid guessed that the man worked as a lumberjack by the splinters of wood in his dirt-covered boots, but it was the way his thick, calloused hands twitched that confirmed it. She had known a few lumberjacks back in Birka, and all of their hands twitched while they drank.

"Could've fooled me. Those look like the full breasts of an ale wench, right, Brother?"

"Full like a pair of ripe melons."

"Really, and do these hands look like they have been gripping pitchers all day?"

Astrid stood and faced the two brothers with her hands out, her elbows bent down.

"Can grip my kokkr, they can!"

His breath was so strong with bitter ale that Astrid wanted to take a step back but only squinted in discomfort.

"Look at them." Astrid waved her hands about.

"Astrid, no," Hammond begged.

"Why not?"

"Not here, not now."

"No better time," she said, as she continued to wave her open hands at the big man.

As the big man leaned in to get a better look, he chuckled.

"My brother is right. My mistake, those look like whore hands."

Distracted as they were by their own laughter, Astrid was able to easily jab the man in the eye and then the nose. The big man reeled backward in pain and bumped into his brother, yet Astrid continued to press him, ready to strike again harder.

"Shite!" Hammond gasped.

"Gah, the girl hit me!" the big man squealed.

"And *the girl* will hit you again," Astrid replied.

Hand over his eye, the aggressive man cracked his biggest smile yet and as he looked Astrid up and down, he bellowed with deep laughter.

"Larger branches than you have fallen on me and hurt less! You pack quite a punch."

"That was nothing."

"Forgive me then, fighter lady," he laughed. "Maybe I should get you some ale? You could teach me to fist-fight proper."

"Make it wine."

Astrid lowered her guard. She knew there would be no further altercation; these men were all too drunk to fight. They were, for the most part, harmless.

"Astrid!" Hammond called out to her back. "Astrid."

Astrid ignored his calls, waiting until the big man and his brother walked off before responding.

"What, Hammond?"

"Your sister is here."

Hammond pointed across the room, and there she was. Arms full, Yrsa poured wine from a swollen wineskin for a table of older men.

"What in Helheim is she doing?"

"Serving—"

Hammond did not finish his statement, as Astrid's blue eyes burned two holes in his forehead.

"Stay here, Hammond."

Once more, Astrid had to push through the merry crowds; the smell of sweat and ale nearly overpowered the scent of the enormous boar being roasted in a fire pit in the center of the room. *Smells like home.*

"Yrsa!"

Just then the old man Yrsa was pouring wine for grasped his chest. With a loud groan, the man tried to stand, his face a bright shade of red. Astrid watched the arteries in the man's neck throb as he strained and gritted his teeth. One of his friends stood swiftly in effort to catch his friend as he fell over.

"Landebert, what ails you?"

The man did not speak, only gasped for air. Before his friend could ask again, the old warrior was dead.

"Landebert has died!"

"Landebert has died?" another man repeated.

"To Landebert!" Yet another man from the table of seniors raised his mug as he spoke.

While everyone else raised their drinks in honor of the man, Astrid stared at his body, which sparkled with a golden aura. It was just as she had seen before, but now, after Yrsa's story, she began to fully understand it; the light—it was the man's soul.

I must release his soul and send it to Asgard.

Astrid moved closer to the fallen man, but before she could reach him, Yrsa knelt at his side.

"Yrsa! Stop!"

Her sister grabbed the old man's shoulder gently, and when she did...nothing happened. Astrid expected to see golden light shoot up through the ceiling of the mead hall, but it did not; in fact, it did the opposite. It receded inside him and abruptly vanished.

Astrid knelt beside her sister.

"What happened?" Yrsa asked. "Did you see that, Astrid?"

"The light vanished. His soul did not ascend."

Astrid shook the man's shoulder, removed her hand, and placed it down again and again, hoping the golden aura would return.

"What? What happened? His soul..." Yrsa backed away slowly. "No. No. No."

"Look at this, two beauties have come to pay respect to the mighty Landebert!" another man boasted. "I had no idea he was such honey to the lady bees."

"Lady bees?" Astrid gave him a cross look.

Yrsa began to shudder and cry. Astrid's view swung between the dead man and her sister's pouring of emotion. She knew with total certainty that something was missing from the situation she observed, but was unable to pinpoint what.

"Rolf, you old fool, these two might be his daughters."

"Oh no, I've seen his daughters and they were cursed to look like their father."

"To old Landebert, slayer of barbarians!" one of the men cheered. "He liked to boast he would never die on the battlefield."

"Instead he died full of ale and meat. A good death, I think," another man cheered, raising his mug.

"A good death indeed."

Astrid took her sister by the arm and led her out of the crowd and toward the exit. She searched for any sign that the dead man's glow had returned as they went, but when she did not see it, she turned her eyes to Hammond, who walked their way.

"I need to get my sister...home," Astrid huffed.

"But the roast boar is nearly done," Hammond teased, but he looked at Yrsa and fell silent.

"This all is too much for me to deal with at once."

"Take her to my home. Helen will feed and help calm her."

Astrid thought a moment. "Perhaps that would be best. Could you—"

"Find my brother, yes." Hammond sighed as he looked back at the barmaids. "Of course."

CHAPTER 41

YRSA SHOOK AND CRIED UNTIL the sun dropped well below the horizon. In all her years, Astrid could not remember a day as long as this one; it moved at a snail's pace—as if two or three days had been squeezed to fit inside it. Seated on the floor near Hammond's hearth, Astrid rested her head in her hands and shut out everything but the heat of the fire against her tired skin. She did not know how long had passed since she had allowed herself to hear, to even think, but she could still smell Helen's cooking; it seemed as if the woman had not stopped preparing food all day.

As Astrid returned to her surroundings, she heard Warren and Hammond whispering. She wanted to know what they said, but that meant she would have to lift her head and return fully to the world of the conscious.

Moments later, she heard her father's voice in her mind. It was the words he spoke to her on the day he asked Astrid to make a heavy sacrifice. Threats had been made against Yrsa, and she refused to move her family into the keep for safety; there was only one other solution Kol felt confident in. *"I trust no man, not even Yrsa's husband to fully protect her. Only you have the strength in both muscle and will to keep her safe, Astrid. I have never told anyone this, but your sister reminds me very much of your mother. To lose her would kill me."*

I will keep her safe, Father.

A tiny, soft hand brushed the back of Astrid's hair. She had almost forgotten that Willamina had not left her side since she sat down.

What is so fascinating with my hair? Astrid wondered. *The smoothness? The length? Willa is seemingly mesmerized by it.* Astrid focused on the little girl's hand as it stroked her head. *This is nice,* Astrid thought; that small gesture gave her reassurance that there would be happiness, balance, and order again.

"Astrid?" Willa whispered. "Astrid?"

"Willa?" she replied, breaking her silence.

"Don't be sad, Astrid."

"I am n—" She began, but the child was right.

"We can be sisters too."

Astrid looked at Willa, the little one had gripped a batch of long strands of her hair in her hand.

"I would like that."

"Do you like to chase rabbits?"

Astrid smiled. "I like to hunt them, so of course, I do."

"We should chase some rabbits tomorrow."

"Okay." Astrid nodded.

"Astrid, do you miss your braids?"

"I do."

"Your hair is so soft."

"Thank you, Willa."

Her conversation with the child had not gone unnoticed. Helen had taken a break from her chores and watched their interaction with a warm smile.

"Come now, Willa, leave Astrid be a moment. You need to sup now so you can go to bed."

"She's no bother."

When Astrid spoke up, both brothers stopped and turned their full attention to her. She shivered and groaned; once again she wished she wore her armor and not a thin dress.

"Are you feeling any better, Astrid?" Warren asked first.

"I am fine. Is she—"

"Sleeping," Hammond responded before she could finish.

"Come, eat something." Warren held up a bowl that was meant for her.

"I am not hungry, Warren."

Warren is not smiling. He has not smiled much this day, Astrid thought. Even when they sprinted through the forest on their way back to Grømstad, in fear of invasion, the man's face had bore a tiny grin. He must have felt the great weight of the day too, much of which was her fault. She considered apologizing to him, yet when they made eye contact, her mouth would not open. Astrid wanted to say the words, but her body would not comply. She blamed exhaustion.

"Look, leave Yrsa here tonight. We have the room and she's already at rest. Must you wake a pregnant woman simply to move her to your home to sleep?" Hammond asked while he patted his fat belly.

"I am well and rested. A night awake will do me no harm. I'm fine with watching Yrsa." Helen added.

"We have put enough on you this day," Warren quickly replied.

"No, I will stay here with her, keep watch over her throughout the night. It is the only way I am comfortable putting Helen's boundless kindness to test. It is no one's job but mine to tend to my sister tonight."

"Fine then." Hammond closed the topic. "Done."

"Are you sure, Astrid?" Warren looked disappointed.

"You could use a night alone, my brother."

"Yes, Warren, go home and rest." Astrid avoided his gaze.

Warren nodded to his brother and thanked Helen again for the good meal and her overwhelming hospitality. As Warren passed Astrid, he smiled, but it was obvious to her it was a mask.

"Good night, all," Warren said.

Much later, when everyone was meant to be asleep, Astrid sat outside Hammond and Helen's home on a chair carved from a whitewood tree. She could hear Hammond's snores, a rumble that sounded like a wild boar's snort. She was less concerned that her sister would wake Helen and Willa now. *How could anyone sleep with that dreadful noise?*

Astrid gazed at the stars as she swung her legs off the high-legged chair.

Could Yrsa be right? Have several hundred years passed? Astrid longed to remember Asgard, Valhalla, Freyja, and Odin. *This is torture.*

Her heart fluttered as she shook her legs back and forth; Astrid was sure she would be sick to her stomach if she did not expel the energy that built inside her.

What's wrong with me, my gods? Tonight, I'm unsure which you want from me: to fight or...

Astrid tried to control her breathing, exhaling with a steady push of air. Her eyes back on the sky, the color of the night reminded her of the past—a late night raid on a tyrant's fortress. Although it was a successful battle, one that should have fulfilled her on many levels, Astrid found herself left with only mixed emotions; much like the ones that plagued her tonight.

CHAPTER 42

ULF'S HEAVY BREATHS WERE ALMOST as loud as the slave girls' screams. Astrid blocked the exit as her eldest brother advanced on the man known as Red Frederek. Squared up to his enemy, in the center of this octagonal room that was lined with beds draped in colorful silks, Ulf remarked how he had never seen such vibrancy outside an autumn forest. Large orange tapestries, bright yellow silks, and fresh, red blood colored the scene—Astrid agreed with her brother, they were beautiful colors.

"Soon you will see only black and emptiness, savage," Red Frederek spit.

"No, you die today, fiend!" Ulf announced.

Known for his cruelty toward women, so much so that his hands were said to be permanently stained with their blood, Red Frederek had amassed a large harem. Astrid found it odd that the man would seek to hide among the very women he abused, though it was apt that he would die surrounded by them.

"Woman-hating coward!" Ulf yelled. "This battle ends now!"

"You are the cowards, you, who wait in the shadows until my army is dispatched...and then rush my fortress."

"We did not come to fight your army, little man. We came to kill you and seize your treasures!" Astrid replied, her voice filled with venom.

"Modri be shamed on you!" he cursed.

"Odin be proud!"

With a broad swing, Ulf's massive war axe detached the tyrant's head from his body and flung it across the room. When the head hit the ground, the slaves cheered.

"Should I have given you the kill, Sister?" Ulf asked, as he wiped the blood off his axe with a bright silk shawl.

"No, he drew first blood on you down at the gates. He was yours to finish."

"True, but now that I think of it, you would have enjoyed ending the life of a man so cruel to women."

Ulf waved his arm around the room at the crowd of scantily dressed women, all of whom bore prominent scars.

"No worries, Brother, I ended his bloodline when I killed his sons before his eyes. I am pleased."

"Very well."

Astrid watched Ulf take record of the women in the room. "Thirty-one by my best count."

"I must say, I'm surprised Jokul has not found this spot yet."

"Aye. I pray he is well."

"When was the last time you saw him seriously hurt during a raid?" Astrid asked, hoping to alleviate her brother's concern.

"Only once before." Ulf smirked. "It was the last time I stood in a room so filled by women."

Ulf cleared his throat and addressed the slaves. "I am Ulf, son of Kol. Tomorrow, I will set you all free."

Where she expected cheers, she heard only gasps.

"Tonight, you face a choice. Remain in the service of Kol or you may go free, but you will be unarmed, unprotected."

"Ulf," Astrid huffed. She would have liked him to chose less aggressive words.

"My father, King Kol of Birka, requires a new woman. He is a strong and wise man, who treats all who serve him well."

Astrid watched as the sea of women began to churn; more than half of them stepped forward.

"I expect only the best for my father, and therefore I must put those who I feel are a good match to an arduous trial. Who thinks they can *best* a man like me?"

Ulf was as big and strong as their father, the only one of Astrid's brothers that was her father's physical match. Ulf was also as kind, but was careful with whom he showed it to. Ulf treated Astrid as her father did, with patience, great care, and boundless love.

"Did father truly ask you to do this?" she asked.

"He did," Ulf said as he scanned the multitude of women.

"Why didn't he mention this to me?" Astrid grew frustrated as she said.

"Why would he?" Ulf said with a raised eyebrow. "What do you know of the needs of men, Astrid?"

She grunted in response to his comment.

"There," Ulf pointed to a woman unlike the others; one of untamed barbarian blood: dark skinned and dark haired. "What do you think, Sister?"

"I do not wish to see these women punished any further."

"Nor do I."

"Then we should go. Remember, we are here to fight not fu—" Astrid was interrupted by Ulf's raised voice.

"I only do as commanded by our father. Now, do you think he would favor the dark skinned one or not?"

"The savage does not speak our language," another slave interrupted.

The woman who spoke wore hair the color of the setting sun, a fiery orange. She may have been ten years older than the rest, by Astrid's best guess, but her body was by far the most exquisite. As Astrid examined her, Ulf hooked his hand into the metal hoop that the rags that covered her breasts hung from. With a quick tug, he tore the dry, rotten cloth from her chest, exposing two full, sagging breasts.

"Do not hurt her," Astrid interjected, her arms crossed over her chest, her sword and dagger still in hand.

"He will not hurt me," the vermillion-haired woman said, not breaking eye contact with Ulf.

"You are brave and willing. I like that in a woman."

"And does your father like those qualities as well?"

"He does."

Astrid watched as her brother stroked the woman's curls over her breasts. Ulf often spoke of how much he loved women with long hair and the slave's reached down past her hips.

The thrill of combat, the splatter of an opponent's lifeblood on his arms, and the sight of a fertile woman: Was this his idea of Valhalla? Astrid wondered.

"I find myself ready for you," Ulf announced as he adjusted himself. "So, tell me, *sunset,* where would your master take you if he wanted your company alone?"

"There are two places: a dark place beneath the fortress we slaves rarely came back from."

"And the other?"

"A secret chamber attached to this one, a place meant to be filled with forbidden pleasure."

"Show me."

The woman's hips swayed as she crossed the room, a motion that made the rags covering her swing open and reveal her ass. Wide and soft, Astrid guessed she had birthed many children in her life, and for the briefest moment, she wondered where the woman's family was. The moment came and went though, as the woman unhooked the last metal ring, bared herself fully to Ulf, and bowed before him.

"Astrid, see to it that no one interrupts me. No one...not even Jokul," he ordered.

"You want me to stand guard, to watch for our brothers and cousins?"

"Family they may be, but that means they are no less ravenous than I." Ulf undid the latches on his armor as he spoke.

"They are no doubt filling the wagons with coin and gems," Astrid said over the clang of Ulf's weapon belt as it struck the floor.

"Not likely. The horn has yet to be sounded." Ulf declared as though his patience was running out. "You may call it, Sister. That should keep them busy while I take care of this."

Astrid had never sounded the horn before. To do so would be a great honor, as only the eldest or leader of the raid was allowed.

"Fine then."

Astrid crossed the space to the small room her brother was in. He had disrobed and joined the flame-haired woman on a bed of furs. The woman was on her back, propped up on her elbows, her legs spread open.

"Brother, wait."

"What, Astrid?" he said over his shoulder.

"This woman…you know she could never replace our mother."

"She's not meant to replace her. She's only meant to ease the pain of loss our father feels."

"I still don't—"

"Astrid, the horn is there, on my belt. Take it. Go and call the plunder."

"Very well."

Astrid untied the horn from his belt and quickly left the room, the sounds of grunts and groans as the pair began to copulate following her out. *Disgusting.*

Astrid took a deep breath and blew upon the horn. She knew it did not sound quite as loudly as when her brother did it, but there was no doubt in her mind it was heard. After she lowered the family heirloom from her mouth, two of the slave girls approached her.

"What do you desire, young mistress?" a thin girl of her height asked.

"How can we aid you?" the second girl, nearly her age, with short brown hair, asked.

"You can aid me by aiding yourselves." Astrid looked away.

"There's wine and bread."

"Yes, and fruit. Would you like some fruit?"

Astrid noticed a mark on each of the girls' stomachs. It looked to be made with a blade. The symbol appeared runic, but the scars left unclean lines, which made it hard to read.

"What is this?" Astrid poked at the tall girl's stomach where the mark was.

"Master—"

"He is *not* your master anymore," Astrid interrupted.

The second slave moved away.

"He carved us with his dagger," the tall girl explained, as she reached out to Astrid's armor-covered stomach. "We were meant to carry his children. He marked us so we would not forget."

"Forget what?"

"The dead master enjoyed killing his women while he fucked them." Another slave-girl spoke as she passed by.

"If we did not give him proper pleasure or get pregnant quick enough, he would kill us. I have seen it with my own eyes; he gutted one girl as she rode him, then slept the night in her viscera."

"I had heard rumors of his brutality." Astrid lowered her voice to a whisper.

"The mark, he had spent two months with us already."

"I see it now. A date…" Astrid squinted as she ran her fingers over the woman's scars. "This date is not long from now."

"Then I'm truly saved, mistress, because on this day he would have surely killed me if I was not pregnant."

"Listen carefully." Astrid grew heated. "Do not repeat any of what I tell you, or I promise, I will cut out your tongue."

The tall girl bowed to Astrid.

"I lied to my brothers. I told them Red was sitting on a mountain of gold. They came here to take his treasure, while I came only to end his life."

"Then I owe *you* my life."

Ulf's grunts had grown louder and harder to ignore. Astrid prayed to Sif it was from pleasure and not pain—the sounds were too close to tell the difference.

"You're worried about your brother."

"He's powerful and skilled with blades and spears. I have seen him hunt bear twice his size with only his fists…"

"He sounds brave—"

"He sounds like she's hurting him."

"Neesa does not know violence, only pleasure."

Astrid gave the girl a confused look.

"You—you do not know pleasure, only violence."

"I am Astrid the White, a proud warrior. The gods have gifted me with skills in combat, hunting, and survival."

With Astrid's hand gently clasped in hers, the tall girl led her back to a spot just outside the hidden room, where she could see in, but not be seen.

"No. I do not wish to watch my brother—"

"Not your brother, look at Neesa." The slave girl pointed. "You see how Neesa accepts her man. She gives pleasure while taking it. Much can be learned from her. She is always in control."

Astrid looked away. "What do I call you?"

"Svana."

"Svana, what is your wish? Freedom or service?"

Head bowed, Svana answered, "My fate is yours to decide."

"Fate is controlled by the gods. I am not a god."

Svana's reply was fast. "No, you're the one who decides if I live or die."

"Then I will see that you are properly clothed and carrying packs full of supplies." Astrid put her hand on the girl's shoulder and said. "I release you, Svana."

"Mistress, these dark lands are very dangerous and I'm not a skilled warrior like you. Freed…I will die."

"Where is your home? If it's near—"

"Gone," the tall slave answered. "Please, mistress, I do not wish to be freed of slavery, only owned by a just individual."

"Ah, I understand. You wish to go next," Astrid concluded.

"I'm sorry. I have spoken wrong. I do not wish to be your father's or your brother's property. I wish to be yours."

"I do not need or want a servant, Svana."

"Then let me offer you my friendship."

"Friendship?" Astrid laughed. "What is to be gained in that?"

"Everything—all that I know."

CHAPTER 43

"Astrid?" Warren whispered from the darkness.

She jumped.

"I am pleased to find you outside. I feared I would have to throw pebbles at the door," Warren said as he eased out of the shadows.

"You would have thrown pebbles at your brother's door to rouse me?"

"I would have." Warren smirked.

"Have you done this before?"

"When I was a child, long before I became a soldier." He smiled largely as she stepped closer to him. "I thought...well, with all that has happened, I figured you would feel safer as the night grew older if had your arms and armor."

"You brought my armor? My weapons?"

Astrid grabbed the bag Warren carried, untied the rope, and gazed inside. The familiar sparkle of her breastplate filled her with pride.

"Thank you, Warren." Astrid smiled largely. "With my armor back on—"

"You will finally feel more like yourself?" Warren interrupted.

"If your goal was to make me happy, you have succeeded."

Perhaps it was the cool night air that reminded her of home, or being reunited with her much desired arms and armor, but either way, Astrid soon found her veins filled with heat and a new strength in her limbs.

"Is this all real?"

Warren laughed in response.

"Tell me, Warren, is this world a lie? Am I dreaming or can this all be real?" Astrid asked again.

"All you see and feel here is real, Astrid. I promise."

Astrid shivered from the energy swelling inside her; so much so that she wanted to release it in the form of a battle cry.

"Do you think the bandits are still out there, hiding in the dark forest?"

"The king's soldiers have searched the forest's edge and the town guards have set up new night rounds to watch for campfires and torches. I have to imagine the bandits have dispersed by now. What would they have to gain by staying?"

If there were no bandits to battle, Astrid considered a return trip to the mead hall—she could easily pick a fight with one of the larger men there. It is what her brothers would do on a night like this, that or…

"Are you still fond of me, Warren?" Astrid asked. "Or have my threats and acting like a fool changed how you feel?"

"Nothing has changed," Warren said seriously. "Astrid, I wish I could spend all my time at your side…day and night."

"Did you find your bed too empty to sleep tonight?"

"Without you, my bed is not worth returning to."

"Then when will you find rest, Warren?"

"I will find rest when the woman I care for is safe and resting. Only then. Not before."

With all the confusion and uncertainty that surrounded her, it seemed to Astrid that there was only one thing she could count on: Warren.

His love, Astrid thought, *the very meaning of unconditional. Such a strong and beautiful emotion could never exist in Hel. I was such a fool to believe I was dead. No, I am alive.* Astrid's body suddenly ached for Warren's touch. *I am very much alive.*

After she smoothed down the wrinkles on her dress, she gripped the bottom of the skirt and yanked it up, over her head.

"Thank the gods." Astrid cheered. "I feel so alive at this very moment, that my skin tingles. Do you feel the same, Warren?"

Warren chuckled. "You may be the very proof the old gods do exist, Astrid."

"What exactly do you mean?" she asked, her thoughts on her conversation with Yrsa.

"You are perfection." Warren closed the distance between them.

"Oh." Astrid smiled. "And what would you do with perfection, Warren?"

"Worship it."

"Then come." Astrid opened her arms.

Warren would not turn down the gift she gave him. He took her in his arms and, after a kiss that lasted so long her legs went weak, he stopped.

"Warren." Astrid rubbed the bulge in his pants. "We will have to drape the heat of our actions in the cool shadows."

"No, not here."

"Where then?" she asked as she gave his manhood another squeeze.

"I have Hammond's storage cellar key."

"Oh, would he mind? Should we ask him first?" she teased.

"No doubt, he's watching us right now."

"No, listen." Astrid cupped a hand behind her ear. "I can still hear him snoring."

Warren laughed.

"We best not wake him, or anyone else. My brother's home has many more neighbors than mine. Perhaps it best if you..." he said with a nod to her dress.

Astrid reattired herself as they ran behind Hammond's house to the base of a large silver birch tree, where the trap door to his supply cellar was. It was pitch dark inside, impossible to see anything, not even the tip of one's own nose, but the smell within was sweet. Warren reached up to

Astrid as she descended, his rough hands grasping her by the waist and helping her to the ground.

"Warren, that scent…"

"Perfume."

"Perfume?"

"An oil that smells like wildflowers."

"To wear such a thing would only alert your enemies from great distances—not very stealthy, Warren."

Warren could hear Astrid fumble with something near him.

"What is all this? Light a torch. I want to see."

"I need to find Hammond's flint. Hold still."

"Hurry."

Warren found the flint and he scraped his dagger against it. The first spark of light let him pinpoint Astrid but did not illuminate her actions. Her back was turned and her head down, but that was all Warren saw. After more sparks, the torch was lit and the black, lifeless room was bathed in the flicker of orange light.

"By the blessed gods!" she shouted. "Everything sparkles."

Warren watched Astrid as she took it all in.

"Look at all the splendor." Astrid's mouth fell open.

"I am," Warren said, his gaze on her.

She smiled back, but Warren doubted his words were enough to pull her mind back to the reason they had come to Hammond's cellar.

"There must be enough treasure here to fill a dozen carts."

"I wager you are right." Warren nodded.

"My brothers would never believe this tiny town has such wealth. Too bad they will never see it."

"Trust me, not all cellars overflow like his."

Astrid dashed from barrel to barrel; it looked like she searched for something though Warren could not imagine what. He had never seen her act this way.

"Astrid, there's still much I don't know of you."

"True…" she replied as she dug into a chest full of small, shiny trinkets.

"You speak as if you and your brothers all worked together. What did you do?"

"We did work together. We… Wait, could my eyes be deceiving me? Look at that!" Astrid laughed. "I traded for one of these earlier today but lost it in the commotion with Yrsa."

Warren stood next to a chest full of hand mirrors, all wrapped in scraps of cloth. "He has another two dozen or more here. I helped him carry them down here."

"Do you think he would mind if I took one?" Astrid asked as she approached.

Warren could smell her sweet sweat, a tangy aroma that made him think of the last time they had joined. He yearned to be back inside her and feared he would explode with desire if he did not do something about it soon.

"Is it true, your brother accumulated all this wealth through trading?"

The cling-clang of coins echoed in the subterranean space as Astrid rolled her hands through a dark barrel.

"He did." Warren answered as he lit another torch.

"Amazing."

"Astrid, you do remember why we are here?"

She dropped the coins and took a step back from the barrel. With a quick tug, Astrid had once again removed her dress.

"There are piles of fabric down here, plenty enough to make a soft bed." Warren pointed.

"No."

"No?"

Astrid pulled over the barrel in front of her, the coins spilling across the floor. "I'd rather you split my legs on top of this."

"Would you?"

"My friend…she liked to say there would be no better place than a bed of treasure for Astrid the White to *fukka*[7]."

---

7 "To copulate" in Norwegian dialect.

"Is that so?"

"It is."

"Far be it from me to say otherwise."

Warren unbelted his pants and released himself as he approached—his kokkr ready. Eyes on him, Astrid lowered herself slowly until, sitting on the coins softly and settling her weight down with a moan of satisfaction.

"Warren," Astrid groaned as she put her arms around his neck and guided him in. "There has been an ache between my legs ever since you arrived with my arms and armor."

"Astrid—"

"I know you care for me. I know that is why you brought me my gear," Astrid finished.

Warren rested his forehead between her breasts; he was torn between the throb of his kokkr, and the desire to make love to her slowly.

"Come, Warren, do not hold back."

Lovemaking would have to wait for another time.

Once more inside her, he growled like a mountain lion. Warren thrust into her, his every motion sliding her over the tiny pieces of metal. He could have sworn Astrid sparkled more than the shiny coins—she was that heavenly.

"More. Do not hold back," she repeated.

He growled and thrust harder, again and again.

"Warren!"

He was so caught up in the moment, he barely heard her.

"Warren!"

Driving his full weight forward into her, Astrid responded with moans of pleasure as the tips of her fingers dug deep into his flesh.

Without warning, Astrid rolled them both over so she was on top and riding him with a force that nearly made him finch.

"Holy Hel!"

She pressed down on his chest with her palms; keeping him in place seemingly turned her on all the more. He reached up, cupping her breasts and could see in her eyes that she enjoyed this as much as he did.

As the muscles in his abdomen began to tense, Warren quickly withdrew from her.

"Astrid—"

"No words, Warren. No words."

CHAPTER 44

WHILE ASTRID WATCHED THE SUN rise over the town of Grømstad, she tried again to remember her past in service of the gods. Ever since Yrsa told her they were former Valkyrie she had wished to reclaim her memories, but had no luck. Last night, she had prayed today would be different. She asked that with the rise of the sun a new comprehension of her past would come—knowledge to be awarded to her by the very gods she sought to remember.

When the sun crept higher and higher, she realized her prayers went unanswered.

I have followed your signs, my gods. I have done what you asked. I have stayed here when I wanted to leave. I have quenched my desire to fight with this new passion to fukka. That is what you wanted? You wanted me to stay to find and save my sister, I know you did. She sighed in frustration. *So you must have wanted me to remember everything too.*

"Astrid?"

Yrsa called as she stepped out of Hammond's house, a blanket wrapped around her.

"Yrsa." Astrid did not find her sister's sudden appearance a coincidence. "How fair you today?"

"Better. I just needed to rest in quiet."

After a brief hug, Astrid asked, "Can you follow me to Warren's home?"

Yrsa nodded and took Astrid's hand.

"Good. We still have much to discuss—"

"We do," Yrsa nodded. "Astrid, tell me, how did you come to find your armor from home?" Yrsa asked, as she stared forward.

"I woke that first morning here with it on."

"Days ago?" Yrsa asked.

"Several weeks now."

"Freyja returned you *here* with your old weapons and armor?" Yrsa stopped walking. "Here, in this friendly, quiet little town?"

"Not here. Close to here."

"Why would she do that?"

"I don't know. I still can't remember anything. I need your help, Yrsa. I need you to tell me everything." Astrid pressed. "I think I was meant to save you so you could tell me everything."

"I—"

Hammond interrupted when he stepped out with a loud yawn.

"Hammond...my sister had a good night's rest, you have my thanks," Astrid called out.

"My pleasure," he said with a wave goodbye.

Helen joined him briefly, with a big smile and a wave over his shoulder to the two sisters. Astrid enjoyed the warmth of their hospitality and hoped to repay them later, but first she needed answers and to see to her sister's safety.

"Let us hurry to Warren's home."

Although she walked arm and arm with Yrsa, Astrid was overwhelmed by a deep sense of separation. It was something she had struggled with since she had reached Grømstad. Simply put, Astrid missed her family.

"How do you deal with the pain, Yrsa?"

"What pain?"

"The pain of being severed from our family...the hurt is greater than any wound I have been dealt."

Yrsa did not answer.

"I wish our brothers were here," Astrid tried.

"I do too," Yrsa stated flatly. "Our brothers. My husband. My children...I wish they were all here, Astrid, yet they are not. They are gone, time has turned them all to nothing but dust."

Astrid wanted to retort, but could not. It was hard for her to accept they were all dead. When she finally faced Yrsa, she saw her sister's eyes forced shut with tears.

Yrsa talks bravely, Astrid thought as she joined hands with her, *but she clearly feels the same sorrow I do.*

CHAPTER 45

THREE DAYS PASSED. THREE DAYS of silence and boredom, rest and restlessness. For three long days, Astrid sat with Yrsa, whose pained eyes told a story of loss and desolation.

If only she would speak, Astrid thought.

Helen visited them daily, each time bringing food and water; her concern was touching. Helen was a good woman. Astrid would have liked a mate like her for Jokul. She had often worried about his wildness, but those worries were wasted now; he, like the rest of her family, was long gone by her sister's account. Yrsa was all she had left.

Warren stopped in several times each day while he tended his fields; his visits were brief but exceptionally sweet.

The town outside hummed; the spring bazaar began tomorrow, and by the end of the day, the population of Grømstad would triple, he said. Astrid was thrilled by the mere thought of it; if she could not go to the excitement, at least some would come to her. She only hoped Yrsa would be in better spirits tomorrow, so they could enjoy the bazaar together.

"Yrsa, please, what ails you?"

Astrid must have asked this question a hundred times since they had walked from Hammond's home days ago, and each time a look of pained confusion appeared on her sister's face, but no reason was given.

"Tell me."

Astrid watched her sister's lips quiver, and could sense she wanted to answer, but she did not. *What is she so afraid of?*

"Please, Yrsa. Speak to me."

Yrsa made a sound—just a sigh that ended in a whisper at first, but then she spoke.

"I-I remember so much, Astrid...but are these memories true, or of my own creation?" Yrsa held her belly tight in her hands. "I traded one nightmare for another, but which was real?"

"What do you mean?"

"The...the thickness...like deep, warm mud..." Yrsa began to sob. "The screams, do you recall them? Never have I heard such desperation."

"What screams? Where, Yrsa?"

"I saw them once. They must have thought me asleep, but I opened my eyes. Did you see them, Astrid? Were you there with me?"

"Who, Yrsa? Who do you speak of? The bandits?"

When Yrsa did not answer and was once again overwhelmed with tears, Astrid clenched her fists and snapped.

"Yrsa!" Astrid yelled in her sister's face. "I need you to talk to me! Tell me something that will help!"

Yrsa gazed down hesitantly at her stomach with a look of dread on her face.

"The baby?" Astrid asked with a lowered voice. "Does all this sorrow come from the baby?"

Yrsa nodded and answered, "yes."

"Gods no," Astrid fell back to the floor, words packed her mind as a gasp of air filled her mouth. "Does your child belong to one of those black-toothed, carrion eating bandits?"

"I-I..." Yrsa rocked back and forth and pulled at the tips of her long hair.

"Tell me, Sister, you must tell me..." Astrid stopped herself before her words took another insensitive turn. "Were you taken by them, Yrsa?"

As she sat up in bed, Yrsa slammed her fists down into the straw and howled like a wounded animal. The sound was so full of bottomless anguish that it tore at Astrid's heart.

"No." Astrid shuddered.

"Emmerich took me," Yrsa whispered. "He...he forced himself on me more times than I can even count, Astrid...more times than I can count."

Astrid kicked the empty chair near her and it overturned and slid into the wall. She felt like she did when she and her brothers entered a fray: strong, confident, powerful, ready for combat. Sword and belt in hand, she marched to the door with the intent of racing directly to the last place she had seen Emmerich and challenge him to fight.

"I will unman him and present his rotting kokkr to you as a gift, Yrsa, I swear this to you."

"No! Do not leave me," Yrsa panicked. "I sense them coming back... they're coming back...coming back for me."

"Yrsa, I must avenge you."

"No, if you leave me now, they will take me away. I'll be gone forever."

"If I do not kill him...he-they will have gotten away with hurting you."

"Please, Sister." Yrsa reached out to Astrid. "Listen to me...they *are* coming."

Astrid held still at the threshold, the sweat of anticipation glistened at her hairline. Inside her, an inferno rose; she needed to kill.

"If you stay, I will tell you more—as much as I know. No matter how much pain it causes me...I will tell you more."

Astrid peered over her shoulder. Yrsa had offered her the one thing she wanted more than revenge.

CHAPTER 46

WARREN HAD A LOT ON his mind and was glad Hammond joined him in the fields. In fact, he speculated that he might have even enjoyed telling his tale…if it was to someone other than the man whose cellar he had invaded the other night—but there was no one he trusted more than his brother.

"So I let her take one of your mirrors," he said as he tilled the soil.

Hammond just stood with his jaw open, a blank look on his face.

"Say something, Brother," Warren urged.

"I do not know which I am more: mad or jealous."

"You should be mad." Warren dug his hoe hard into the ground.

"I am, but the jealousy seems to outweigh it."

"I am sorry."

"I thought something was amiss that morning."

"Is anything else missing?"

"Other than my confidence in you? I have no idea." Hammond's eyes turned suspicious. "Why do you ask?"

"I had the strongest sense that once we got to your cellar, I was no longer the thing Astrid desired most." Warren swallowed his pride again. "Like she would have rather robbed you than…"

"Rode you?"

Warren smiled but then quickly wiped it away. "I must tell you, we… well, the deed was completed on a bed of your spilled coin."

Hammond howled—Warren was pretty sure in envy-filled annoyance.

"Why have I never thought of that?"

"Helen would—"

"Not with Helen; she would never do such a filthy act. But that one girl in the mead hall...the one with the freckles that dive deep down between her breasts...for a new dress, I bet she would. She loves the gifts, that one does."

Warren wiped his brow with a handkerchief. "Hammond, must you whore about?"

"This coming from the man who admittedly beds women in *my* storage cellar." That effectively shut Warren up. "Not to mention that it was while I was tending to the care of her sister."

"You were sleeping. We both heard you snoring. Elk make less noise mating."

"Just remember I sleep with one eye open, Brother, like any good merchant should."

Warren laughed. "Fine then. How can I repay you?"

"Repay me?"

"Yes, you, the man with enough coin to purchase a castle."

"Well, perhaps you could take Helen and Willa with you tomorrow to the spring bazaar. You *are* escorting the lovely sisters, aren't you?"

"I had hoped to."

"Good then. It's settled."

The brothers nodded to one another.

"You have lots of business to attend to tomorrow?"

"All day tomorrow and the next," Hammond replied firmly.

"I will see that your family is kept safe and well-entertained then."

"Thank you. Oh and please, stay out of my supply cellar."

"I will."

Hammond gazed back at Warren's home a moment. "Do you really think I need to take an inventory? That our beautiful warrior might have stolen something?"

"Just count your coins."

"Not after what you did on them. Better to suffer the loss, I think."

"If I was you, I might change the lock."

Hammond looked at his brother knowingly. "Something grander bothers you."

"You are right. Sometimes I wonder if there's a darker side to Astrid that I might not have allowed myself to see before."

"And what of it? You have been responsible for killing a hundred men. Some might call that a dark side."

"What I did, I did during the wars, for our king." Warren's voice rose as he spoke; he did not like his service being questioned.

"Fine, yes, but there's more to this."

"It's nothing." Warren went back to work, hoping his brother would not persist.

"Spit it out."

"Fine," he quickly conceded, looking back up at Hammond. "Did you ever stop to consider that maybe Astrid was one of them? One of the bandits? A scout, perhaps?"

Hammond laughed loudly, took a deep breath, and then laughed again. "You worry too much, just like our dearly departed mother. Astrid is no bandit, Warren. Put a stop your fantastical worries."

"I don't know what I'm thinking." Warren nodded. "You are right."

"Of course I am." Hammond put his hand on Warren's shoulder. "You might be the fighter, dear Brother, but I am the thinker."

Side by side, the two brothers looked toward the center of town. The traveling merchants had arrived in full, and the place crawled with people, like ants up and down an anthill. Together the brothers reminisced about the spring bazaars they had attended as children. It was undeniably the most enjoyable time of year in Grømstad. There was something for everyone: music and games of sport, new and foreign wines to taste, and exotic women to dance the night away with. Warren particularly remembered a drunken brawl from the past, a misunderstanding tied to an act of adultery that resulted in the death of two young men. Hammond reminded him that at least one person died during the daylong festivities, more often than not a victim of too much sin.

"To breathe your last breath with lips wet from too much ale, all while celebrating the harvest—this is an honorable way to pass, Brother," Hammond stated as he rested his hands above his gut. "The old gods would be pleased."

"We shall see."

"Do you remember when old man Ekkebert ran about the town naked shouting about something...what was it he was saying?"

"He thought he was covered in spiders and screamed for someone to set him ablaze before they consumed him."

"That's right, 'burn me, burn me' he yelled." Hammond laughed. "Wasn't it Uncle Kelt who knocked Ekkebert out with a single punch to the old man's red, bulbous nose?"

"Fists the size of anvils and just a solid."

Warren joined Hammond in a good long laugh.

"You see, Brother, you can still laugh. All is well in the world."

"You are right, all is well."

"Rest up. Tomorrow you will have the four finest girls in all of Grømstad on your arm. For that, a true soldier's resolve will be needed."

"I am fit for the test."

"A true soldier's resolve," Hammond smirked as he repeated. "That and all your coins."

CHAPTER 47

YRSA TOOK A LONG, DEEP breath and exhaled slowly through her nose.

"Let me start with my first memory." Yrsa looked at Astrid blankly. "I was drowning."

Cold water filled Yrsa's mouth, chilling her tongue and freezing her teeth. She swallowed and tried to scream for help, but the act only gave her another mouthful of water. Yrsa thrashed about, and tumbled over and over in the water. She had no idea which way was up; everything was dark, a shade of green she had never seen before.

When she choked a burst of bubbles rose around her face. There was something beautiful about the white bubbles. *Look how quickly they rise up.*

Up. There was her answer.

Yrsa pushed her arms down and kicked as hard as her drained body would allow. The moment she breached the surface of the water, she gasped for air and her voice burst the silence.

"Help!"

How did I get into the water? she wondered. *I didn't go to bathe or take a swim. I was not aboard a longboat...or was I?*

Try as she might, there was no memory; in fact, the last thing she remembered was being in her home with her sister. Birka was aflame— bright lights, warmth, and then...nothingness.

She would have to expel more effort to swim ashore, and Yrsa was unsure she had the strength to do so. She was not a fighter like her sister; she was a milkmaid, a baker, and a caretaker to…his name was gone from her mind.

What happened?

As she began her paddle to shore, she realized her arms were bare to the shoulder—she wore not a stitch of clothing. In the calm water—a large lake by the best she could tell—Yrsa trembled from the cold. Her skin may have felt like ice, but her willpower burned hotter with each heavy beat of her heart.

I need to get out of the water. I must get out of the water.

Yrsa kicked harder and harder; she pushed her body past the limits she thought it had and darted through the water like a sea snake.

"Gods…you do me a favor this day, granting me…the strength I need," Yrsa said between shallow breaths. "I promise you…I will not forget this boon, and see it…repaid once I am home."

As she reached shallow water and was able to stand, she prayed that the gods would not forsake her.

"Help!" she called out. "H-help!"

Yrsa shivered, her arms wrapped tightly around her chest and waist as she dripped on the smooth, greyish-green pebbles of the shore.

"Anyone there?"

If this is the lake not far south of Birka, there should be a small village nearby, just beyond those trees, one filled with kind farming people who should hear my calls. Yet there's no response.

Yrsa looked again at the lake; it was much larger than the one she had originally thought it was. *Where am I?* she wondered.

"Can anyone hear me?"

The cold air stole her newfound strength. She was suddenly lightheaded, and unsteady on her feet. Carefully, she lowered herself onto a patch of sandy earth and tried to catch her breath and calm her nerves.

"Modi, give me courage," she whispered as she looked up into the dark sky.

Within moments, the air around her seemed to lose its chill, and her shivers were gone. Her skin had magically begun to warm up.

"The gods *are* with me tonight."

Warmer now, she no longer needed to hurry to seek refuge. Instead, Yrsa stared up at the stars which had given her comfort in the past. *For winter,* she thought, *the sky is amazingly clear.*

"Such grandness. I feel as though I could..."

Hands up to the stars, Yrsa did something she had not done since she was a child; she reached out to trace the constellations and it was then she noticed her arm and the strength in it.

"Whose arms are these?" Yrsa knew they were her arms, but marveled at the might apparent with each flex.

This must have been a dream, Yrsa thought, as she was no longer cold and not nearly as worried about being without clothes as she was moments ago. In fact, the further she investigated, the more changed she realized her body was.

"Ulf? Vignir? Hak? Jokul?" she called to each of her brothers. "Are you there?"

This time she got a response. Cautiously, a man in a dark cloak stepped from the shadowy thick bushes not far from her. The way he crept forward made her think of the times she had seen her brothers hunt. This was no farmer, and he had not just come upon her. He had watched her for some time; she could sense it. Yrsa began to shake again, but it was not the cold that chilled her, it was fear.

"What do you want?" Yrsa asked as she covered herself with her arms.

The man drew his sword, a long, thin blade; pointed it at her and motioned with its tip for her to sit. His voice was foreign, a language she did not think she was familiar with at first, yet as he continued to rattle off words, her ears filled with a crackle, like the snap of dry hay...and then suddenly, Yrsa could understand the man.

"Do you not hear me, woman?"

"I hear you." She kept a close watch on the man who appeared to be dressed in rogue's attire. "Who are you? Where did you come from?"

"Me? Here on land. You...you fell from the sky," the man answered cryptically.

"I what?"

"I saw you fall from the sky." He pointed to the canopy of stars above them with his sword.

"I did not."

"Are you calling *me* a liar, woman?" The man stepped slowly forward.

"My apologies. You have me at a disadvantage. My clothing has been washed away and I need assistance finding my way home."

"I watched you fall. I almost swam out to aid you. You were underwater so long that I was unsure where to find you—"

"I almost drowned."

Yrsa began to stand again, and this time, the man sheathed his sword.

"Should've drowned. No man stays under water that long, let alone a frail thing like you."

Uncomfortable with the way the thin, middle-aged man stared at her body, she asked, "Could you spare your cloak, sir?"

"Tell me now, what are you?"

"What am I?" Yrsa sneered. "I'm nothing."

"Nothing," the man repeated with a frustrated chuckle.

"I am Yrsa, daughter of Kol. Wife of...wife of...I come from the fortress city of Birka."

"Daughter. Wife. Birka. None of these answer my question." He took another step toward her as he spoke. "*What* are you?"

"I told you!" Yrsa stomped her foot.

As the man looked her up and down again, he seemed as much in awe as he was confused. With one hand on the handle of his sword, he untied his cloak and handed it to Yrsa.

"You have my thanks, sir."

"Are there more of you?" he said with a gaze past her to the water. "Here? Now?"

"I think I am alone...I was home." Yrsa remembered the attack on Birka. "My home was invaded. In Odin's name, it was invaded by—"

"Invaded? An army? Where?" The man was clearly concerned. "You must tell me! Now!"

"I am unsure."

He grasped her by the arm and pulled her toward him. She could see the panic in his eyes. Dragging her behind him, the man moved back toward the wooded area he had come from. Yrsa didn't know whether to scream and fight or go with him.

"Please, sir, what do you want of me?"

"Stop calling me sir. My name's Emmerich, and if there's an invading army nearby, we must move. My men will need to know."

"Your men?"

"I'm forming an army myself."

"You are—"

"I like to consider myself a leader. I'm accustomed to people following me. Will you follow me, Yrsa of the falling stars?"

His title was electrifying and romantic, but she still did not understand why he would think she fell from the sky. Regardless, if he led an army, she would need his help to liberate Birka from its invaders.

"Where are we going?"

"To town. I have friends there, riders who will get this news to my men."

"I am worried about my kin. Could your men find out what happened to Birka?"

"Birka. Yes. Of course."

Wrapped tightly in the man's cloak—a kind of stitched, light leather unlike that prepared in her homeland—Yrsa began to wonder if she was making a mistake.

What was it my brothers always said I should do if I was captured or seized by the enemy? She could not recall—too much was happening at once. She pulled the long cloak tighter, wishing she had a belt or something else to secure it.

The town Emmerich escorted her to was not far away, nestled in the forest. It was late, and the place was quiet, with the exception of an inn and a tavern that sat across from one another. That edge of town was filled with loud voices.

"Come, my scouts are waiting for me inside the inn. I will give them your news and then see you to a room."

"I would benefit from some clothing too."

"You might."

The laughter from the tavern across from the inn soothed Yrsa, and she began to remember why. *These sounds of mirth…yes, I come from proud people, people who have celebrated many victories.*

For a moment, Yrsa wondered if she would find people she knew here; since *she* was in this place, wherever it was, then it was equally possible others from her family could be too.

The inn was mostly filled with men, hunters by the looks of the hides they wore and the dirt and leaves that decorated their boots and legs. Yrsa recognized the bows; she had seen their likes before, but from where? The details escaped her.

"Sit at the bar," Emmerich ordered, and she complied without thought. "Keep still and quiet."

As Yrsa rested on a stool, she squinted at the intensity of the closest torchlight; the fire pulsating—she felt it wanted to reach out and lick at her cheek.

Mesmerized by the flames, she counted six torches on the back wall, and a candelabrum with ten candles that burned equally bright at the middle of the bar.

"Need a drink?" the toothless barkeep asked as he limped over to her.

Yrsa nodded first, to heed Emmerich's words, but when the barkeep simply yawned and stared back at her, she spoke.

"Aye."

"Wine or ale?" the barkeep mumbled after he slammed a wooden mug down on the bar in front of her.

Yrsa wanted wine, but she was unsure how to pay the man, so she looked for Emmerich. He stood in the opposite corner of the large room, with his back to her. His gestures were grand, and Yrsa could see he was telling the story of how she fell from the sky.

This feels wrong, she thought as her heart began to race. *Odin, tell your faithful servant what she must do.*

"If you ain't drinking, take your pretty arse and sit it elsewhere," the barkeep grumbled. His breath smelled like he had drank piss.

"Where am I?"

A few steps away he answered, "Heinrich's Inn."

Leaning over the bar, Yrsa whispered, "What town?"

"You don't know you're in Forrest's Glen?" the barkeep laughed and called out to another man at the bar. "She don't know this is Forrest's Glen!"

"Maybe she's new. You working?"

Emmerich's footfalls echoed with each stomp in her direction. Her body seized and trembled as Emmerich pointed a dagger at the man who had just spoken.

"Back off her."

"She yours? How much you want?"

"You cannot afford her." Emmerich snatched Yrsa by the back of her neck. "This one may just be priceless."

"You put that blade away or you leave." The barkeep's voice rose as he spoke, and when he was done, he belched.

Emmerich looked back at his men and gave them a nod. With it, they were off. Once they were out the door, he sheathed his dagger at the small of his back.

"Everything is good here."

To Yrsa it sounded like a statement, but when the man at the bar and the barkeep both answered yes, she realized it had been a question.

"Let us go to our room."

Our room? She felt Emmerich long finger's tighten around her neck when she did not move fast enough. Yrsa held her breath as she shuffled in the direction he steered her, through the bar and to a back archway. The hallway was dimmer than the bar itself, which at least provided relief for her eyes. She blinked, trying to clear her vision, and unexpect-edly found herself standing before a closed door.

"Kind of you to escort me—"

"Hush."

Emmerich jammed a large metal key into the lock and forcefully twisted it with a grunt. He swore under his breath, until it turned, and the lock finally released.

"Go!" Emmerich pushed Yrsa into the dark room and followed quickly behind.

When she heard something wooden slide across the floor, she spoke out in alarm.

"What is that?"

"Stay still."

As she heard the man creep about the room, she considered escap-ing, bolting for the door like a rabbit that raced toward its hole, but her legs had turned to mush and she stumbled to the ground.

What do I do? Do I call for help or stay quiet and still? Where's my family? I need my family.

One by one, ten tiny flames came alive on a candelabrum, and then two more on loose candles. She could now see the room held a straw bed in the center and an old sitting stool. On the floor, in the back corner of the room, a piss pot sat, empty as best she could tell, as there was no hint of the sour aroma of urine in the otherwise stagnant room. Panic gripped her when she spotted a satchel propped up against the wall, the handles of many weapons poking out its side.

He's going to kill me, was all she could think.

"Stand."

"What?"

"Stand." His voice was firmer the second time around.

Yrsa stood, wobbling a bit on her weakened legs. "I must warn you, your actions have put me very much on edge."

He did not respond; he only stood across from her and stared.

"What do you want from me?"

"Just tell me this, Yrsa. What kind of woman drops from the sky, glowing like a bright yellow, falling star?"

Yrsa did not know how to answer.

"Glowing?"

"You...you appeared much different when you stood awash in all that torchlight." Emmerich pointed out toward the bar. "The pale moonlight did not do your beauty justice."

"I—"

"You are no stranger to being called beautiful, I wager."

"Emmerich—"

"Take off the cloak."

She pulled the article tighter.

"Take it off and show me your glow!"

"No!"

In two steps, Emmerich had boxed her in.

"My scouts, they did not see you descend, but I did. I saw a bright golden light as intense as the sun but much, much smaller through the trees. It was you, falling to the earth."

"I...no...I was in the water."

"You fell from such a distance and so slowly that I had time to run all the way from town to the lake, tracking your descent into the water."

"No..."

"Yes, and the whole way, you streaked through the sky. Even when you were lying on the ground, reaching for the stars, you shimmered with the golden light...but then it vanished."

"You mistake this glimmer as special when it was nothing more than the moon off my wet skin."

"I make no such mistake. Now tell me, what are you?"

"I'm nothing!" she yelled in his face.

"Show me your skin so that I might make that judgment."

"No!" Yrsa screamed.

"Do it, or I swear to the old ones I will gut you right here...and I will do it slowly."

Yrsa could tell by the look on his face that this was no bluff, and when his hand shifted from his belt to the handle of one of his daggers, she complied. With the cloak on the dusty floor, she was once more naked before Emmerich.

That feeling of power you had when you pulled yourself out of the water—don't forget it, Yrsa. Use it, damn you.

"No glow?" Emmerich questioned.

"I told you." Yrsa's voice became stronger as she spoke. "Whatever you saw fall from the sky was not me."

"Very disappointed," Emmerich said. "Still, there's *much* value here."

He reached out and grabbed her left breast in a tight squeeze. Caught off guard, Yrsa shouted and slapped his hand down.

Now is the time.

Like she had seen her brothers do so many times, Yrsa clenched her fist and swung at her attacker's nose. Emmerich read her movement easily and swiftly dodged her punch.

"So be it, lovely. Let us *fight* before we *fukka*."

His fist struck her cheek with such force that the shadowy room went fully dark, though as her eyelids fluttered, she could sense another strike was on its way. Emmerich drove his fist into her stomach, and she fell to her hands and knees.

What is this strange glare in my eyes? she wondered. *Is the room on fire now?*

"There it is!" Emmerich's voice was peppered with cheer. "Look upon yourself! Am I imagining it now, woman?"

The ache in her stomach made her want to retch, but she sat up, against the raw pain, and set her eyes on her arm.

"Odin's eye! I-I glow."

"That be the trick. A touch of fear brings it forth."

Yrsa watched in shock as Emmerich fumbled with his belt to free himself from his pants. With his kokkr out, he lifted her from the ground.

"No..." she whispered. "Please, I'm nothing...please..."

He turned her around and shoved her into the stone wall. Her already bruised cheek scraped open on the coarse wall—blood painted the stone bright red.

She tried to push herself away, yet the cold prick of sharp steel at the small of her back where her spine and hip met paused her.

"Move any further, and my blade will pierce that soft skin of yours."

Emmerich stepped to the candelabrum and yanked a candle free.

"There's a similar glow, this flame and you."

"Let me go!"

Yrsa began to squirm again, and as she did, he turned the candle over and jammed it into the small of her back. She screamed; the pain was immeasurable and had her clawing at the wall.

Emmerich laughed as Yrsa's aura increased and the room grew brighter. She could hear him sheath his blade a moment before he leaned his forearm on her shoulders, and pressed her bare chest into the cold, rough wall.

"What are you doing?"

Emmerich held two candles in his hand, the wax from one dripping onto the crest of her buttocks.

"Stop!"

He did not listen. He pressed both candles to her skin. The pain was somehow less this time, but the smell of burnt flesh overwhelmed the small room.

Tears streamed down Yrsa'a face, but through the sting, she suddenly remembered: she was a mother; she had two children.

"My family," she sobbed.

Another candle scooped up into his hand, Emmerich plunged it like a dagger between her shoulder blades, and pain rippled through her.

"You call yourself nothing, but you are far more than nothing, woman."

Yrsa watched as he withdrew the smallest of his daggers from his boot and gazed at himself in its polished metal.

"Daggers have always been my weapon of choice. They award an intimacy to killing, you know," Emmerich said, before he pierced Yrsa's right hand, pinning it to the brittle stone's mortar.

Yrsa shrieked, the pain so unbearable she felt faint.

"Tonight, I will find out exactly what you are, no matter how much pain and fear I must feed you."

When Yrsa finished her story, Astrid was statue-still. It was not until Yrsa looked away, that Astrid finally took a breath and growled.

"I will cut out his swine heart then stomp it beneath my feet."

"The gods will see that Emmerich gets what he deserves. I am sure of it."

"No. My wrath should be feared more than theirs."

"How can one woman stand against an army?" Yrsa asked as much to herself as Astrid.

"I will—"

"You will die."

"Then I will die…again."

CHAPTER 48

AFTER A LONG NIGHT, YRSA fell asleep. Exhausted herself, Astrid curled up behind her sister and held her tight.

In the blink of an eye, it was morning, and Yrsa was up, seemingly in better spirits. She shuffled about Warren's house, cleaning things that probably had not been touched since the death of his wife. She hummed and even smiled.

Astrid, on the other hand, was overwhelmed by her sister's tales and filled with a sense of foreboding.

Yrsa had mentioned Emmerich led an army. If such an army existed, it could have demolished Grømstad the other day; *no, that attack had been by a small force.* Yrsa had also explained last night how Emmerich's people marched here from the south—that was where she had been caught. That, along with her claim that she and Astrid had been servants of the goddess Freyja for many years, suggested these bandits were not to blame for the attack on Birka or that of Sven's outpost in the north.

Something is wrong here.

"Yrsa," Astrid yawned from the straw bed, "tell me again, how long did Emmerich question your mortality?"

"Many, many months."

"Yet, you never once admitted to him you were a former Valkyrie?"

"It was many weeks before I remembered it myself."

"You were still healing then?"

249

"Yes, which made for much longer…" Yrsa paused to steady herself. "Every time he stabbed me and I healed he had reason to stab me again. Torture, my dear sister, takes on a new meaning when your wounds repair themselves so quickly."

"I can imagine."

"When he burned me with the candles and there were no marks the following day, he was surprised. When he broke my nose and it healed straight, he found it remarkable." Yrsa held up her hands to show Astrid. "When he cut off several of my fingers and fed them to his dogs, he just plain forgot."

"As if the memory was stolen…"

"Aye. My fingers grew back, and the following day, he cut them off again, saying he must have forgotten to punish me earlier." Yrsa grimaced as she spoke. "This went on for a while."

"How long?"

"Almost three weeks."

"Yrsa?" Astrid felt vulnerable off her feet so she finally stood.

"I am better now."

Astrid could see it now; the weight was no longer on Yrsa's shoulders, crushing her into the ground. Now, the burden of her past experiences with the bandits was shared. Astrid knew their father would have been proud of the strength of body and mind Yrsa displayed; now all that remained was vengeance, and that belonged to Astrid.

Yrsa smiled and sighed. "Let us ready ourselves for the day."

"Agreed."

Astrid could not imagine the shame and despair her sister endured each day, a simple glance down a painful reminder of the horrible acts.

Eying her arms and armor, Astrid once again imagined rushing out into the dark forest to confront the bandits. One on one or one against a thousand, it mattered little. It would be a glorious death, one she knew the gods would be proud of.

"Yrsa," Astrid called out as she dressed. "Thank you again for braiding my hair last night."

"I enjoyed it. It seems like a lifetime since I had braided it."

"I could try and braid yours tonight."

"No, my hair will not take to braids while I am with child." She rubbed her stomach as she spoke. "Don't you remember?"

"I don't."

"Well, you were young and so focused on our brothers."

Astrid just stared at her sister's belly. *If our brothers were here, now, I fear they would have seen to it that your unborn child was slain. Even if they had to pierce your belly with a reed-thin blade, risking your life, dear sister, the men would have wanted to do so, and father would have allowed it.*

"It's a good thing you are here with me, Yrsa. I will not allow any more harm to befall you."

"Your promise to father no longer stands."

"Yes it does."

Yrsa hugged Astrid, but Warren waited outside, so Astrid cut the embrace short. The town already sung with the sounds of commerce and festivity, a tune that floated in through the open windows with the scent of baked goods.

"Do you smell that?" Astrid asked Yrsa.

"Yes."

"Helen brought some muffins she baked to feed the men Hammond has selling his goods."

"How do you know?" Yrsa asked.

"I heard Helen telling Warren outside."

"Oh." Yrsa shrugged. "My hearing has not been the same since..."

"Since when?" Astrid asked as she tied up her boots.

When Yrsa did not answer, she asked again.

"Since the healing stopped and...I...I forget."

"The healing stopped? When?"

"When I realized I was with child."

A knock startled both women. Astrid opened the door and Warren walked in, Willa on his heels.

"Astrid!" Willa hooted as she raced in.

"All hail, Willa."

"Your hair…" The little girl was in awe.

Astrid knelt before the child. "My sister braided it for me."

"It looks beautiful."

Willa's smile lit up the room. It was hard not to feel good in the little girl's presence, but Astrid's attention was split. Warren paced; his eyes had not left her since he entered.

"You look like you have been busy." Warren smirked. "What is that you are wearing?"

Astrid was adorned in one of his Helen's old dresses, yet she had altered it. "While Yrsa and I talked last night, I weaved some strips of hardened leather into one the dresses Hammond left the other day. I even reinforced it with hide scraps."

"Astrid, you—"

"Turned this useless fluff into rough leather armor? Aye." Astrid tapped her stomach with her fist, and each strike made her breasts jiggle.

"Outstanding."

Astrid watched as Warren's eyes traveled down her long body and paused on her sword belt.

"You cannot wear your sword today."

"Why? When are you people allowed to be armed?" Astrid grumbled as she unhooked her belt.

Warren pointed to her bear-skin boots, filthy with blood and dirt.

"And you need new boots, I think. Why not wear the sandals Helen gave you?"

"These have served me well for many years."

"They smell disgusting," Yrsa remarked, with a pinch of her nose, making Willa giggle.

"*You* smell disgusting," Astrid teased.

"Let us see if we cannot find you new boots today, agreed?"

"I—"

"She would love new boots," Yrsa interrupted.

"Great, we shall search until we find a worthy replacement, and while we are looking, if we should find you a few nice dresses, ones that are not so much like *farmer's clothes*, I will purchase those for you as well."

Regardless of being the daughter of royalty, Astrid was not used to anyone other than her father tending to her needs like this. When she wanted something, she either took it, traded for it with her own coin, or requested it from her father. Yrsa, on the other hand, was accustomed to a husband that provided for her.

"I do not—"

"Do forgive my sister," Yrsa interrupted again. "She's all fight and no etiquette. She would be honored by your gifts, Warren."

"And would you accept the honor as well, Yrsa?" Warren smiled.

Yrsa bowed.

"We best be going." Warren pointed to the door.

"Yay!" Willa cheered as she dashed out the door to her mother.

The scenery had changed overnight. Warren's house no longer looked down into a meager town, where an occasional man or woman could be seen. Now it looked into the center of a city that bustled, one that reminded both Yrsa and Astrid of home. Even the familiar moo of cows and the high-pitched chirp of playful birds were lost to the thousands of voices of men, women, and children at the spring bazaar.

Several dozen large tents had been constructed around the center of Grømstad and spread out to the far border, where the mead hall was tucked away. The red, white, and black tents looked like colorful sails of a long ship, especially when they shimmered in the light spring winds.

From this distance, the people who walked around looked to be one large mass, swaying from side to side.

Hammond and Warren were right in saying the population tripled with the bazaar, Astrid reflected. *How I would like to see Emmerich and his bandits try to attack now.*

As they strolled down the path into town, Willa jumped at Astrid's braids as they swung side to side.

"Sweetheart, stop that. You would hurt Astrid if you hung by her hair."

"Sorry, Mother. Sorry, Astrid."

"No worries."

"The braiding is very nice work," Helen noted. "What is your secret, Yrsa?"

"I vigorously brush Astrid's hair, each section, many strokes."

"How many strokes?"

"I do not count," Yrsa answered. "All I know is that it removes all that dirt and those unsightly knots."

Astrid smirked and shook her head; *just like home.*

Warren chuckled. "I like your hair, Astrid, dirt, knots and all."

"Thank you, Warren."

"Oh, Warren, you should have seen it when we were…" Yrsa's voice trailed off mid-sentence.

"Were what?" Warren asked.

"Nothing," Astrid replied. "Look, rabbits, Willa!"

"So many rabbits!" Willa gasped as she faced the small, fenced-in area filled with livestock.

The voices of several hundred merchants and townspeople flooded Astrid's ears as they drew closer to the entrance of the spring bazaar, through an enormous, flowered archway wide enough to fit six mule-driven carts and tall enough for a *Valslöngva*[8] to have been pushed under it. Helen's voice grew loud and stern when she instructed Willa to stay

---

8 Catapult or "war-sling".

close, and Astrid overheard Yrsa remind Helen that she had children long ago. *Had...long ago,* Astrid thought. *Feels like yesterday.*

Near the entrance of the bazaar, livestock, grain, and seed could be found. Two of Hammond's men also worked nearby, and Helen gave them each a muffin as they passed them.

"Where are the dresses?" Yrsa asked Helen as they passed by some clucking chickens.

"They are just past the center of the bazaar," Helen answered. She looked to Warren for confirmation. "Warren?"

"I'm sorry. I was just thinking of how the king himself would be jealous of me, escorting the town's three most beautiful ladies." He grinned.

"Such a charmer," Helen replied.

"You are too kind." Yrsa smiled back.

"Too kind, but his counting is off. He forgot poor Willa," Astrid teased.

"Sorry Willa. Aye, the garments are just beyond the center, Helen." Warren pointed.

Helen and Yrsa, hand in hand with Willa, shuffled towards the dense crowds.

"We best hurry," Yrsa shouted.

"Wait for me." Warren laughed. "Astrid?"

She did not answer. Through the crowd was someone Astrid swore she recognized. The sight caused her to stop dead in her tracks. She stood still until a break in the congestion showed him clearly: Sven.

"Odin in Valhalla!" Astrid blurted as the crowd swallowed Warren up. "It's Sven. Sven of the northlands!" she called out to the man.

Astrid watched Sven turn and walk away from her, heading out of the crowds toward the edge of town.

There was no time to gather Warren; Sven would vanish from sight if she did not follow. What she could not fathom was how a man she had seen slain could be there now, alive and well. Perhaps he held answers to the questions Yrsa could not shed light on. There was a new sensation in the air, one that heated Astrid's skin and raised her heart rate. *This must be another sign from the gods*, she thought, and she had no other choice but to give chase.

"Odin, if this is your sign to me, a new task to fulfill in your great name, then I pray the reward is worth the risk."

Astrid dashed off through the crowd, chasing Sven. Through the masses where vegetables and fruits were being sold, Astrid trudged until she was almost halted. Nevertheless, she stood taller than most of the surrounding men and was able to keep an eye on Sven as he wove in and out of the people.

"Move!" Astrid grunted as she shoved two men apart so she could squeeze through. "Damn you!"

She had never encountered such a true barricade of human bodies. She was trapped. Shuffling forward at an incredibly slow pace, made her blood boil. Astrid began to sweat and when a young man fondled her as he passed by, his giant grin an admission of guilt, she snapped.

Her burning anger turned the crowds into simple objects she had to move, and one by one, she started to shove them aside. With rage-born force, she knocked down part of the wall surrounding her, and then separated more of it until she could see a break.

As she stepped over people, a rough hand grasped her wrist. Turned, Astrid faltered when she came eye to eye with the man she had punched in the tavern the day before. "You're not Warren."

"You...you shoved my mother!"

Astrid gazed down at an old woman at her feet, just then realizing what she had done.

"I am truly sorry."

"You will be."

The large man's swing was wide and slow. *Too much meat on you makes you sluggish,* Astrid thought as she easily ducked his punch.

Prepared for another wild swing from the burly man, she stepped to the side, her back to the most crowded area. Astrid waited for the man's shoulder to drop. *There it is.* The strike was imminent. As his fist arced toward her face, she rose from her defensive stance, crossed her arms over her chest, and braced for the impact. His fist hit the mark—the spot where her forearms crossed—and the force did exactly what she had hoped for: propelled her backward through the barricade of people. She fell to the dirt, tucked her head, and rolled over, her head snapping back, whipping her braids over her back like a cat-o'-nine-tails.

Free of the masses and sure that her assailant would not pursue her, Astrid peered over the heads of townsfolk and merchants, in search of Sven.

"Sven!" she called out. "Sven?"

After the third turn she spotted him; he was moving in the direction of the hills and forest. She dashed through the moving crowd, going faster as the crowd thinned.

"Sven!"

Just when Astrid thought she would catch up to him, the man vanished into another crowd. As she ran up on a group of elderly women, she said, "A man was here. Where did he go?"

One of the women trembled and Astrid oddly knew it: the woman was not only afraid of her. *There's something else in this place, a scent—one of ash, fire, and…death.*

Ahead of the group, between her and the edge of town, was a young woman. She was on her knees, her arms wrapped around herself as she rocked back and forth.

"Are you hurt? Do you need aid?"

The girl, a few years younger than Astrid, looked up, her face red and puffy. She mumbled one word through her tears.

"D-demon," she said.

The young woman pointed, and as she did, Astrid could see her wound. Her arm was blackened from wrist to elbow, the skin like scorched earth—and it smelled much the same.

"By the gods," Astrid spit, overcome with the stench of the wound. "I will find you help…"

Astrid's words trailed off into silence as she once more spotted Sven. He was stepping into the shadows of the forest, about to escape.

"Ho, you there!" Astrid shouted to the old women. "This girl needs help. Bring the healers."

"W-where are you going?" the girl asked as Astrid stood, eyes on the forest.

"I have to catch him."

"No, don't leave," the girl begged. "They are coming."

Astrid turned sharply on the girl. Those were the very words Yrsa used.

"Who is coming?"

The girl did not answer; only groans left her mouth now. Astrid shook her head, she knew there was no time to waste, so she wished the girl well and sprinted off towards the forest.

CHAPTER 49

ASTRID HAD FOLLOWED SVEN FOR a while, staying safely behind him and downwind. He moved like a man with purpose, his steps clean and softly put in the earth. Yet every so often he shivered from head to toe, reminding her of newly forged steel when it was struck by a blacksmith's hammer. When Astrid would get to a spot where he shivered, she would see no proof of it on the ground, no broken twigs or snapped stems. His behavior should have left clues, yet he left no different tracks than any other man with one exception: for a man of average height, it seemed to Astrid that his gait was off, his feet too far from one another.

Jokul would have been sure; he was the master tracker. He would have known what to do.

At this distance, the temptation to call out to Sven was great, but she wanted to see where he was going first. Astrid had kept her bearings; they had not traveled in the direction of bandits, but toward where she and Warren had met him, though the spot was days away.

Sven slowed as he trudged up a steep incline and then paused to look over his shoulder. In all the time she had followed him, Sven had not looked back, and now when he did, her complacency betrayed her. Astrid dove to the leaf-cluttered ground and flattened herself as best should could; what little brush was there would have to mask her body.

Sven's face did not change; he seemed to be gazing past her. After a long moment, he took a dozen or more steps on his original path, his strange tremble more frequent now. When he reached the top of the hill inside the forest, he suddenly stopped altogether.

Still flat to the forest floor, Astrid watched him. Sven had suffered one of the most gruesome neck wounds she had ever seen.

No way he could have survived…we buried him…however, my own neck was slashed, and I live. Did the gods gift him with healing too?

Still, there was another theory, one that made her less comfortable. *What if that is not Sven at all? Father's tales of ghosts, lost souls of men in search of the afterlife—is that you, Sven?*

Astrid slid her fingers into her boot like a weasel that dove down a rabbit hole and, dagger in hand, breathed a sigh of relief. Dead or alive, it mattered little; she would be prepared.

Astrid stood slowly and carefully wiped off the leaves and twigs stuck to her. *Better they fall softly now, than loudly as I am mere inches from the man.* She scaled the hill behind Sven, who had not moved; she would catch him soon. The thoughts of what to do with him once he was apprehended began to stir. She would need something to bind him with whether she took him back to town or left him here to be questioned. *I will know the truth about you soon, Sven.*

Her heartbeat echoed in her ears. Astrid was trying to catch her breath when a new breeze blew over the hill and delivered a hint of the same smell she had encountered in town: death.

More concerned now, Astrid pushed on, nearly close enough to reach out and touch him. She breathed shallowly through her nose. She had not meant to stand behind the statue-still man for so long, and as she finally reached out to touch him and her fingertips grazed his shoulder, a shout echoed through the forest.

"Astrid!"

Astrid jumped. Her hand landed fully on Sven's shoulder—and the man crumbled like a rotten scarecrow. A powerful gust of air forced her back and she tumbled over. On her back, she slid down the hill overtop a bed of dry leaves and twigs.

"Astrid!" Warren yelled.

Warren jumped over a pile of rocks and dropped to his knees where she lay, arms out to her side.

"Are you hurt?" Warren gently grasped her shoulders.

She stared up into the sky and laughed. Amused, Astrid let out a resounding, "Shite!"

"Astrid?"

"Tell me what you saw."

"I cannot explain what I saw..." Warren grimaced. "There was a man here—"

"It was Sven."

"That couldn't have been Sven. He's dead." Warren cautiously looked around as they spoke. "Who I saw was much bigger than Sven."

Astrid reached up, pulled Warren down into a hug and laughed through happy tears. "I sent Sven's soul to Valhalla. I did. Back in the forest after he died. Now, I believe the gods returned him here to give a message to me."

"Astrid..." Warren said. "We buried him."

"Warren, there's only one meaning behind all this mystery."

He sighed and asked. "And what is that meaning?"

"This is not Helheim. This is not a dream. I'm not going mad." With his scruffy face squeezed between her hands, Astrid planted a kiss on his moist lips. "Yrsa's claims are true, Warren. Yrsa's claims are true!"

CHAPTER 50

ONE KISS LED TO ANOTHER and another, but the timing did not feel right to Warren; he needed to make it clear that he had abandoned Yrsa, Helen, and Willa to pursue her. Yet, when their lips separated, he was overcome by the sweetness of wildflowers and the musk of Astrid's groin. Caught in a sudden undertow of desire, he spread Astrid's legs with his knee and then climbed on top of her, one hand under her neck, the other diving under her skirt.

"Warren," she huffed, his hand held with both of hers. "Your fingers are magical, true gifts from the gods; imbued with Tyr's speed and Thor's lightning, they send sparks through me."

"I love you, Astrid. Do you love me?"

Eyes sealed shut, her lips moved, "You…you make my body burn…"

As he worked his fingers, Astrid moaned loud enough to scare the birds from the trees. Back arched, Warren could see it—arousal flowed through her body, sensations peaked and grew greater by the moment. Eyes still closed, Astrid clenched her teeth until a pleasure-filled squeal finally opened her mouth and she commanded, "Join with me."

With little effort, Warren was inside her. He had never desired a woman more than he did Astrid in that moment; he would have killed to have her.

With her legs locked around his waist, it was not long before Warren lost himself in the pure ecstasy of being inside her. Even with her head tiled back, he could tell she was going to release—the thought was more than he could bear.

Unable to move, Warren found himself spilling inside her, his animalistic thoughts quickly heavy with panic. In a burst of speed, he pushed himself back until he was seated on his knees.

"Astrid I—"

"I call upon you, great Frigg," she interrupted.

"I was overcome."

She cupped her lisk with her right hand and asked, "What have you done?"

"The pleasure...I was selfish, please forgive me."

Full of regret he had looked away, but looking back, he was shocked to see a warm, almost playful smile on her face. She had never looked so lovely—her cheeks were red and her eyes shimmered. Warren swore she almost glowed.

"You...you have made me yours on this day, Warren."

But in the space of a moment, her happy look turned into a blank stare. Warren stood up and scanned their surroundings; he did not want to be struck when vulnerable. As he moved, he accidentally kicked her leg, and it wobbled like a dead man's limb.

"Astrid, do not tease."

As he watched her for a sign, a cone of blue light enveloped her, painting her with its color.

"What is this?" Warren looked up into the light.

There was a flash and, momentarily blinded, he staggered back, stumbled over a rock, and fell to the seat of his pants. As he cleared his suddenly bleary eyes, he realized Astrid was gone. Left in her wake was only dirt and crumbled, dry leaves.

"Astrid?" Warren rubbed his eyes.

He spun around, expecting to find her, but there was no hint of her. With each turn, each tree he looked behind, each patch of earth he searched for footprints, Warren's heartbeat grew faster.

Astrid was gone.

CHAPTER 51

"Sweetheart, wake up," Astrid heard her mother call to her. Astrid slowly awakened, peeling her eyes open and taking in her surroundings; she was in her quarters in Birka's fortress. She had not lived in that room for some time, but to wake in it now felt right.

When Astrid stretched her legs, her feet bumped into her mother, who was seated at the bottom of the bed—impossible as it may be.

"Mother?"

"Astrid, my dear love."

"Mother, you-you're alive?"

Backlit by the bright torchlight of the hall, even in shadows, her mother's beauty was magnificent.

Astrid sat up when she heard her father's hounds bark in the distance and smelled the scent of bread baking in the hearths. Her brothers liked to tease that her bedroom was the furthest away from their parents, that nearness to the royal chambers equaled importance, but she liked being above the kitchens, where the only odors that rose from the floor where those of food and not filth. Astrid raised her nose to sniff the air, smiled, and enjoyed the moment.

"Astrid, listen carefully."

Her mother's voice sounded different.

"How is this possible?" Astrid squinted to get a better look but she could not make out the details of her face.

Her mother stood and moved around the bed, into the light from the hall, and suddenly, Astrid realized—this was not her mother at all; this was someone else. The appearance of this woman did not frighten her; Astrid was sure she knew this stunning woman, but the name was lost to her.

"It pains me that I had to do this to you, Astrid."

"Do what?" Astrid asked, reaching out to touch the woman. "Who are you?"

"I had to trick you, your mind...it was too fragile, any other way...I fear you might have been wounded by reality."

"I know you. I am sure of it."

Astrid pulled herself out of bed, realizing she was in her armor. *Why would I sleep in my armor in my own bed?*

"Look at me, Astrid. Listen to my voice."

As she spoke, the familiar woman shed the heavy, wolf-fur robe she wore. Underneath the furs was a thin white gown, transparent in the bright light, which seemed to intensify with each moment. On the woman's right arm were three golden armlets and on her left were three equally extravagant golden bracelets. It was not until she disrobed that Astrid saw the fullness of the mass of her curly blonde hair which nearly reached her ankles.

"I..." Astrid could feel the woman's love; it felt like that of her mother's and much, much more.

"The answer is in your heart, Astrid," the woman said, as she touched Astrid's chest.

The realization came with a great sense of humility. Astrid dropped to her knees to honor her god.

"Great Freyja," Astrid whispered as a tear formed.

"Please stand, child."

Astrid continued to bow and keep her eyes averted.

"How is it possible that someone as insignificant as me is worthy of your attention, my goddess?" she asked.

Freyja grabbed Astrid under her armpits, lifted her up, and placed her finger under Astrid's chin, to raise it so their eyes could meet.

Before she gazed directly upon Freyja, Astrid spotted her god's necklace, Brísingamen, its jewels so bright they seemed to burn with their own life—*especially the red one*, she thought.

"Astrid, my daughter, my soldier, welcome home." Freyja smiled and as she did, Astrid cried tears of joy.

She looked around the room, the place she had been raised and that held so many fond memories, and it suddenly made sense.

"I am dead."

"Not dead."

"This is not Birka. My home was destroyed, this—"

"Is a simple illusion," Freyja said with a wave of her hand. "Your mind, it is still in the early stages of metamorphosis. Had I not tricked you it would have splintered."

"I do not understand."

"No, I am afraid you do not." Freyja paused. "Perhaps I am being too gentle. You *were* my strongest."

The light from outside her room suddenly flashed; Astrid closed her eyes, and when she reopened them, she stood in a lush meadow.

"Is this—"

"Fólkvangr." As she spoke, Freyja raised her arms and smiled. "I summoned you home. Not only were you one of my most skilled and trusted Valkyrie, Astrid, but also one of the most recently returned to Midgard."

Astrid glanced around, letting the surroundings sink in. The field, its bright colors, the warmth of the air, the sounds of nature—it was all too beautiful to take in at once. Overwhelmed with it all, Astrid went numb.

"My sister...her stories were true." Astrid nearly choked on her own breath with excitement. "I served you?"

"You did."

Astrid wanted to give out a battle cry and she would have had she not been so humbled by Freyja's presence.

"There's much I have to ask, my goddess."

"And more I have to tell, I am afraid, my daughter." Freyja frowned. "I fear there is dire trouble in Midgard."

"Trouble?"

Freyja waved her hand and out of the tall grass beside Astrid, a moss-covered boulder rose.

"Please, be seated."

Freyja paced back and forth, her gown slipping off her shoulder. She stopped, fixed her dress, and spoke with a new sense of urgency.

"Not long ago, we gods became aware of a new breed of demon. These demons, the Ashvolk, claimed to be god killers and boasted that the blood of Valkyrie gave their kind strength. When they first made themselves known, the Ashvolk were not strong enough to kill a Valkyrie one on one. My legions diminished their numbers to just a few, but those few became stronger. They had vanished from the realms for many years before resurfacing in Midgard," Freyja explained. "No longer hunting active Valkyrie, they searched for those who were recently retired and returned to mortal life. Hundreds of women across the lands were killed and consumed within a period of a few months. Heroes were dispatched and armies roamed the countryside in search of the demons, but none were stalwart enough to overcome the Ashvolk. Soon the demons grew so adept at hunting Valkyrie that they could sense the women about to be called to service. It was during one of their hunts that they followed the scent of maiden blood to Birka."

"Birka…" Astrid repeated in a whisper.

"I set a trap within the fortress city."

"A trap?" Astrid finally understood what Freyja was suggesting. "You…you used Yrsa and I as bait?"

"I did."

Astrid stood; her nerves no longer allowed her to stay seated.

"Birka was razed because demons came in search of my sister and I? Yet when there was a fight to be had, you snatched me off the battlefield?"

"I did not wish you killed there. It would have been—"

Her emotions boiled over.

"All of those families died because of me!" she screamed.

"Not you, my daughter. You are blameless in all this."

"Then who, my goddess? Who? For they deserve the point of my sword."

Freyja was silent a moment, then, with a nod, she peeled the straps of her gown off. "Are you not warm under all that metal, Astrid?"

Astrid did not answer; she did not know how to.

Freyja continued after a large, green leaf floated atop the breeze to her hand, which she quickly used to fan her cleavage. "The meadow, it gets so hot here after a battle."

"Battle?" Astrid looked up.

"The dead I receive here help train my Valkyrie. The lords and generals, they enjoy staging a battle from time to time." Freyja fanned the nape of her neck.

Astrid could not help but be mesmerized by her alluring appearance. The longer she stared, the more her anger seemed to drain away. *Did all the gods have such power?* she wondered.

"Would you like to know more?"

"Please, my goddess."

Freyja fixed her gown back up over her shoulders, smiled, then plucked a large sunflower which had bloomed at her feet while they spoke.

"I ordered ten of my finest women to annihilate the demons."

"Why Birka? Why us?"

"Because the demons are weaker in the northern cold, and the stone in your lands...something about it makes it harder for the creatures to sink down into the earth when they move or try to flee." Freyja plucked the petals from the sunflower one at a time. "You would not know this, of course, but your family is born of a long bloodline of Valkyrie. Your father's mother served me, and so did her mother's mother."

"My father's mother?" Astrid repeated, shocked, but her mind quickly snapped back to task. "Please, tell me the day was won."

"Know this, Astrid: the deaths of your family were not in vain, most of the Ashvolk were killed that day. In fact, one demon was slain by your brother. He even faced it alone."

While she was proud to hear one of her brothers defeated a demon, she had heard Freyja's entire statement.

"*Most* were killed?" Astrid covered her face with her hand. "So this is why you called me back here…you wish me to find and destroy the rest of the demons?"

"Precisely."

Astrid would have liked to think she knew the answer to her next question. She would have liked to think it was because she was the best, but there was a voice inside her mind, her father's, and it asked her questions any commander would have. *If Freyja has legions of Valkyrie, then…*

"Why me?"

"Astrid…times have become very…unsettling here. The gods you know, they do not have the power they once did. As a result, the mortals have lost their faith in us. Disease and war now own their fears. Odin, the poor, misguided old man, thought the best solution would be to end my charge, take away my soldiers. He thought if it is Valkyrie blood that makes the demons stronger, then there should be no more Valkyrie. He was wrong. The demons adapted, as I told you; they could sense who had been under my charge."

"The Allfather was mistaken?"

"Now is not the time for blame."

"He ordered an end to the bloodlines? All of them?"

"All of them, Astrid, there are no more Valkyrie. You are the last."

Freyja's words echoed in her ears. *The last one. How could all I have grown to have faith in be so changed?*

"Before you speak, I know you have doubts. Worry not, this is no trick. Rest assured the king of mischief himself is still bound. The demons are real."

Astrid did not know what to say. Astrid should have been elated; she had just learned she was the owner of one of the greatest gifts of honor a god could bestow upon a mortal. But the more Astrid thought about Freyja's gift, the less she wanted it.

"There have been moments, as recent as this morning, when my will to fight has slipped away. My goddess, when I was younger, I stayed awake many nights wishing I could honor you as a Valkyrie, yet now I do not know. I find my thoughts of battle mixed with love and leisure. I misread the signs. I-I am so truly sorry."

"Do not be sorry, Astrid. You feel what I have made you to feel. It was my powers at work that were taking away your will to fight, transforming you from a warrior to a woman who could choose a life of quiet love over one of howling violence." Freyja reached for Astrid's hand as she spoke. "Just look into your heart and soul and you will find your true self."

Astrid felt a tickle run from her hand, up her arm to her chest, and shivered. *Freyja's words make sense*, she thought.

"You need me to fight again."

"I do."

"I will require information, as much as you can give quickly, Goddess Freyja."

"All you need will be provided."

Astrid nodded.

"Do you know where in Midgard the demons are hiding?"

"I do, because on this day, the surviving Ashvolk demons have stolen your sister."

CHAPTER 52

FREYJA'S WORDS PIERCED HER HEART. Astrid loved Yrsa; she would not lose her again.

Before the sting of shock could wear off, Freyja explained that once, in the recent past, the Ashvolk had held a former Valkyrie hostage. They did not kill her because she was pregnant; Freyja was sure the demons wanted the woman's baby.

"Do you know who rescued that maiden?"

"Me?" Astrid wished her memory of past events were clearer.

"No, Astrid, that quest was given to your sister. She had reached her quota of souls, and instead of returning to Midgard, she chose to stay here and represent me in Asgard. When the news reached us, I awarded her this final task."

"Such a notable quest should have been mine. Yrsa is no warrior."

"You are thinking only of life. In life, the blood of a warrior may not fill your sister, but here, she was much more. Yrsa succeeded in her task, saved the woman and her child, but I fear she witnessed many horrors in doing so. When she returned, her fighter's resolve was damaged. I had no other option save returning her to Midgard."

"Yet you returned her to life with her memories of being a Valkyrie intact. That means she must remember how to fight too."

"The mortal memory is a slippery serpent. While she recalls some facts of her time in my service, her mind has filled the gaps with dreams and fantasies. It saddens me to say, your sister is not well."

With no petals left on the sunflower, Freyja crushed the thing with her hand, reducing it to flakes and oil.

"I like this smell." Freyja sniffed her hand. "But yours is more alluring. Astrid, do honor me by telling me, what where you doing when I summoned you back?"

As steeled for combat as she now was, Astrid could not contain a smirk.

"I was with a man."

"Yes, I thought so. The scents of lovemaking have clung to your skin like honey."

Freyja stepped closer to Astrid as hers eyes sunk down the fighter's body to her hips. Embarrassed, Astrid looked away.

"No, do not be ashamed, my daughter. Whenever I call a mortal to audience, my powers fill them with lust. The sensation has been known to *affect* time."

"Our encounter did feel ill-timed," Astrid admitted. "Warren must have been confused."

"Warren, is he your man?"

Astrid paused before she answered, "He is."

"Then what you did with him when I summoned you was out of your love…while slightly empowered by mine."

"He desires me unlike any man has."

"Good, remember that. He will make a useful ally when confronting the demons."

Astrid enjoyed Warren's company on the battlefield, but this worried her. *Could he face and defeat a demon?* she wondered.

"I do not wish him killed, my goddess."

"And if he is?"

"I would see him returned to Valhalla."

"Yes, you would. No greater honor than to be ushered by the woman you love to the hall of the gods, I would think," Freyja said with a sly smile.

"You are right. Odin be praised."

Certain that every moment spent away from her sister was a moment lost, Astrid decided it was time to return to Midgard.

"Yrsa needs me. I must go." Astrid stood.

"Not until you are fully prepared," Freyja replied firmly.

"Return my sword to me. It and the fighting spirit of my kin are all I need."

"You need much more, Astrid, do not be foolish."

Freyja pressed Astrid back to her seat.

"Before we proceed, you must know this: I will remake you a Valkyrie and return you to Midgard, but with the memories of your past here, your training...you will begin to feel different than you do now."

"Different?" Astrid did not like the sound of that. "Again?"

"I cannot promise that your love for Warren will remain. You were a feisty and sometimes arrogant soldier, Astrid," Freyja chuckled. "Even here you deflected the amorous intentions of men."

The goddess's words filled Astrid with a sense of dread that rose from the pit of her stomach. She was being challenged—given an ultimatum.

"The love of my sister or the love of my man. Why must I choose? What if I want both?"

"With each passing moment, you are sounding more and more like the young woman I trained." Freyja smiled. "I will tell you what I always have, Astrid...life and death are yours to take."

CHAPTER 53

990 AD, Scandinavia

WARREN'S SOLDIER'S INTUITION TOLD HIM to run; there was something direly wrong. Astrid's sudden disappearance was a bad sign; he knew it. As he raced back to town, Warren cursed his decision to leave Yrsa, Helen, and Willa, and prayed his rashness was not the biggest mistake of his life.

As he neared the settlement, he heard a commotion that was not the normal buzz of the spring bazaar; it was the sound of mass panic. He imagined a series of events: Grømstad in flames, hundreds dead and dying, the full force of bandits, whatever it was that had decimated the men in that field—that left only parts and gore. Warren expected the worst and painfully accepted that he had once again failed a woman who loved and trusted him.

When he came upon the crowd, there was no sign of battle, yet he could hear the screams of a fight. Deep into the mass of people, he soon discovered the catalyst of the mayhem: two young men fist-fighting. They were both bloodied and unsteady on their feet, and Warren could tell the contest was almost over.

"A fight caused this much stir?" Warren asked the butcher, as they watched the boys throw their final punches.

"And over an ugly lass if you ask me."

"Two boys fighting should not have created such a crowd." Warren scanned it for Helen and Yrsa.

"There's something in the air today," the butcher said, then cheered as one young man was finally toppled by the smaller. "You know what the smell of blood in the air can do to a predator."

"Yes, I do."

"Warren!"

Warren nearly stumbled when he turned toward the sound of Helen's voice. There she was, on the other side of the crowd, not far from where he'd left her.

"I see you, Helen." As Warren made his way to her, his frayed nerves began to mend, but the closer her got to his brother's wife, the clearer it became that Yrsa was not with her. Warren dashed the last few steps and yelled to Helen, "Where is she?"

"Who, Astrid or Yrsa?"

"Yrsa?"

"In that tent, trying on new garments. Willa joined her," Helen said. "Why? What's wrong, Warren?"

"Astrid vanished in the forest. There was a beam of blue light... there's no good way to explain it, but she stood before me one moment and was gone the next."

Helen's face turned white. "Warren, you are scaring me," she said, grabbing his arm. "What are you saying?"

"I'm not sure, other than in that moment, I realized I never should have left you all here alone."

"Alone? We have hardly been alone. Warren, we have been here, surrounded by a town overflowing with people."

Warren looked away from the tent and could have sworn he saw a flicker of the blue light through the trees in the distance. The town butcher was right; there was something in the air. He could feel it—that sense that there would be violence. It was that same heaviness he sensed when he took up ranks in the army—as he prepared to do battle—and he knew, in a heartbeat, all that was grass green, soft, and pretty would become awash in bright red blood.

"No."

Warren charged forward, tore back the flap of the tent, and looked inside. Yrsa was not there. Willa was tucked in a ball, sobbing so hysterically that her tears had soaked the front of her dress.

"Willa!" Helen shrieked as she ran to her daughter.

When Helen scooped up Willa in her arms, her daughter's tears slowed, but only slightly. The little girl trembled so hard Helen had to squeeze her tight just to settle her.

"Yrsa!" Warren shouted. "Yrsa!"

"Are you well, sweetie? What ails you?"

"Yrsa! Damn you, answer me!" Warren nearly ripped the flap off the tent as he stepped out of it.

"Shush, baby, mother's here."

"Helen, ask her where Yrsa went."

Warren paced the small spot in front of the tents as he spoke. When Helen did not respond, busy cooing, Warren marched up to them and repeated himself.

"Warren, please."

"Yrsa!"

Warren grunted in frustration; he had attracted the attention of many passersby but had not spotted the one woman he searched for.

"Helen! Ask her!" Warren ordered. "Ask her!"

"Fine!" Helen snapped at him, covering her daughter's ears.

"Please."

"Willa, darling, what happened to Yrsa? What happened to your friend?"

While Helen stroked Willa's head, Warren continued to pace, praying the child would calm down enough to answer. After a series of wet sniffles, Willa finally squeaked out four words.

"The...the monster...t-took her."

Warren did not like the sound of that, but before he could ask a second question, Willa wrapped her arms around Helen's neck and shoved her face into her mother's collar.

"We should find Hammond."

"Yes," Warren sighed, only then realizing he'd been holding his breath. "Can you find him alone, or should I stay with you?"

"I see Adora, the wife of one of Hammond's business partners from the kingdom over yonder. I will be fine with her and her lot until I find him."

"Are you sure?"

"Go." Helen gave a weak smile. "Find Astrid and Yrsa."

He watched Helen and Willa join up with the other family and then turned his attention back to the milling crowd. He would search every tent in the entire bazaar if he had to; Warren refused to lose them both in one day.

Before he left the spot Yrsa had vanished from, Warren heard what sounded like a mass of people on the move—the noise so similar to that of an army at charge, his blood ran cold. *This is it,* he told himself.

As Warren looked about, time seemed to move at half speed; a dozen or more large objects flipped end over end through the sky as high up as the tallest building in town. Bodies—he had seen such a horrid sight once before, when his men were struck with siege-weapon fire, but then it had been parts of men, not their full bodies that flew over his head.

A thousand screams filled the air, like the roar of the ocean. People were running away from the far end of town.

A cloud of dirt rose fast, boiling up from the ground like the geysers of southlands. The ground must have rumbled, but the only thing that shook the earth where he stood were the hundreds and hundreds of feet that pounded the ground as they ran by him.

Something large exploded from the center of the dust cloud, black as coal with jagged lines like limestone rock. Warren might have mistook it as a giant stalagmite had it not begun to move; the thing's head twisted, and its eyes red as lava searched about.

Seeing it, Warren could think only one word: *monster.*

"Run!" a woman yelled as she rushed by him.

He intended to do just that, but not in the same direction everyone else was going. He'd seen several weapons dealers not far from where he stood earlier in the day, so he ran forward, against the crowd that surged in the opposite direction.

As the dust cloud began to settle, Warren gasped and screamed "Demon!" partially hoping that he would then wake up in a sweat, Astrid beside him, and Yrsa safe in Hammond's home—but he did not. This was no nightmare; this was real.

With a growl, black oil spilled from the demon's mouth to the ground where Warren watched it bubble. When the beast looked his way, he ducked under the nearest table; he was still a few feet from the weapon merchants. Warren peered around the side of the table and caught sight of a large shield; it would be the first thing he grabbed when he reached the spot.

The horrified shriek of a young man made his heart sink. It reminded him of the battlefield. Warren had hoped not to lapse back to those horrible days, but with all the combat he had seen in the past week or so, he was relieved to have his training and experience.

As he crawled to the opposite side of the table, he spotted the demon; it moved quicker now, its body lined with glowing red veins that looked like they pumped the same red lava that its eyes were made of. The demon attacked a man that had fallen during the chaos, a total lack of emotion on its inhuman countenance.

Warren turned away and saw a child behind a pile of large pots. He scrambled to his feet and dashed through the aisles to the shield. It was a large wooden shield reinforced with metal plates.

If I survive this, I'll have to ask Hammond if this is one of his goods, he suddenly thought. *Otherwise, I'll have to find the merchant who owns it and repay him for this theft. Damn it, Warren, focus.*

He snatched up a sword belt, one he knew he could quickly wrap around his waist, and the screams of horror that had only moments ago filled his ears had faded. People were smart; they had distanced themselves as best they could, but that did not mean he was the only brave man around. As he holstered a long sword, he spotted a cadre of royal guards charging the demon. Warren only paused a moment, just long enough to wonder if he would not have to fight after all, but the demon answered that question in a heartbeat.

The royal guards had to get close enough to swing their swords—and were sliced to ribbons by the demon's jagged claws. *Their armor might as well have been made of farmer's cloth*—Warren looked at his outfit—*like mine.*

He stared at the table of weapons, his eyes finally alighting on exactly what he needed: a very long, iron spear.

"Perfect," he declared as the weapon's weight settled in hand.

Warren swiftly positioned the spear at his waist and began his forward charge. The demon had its back to him, but as Warren drew closer, he saw how thick the creature's backside was. He would need to attack its chest, and there was only one way to do that.

"Die!" Warren screamed as he rushed around to the front of the demon. "Die!"

Warren had to raise the spear to aim at its belly, and still, he missed his mark. The sharp tip of the weapon struck the demon's hip and glanced off it with a spark, like a sharpening stone across steel.

The way the thing turned its head and looked at Warren made him feel as if it recognized him; the sensation chilled his blood. He could imagine all of Hel filled with the souls of evil men, some of which he slew. *Could this be the embodiment of one of them? Or worse, a conglomeration of them all?*

He had no time to ponder further as its claws came at him. With his spear laid down, Warren rolled on the ground over his shoulder, under the demon's swing. The battle excited him, and he channeled that energy back into the fight, just like he had in his younger years. Spear aimed between dodges, he took two pokes at the demon's hide.

In the midst of a growl, the demon coughed and vomited a spray of black oil that burned the wood but not the metal plates of Warren's shield. Warren dropped it and clutched the spear in both hands. He had no protection from the demon's ooze now, but it was the claws that scared him most.

Warren jumped back to avoid a downward claw strike and then forward to plunge the tip of his spear into the demon's shoulder. Before he could celebrate his success, the monster had grasped the shaft of the spear with one hand and sliced through the metal with the claws of his other.

Now that the spear was destroyed, Warren did the only thing he could: he tried to move the beast away from the child.

"You're as stupid as you are big!" he shouted.

The demon followed Warren as he backpedaled.

"Fight me!"

Preoccupied by the child's safety, Warren allowed himself to get backed into a corner between two overturned tables, instantly aware of the irony in his comment. *Great work, Warren. You're trapped now.*

"Come on, demon," he yelled. "Let us end this!"

Behind the monster, he spotted a flash of highly polished armor. *I owe the royal guards more credit.*

He steadied himself and watched the demon carefully, ready to parry its next strike with a sword he had grabbed from the ground, but it did not attack. Shoved forward by a powerful blow to its back, the thing turned and stumbled—finally Warren had a clear view behind it.

"By the great heavens…" Warren muttered.

In a defensive stance, covered in armor unlike he had ever seen, her family sword brandished, was Astrid. *She looks like…no, it's not possible,* he told himself.

Astrid sparkled from head to toe. Her new armor shimmered as if it were an amalgam of silver and gold. Even her skirt, which was made of heavy leather pleats, was reinforced with golden lining.

No longer the target of the demon, who gazed eagerly upon Astrid now, Warren dashed to save the little girl as she wept loudly. As he ran around the demon, he saw that Astrid's eyes were filled with a fire he had seen before when she fought—but now that fire was combined with a fresh, icy calm. As he looked upon her currently, he did not worry about her like he had when they faced the bandits; somehow, he knew all would be well.

"You're safe now, child." Warren fell to his knees when he reached the little girl. "I'll take you to your mother."

Warren scooped up the child, held her tight to his chest as he jumped to his feet, and scanned toppled tables, destroyed merchandise, and broken bodies until he found exactly who he was looking for: a young blonde woman as red-faced with tears as the little girl—the girl's mother.

A rumble alerted him that the demon had done something, but he could not look back; Warren had to press forward. He sprinted through the aisles until he reached the child's mother, her arms outstretched.

"My baby!"

"She'll be fine."

"Thank you, thank you."

The young woman tried to take his hand in gratitude, but Warren stepped away.

"Please, run, all of you! Get away from here!" Warren shouted. "Go, damn you! Go!"

As soon as the onlookers moved away, Warren faced the fight. On the ground beside the coal-skinned monster was its left arm. Astrid was winning.

CHAPTER 54

"Demon, you have one last chance: tell me what your ungodly kin has done with my sister and I will make your death quick."

The demon growled, a black mist of saliva spraying through the air. "Will drink your maiden blood."

With a broad swing of her sword, Astrid cut a deep gash across the demon's barrel-shaped chest, but the demon showed no pain, and wrapped its arm around her, pinning her to it, back to front.

"Lord will consume you both…and then devour the gods you worship," the demon grumbled.

It's mouth open wide, the demon leaned over and tried to fit her head into its maw, but her large feathered headdress got in the way. The demon's black teeth squealed against the metal of her thick helmet, crushing the helmet in its mouth as Astrid squirmed down, freeing her skull.

The demon's grip loosened, and Astrid quickly grabbed the dagger on her belt and jammed the blade into the thing's side.

Wounded, the demon released Astrid and she dropped to the ground where she landed with a dancer's grace. On one foot, she spun around, swinging her sword at the demon's waist, where the blade cut into it nearly halfway. Through a howl of pain borne of the depths of Hel itself, the demon woozily staggered back, attached to Astrid by her sword.

Astrid glimpsed at Warren in time to see his smile fade and his warrior's face return—and, with sword cocked back, he dashed in to help.

"Stand down, man!" she ordered him.

Finally able to free her weapon from the demon's belly, Astrid watched as it fell lifelessly to the ground.

"I'm here to help."

"Back off, Warren." She waved her hand as she stared down at the demon.

"Astrid?"

"Now!"

Warren took several steps back, "Is it dead?"

"Not yet."

Astrid approached the downed demon cautiously. Freyja had told her that the larger Ashvolk demons would only die if their heads were separated from their bodies and then crushed. Otherwise, in a short time, they would regenerate. Freyja had also warned her that, when near death, they became increasingly dangerous.

"What do we do? Are there more?" Warren asked as Astrid circled widely toward its head.

She kept an eye on the demon's body for movement—if it were to even twitch, she would be ready.

"Astrid, answer me."

In position, she snapped, "Just stand back."

With a downward slice, Astrid cut the head from the demon's shoulders, but the moment her sword struck the earth, its last arm scooped her legs out from under her. Her right foot kicked the demon's head as she fell, spinning it toward Warren.

"Astrid!"

The wind knocked out of her, Astrid could not respond. She braced herself with her sword and attempted to stand, but was struck once more by the demon's arm as it wildly swung about.

"Astrid!" Warren shouted a second time, his sword raised.

"The head!" she finally coughed out. "Bash the head."

Astrid observed the cut-off arm begin to pour out an oil-like ooze. Like long vines, the ooze reached for the demon's body; the demon was trying to make itself whole again.

Kevin James Breaux

"Hurry!" Astrid shouted as a sharp scrape filled her ears.

The hand that had her was trying to pierce her armor with its nails, but the dagger-sharp spikes only slid up over the metal toward the bare skin of her neckline. Astrid knew a scratch from the demon's claws would burn and a deep puncture could possibly kill her.

Motionless, Astrid watched as the two claws reached her collar bone. "No..." she shook.

With the word hardly off her lips, the demon unexpectedly crumbled into brittle rock and ash; she was suddenly freed and unharmed.

Warren stood with a large war hammer in hand, its heavy head sunk deep into the ground before him. The look of surprise on his face quickly shifted to a smile when their eyes met.

"Did you see that?" Warren asked.

Astrid breathed a sigh of relief and nodded. "It turned back to helstone and ash."

"The head...I swear it looked at me before I crushed it."

Astrid brushed the dirt from her armor as she stood and took note of the area. There were many dead and a sickening scent of smoke hung in the air. Freyja had told her that upon her return, her senses would amplify and the sensitivity might overwhelm her. She'd also instructed Astrid to wait until night to hunt the demons who took her sister, to find someplace quiet and hide there until fully ready.

So far, she had found neither luxury.

CHAPTER 55

THERE WAS STILL ENOUGH CHAOS in town for Warren to escort Astrid away unnoticed—covered in a long riding cloak that he had snatched from a merchant's table.

Warren was sure Astrid was ill regardless of her assurance that she was not. When she asked him to take her someplace quiet, and then nearly fell faint in his arms, he knew exactly where to go. Warren drug her through a large crowd that had been on the opposite side of town and unaware of what had happened. Once lost in the mob, Warren and Astrid slipped into the forest and snuck to Gathon's supply cellar.

Warren had hidden the key he had discovered days ago, and although he knew it was a crime, he had already slipped back inside the place once and stolen several more pouches of coin. He knew the place would be picked clean by the guards over time, and felt he was owed as much as anyone for the years he put up with Gathon's passive-aggressive behavior. After all, the man nearly ended him and Astrid.

I wish I could kill Gathon again, Warren thought as he unlocked the chain around the cellar door. *I wish I could kill him again and again...*

Astrid was mumbling to herself. Her words had not ceased for the last hundred or so steps, but he could actually hear her clearly enough to understand now. She shifted back and forth between complaints and what sounded like rehashing of a conversation she had had with someone. It was a negotiation of sorts, Warren guessed, and apparently Astrid wanted more than this other person was keen to give.

Down in the cellar, Astrid gradually perked up.

"Where are we, Warren?"

"Gathon's cellar," he answered as he lit a torch.

Astrid looked about. "Gathon, the corrupt guard? You brought me to where he kept his slaves?"

"Yes."

"Interesting choice, Warren."

"You wanted someplace quiet," Warren replied. "No one will know to come looking for us here."

Astrid paced the small area that was filled with barrels until she spotted the tunnel. She walked down it to the first small room, which had a table and four chairs in it; a vase with a dying flower acting as a centerpiece. A map of town was pinned to the wall, and had some notes scribbled on it.

Warren followed closely with the torch and lit as many candles and other wall mounted-torches as he could locate. With all the light, the place was much cheerier.

"Cozy for a slaver's dungeon," she said sarcastically.

"Do you feel any better?"

Seated, Astrid released a long moan. "Much better."

"Sore from the fight? That thing was strong, but you bested it, Astrid." Warren smiled.

"It was strong, but lacked skill."

"That was a demon, right?" Warren wanted to hear someone else say it.

"Ashvolk demon."

"I knew it, a damned demon."

"She told me change would come with many sensations, emotions, and pains. Not long, one night at most," Astrid said, her eyes on her hands, as she clenched and unclenched them. "I did not expect to return to a fight. I am sapped."

"Astrid." Warren paused. "Where did you go?"

"Go?"

"In the forest, after we…you vanished before my eyes."

"Water," Astrid demanded.

"Let me find you some."

While Warren was gone, Astrid was able to define what her senses were trying to tell her. Freyja warned her, her feelings about Warren might change, but what she should have said was her feelings about all mortals would change, as Astrid felt far superior to them in general—so much so that she had to repeatedly remind herself that Warren was not her servant, but her lover.

"Here, I filled this waterskin with fresh water. There's a large vat down here. It looks like Gathon found a way to direct rainwater down into a storage tub."

"You bring me bath water?" Astrid sniffed the tip of the waterskin before she drank.

"It's clean."

"It best be."

His eyes squinted and a puzzled look formed on his furrowed brow. "You look different," he stated bluntly.

Astrid peered down her nose at the man. He surely sensed it; Freyja said all mortal men would, and those who had faced combat would feel it much more.

"How do I look, Warren?" she asked.

"Beautiful. I mean you always look beautiful, but now even more so. I cannot take my eyes off you. Astrid, you are the most lovely woman I have ever seen."

"I bet."

As he pointed at her gold and silver armor, he asked, "Where did you get this new armor? It-it is too high a quality to be sold here at the bazaar. Such a design with those precious metals would be worn by a monarch or a…" He paused.

"A what, Warren?"

"Is that your family sword?"

Warren stepped back.

"Easy, Warren, I can feel your shock and worry as if it is my own. I asked you to take me away from the masses so I might escape those kinds of panicked feelings. I need time to—"

"You're a Valkyrie," he finally said.

Freyja had explained that she could not announce herself as such, that by doing so would make the bloodline weak. It had been a problem of old, and as the last living Valkyrie, she could not risk it. However, when a mortal man reached the conclusion himself, she would gain strength. Now that Warren realized what she was, she could openly speak about it.

"Yes, Warren, I am."

"Why didn't you—"

"I was no longer in the service of the gods that day you found me— that I staggered to the edge of your farm. In fact, I had just been released, returned to Midgard to live out my life."

"You knew."

"I did not." She shook her head. "You know how confused I was. I thought I was dead. I thought this was Hel. I did not know the truth until Freyja recalled me."

"That light…that was your ascension to Asgard?"

"It was."

Warren sat down across from her with a sigh and slumped into his chair.

"So the old gods *do* still exist. I cannot believe it. I have so much to ask."

"I cannot answer your questions, Warren. I must rest before I begin my search for Yrsa. She was taken by—"

"Yrsa! Curse me, Astrid. I lost her. I should never have left her side. I could not stop myself. I knew better, but I was drawn to you when you left, chasing Sven."

"Neither of us should have left my sister." Astrid frowned. "It's not your fault. Freyja's calling, you see, it affects the minds of mortals, filling them with lust."

Warren adjusted his manhood before replying, "So she lured you into the forest with Sven—"

"That was not Sven."

"So then it was Freyja who lured me out in the forest so that we could—"

"Focus, Warren. Yrsa was taken by the Ashvolk Demons. They seek Valkyrie blood."

"Are you saying she's a Valkyrie too?" Warren's voice elevated.

"Listen carefully. There was a time that we both were in the service of Freyja. At the moment, just I am, which means Yrsa is powerless and in grave danger."

"I will do whatever I can to help."

Warren began to stand, but Astrid pulled him back into his seat by his arm, a look of impatience on her face.

"First, I need you to listen."

Warren nodded. She wanted to keep her talk with him simple, so she began with Freyja's tale of the Ashvolk demons and how they had raided the lands of retired Valkyrie for decades. Warren had many questions, but Astrid did not answer them; there was no time.

"There are three different kinds of Ashvolk demons. The one we faced out in town was a soldier. Big, strong, single-minded, its only purpose is to fight and kill. I am told there are several more of these present in our area."

"Several more?"

"The other kind of Ashvolk demon serves as a spy or scout. They are intelligent and fast. These can alter their form using demon magic."

Warren looked appalled. "How so?"

"Their limbs can grow and stretch at will."

"And they all desire the blood of a Valkyrie? Your blood?"

Astrid nodded.

"Which leads me to the last of the Ashvolk, their leader. The thing was once a simple soldier, yet through the years, this one grew more powerful through the consumption of maiden blood. Now the lord of the Ashvolk demons is nearly strong enough to slay a god."

Warren shivered.

"They have Yrsa, but Freyja says they need me too. Only after consuming us both will the demon lord be at its fullest potential."

"So they'll be using Yrsa for bait," Warren concluded.

"They will."

Warren and Astrid sat in silence a moment. Astrid drank the remainder of the water while Warren sat still, wearing a ponderous look on his face that slowly turned to one of total horror.

"The slaughter we witnessed in the forest after Sven's death, was that—"

"That was the Ashvolk. They massacred all those people in search of Yrsa and I."

"If they are so powerful how can we stop them?"

The way he said "we" made her both concerned and mad. Astrid did not want him any more involved than he already was. Her mind was still a muddled mess of emotions and sensations. To top it off, there was some deeply evil energy in the storage cellar; *something worse happened here, something Warren has not told me. I sense agony and fright;* but there was another feeling that was so strong it made the water she drank taste sour.

"Warren, you need to check on Helen and Willa. Make sure they are unharmed."

"You are right." Warren stood quickly. "Will you be—"

"I will be fine here, go."

While he climbed the stairs out of the cellar, Warren called out, "I love you." The words sounded distantly familiar. She felt like she loved Warren but her mouth would not open and release the words. *Odin,* she prayed, *protect my heart through this transformation so I might keep a small portion of love inside it when this battle is over.*

With Warren gone, Astrid could finally relax. She did not want him to know she was in pain. The demon did not shed her blood, but her muscles ached as if she had fought all day. *Freyja*, she thought, *it will serve you well to send me the help I requested, or you might have to fight these demons yourself.*

Astrid sighed and stood. She could feel the leftover emotions in the cellar; they hung like the scent of death in the stagnate air. Several women had been tortured down here. Gathon did more than just trade slaves; he hurt these girls for pleasure. Had she known this before they fought, she would have made the extra effort to cut him where a man most fears a blade.

Astrid moved down the tunnel and read the past through her senses. She tracked the feelings of anguish like one followed the aroma of baking bread until she reached the end of the tunnel—the last room. Her eyes fixed to a straw bed that sat against the wall with several chains and a set of shackles strewn across it. This space, it was colder than the others, with a damp smell about it. It angered her, but the pureness of the fury felt good. *This place...I thought it stupid of Warren to bring me here, but now I know differently.*

CHAPTER 56

WARREN RETURNED TO GATHON'S CELLAR in the early hours of the night, his desire to see Astrid again as great as his need to tell her all he had seen. The town had settled, and to his surprise, many of the onlookers had dismissed what they saw. In fact, as unlikely as it might have seemed, Warren guessed more people had filled the town for the bazaar than fled it when the attack was over. Whether the king would arrive in the morning, Warren could not discern, as the advance guard was not eager to say one way or another. Regardless, he hoped the king would turn back.

His brother walked with him; no matter how much Warren begged Hammond to stay with the girls, he would not. His brother would not accept that Astrid was Valkyrie and had to see her for himself. His stubbornness infuriated Warren.

"She needs rest, Hammond. Do not pester her with questions."

"I only have the one."

"Well then be quick with it," Warren grumbled.

"What is eating you?" Hammond asked.

"Nothing."

"Are you sure?"

"I told you, nothing."

Astrid emerged from the back tunnel into the torchlight. Hammond would have spoken had his mouth been able to do anything other than just fall open. Astrid was the very image of a goddess. The length of her body sparkled in the firelight, and her hair was tied back in two long braids that were thick as rope. Hammond's eyes traveled up her body, tearing up at the sheer magnificence of her armor.

"Your chest—" Hammond began.

"Hammond!" Warren shouted.

"—armor. It's astounding." He imagined the metals in her coverings must cost a fortune.

"Oh."

"Wait, where are your wings?" Hammond asked.

Warren grunted and nudged Hammond.

"He does not believe that you have returned to us an ancient Asgardian Valkyrie. He argued my every point as we walked across town. He thinks I am drunk on brew."

"That's not entirely true. I can now agree with you, Warren, that Astrid's normal wealth of beauty has doubled."

"Thank you, Hammond." Astrid clearly enjoyed his compliment.

"That being said, there's no way you are a Valkyrie. The old gods—"

"Exist," Warren finished for his brother.

"I was going to say, they no longer send Valkyrie. You have fought dozens of battles, Brother. If there were beautiful shieldmaidens present on the battlefield, would you not have seen one already?"

Warren wiped his face, and pleaded, "Astrid, please tell him."

Hammond watched Astrid place her hands on her hips and nearly laugh.

"Regardless, old boy, I have seen a lot of Valkyrie art in my day…sold lots too. Paintings, drawings, pottery, all the likenesses depicted a half-naked woman with large feathered wings. Astrid is neither half-naked or winged. I am sorry—"

"Have you ever considered that the wings of a Valkyrie are only seen by dead or dying men?" Astrid interrupted. "Let me spill those swollen guts out of yours, Hammond, and I promise, as you die, you will see wings."

Hammond smiled, thinking her words a joke, but the way she placed her hand on her sword suggested more than just bravado.

"Hammond, why must you be so stubborn?"

"Me?"

"Yes." Warren nodded.

"You can call it stubbornness, but it is my unwillingness to make decisions based upon words that has made me such a good merchant. I like to see, feel, test the weight..."

After he followed Astrid's glance to Warren's sword belt, Hammond was not surprised when she said, "Warren, give your brother your dagger."

"Why?"

"Just do as I say."

Hammond grabbed it and waved it around as he spoke. "Fine craftsmanship. I gave this to him, but I fail to see what this proves."

Astrid took a sudden step toward Hammond. "It proves nothing... yet."

Astrid grabbed Hammond's thick wrist and directed the dagger into the curve of her inner thigh. Hammond could not stop it and watched with alarm as the knife scraped hard against Astrid's bare flesh.

"Where is the blood?"

She raised his hand, so he could see the blade, and replied, "No weapon in the hands of a mortal man can harm me."

"Amazing..." Hammond breathed, looking from her thigh to the clean edge of the dagger.

"Astrid, this is incredible. You did not tell me—" Warren began.

Hammond abruptly plunged the dagger into Astrid's stomach, where her midriff was bare of armor, only to find the dagger stopped again. No matter how hard he pressed forward, even when he added his other hand to the dagger's small handle to lean his full weight into it, he could not pierce her.

With a look of determination, Hammond prepared to strike again, but this time his attack was halted by Warren, who slammed him against the dirt wall.

"Off of me!" Hammond shouted.

"What are you thinking?" Warren snatched the dagger from his hand.

"The blade cannot pierce me. I am in no danger," Astrid stated. "Care to try?"

"No!"

"I figure Warren has a different weapon he desires to pierce you with. Right, Brother? That's why you are so irritable now, isn't it?"

"Shut your mouth, damn you."

"Damn me?" Hammond's face turned red and his arms began to shake. "I left you with a simple task: protect my family. You promised to keep Helen and Willa safe, but then you go and abandon them both."

"Just as *you* have abandoned them now?"

"How dare you?" Hammond grumbled.

"I kept them safe." Warren declared. "Were they hurt?"

"Lucky for you they were not." Hammond stated. "Now, I am forced to pay my men to keep them protected. You, Warren, the big, strong soldier, could not follow a simple command."

"Stop! I will hear no more," Astrid shouted.

Holding silent, the two brothers stared at each other.

"Hammond, please follow me. I need to speak with you alone."

Warren hated to watch his brother and Astrid turn their backs on him and walk down the tunnel. He hated it even more that he could not hear them speak.

What are they doing? Why did she take him down there and not me?

His jealousy began to flood his other senses. He wanted to call out to her, but to speak would shatter the silence, which had become as strong as steel and conversely comforted him. Instead, Warren thought of the fight with the demon. The thing had been so big and strong, not to mention terrifying to look at. If there were more of them out there, something needed to be done now.

It was not long before Hammond emerged from the shadows of the tunnel.

Something is wrong, my brother, he looks so sad and stern. What could Astrid have said to him?

"Warren, please join me," Astrid called out.

Warren watched his brother leave first, without a word.

"Warren?" Astrid called again.

"On my way."

Astrid stood in the back, the firelight painting her skin a orange hue; he would've sworn golden sparkles rose from it. She had her back turned to him as he approached, and Warren took the opportunity to steal a long look at her legs. He imagined them wrapped around him, her bare waist clutched in his hands, just above the crests of her hip bones. He wanted to dig his fingers into her warm flesh as he bent her over. As he closed the distance, his kokkr grew harder.

Was it the demon, fighting something so gruesome and horrifying, that has my blood stirring? Or is it finally meeting Astrid's true self that makes me want her all the more? Warren had questioned who she was since he had met her. Now that he knew, he realized that he had grown to love her regardless of who or what she was.

"I can feel your passion, Warren. Like heat off freshly baked bread, it comes off you in waves."

"Is that the power of a Valkyrie?"

Astrid smiled as she faced him. "All my powers, my strength and weaknesses, are unbalanced right now. The transformation from human, it is not instantaneous, but lucky for me, Freyja said it had not been long since my powers were removed, so returning them should be speedy."

"You *sound* like you are feeling better now."

"No, I am feeling worse. Are you listening to me, Warren? I am changing."

"Becoming a Valkyrie again. I stand impressed. You are lucky to have the old gods with you, Astrid." Warren placed his hands on her shoulders and leaned in to kiss her.

"Lucky?" She broke his hold. "Warren, you still do not understand."

"Then tell me. Together we can overcome anything, even demons."

"Warren, stop." She waved her hands up and down her body.

"Relax. The chaos has calmed in town. From what I overheard, people do not even know what they saw."

"No...listen to me."

"Astrid, you will be safe here until your strength has fully returned. I will guard you..."

Astrid merely sighed. "Warren—"

"Once rested, we will search for Yrsa together."

Warren's eyes drifted from her lips to her cleavage, and he once more became engulfed by his desire.

"Warren, listen to me."

"Sorry, Astrid, truly, I just cannot contain my love—"

"What I see in your eyes is *not* love."

"You're right. It is a burning desire that must be fed. And I only want to be fed by you."

Warren grasped Astrid by the waist and tried to pull her into him, but she held him back.

"Warren, you need to understand something. The more that returns of my former life, the less I care of the time I have spent here...with you. The more I become who I was, the less I will be who you know. I cannot promise you—"

"Reach deep down inside yourself, Astrid, underneath the rebuilding of a warrior of the gods to the woman who was mine and not theirs."

While her hands went to work with the fasteners of her armor, she said, "take me while you can, Warren. Make it fast, before I forget the value of mortal love."

CHAPTER 57

BEFORE ASTRID'S BREASTPLATE WAS OFF, Warren had lifted her skirt and entered her. The thickness of his kokkr was a surprise, even after it had been inside her not a half a day ago—she had simply forgotten its size. Its presence stole her breath, and when she inhaled again, her body shivered. Astrid had not expected to be joined while she still stood and found it remarkable.

She tilted her head down, resting her forehead on his chest and tried to focus. Each of his thrusts ended with a grunt. She did not need the powers given to her by Freyja to perceive that Warren was lost in pleasure.

With a hard twist and another tug, the armor that contained her full breasts was off and her soft flesh was promptly in his large hands.

"Enjoy them, Warren," she whispered with a hint of sadness in her voice. "Enjoy me."

Astrid turned, planted her hands on the dirty wall where two support beams braced the ceiling, and then welcomed him back inside her.

Attached to each beam in front of her was a metal chain, a rusty shackle at its end. Astrid had to keep their purpose far from her mind.

"I've never felt this way before, Astrid." Warren grunted through clenched teeth.

"Freyja's gift…" Astrid tried to explain, but her words turned to a moan. "Mortal men are weak in the presence of her powers."

Freyja's words rang in her ears: *"Virtuous men, especially soldiers, will follow your every command as long as your will does not go against their true nature."*

"Chain yourself," Astrid ordered.

"Chain...myself?"

"Aye, take these shackles and connect them to your wrists, Warren. Do it."

Astrid was surprised that connecting the shackles did not slow his thrusts. The rattle of the chains was as loud as the slap of Astrid's buttocks against Warren's lower abdomen. The chains on the shackles were long, long enough to reach the bed or walk straight out from the wall a good ten paces. At the moment, the cold chains rubbed against her legs and drug on the ground as Warren gripped her waist and squeezed tight—*the man mates like a wild animal. His lust is nearly overpowering.*

Astrid grabbed the keys hanging off a nail and palmed them. "Lay down so I might mount you."

When Warren withdrew himself, he left a tender ache in his absence. Astrid looked at him as he lay so anxiously waiting that he patted his muscled thighs with his hands. It was in that moment that Astrid was confident she had made the right decision.

Warren may be furious, but I pray this gift helps ease him.

Carefully, Astrid mounted Warren, her hand gripped around his manhood to guide it back inside her. No sooner did his tip touch her wetness than he plunged deep inside.

"Slow."

"I cannot control myself. I need you, Astrid."

Astrid lay down on Warren and breathed heavily into his neck. She had succumb to arousal too now—the sensation so great she never wanted it to stop—just build and build; but she had to regain her focus. Warren's hands squeezed tighter around her waist. *There...think of his hands...their grip on me.*

His strong hands would have left bruises, she realized, had it been possible for a Valkyrie to be hurt by a mortal's touch. Regardless, Astrid began to feel slightly sore where his fingers dug into her waist, so she pushed his hands down over the belt of her leather skirt.

Astrid cleared her mind long enough to look up and focus on the shackle around his right hand. It was closed but not locked. Arms outstretched, the key still hidden in her hand, she inserted the metal shaft into the hole, and with a slight turn, the shackle was now locked tight.

"Astrid!" Warren yelled in pleasure.

He wrapped his arms around Astrid's waist and squeezed her as he released. Then, with one last thrust, he palmed the back of her head, and buried her nose into his collar.

"Warren."

"Yes, Astrid?"

"I am sorry."

"Sorry? You were perfect."

She pulled back to make eye contact with him, reached up, and locked the last shackle.

"I'm sorry that you cannot come with me to search for Yrsa. I'm sorry that I had to trick you."

"What?"

Astrid jumped up. With sword and breastplate in hand, she tried to regain her composure.

"Astrid, what's happening here?"

Back turned to him, she strapped her breastplate on.

"I realized as we talked earlier that if I waited much longer, I probably would have had you join me in the fight. The demons are powerful—and you would've died. I did not—*do not*—want you to die, Warren."

"To fight is my decision." Warren rattled his chains loudly as he stood.

"No longer. I have taken you out of the fight."

"Astrid, you cannot do this to me."

"I already have."

"You would leave me in a slaver's dungeon while you fight? You would have me stay here while you risk your life?"

What a sight he was, pants-less, still moist from their lovemaking. *He is not a warrior*, Astrid told herself. *I need a true champion for this battle.*

"I instructed your brother to find his family and take refuge in this place until the demons are all defeated. When it is safe above, I will return."

"If you live. What if you die, Astrid?"

"If I die, you all die."

CHAPTER 58

WHEN ASTRID REENTERED TOWN, SHE wore the cloak that Warren had stolen for her, with hopes to not cause a stir. It was true what Warren had claimed: the townsfolk had fared better after this ordeal than expected. Although the bazaar portion of the festival was closed for the evening, there seemed to be large groups of people around fires, for meals. As she passed a group of fifty or more men, she heard the familiar sound of a tall tale being told. There was no sign of panic here as far as she could tell.

After witnessing a demon, shouldn't they be scared? Or do the demons have the same powers I do, do those who witness them soon forget?

In search of some sign of upset, Astrid moved around the town. There were a lot of people present; she should have found at least one mourning the death of a relative or friend. As she made her way to where the demon was defeated, she searched for those grieving the dead. She finally heard a shout from a young woman, and dashed through crowd, until she found something entirely unexpected.

At the center of the crowd stood her youngest brother, Jokul, his cheek freshly slapped red. He wore his battle armor decorated with the symbol of the sons of Kol and carried his two-handed family sword—just as when she'd last seen him. His furs—which were a bit much for this temperate night—and his size—being a good foot and a half taller than most—made him look out of place, but there were enough other strangers in Grømstad that he would blend in. At least she hoped.

"I asked Freyja to release the brother who killed the Ashvolk demon in Birka and instead she teases me by sending you?" Astrid said in greeting.

Jokul smiled as he watched his sister approach.

"Hail, Astrid the White," he cheered.

"Did Freyja send you back so you could chase women?"

"No, but I have been gone from Midgard a long time, Astrid. I cannot decide which I want to hunt more: deer or the freckle-faced maiden who slapped me."

"Always looking to plunge your arrow into the backside of some young hide…that is my brother Jokul," Astrid cracked.

Arms open, Jokul announced, "I have missed you so, Sister."

"I have missed you too, Brother."

Their embrace reminded Astrid of the last time she had held him in her arms: his death.

"My sister, the Valkyrie."

"You know?"

"Aye. I remember it all."

"I wish I could say the same. I'm just beginning to…" Astrid started to make sense of the odd vision she had of Jokul as an old man as they hugged. "I ushered you to Valhalla."

"You did."

"You were old and that trimmed beard of yours was long and grey," Astrid remarked, finally remembering. "You were as handsome as father."

"Aye, last survivor of our immediate family. But don't you worry. The Kol bloodline lives on. You see, I cluttered the countryside with my seed, had at least eighteen children"—Jokul laughed—"that I know of."

"Ulf always liked to say, 'Like a bee, Jokul is gone before the ladies know what stung them.'"

Astrid stared at her brother's face. He was young again; Freyja had returned him in his prime. The red splotch on his face, above his thick blonde facial hair, had already begun to fade. In his youth, Jokul had never worn a long or bushy beard; he bragged that his face was too good-looking to hide. Astrid agreed and liked to joke that he was the prettiest in the family. Still, Astrid never understood why he cared so much about his beard when he never brushed his hair, which was as long as hers and the same bright color. Even now it appeared knotted and tangled. She would offer to brush it later if all turned out well. *Perhaps,* she thought, *without my other brothers around to mock him, he might let me.*

Jokul went back to staring meditatively off into the distance.

"The mountains are all wrong here," he stated, as he glared out in the direction the snowcapped peaks should have been.

Astrid nodded in agreement and asked, "You truly killed the demon in Birka?"

"Who else did you think performed such a magnificent deed?"

"Well…"

He patted the flat of his sword on his gloved hand.

"I slew it with this very blade. Nevertheless, when the ever-lovely Goddess Freyja paid us a visit, she asked which brother could sneak past Odin's guard to escape."

"Ah, with that, the decision was easily made."

"You know me," Jokul said, "at home underground."

"You must tell me where you faced the demon. How did you fight it? What happened in Birka that night?" Astrid fired at him.

"Do we have time?"

"Yes and no. The demons have Yrsa, but the goddess thinks they will not harm her until they have me too."

"They set a fine trap," Jokul said, his attention clearly split as he looked about more.

"That they did," Astrid said with a nod.

"Freyja told me much but kept as much from me."

"Then let us compare quickly."

As a crowd passed by, Jokul rubbed his ear and frowned.

"Perhaps after a few mugs this buzzing in my ears will go away."

"You have the buzzing?" Astrid asked as she remembered the sensation.

"It did not begin until I started talking to that young woman." When he pointed his sword at her, the woman shied away with a giggle.

"Trust me, it will end soon." Astrid placed a hand on his big shoulder. "It *is* very good to see you again, Jokul."

"It is good to see you too, Astrid."

Astrid slowly led Jokul to the old building across town. She was happy to find her brother so strong and prepared, but if he felt at all as she did when she had first returned, then she knew he was just as confused.

"This is not our year," Astrid stated.

"I had guessed as much. Not our year and not our home."

"Aye."

"Home. In Valhalla 'home' has a different meaning. Feels like ages since I thought of Birka so longingly," Jokul replied.

"Wish I could say the same. Birka has been on my mind with nearly every breath I take."

"You always loved that place more than any other," Jokul smiled fondly. "You should know this, Astrid, Father is extremely proud that his daughters were choosers of the slain, Valkyrie. He brags to all that will hear his voice in Valhalla."

Astrid stopped dead in her tracks. "Are you sure he's proud?"

"The amount of pride he owns outweighs all the coin in Birka's treasury."

She knew he did not mean to, but Jokul had struck a nerve, but he quickly changed the subject.

"So where are the others? Freyja said we would have at least one more here to help us. She might even have let it slip that there was a man, a lover—"

"He will not be aiding us."

"Why not? Tell me you did not bed a coward."

"Jokul, stop."

"Ah, it has been a long time since my ears heard that tone, my sister," Jokul nodded. "Very well."

A moment of silenced passed as they continued their walk. Astrid could feel Jokul's eyes on her.

"Spit it out before I punch you in the nose."

"Astrid the White, the fifth son of Kol, has a lover. I always thought you would die a virgin."

"I did."

This time Jokul came to a stop.

"You died, wait, I thought…I mean Freyja did not have time to explain it all to me, but…"

"It's a long story."

Suddenly, it seemed as though the amount of people in town suddenly had doubled or even tripled. It looked like the roast, which had been planned and then canceled, was back on. Astrid overheard one man, a royal guard, saying that the king would arrive midmorning. *Why have they not warned the king? Why would they allow him to come to this place after what has happened? If they are so determined to have this festival now, let them try—as long as they stay out of my way when the fighting starts.*

"I am feeling stronger by the moment," Jokul stated.

"Good. As soon as you are right, we must begin our search for Yrsa."

"Aye, after a drink or two, I wager I will be fine." Jokul smiled. "This reminds me of that time we all got sick the night before that raid. Do you remember, Astrid? Only Vignir could stand—"

"Tell me, how did you come to face the demon?"

"Aye, the fight." Jokul nodded deeply. "After getting Gyrd and the kids to safety, I returned for you and Yrsa. I found the thing in the tunnels. It was tall and skinny, and I would not have seen it hiding in the shadows if it had not been moving so erratically, twitching."

The tunnels under Birka had been built hundreds of years before the fortress. The legends stated they were there when the city was no more than a village and were built by the gods themselves so that Odin could sneak in and out to take his pick of women. Jokul knew the tunnels well—so well he took wagers all the time that he could traverse the long and twisting corridors blindfolded. He liked to tell his friends he was born in the ancient tunnels, though it was not true.

After he had helped Gyrd and Yrsa's children escape, he had sprinted down the tunnels back to the fortress. His brothers were set to defend their father, and he would have liked to have been with them; if the sons of Kol were to die that night, it should be at each other's side, he thought. Nevertheless, his father had given him a strict order.

The torches at the opposite end of the tunnel had blown out though no breeze blew down there, especially not strong enough to extinguish a flame. The thought stuck in his head.

Jokul moved quickly, staring into the dark of the tunnel until he spotted movement. Jokul, a skilled huntsman who often enjoyed a midnight hunt with his brother Hak, knew his eyes had not played a trick on him. Something solid had moved across the corridor.

Jokul continued to the exit, slowing his pace slightly, so as to not give away that he knew something was there—his senses were at their sharpest. Doing his best to block out the sound of his boots as they slammed against the stone floor and echoed down the hall, he listened for breathing.

"Ho there?"

Close to where he thought he had seen something, he smelled burned, damp wood. Jokul slowed even more, to a measured jog, his eyes fixed on a shadow-filled alcove where a torch should have glowed. He watched the wispy smoke vapors rise from the air, and the shadows themselves seemed to pulsate.

No one should be in the tunnels but him.

"Die!" Jokul shouted as he plunged his sword into the shadows.

As he withdrew his sword, he saw no blood; only a shiny black substance coated the tip. Suddenly, from the deep shadows staggered one of Birka's gate guards, a man he knew by name. Jokul had made a dire mistake, but his mind returned to why the man was down there. The tunnel was so dark that the man's face was hard to read, but Jokul could see his mouth was open, as if to say something.

"Tuvid? Oh, no. Tell me I haven't wounded you too badly."

Tuvid stumbled forward and stood in what little light remained, but it was enough for Jokul to see the man was already dead; his jaw hung open lifelessly and he had a wound the size of a fist in his belly and another on his leg.

"What…"

Tuvid's body fell forward, and dropped to the floor not a foot from Jokul. The smell of burnt corpses began to overwhelm him, and as he stepped away, he caught a hint of movement, a twitch from the dead man's back. Suddenly reduced to a mound of oozing black oil, Tuvid's body melted away and up from the puddle on the ground stretched a large black spike. Had he not seen it a breath earlier, Jokul knew it would have impaled him on the opposite wall.

It slammed into the stone so deep it dislodged mortar that had held tight for many centuries. No sooner did it strike than it withdrew and returned in the form of two spikes—aimed for Jokul's head.

"What ungodly thing are you?" Jokul yelled as he parried both spikes.

From the puddle rose a tall figure, black oil dripping from its limps; the thing had red eyes and a latticework of glowing lines across its shiny body. It nearly stood as tall as the tunnel itself.

"Has Hel sent her minions to Birka?"

Jokul was shocked when his hardest swing was deflected with a swipe of its long, wiggling arm. The clash of his weapon against it chimed so loudly it was almost too much to bear.

Again and again, Jokul swung his sword, unable to find the monster's weakness. It blocked all his attacks with both arms, as they elongated, shrunk, went as rigid as spears or loose as whips at any given moment. Backed into the wall, Jokul had a grave thought flash through his mind; *if I fail, if I die here, then my sisters might also die.* He could not let that happen.

Blood spurted from a wound on his arm and Jokul turned the pain into rage. He launched himself at the monster, tackling it, and hacking away at the thing's chest and neck with a dagger from his boot. Surprisingly, it did not fight back.

Jokul stood up, thinking it dead. Covered in sticky black goo, he gazed at the thing's wounds. The hole he had seen in the gate guard's belly—the monster had a similar wound, identical he would wager. While he stared, it began to melt, the features of its monstrous face faded before his eyes. But before it could disappear he lopped its head off. It was dead now; he was sure of it.

By the way his hands shook as he told the tale, Astrid could tell it was a memory full of horrors. Jokul may have liked to boast about women, but fighting was serious to him. He did not take as much pleasure in a kill as her older brothers did, though it was rumored that he kept a tally of the lives he claimed. She wondered why, if it was not to brag, but never asked him. Hak had told her once that Jokul wished to repay each death. It was an honorable thought, but equally foolish; a life could only be repaid with another.

By the end of Jokul's story, they had reached the door to the Grömsala. Astrid watched as his eyes traced the building's every detail, and she could not help but wonder if her brother would find it as similar to home as she did.

As he opened the door, a scream rang out from the forest.

Astrid and her brother looked at each other. As much as Jokul wanted a drink and Astrid wanted more answers, they both needed to know what the scream meant.

"Let's make haste." Astrid drew her sword and kept it at the ready.

As they ran, they abandoned their riding cloaks, the heavy wool and fur only slowing them down.

"Help her, please!" a man's voice called from nearby.

"What happened?" Jokul asked as they approached.

"I was relieving myself when I heard moans. I found her. She's bleeding out."

"Where?" Astrid impatiently asked.

"I-I swear, I saw the trees move, as if they walked away from her." The man shook as he said.

"Calm down," Jokul grasped the panicked man's shoulder.

"So much blood!"

"Quiet," Jokul shushed him.

"The Ashvolk are near," Astrid whispered to her brother.

"Their trap is set," Jokul agreed.

"Where?" Astrid asked the man again, yanking on his wrist. "Tell me where!"

"Twenty paces forward, maybe another ten to the right."

Astrid and Jokul entered the forest as soon as the man was done. Jokul took the lead, his movement calculated and precise. He was the better hunter. Crouched down, her brother ran his gloved fingers across the grass and dirt. Then, fingers to his nose, he sniffed as he rubbed them together.

"Blood."

Astrid looked over Jokul's head as tree limb swung down at him.

"Look out!" She shoved him forward, taking the brunt of the strike across her chest.

Astrid fell backward as her brother rolled to his feet. She understood now. The tree was not a tree; it was a demon. All of a sudden, the thing took shape; it's body, black as the night sky, vibrated.

"Careful of its arms!" Jokul yelled over his shoulder.

His warning came not a moment too soon. The Ashvolk demon reshaped its arms into three tentacles on each side. The limbs writhed like snakes until the arms lashed out at Astrid and Jokul. One of the vine-like limbs swept Astrid's feet out from under her the moment she stood.

"Don't look it directly in the eyes!"

"What?" Astrid hacked at the limb that had tripped her as it slithered about.

"Trust me."

After rolling backward over her shoulder, Astrid was able to finally stand out of range of the demon's tentacles.

"Anything else I should know?"

The demon turned into an ooze-like substance as Astrid spoke, and poured into the ground where it instantly soaked into the earth.

"Indeed, much more."

Back to back, the two scanned the perimeter, awaiting the demon's return. Astrid breathed heavily until the ground rumbled—an attack—yet where one of the tall, scout demons was expected, two appeared.

"It's here."

"Here too."

"Do we face two or one of these demons split in half?" Astrid asked her brother.

"I do not know, but I will ask the beast when my sword is hands deep in its chest."

Astrid smiled.

"Fight well, Brother."

"Die brave, Sister."

The glow from Astrid's armor intensified as she charged the tall demon, and the demon shielded its eyes as it hissed at her. Astrid averted her gaze from the beast's gaze and focused on her new target: its legs.

Before she could reach the demon, multiple tentacles had sprung from each of its arms, a net created instantly. The demon dropped its meshed limbs over her head to ensnare her, but Astrid ducked under it while she raised her sword. With the tip of her blade up, she cut the web, and the severed pieces fell behind her where they wiggled on the ground.

Unable to get her sword into position for a kill shot, Astrid settled for a glancing blow across the demon's shiny, smooth shoulder. Her blade scored its flesh; the skin peeled open like a grape and spilled radiant red blood. Before she could take another swing at it, the monster reformed its damaged limbs into a ball and struck her with it like a giant mace.

Her breath was forced through her teeth and her vision went black as she flew through the air into a thick tree. Astrid grunted as she tried to stand, but she was seeing double. When her vision returned to normal, she watched Jokul attacking with both sword and axe, swinging wildly at the demon he fought. *Where did it go? Where's my opponent?*

Astrid watched the rustling of leaves at her feet as what looked like a black briar sprouted. The vine shot up and lashed her from hip to jaw. Dazed, droplets of blood spilled from her chin to her chest.

Astrid adjusted her grip on her sword and inspected the tentacle that entangled her right foot from boot to midthigh. She plunged her sword into the ground, retrieved her dagger from her belt, and began hacking at the limb, but as she did so, another one gripped her left leg.

"Jokul!"

Her brother stood in what appeared to be a pile of severed demon appendage, but the thing still came at him, still pressed forward. Years of her father's instruction returned, his voice clear in her head. The demon that fought Jokul did not want to win the battle; it only wished to divert attention, keep him busy so the other one could seize her.

Another two snake-sized vines wrapped themselves around her boots; she was caught, and if she did not free herself soon…

At her feet, the black oil returned, oozing up around her. Soon she was ankle deep in it; she could feel herself sinking, and no matter how fast she cut, she was not able to escape.

"You will not take me, demon!"

Bubbles popped at the surface of the oil as the demon's features slowly rose to the top. When it was a fully formed face, it opened its mouth again. As it spoke to her, Astrid's ears buzzed.

"…with your blood our lord will be strong enough."

"No, I will not be eaten!" Astrid screamed.

Astrid wanted to jump from the oil, but her legs were sunk now nearly to her knees.

"Odin, give me the strength!"

With a burst of golden light, Astrid felt a sudden weight at her back and a gentle shove; it was her wings. With two flaps, her wings pulled her out of the oil and lifted her a foot off the ground. Now, as she looked at her wings, she remembered their gloriousness; the sensation of flight was as grand as anything she had ever known. Yet, with a span of nearly twenty feet, it was difficult to flap them in the confinement of the dense forest.

"Astrid!" Jokul yelled in surprise.

The demon he fought lashed out with its last tentacles, staggering him, but Jokul did not fall; instead, he lodged his axe into its back as it turned to face Astrid.

"This one fights harder than the one in the tunnel, but it will meet the same fate."

From the oil beneath her, two spindly arms grabbed for her feet, but she was ready and sliced them off as soon as they touched her.

"This one seems invincible!"

"It needs to take shape. Then you need to damage it enough…take its head."

Astrid flapped her wings again, rising higher until she collided with a low branch and dropped her sword. The weapon fell, point first, into the oil and the demon screeched in pain, retracting its limbs.

Bit by bit, the Ashvolk scout rose from the black oil; its long arms grabbed at the ground as the puddle receded. Astrid's hand dove into her boot for her dagger, but these were not her bearskins. As she floated above the demon, she realized she was weaponless…

But her hands tingled and had a curious golden glow. She pressed her palms together and remembered: her holy spear. She pulled her hands apart and in between them formed the long metal shaft of a spear, which crackled with golden energy.

The Ashvolk scout was all but out of the puddle of oil now, only his left leg remained, his red eyes set, his purpose clearly to attack.

Her spear in one hand, Astrid flapped her wings hard twice, and fell on the demon below with her spear, driving it through the demon's chest and pinning it to the moist ground.

She left the demon trapped by her spear, lifted her sword off the ground, and swung her blade straight through the neck of her sinister opponent.

As soon as she knew it was dead, Astrid refocused on Jokul's fight. Her brother had chopped off the last of the demon's tentacles as it flapped about, and finally drove his sword through its open mouth; tearing its head in two.

"You fought well, Sister," Jokul said as he approached her, his eyes on her wings.

"You too."

"Many thanks to you." He patted her shoulder as he moved around her.

After two deep breaths, she asked, "Your meaning?"

"I was feeling weak there for a moment, but seeing you...your wings, that glowing spear, the way you fought...I swear to Odin, you gave me extra vigor."

Astrid nodded as she wrenched her mind out of the battle just fought. "Where does the blood trail lead, Brother?"

"This way." He pointed.

Astrid sheathed her sword and picked up her spear. *How do I return this...where do I return this?* she asked herself while examining at her hands. *Freyja's powers are not giving me my memory back quick enough.* Astrid knew Freyja had not shared all the information. *Perhaps there's something she does not want me to remember.*

"Astrid, look!"

Jokul pointed to a pair of legs stretched out, motionless, on the forest floor. The rest of the body could not be seen from where they stood, but by the bright red blood that coated the bare legs from inner thigh to ankle, Astrid had little hope the woman was alive.

"Do you think more demons are here, waiting for us?"

"Most likely."

"How do you want to proceed, Astrid?"

The longer Astrid looked at the woman's legs, the more enraged she became. Man or demon, no matter, the way they subjugated women with violence sickened her. *The cellar—that horrid place—it will empower me further against the rest of the demons.*

"I must see if she's alive."

"Such blood loss, I highly doubt—"

"Jokul, I must."

"Withdraw your wings. The way they shimmer, even a blind man could spot them from leagues away."

With a sigh, and a gaze over her shoulder, she replied, "I wish I knew how."

"Pull them back into your body." Jokul pointed to two slits in her armor at her back.

"I'm trying," Astrid said, frustration mounting. "Forget it. Let them come."

Astrid stepped out of the tall brush where they had hidden, and brazenly walked a direct path to the woman. If this was a trap and more demons attacked, she would face them proudly—*to kill demons was the reason Freyja sent me back to Midgard. So be it.*

When Astrid finally reached the woman, her breath was stolen at the sight. The injured woman was none other than Yrsa. Blood spilled from a large open wound across her sister's stomach to pool where she had been laid out in the bushes.

"Jokul, it's her. It's Yrsa!"

Jokul ran over as Astrid reached into Yrsa's wound, although the hollowness of the cavity was a clear indication that her baby was gone, she had to be sure.

"Gods no."

"Yrsa, Sister, I never should have left your side today. I should've been here to protect you." Astrid brushed the blood-stained and sticky hair from her sister's face.

"Astrid she—"

"The Ashvolk tore her baby out," Astrid spit with anger.

"They killed her," Jokul muttered.

"No, look. Her lips yet quiver. She lives."

"Not for long, Astrid." Jokul pointed. "She's been disemboweled."

Astrid did not listen to her brother.

"Yrsa, hear my voice. Do not die; stay strong."

Astrid dropped to her knees in the pool of her sister's lifeblood. She placed one hand on Yrsa's chest and the other below the large gash in her belly.

"Astrid—"

"I can save her, Jokul. Freyja gives all her followers the ability to heal—"

"You know this is a trap." He raised his voice as he looked about. "They hope to kill one sister with the body of another."

"Jokul! Silence while I remember how to do this."

"The demons—"

"Watch our backs!"

The golden light filled her hands as she touched her sister's cold flesh. *Jokul's right, but I must try.* Astrid steadied her shaking hands, and pushed them tight to her sister's body. *Yrsa will not die today.*

Astrid focused on the love she had for her family. Her kin were what mattered most to her. Astrid could see Freyja's gift at work through her tear-filled eyes. It warmed Yrsa's skin where her hands were pressed and slowly the bloody wound closed until it vanished from existence.

"Is she—?" Jokul asked, while he tracked movement in the distance.

"She will live."

"Can we move her?"

"I think so."

"Then we best hurry. Something massive moves our way."

CHAPTER 59

ASTRID FOLLOWED JOKUL BACK TOWARD town with her sister in her arms. Yrsa's dress, what was left of it, was tattered and blood soaked. With her head turned to the side, her hair matted across her face, and her arms and legs dangling so, Yrsa appeared dead. Astrid's healing touch had mended her wounds, but she was still weak from loss of blood. She needed shelter, water, and care, and Astrid knew where that all could be found.

While she healed Yrsa, her wings had receded into her back and Astrid wondered if the two powers—healing and flying—may coincide. It would be good to know. Astrid hated being at such a disadvantage, *until I remember more, I will have to rely on my old skills as a fighter, and that does not bother me at all.*

Once out of the forest, Jokul looked back and grunted. "I have never been so afraid of a forest before in my life."

It made her think back to the moment the mere sight of the dark trees had made her panic; there was evil in the woods. She was sure of it, and now she knew what it was.

"It must be the demons. I am surprised you sense it too," she replied. "Are you certain we are not being followed, Brother?"

Jokul laughed nervously but quickly caught himself and reined it in.

"With the amount of blood Yrsa is leaving on the ground, a sightless rat could track us."

"We better hurry then. The battle is surely upon us."

It had not been their purpose, but they reentered town where it was most busy. Torches burned all over, and the scent of roasted meat was thick in the air. It must have been midnight, and the festivities were at a new peak. More tents lined the town's edge in the distance, and by Astrid's estimate, it seemed that nearly twice as many people milled about now than during the day. *Where did all these new people come from?* she wondered, trying to take a rough count.

"Y-Yrsa?"

She had only just stepped out of the shadows a moment ago, but already all eyes were on her and her sister. Jokul placed himself in front of them, but it was too late. Hundreds of voices could be heard now, but one was louder than the rest: Emmerich.

"Is she dead?"

Emmerich stepped out from the crowd and lowered his hood. He looked close to tears, a total contradiction to what Astrid knew of him.

"Emmerich," Astrid grumbled. "You cowardly bastard."

The bandit leader did not pause in his approach; he did not show distaste for Astrid's insult or concern for his own safety. He had eyes only for Yrsa.

"What happened? Did she die in child birth?"

"You risk your life being here now, Emmerich."

"Please, you must tell me what happened to her...I...I loved her."

"You what?"

Astrid was so puzzled, she did not order Jokul to kill the bandit leader. Instead, she stood still while the man closed the distance, hand outstretched to touch Yrsa's face.

"What happened to my beloved goddess?"

For days, Astrid wanted nothing more than to stab him through his heart, but the look of concern and sadness in his eyes stayed her hand. *Emmerich must be spellbound by the last remnants of Freyja's powers*, she thought as a scowl formed on her face. *There's no way this wicked man could have true feelings for her.*

"She had her baby cut out of her. She-she nearly died."

Emmerich's pained eyes searched for a wound. "I see only layers of blood, no—"

"I healed her." Astrid lowered her voice so only he would hear her.

Emmerich looked Astrid up and down, shook his head, and took a step back. "What is happening here?"

"Enough." Astrid gave him a look she hoped would stop him. "As much as I want to cut off your kokkr and feed it to the dogs, that must wait. I need to take my sister to safety, so leave my sight."

Astrid took several steps around Emmerich before he spoke again. "No."

"Did you not hear my sister, you troll bastard?"

Jokul drew his sword and pointed it at Emmerich's chest. His action started a domino effect; suddenly, throughout the crowd, several hundred men threw back their hoods and raised hidden arms, weapons of all means from bows to axes and swords.

"So, that is your game. Your army has been here all along," Astrid stated.

"Since nightfall."

"For what gain?" she asked. "To steal the coin made at this bazaar?"

"Does it matter?" Emmerich answered hardheartedly.

"You two might want to wage this disagreement later. A much larger problem approaches." Jokul pointed to the treetops where he and Astrid had exited the forest moments ago. "Do you not see it? The trees bend, yet there's not a hint of breeze. No, something else is moving them— something colossal."

Her brother's outstretched finger pointed to the general direction of the commotion. When the ground beneath their feet began to rumble, Astrid spotted movement across the fields adjacent to the town.

"Something else comes, Astrid. Several targets, like wild boar they run—parting the tall grass."

Astrid shivered. "I see them."

"Let me carry her." Jokul's sounded eager. "She must be heavy."

"I have her. It is my duty."

Astrid began to step away when Emmerich shouted, "Do not turn your back on me! Men, be ready!"

"Listen to me, Emmerich! There are demons here, ones that wish to consume my and my sister's blood. To do so will make them so strong they can defeat the gods."

"You truly want me to believe that nonsense?"

"I don't care what you believe, you are nothing to me," Astrid explained. "The demons will slaughter everyone, destroy everything."

"Madness."

A crash echoed from the forest as a large tree fell, several others following it.

"Consider yourselves warned," Astrid shouted to the bandits that surrounded her. "I would kill you all myself, but there's no time. I will have to take comfort in the fact that the demons will no doubt dine upon all your flesh tonight."

"What—" Emmerich began.

"You are lucky my arms are full," Astrid interrupted.

She once more began her march toward Gathon's supply cellar, her mind on the many ways she would have liked to kill Emmerich.

"What can I do?" Emmerich called out.

Astrid stopped, Jokul's eyes on her. She wondered what he thought, what their father would have done in this moment.

"Speak, but chose your words carefully. They are your last."

"What can I do to help?" Emmerich's voice softened.

Astrid placed her sister in her brother's arms and stomped over to Emmerich. While looking him in the eye she shoved him to the ground.

"You? You cut my throat, you made me question the world I live in, and now you wish to help me?"

"Not you...her. I want to help my beloved Yrsa."

"Your beloved?" Astrid's heartbeat accelerated. "You want to help her? *You* kept her prisoner!"

"I loved her."

"You raped her!"

"I loved her! I would do anything to keep her safe!"

"There's no time for this," Jokul said to Astrid. "The battle begins now."

Astrid exhaled, frustrated. "Do you remember your way to Gathon's cellar? The place where *he* was trading *you* slaves?"

Emmerich sneered but she had left him no choice but to answer. "Yes."

"Then take my sister there. She needs rest."

"And my men? How can they help?"

"Order half of them to defend against whatever it is that advances through the tall grass north of here. Tell the other half to move the citizens and visitors down into their cellars for protection."

The rumble under their feet grew louder. Screams of fear could be heard around town. Astrid looked at her brother, Jokul had not taken his eyes off the trees as they bent in the distance. He was right, she knew it; there was no time for this.

"Give her to me," Emmerich said to Jokul, but he only responded with a cross look that would have frightened most men.

"Do it," Astrid commanded her brother.

"Hurt her and Astrid will be the least of your worries."

After he placed Yrsa in Emmerich's arms, Jokul withdrew a dagger and ran it across the bandit leader's outer thigh, above his knee. The cut was shallow, but it was enough to slice his leathers and cause a bleed.

"What the—"

"I know your blood now, little man," Jokul said.

Carefully, he ran the flat end of the blade over his tongue.

"I will find you…no matter where you run."

Bewildered, Emmerich stood in silence.

"Go!" Astrid shouted.

As Emmerich rushed off in the direction of Gathon's cellar, Astrid heard him relay his new commands to his soldiers. His people, they were everywhere Astrid looked; they would have taken the town and killed the king for sure.

"More men on our side. You made a wise decision not killing him," Jokul laughed. "Have faith, Astrid, we might live through this after all."

"I believe I have seen what the demon lord does to men like this. *They* will be slaughtered."

"Well, then you best know what *you* are doing."

"I do, Brother. We fight like this place is our home."

Jokul nodded.

"I was not given a chance to defend Birka from these wretched things," Astrid stated, a sneer on her face. "I owe them."

"Aye, we both do."

CHAPTER 60

EMMERICH'S BANDITS CARRIED OUT HIS orders as well as any conscripted army. It was good to see, as the sense of dread of the citizenry and bazaar was all around her. Still, Astrid held strong. She marched confidently across Grømstad to the town hall in search of the elders.

Did they flee at the first sign of danger? Will they be here? She was unsure. *Their voices might cut through the growing panic and help bring some much-needed order to the town. I hope.*

The closer she got, the more she could sense something different and nevertheless familiar. A distant pulse of power grew stronger with each step. *Is this yet another of my abilities being born in to existence? What draws me here?*

Screams broke her concentration. Jokul and the bandits had begun to engage whatever it was that moved in the tall grass north of town. She would have liked to fight alongside her brother, but she knew he was capable enough to fend for himself.

"Fight brave, Brother."

"Brace yourselves!" Jokul shouted as the things in the tall grass reached the dirt path he and the bandits were on.

All was calm for a moment, long enough for a few of the bandits to drop their guards. Then, suddenly, the unseen foes sprung from the grass, and, with long frog-like tongues, the beasts snapped and lashed out at them with incredible speed.

"Sea serpents!" one bandit yelled.

"On land?"

"Where did they come from?"

The beasts were long, the tips of their tails still hidden in the grass on the other side of the path when they struck across it, rearing their heads back to strike again. Jokul figured the demons were easily thirty feet in length. The main section of the serpent's body was segmented, like an earthworm, but covered with thick grey scales. A sword would do the beasts no damage, nor an axe. Not even fire, he surmised, since these creatures were born from Hel's own flames.

Jokul stood at the rear of the line watching the three serpents snap down in violent strikes, man after man crushed in their jaws or tossed in the air to heights no man could survive a fall from.

He motioned for archers and watched the first volley strike and then ricochet off the serpents' thick, ash-colored hides. It was not until an arrow struck between the largest beast's scales that he saw one injured. There it was: a small weakness. He breathed a sigh of relief.

"Spears, rush them with spears! Attack from behind! Aim for the space between their scales!"

Jokul found himself in command again; it had been a long time, and when he had last done so, he had not looked or felt so young. The sensation was exhilarating. The men around him rushed off, back into town where the weapons dealers were, filling their arms with as many spears as they could carry, while the front line tried their best to hold back the serpents' advance.

Jokul cringed as one man was ripped in half. His guts sprayed the ranks; it reminded him of the day he and Ulf had fought back to back, their axes raining gore down on each other after each chop. How he would have loved to have one of his brothers there to see him now. Over his shoulder, he searched the area for Astrid; she was gone on her mission, not there to witness his glory either.

The guards were no longer at the entrance to the town hall, so Astrid walked through the main doors unmolested. Her armor sparkled and lit her way in the darkness, until she reached the elders' room, which had a single candle aflame on the center desk.

"I was right to name you shieldmaiden." It was the only elder to remain in the meeting hall, her voice loud and strong, her words clear.

"I am Valkyrie if that is your meaning."

"You know it was, or you would not have risked yourself by saying it." The elder's voice cracked. "I see your armor was returned to you, and you discovered your spear."

"How do you know so much?"

"I knew you, Astrid. We served together once."

"You were Valkyrie?"

"A long…long time ago," the woman said with a sigh. "My service ended sixty years ago."

"Did the elder council know?"

"They did."

"You told them?"

"I had no choice. I came here, as you did, long ago, drawn to something…and when I found it—"

"Drawn to something?"

"Yes, and it's past time you saw what I did all those years ago."

"Past time? I have no time; the demons have begun their assault. I came to seek aid. You must speak to the townsfolk—"

"The Ashvolk will not attack until their pet serpents have finished their job. You have some time…please."

The old woman stepped into the light. She was frail, an age so great, Astrid could not guess it. The woman's grey hair was thin, straight, and long—it nearly brushed the floor as she shuffled forward. Astrid would have liked to ignore the elder's request, but she was drawn to this place, there was not use denying it.

"You know of the Ashvolk too?"

"It is because of them that I was retired. Odin forced Freyja to trim her numbers. I was an unfortunate casualty in the gods' disagreement."

As the elder and Astrid joined hands, she could feel the connection.

"Quickly, show me," Astrid said. "Show me before this town is razed."

"Grømstad was built on a tomb. Few know this, as it was ages ago. The tomb lays several levels under this building now, hidden…"

"Whose tomb?"

The elder smiled before she answered, "The tomb is that of a veteran Valkyrie warrior. The first to fall to the Ashvolk, years and years before you were born, Astrid."

"Incredible."

Astrid followed the elder down a long, narrow, spiral staircase into darkness. How the woman could see was a miracle. Still, Astrid trusted she moved in the right direction, as the sense of something powerful nearby was in her heart and soul.

"So discouraged and worried were the gods that they did not take this fallen Valkyrie home. They left her here in Midgard to rot. Some of the land's men, those who realized who she was, built the tomb to protect her body after death. It was one of those men who founded Grømstad years later."

"Was Freyja disappointed in this Valkyrie? Or did she not want the proof of her passing to be known to the new generations?"

"Only she knows this answer," the elder replied. "Do you feel it? Can you sense it better now? We are close."

"I do feel it."

The staircase ended in a room darker yet. The scent of mold was strong, but there was also a scent of death on the air that made Astrid's skin crawl. The golden glow of her armor was swallowed up by the deep shadows of the room. She no longer lit the way; instead, she stood out like a beacon.

"Go ahead, Astrid. Illuminate the room."

Astrid adjusted her grip on her spear. "With what? I carry no torch."

The elder laughed. "You have forgotten how?"

"Not so much forgotten..."

"The key to being a Valkyrie is in the gift Freyja gave you," the elder said. "Your armor, my dear, do you not remember Freyja giving it to you?"

"I do."

"What did it look like? Her gift to you? Remember what it looked like, Astrid."

"It was not armor at all. Freyja handed me a golden circlet. It was like twine but smooth, and when I put it on my head..."

"You were unexpectedly armored."

Suddenly, Astrid remembered. A Valkyrie's armor, it could be reformed at will and hidden in the form of an ornate golden circlet. Astrid concentrated on her armor, and it responded, reshaped, moved like molten metal to cover her bare stomach.

"You do remember. Well done."

Astrid joined her hands, like she had when she summoned her spear; this time, three glowing balls of light formed in her palms and she threw them to the ground, where they popped and lit the entire room.

"Good, Astrid, now I can direct you."

The room was littered with debris, as if the town had stored all its old and broken wares here for years. Astrid looked around but could not spot anything that looked like it had any value: broken pottery, rotten chairs, moth-eaten clothing stuffed in and overflowing from crates. Nothing.

In the center of the room was a pile of wood that looked as if it could be used as a pyre.

"Under the wood."

The room shook, a clear reminder that their time was limited.

"We're taking too long."

"Trust me, this will aid you."

Astrid rested her spear on a large crate and withdrew her sword. With it held tightly in both hands, she began to swing it at the pile of wood. After several swipes, she had cleared enough to see a sarcophagus.

Built from the ground up, carved out of granite, the tomb had elaborate designs: words, dates, and pictures. Astrid wished she could read them all.

"Her final resting place."

"You brought me to the corpse of a Valkyrie? This is what is so special? Well, if I fail to defeat the demons, your town might have a second body to hide down here."

"Not the corpse, Astrid. Open it and gaze upon a treasure most unique."

Astrid heaved the slab, pushing it more than halfway off, where it teetered a moment before falling. The crash echoed so loud in the chamber it stole her thoughts.

"You *are* strong," the elder said.

Astrid gazed inside and gasped, as she backed away. Within the stone coffin was the naked body of a young woman with long blonde hair. *This is impossible,* she thought. The Valkyrie had not decomposed; she looked freshly dead, or even as if she were in a deep slumber. Astrid thought trickery may be at hand, but when she spotted the circlet atop the beauty's head, she realized what had called to her.

"Freyja's gift... This Valkyrie, her armor...it was left here?"

Astrid could hear the elder's soft weeping. She sounded so very sad, it nearly made her want to cry too.

"Take the circlet, Astrid. It is yours now to keep safe or..."

"Or what?"

"Bestow it upon someone. As Freyja's favorite, she has no doubt given you such ability."

Another loud rumble from above spurred Astrid to action.

"Are you saying I can give someone that which is normally Freyja's to give?"

"Only a veteran Valkyrie can."

"Perhaps I could heal her..." Astrid touched the dead woman's shoulder.

"Heal her body, possibly, but her soul has long passed."

Astrid considered her actions a moment. "So be it."

She carefully lifted the circlet off the woman's head, and when she did, the body rapidly decayed, turning to dust.

"What-what just happened?"

"Her power was in the circlet. Once removed she—"

"She was dead," Astrid mumbled.

"Long dead."

Astrid wanted to make sense of it all, but there was no time to figure it out. "Can I wear it?"

"To bear two, I cannot be sure such a thing is possible, but I do know this: Whoever you award it to will become a new chooser of the slain."

"Yrsa. I could remake her Valkyrie?"

"If you would have your sister face the Ashvolk again today."

"Then who…" Astrid looked at the elder. "You?"

The woman's dry lips parted in a smile.

Is this what she wanted all along? Astrid tightened her grip on the circlet. *She hopes to become young, beautiful, and powerful again. But at what cost?*

"So this is why you brought me down here? To remake you?"

"Yes." The elder held her hands out for the circlet.

"To what end?"

"I do not understand."

"Why do you want this now? The Ashvolk have stolen my sister's baby and nearly killed her. The demons have come to consume the last of the maiden blood. Do *you* wish to die here?"

"Today is the day of my death regardless. I cannot escape these demons. If they do not sense I am former Valkyrie already, they'll surely kill me when they raze the town. With my powers back…I at least stand a fighting chance."

"Then you wish to fight?"

"You question me, Astrid, like I have never owned your trust. We chose together, we were sisters you and I."

Astrid knew her words to be true but still guessed her motives were not pure.

"Please, together we might be able to defeat the demon lord."

Another rumble shook the tomb, and they both lurched to the side. Astrid considered the option of keeping the circlet, but the elder was right: together they might be able to win this day.

"Fine."

"You will not regret th—"

"Kneel," Astrid said firmly.

The elder gazed deep into Astrid's eyes for a breath, a silent protest, yet she complied. It took the old woman some effort to get down on her knees, but once there she bowed her head, and awaited the circlet.

"I bestow upon you Freyja's most cherished gift. Today you become a chooser of the slain, a warrior for the gods, a Valkyrie."

Once the circlet was placed upon the elder's head, the transformation began. The color returned to her hair, pale grey turning black, the color racing from her scalp down to the ends that rested atop the dusty floor. The elder's shoulders began to twitch as muscle began to build and stretch beneath her skin. After a grunt borne of pain, the old woman laughed, her voice absent its gruff scratchiness before the chuckle ended.

"I feel it, Astrid."

"What do you feel?"

"My youth."

Astrid watched the wrinkles vanish from the old woman's hands, as they retreated up her arm and then under her cloak. The elder struggled for breath as her legs slid out from under her, and she dropped face first to the floor.

After she grunted and cleared her throat, the elder spoke with the voice of woman younger than Astrid.

"I feel so strong."

Slowly, the woman stood as she looked through her tousled hair, her green eyes as vibrant as gems.

Her gaze…so sinister, Astrid thought. *Have I made a mistake?*

"Do you remember my name, Astrid?"

She could almost recall the name. While Astrid untwisted her tongue, the elder removed the loose cloak she wore to reveal taut, pale skin, a lithe form, and her newly acquired armor, which was formed like Astrid's with above the elbow armguards and knee-high leg guards.

Now Astrid knew her name.

"Erna."

"You do remember."

"Daughter of the mountains," Astrid continued. "That is what you called yourself."

"Born in the caves of Esja, in a land far from here," Erna boasted, as she stretched her arms and legs.

"I remember the tale now. You told it well."

"I did." Erna said as she cracked her knuckles. "Now, to find a sturdy mace…"

"We can find you one above. We best hurry. There's a battle to be fought."

Erna gazed deeply as she nodded. "Yes, Astrid, there is."

CHAPTER 61

JOKUL HAD GROWN TIRED OF leading from the back of the bandit ranks; he had watched too many of the lawless men throw down their lives and die in glory. He too wanted to take that risk. Of the three, only two of the serpents survived. The spears had done the job, but many of them had broken in doing so; a new tactic was required. Jokul rushed forward, axe in hand, dodged one serpent's strikes, jumped, and finally wedged his axe between the scales on the neck of the other.

"Ho!" he screamed in excitement.

He tackled the tired serpent and wrapped his arms around its neck as it reared up, into the air. With plenty of damaged scales to hold on to, he was able to keep his grip and not fall off, regardless of its efforts to shake him free.

"Need help, friend?" Emmerich called from the ground, an undamaged spear in his hand.

Jokul motioned for the bandit leader to toss the spear, and once it was in his hand, he turned it on the serpent and plunged it deep between the scales his axe had peeled open. As the serpent hissed in pain, Emmerich hacked away at its underbelly with his two daggers, the beast's lifeblood showering over him.

"We have this beast!" Emmerich called out. "Finish the last one!"

The remainder of his men focused their efforts on the last serpent, but before they could fatally wound it, it slithered away.

After he hacked out one of the serpent's teeth with several blows of his axe, Jokul turned to Emmerich and cheered.

"Good fight. Take a trophy."

"Good? There was nothing good about it."

"We yet stand, two of the serpents bested, dead at our feet."

"Look at how many of my men were killed."

The ground was cluttered with bodies parts. Many of Emmerich's soldiers had been ripped apart by the serpents, making it hard to assess the total damage, however it was obvious to Jokul that at least a third of the group had been killed.

"Honorable deaths, one and all. I'm sure a Valk...I'm sure they will find passage to the afterlife."

Emmerich shook his head in disgust. "You know, I had estimated fewer casualties than this for my planned assault on this town. Now I—"

"How was Yrsa when you left her?" Jokul interrupted as he wiped blood off the tooth he had just taken.

Jokul could see it in the bandit's face, the way the mere mention of Yrsa changed his stance—he did care for her.

"She's resting now, as well as can be, I guess," Emmerich's face twisting into a scowl. "You would not believe the reception I was given."

"Not good, I take it."

"Not good."

"Keep your heart and mind clear, bandit, and after the fight is won, all will cheer your name, friend and foe. Trust me." Jokul patted Emmerich on the shoulder as he passed.

"And what of my child, Yrsa's baby?"

"No time to think of it—"

"No time?"

"No. Ready yourselves," Jokul advised. "Now that we have killed their pets, the true demons are sure to be the next wave."

As Astrid walked to the scene of the fight, her eyes darted from her brother to the bandit leader. Jokul had patted the man's shoulder, and her brother had showed concern and expressed camaraderie with him.

He has no idea what this wicked man has done to his sisters. Perhaps I should tell him. The thought put and extra spring in her step.

"Hail, Sister, how do you like your gifts?" Jokul waved his arm in the direction of the two dead serpents.

"Is that what you were fighting?"

"Aye."

Eyes still on Emmerich, she said, "I have never seen the likes."

"Rare fiends, these serpents," Jokul bragged. "Born in Helheim."

"And they were the source of all that rumbling?" Astrid asked.

"Oh no...not them. Whatever bends the trees, moving slowly toward us, *that* is the rumbling you hear, Sister."

"The demon lord, he comes," Erna said.

Erna stole all attention as she walked into view, her new mace hefted over her shoulder. She swung her hips as she moved, in a way that better fit a whore than a warrior of the gods, and wore a smile that stretched from ear to ear. It was obvious to Astrid that Erna ate up the attention like a starving man.

"Who is this?" Jokul asked Astrid.

"I am Erna, born of the caves of Esja. Like Astrid, I am also a..."

"Valkyrie?"

"Thank you," she said with a slight bow to Jokul.

"What?" Emmerich gasped.

"Is this true?" Jokul grabbed his sister's arm and pulled her toward him as he asked.

"It is true. She's here to help."

"Our numbers strengthen again." Jokul cheered. "Bring forth the demons. We are ready."

"Another one? This place attracts Valkyrie like shite does flies," Emmerich grumbled.

Erna walked straight to Emmerich, her long hair swaying side to side. When she reached him, she cocked her head and smiled; then, in a flash of movement that made the bandit leader jump, she snatched one of his daggers from his belt.

"Give that back!"

"When I am done with it," Erna stated bluntly.

She gathered up her ankle-long black hair, slowly raised the dagger over her head, and began to saw at the rope-thick handful of locks until it was cut. The jagged line of her hair fell to just above her shoulders, and laughing, Erna shook her head like a dog who had just come in out of the rain.

"Much better. You cannot imagine the weight of all that," Erna said, handing Emmerich back his dagger with a wink. "You have my thanks."

"Erna." Tired of the show, Astrid pointed at Emmerich. "That man is the leader of the bandits who have besieged your town all month."

"Is he?" The look of desire did not leave her eyes. "I had no idea he was so handsome."

Astrid motioned for her brother to join her as she walked away.

"Where did you find this one?"

"Never mind, just listen, Brother. When this is done, if she lives, we might have to kill her."

"Truly?"

Looking at Erna, Astrid took a deep breath and steadied her nerves. "Just be ready."

Jokul nodded. "And what of your friend, the bandit leader?"

"Today is his last."

CHAPTER 62

"I will kill him!" Warren screamed as he thrashed around, still chained to the wall.

"Relax, he said he is helping," Hammond answered as he searched through an unlabeled crate of valuables.

Warren grunted with frustration.

Why would Astrid do this to me? Why would she want to humiliate me in front of my family? Why would she deny me the right to fight alongside her—to protect her?

Each time he thought of it, he got angrier, yanking at the chains and growling like a rabid dog. It made Helen nervous, so she kept Willa away, which only fueled his frustration more. *Astrid has made me look like a fool.*

"She did this because I failed her!" Warren yelled to his brother. "Yrsa—"

"Yrsa is alive. Her wounds are not your fault."

"She would rather fight side by side with the bandits than the man who loves her. Does that seem right to you, Brother?"

"No, but I am putting my trust in her. She's the one in league with the old gods."

Warren pulled at his chains and grunted again. He could imagine summoning godlike strength and breaking his bindings. *But then what?* he thought. *Astrid does not want my help.*

Helen had removed all of Yrsa's bloody, soiled garments, and Warren had heard her say over and over how she could not believe the woman was still alive. Considering the amount of blood that soaked her tattered dress, he agreed.

With the wet washrag resting on Yrsa's belly, Helen began to weep.

"A child journeyed inside her no differently than Willa did inside me. Now…"

"Try not to think of it, Helen," Hammond said.

"My first thoughts were wanting to hold my child in my arms, Hammond. Yrsa will want the same. What do you suggest we tell her then?" The statement made Helen cry even harder.

Helen's tears made Warren even angrier.

"Hammond?" Helen called to her husband.

"Yes," he answered, walking toward her.

"She bears no wounds…"

"The bandit said Astrid would explain it all to us afterward."

Helen was quiet a moment before she responded, "Will *we* be alive afterward?"

As Hammond and his wife spoke, Warren pulled harder on his chains, and the right side began to break free from the wall. Excited by the notion of escape, his muscles quaked.

That's not all me; the ground above is shaking.

When the quake grew stronger, everyone jumped into action. The bandits had ushered all the families they could to their supply cellars, and now, those who remained had taken up arms. Astrid had no idea of their numbers, only that when the battle was over, there would be a lot of brave men she would need to help ascend to Valhalla.

Astrid climbed atop a table still covered in an assortment of fabric, to take control of the mumbles and meandering.

"Listen! There are three types of Ashvolk Demons. The tall, thin ones that can be hard to see at times turn into oil and lash out with many tendril-like arms. I believe not many of these remain, but be aware: they are fast and hard to kill. Chop at them until they no longer move then take their heads."

"Only fight them if they are solid; otherwise, your efforts are wasted," Jokul paced the ground below her.

"The kind which attacked here yesterday, large and stony, are strong and resilient, but stupid. Overwhelm them, keep moving, do not allow yourselves to become easy targets. There may be several of these, but do not worry. They can be defeated."

"My archers—" Emmerich began.

"Arrows will not be enough to pierce the bigger demons' skin," Astrid quickly answered.

"We have a battering ram in the forest. I could send some of my men to fetch it," Emmerich stated.

"Do that."

"Is it the demon army that makes the ground quake?" one of Emmerich's bandits called out.

"No, not the army, just one: the demon lord. He will be the largest and most dangerous. Do not engage him; leave him to me."

"Us!" Erna shouted.

Astrid did not even reply.

"Bandits, know this: today's fight will absolve your wrongs. So fight to live, for a new life is your reward."

She looked at Emmerich as she finished. They each knew this alliance would end in one of their deaths—if not at the hands of the demons, then at the end of the other's blade.

"Fight well!" Astrid shouted.

"Die brave!" Jokul cheered in response.

"One hundred coins to the man who slays the first demon!" Emmerich added.

Astrid jumped down from the table, and Jokul quickly approached.

"Do you think that offer includes me?"

"I hope so because my coin is on you." Astrid smiled then took her brother's arm. "We will share a drink when this is over."

"Today we make the Allfather proud. Today we avenge Birka."

"For Birka." Astrid nodded.

No sooner did the words leave their mouths than two of the larger demons breached the ground, one in the middle of the largest rank of bandit soldiers, the other behind Erna, who stumbled backward into its grasp. Men flew through the air like dolls thrown during a tantrum. Astrid had already forgotten how big the soldier demons were; the one that squeezed Erna in its massive fist stood two stories at least.

"Two, is that all?" Jokul asked as he charged in to aid Erna.

I doubt it, Astrid thought.

Erna was desperately trying to break free, each swing of her mace aimed at the demon's hand, but it appeared as though she could not muster enough strength to hurt it.

"No! It can't end already!" Erna's feared-soaked shout rang out.

As Astrid watched Jokul jump in to help Erna, her heart filled with dread. *Odin, bless him, for I do not wish to see my brother hurt.*

Jokul displayed no fear—in fact, he looked like he enjoyed himself and, her wild-eyed brother's attack must have hurt the demon, as its grip loosened and Erna fell free.

"Careful, these things bleed lava!" Jokul announced as he pulled her away from the demon.

"They don't. Their blood may look as such, but it's nothing special," Erna disagreed. "This is not my first fight, handsome."

"Should I leave this one all to you then?"

"No, no."

"Good then, I wish to win that wager."

With axe raised high, Jokul dashed back in, past two other bandits who had engaged the demon. *He seems to be faring well. I should*—Astrid suddenly heard the strange buzz from before. She looked in the direction of the town hall, her mind thinking of the tomb for a brief moment before she saw the roof buckle. There was a fluttering in the pit of Astrid's stomach as she marched off toward the destruction; the demon lord was near.

The ground shook so hard Astrid nearly lost her footing as she watched the chimney fall inward, a giant hole left in the roof of the town hall. There was only time for Astrid to gasp before one of the largest Ashvolk demons rose up and reduced the building to splintered timber and chunks of stone.

This demon seemed angrier than the others; *does it sense the ruins where the dead Valkyrie was? Or perhaps it smells Erna and I there.*

The demon grasped a handful of broken stone and pitched it in Astrid's direction, the debris raining down on her like sleet. Exasperated, she finally entered the fray; dashing across the space that separated her and the demon, ducking debris as she did, she aimed her spear.

Stuck inside the rubble itself, the giant demon swept its arms left and right to clear a path so it could move and as Astrid grew closer, it grasped another handful of stone from the broken hearth and tossed it at her. This spray was much thicker than the others, filled with pebbles and chunks of rock the size of apples—too difficult to evade. One piece of rock sliced her cheek open, while others struck her torso. She would have screamed in pain if a battle cry had not already exited her mouth.

Astrid launched her spear, and the weapon sailed at the demon's mouth. As it closed the distance, Astrid raced up a piece of wood that had fallen like a ramp toward the demon, her two-handed long sword drawn and raised above her head.

The spear hit its mark; Astrid could read the demon's panicked red eyes as it bit down on the metal, and several of its teeth broke off.

The massive demon pawed at the spear, giving Astrid the time she needed to swing her sword in hard and fast. Her strike took three of the demon's fingers off its right hand before her momentum sunk her long sword into the coarse rock-like skin of the Ashvolk's shoulder. But the thick skin slowed Astrid's blade, becoming lodged, she pressed her bootheels into the demon's chest, and pushed until her weapon quickly dislodged.

Astrid fell to the debris-cluttered ground, only then, when she looked up, did she finally realize the size of the demon, "You! Demon Lord, tell me now, where's my sister's child?"

With its mouth open, ooze spilled from the wound in the back of its throat. Finally free of the spear in its mouth, the demon spit radiant red blood.

"Not lord," it answered.

"Do not try and deceive me!" Astrid pointed her sword at it. "I know the largest Ashvolk demon is the lord."

"Not largest, Valkyrie."

The demon tried to swat Astrid but missed her as she rolled backward onto the broken wood that was once the town hall. Her spear back in hand, Astrid crossed the two weapons, both points aimed at the thing.

If this brute is not the biggest demon, then just how big could the demon lord be?

Once again the demon tried to free itself from the hole; harder and harder it yanked until a cracking sound was heard and the ground itself started to drain, like the silt of a quicksand pit. Astrid all of a sudden started to sink, a rumble beneath her a moment before the ground dropped entirely out from under her feet.

As she began to plummet, she did the only thing she could think of and stabbed her long sword into the demon's hip. Slammed into the side of its leg, Astrid looked up as she swayed to the side, full of momentum.

The large Ashvolk had managed to hold on to the edge above as it crumbled, and as Astrid hung there, her lower half swayed with each movement the demon made. There was only the darkness of the tomb beneath her—deep and seemingly bottomless.

If this thing falls will it survive? Will I?

The thought sobered her and forced her action. With a deep breath, Astrid withdrew the dagger from her belt, reached up, and plunged it into the thing's lower abdomen to pull herself up further.

CHAPTER 63

"Duck, damn you!" Jokul yelled at Erna.

"Sorry."

"Keep your eyes forward, or they'll be plucked from your skull by the enemy," Jokul told her.

"I know. I know."

"What has your attention, girl?"

"Nothing."

Mace up, Erna made a sudden dash at the demon's flank, her weapon's spikes sinking deep into its side. Before Erna could withdraw her mace from the demon's thick hide, Jokul watched it swat her away with one of its big hands.

Axe raised, he shouted, aimed his weapon and prepared a charge, but sooner than he could move, two bandits ran the demon through from the back with long metal pikes. The demon spun suddenly, shaking the men's grips from their weapons and throwing them to the ground, which turned the non-bladed ends into dangerous obstacles that Jokul now had to dodge. Forced to step away, he watched as the demon reformed each hand into two-pronged spikes, which it promptly used to impale both bandits.

"Low–high." Erna suggested. "I will take low. Ready?"

Jokul nodded and choked up on his battle-axe. As the Ashvolk turned, Erna and Jokul rushed in, Erna swinging her mace, and dealing the demon a crushing blow to one of its legs. At the same time, Jokul had slashed, and the impact of both their strikes sent it hard to the ground face first.

"Chop it up!" Jokul ordered as he hacked at the back of the demon's neck. Four of the nearby bandits rushed in with their swords and began to slice at the beast as well. It struggled to stand after each strike, but never got its barrel-shaped chest more than several inches from the ground.

Jokul drew in a deep breath, raised his axe over his head, and with his mind on his fallen family, dropped the thick blade down, severing the demon's head from its stony body.

"It's done," Jokul stated.

"I forgot how thrilling a good fight could be."

Erna, who bled from her lip and nose, sauntered over to Jokul.

"Have you seen Astrid?"

"I lost track of her," Erna replied.

"There, look. The town hall!" a Grømstad man shouted.

Where the town hall had once stood was a large hole, and it was still widening, more dirt crumbling inward by the moment. Little more could be seen through the dust clouds filling the area.

"Erna, didn't Astrid rush off in that direction?" Jokul pointed.

When she nodded, Jokul was off, full sprint toward the remains of the town hall.

As the demon's grip slipped, the ground above him slid through his fingers and showered down on Astrid. *I can't hold on much longer, I must—*

The air was cool on her face as she released her sword and fell free of the demon. She could smell something in the sky. The temperature had suddenly dropped; it was going to snow.

Astrid summoned her wings and caught an updraft as the demon collided with the stone floor of the tomb. The blast of air shot her out of the hole, and she sailed above it all.

She could see her spear on the edge of the hole, as it teetered on the loose earth; she would need it now. Astrid swooped down and grabbed it as she launched herself at the demon in the depths of the Valkyrie tomb.

With the precision of a marksman's arrow, Astrid pierced the demon's right eye with her spear and immediately flew out of the hole again.

She heard her brother screaming her name as she floated above the dust and debris. But before she could see him, she dove back down, this time sinking her spear into the demon's other eye. This eye erupted—a thick yellow goo combined with blood and splattered all over her lower body. Astrid gagged, quickly flew back out of the chasm and shook the mess from her limbs.

"Astrid!" Jokul shouted as she rose into view.

"Is that it? Is that one the demon lord?" Erna asked, as she moved slowly behind Jokul.

"No," Astrid answered.

"How can that be?" Erna gazed down into the hole. "By Odin, the size of this demon is unbelievable."

"Do you need my help, Sister?" Jokul asked.

"I'm unsure how to kill it."

"Wait, I know." Jokul spotted at least a dozen bandits who had come to watch Astrid. "You men, come with me."

"I would carry on if I was you. Better to keep that thing wounded and down there," Erna offered.

Astrid peered down, her aggravation plain on her face.

"Cheer up, Astrid, we are doing well."

CHAPTER 64

WARREN COULD NOT TEAR HIS frantic mind from the battle above ground. *Is Astrid still alive?* He could not allow himself to think otherwise.

With another hard pull, he loosened the bracket that held the chains to the wall a bit more. He could hear Hammond and Helen whispering down the tunnel. They were talking about Yrsa; as best as he could tell, Astrid's sister was still unconscious. He could see her but could not make out the details; the alcove she was lying in was too dark. Still, Warren knew Yrsa's wounds had to be grievous; her baby had been taken from her.

I should have been there. I could have helped. It should've been me carrying Yrsa here, not that bastard bandit. Enraged, Warren rattled his chains. *She's too afraid of what I might say to her. That's why she did not return with her sister.*

"Damn you, Astrid!"

A rumble rocked the entire cellar, spilling barrels and knocking bottles and bags off shelves. Warren did not want to die buried alive, his mouth and lungs filled with dirt.

"Hammond! Hammond!"

"What?"

His brother rushed down the tunnel to him; face wet from worry.

"Hammond, do you remember the earthquakes from a few years ago?" He said, knowing now would be his best chance to gain his freedom.

"What? Yes, yes I do." Hammond looked up at the loose dirt as it rained down on him.

"We're all going to die down here. You know this, right?"

"No, we should be fine. We should be safe."

"Am I the only one who hears that rumbling?"

Several thumps came from the cellar's trap door. Hammond nearly jumped out of his skin at the last bang.

Did Astrid really believe my brother could protect us all? Warren wondered, the thought left a sour taste in his mouth. *No, they need me. They need me now.*

Helen quietly joined the men in the back room.

"I believe we have a visitor," she whispered.

"Let me loose," Warren demanded. "Now!"

"No one knows we are here except, Astrid," Helen said to Warren as she watched his face go gaunt. "The bandit leader?" she gasped.

The knocking hadn't stopped and was now followed by the sound of metal scraping against metal. All three held silent as the wooden stairs creaked beneath someone's heavy feet.

"Damn you, Hammond, release me now," Warren said through gritted teeth.

A voice was heard from across the tunnel. As they feared, it was Emmerich and he called for Yrsa.

"Where's Willa?" Hammond's eyes frantically searched about.

"She was waiting for Yrsa to rise."

"Helen," Warren urged. "Tell Hammond to release me now."

Both Helen and Hammond looked at Warren.

"Yrsa!" Emmerich cried out.

The footfalls atop the wooden planks of the supply cellar floor echoed all the way to the back. Emmerich was moving closer, although very slowly.

Helen could feel her heart pound in her chest. She had never been this terrified in her life and the fear amplified when, eyes on Warren, she realized the best fighter in the room was locked up.

Another crash from above shook the place, this time loose dirt from the ceiling extinguished several of the torches when it poured over them. Now darker than ever, the cellar felt smaller.

Helen gazed in silence at the end of the tunnel. The air was murky from copious amounts of dirt and dust. The glint of light off of metal was the first thing she saw of the bandit leader as he emerged from the shadows. Emmerich looked as if the color had been washed away from him, leaving only a darkness that spread from his chest to his stomach and massed over his legs. When Helen realized it was blood, she screamed.

"Yrsa?" Emmerich called out when his eyes landed on Helen.

"What's wrong with you, man?" Hammond replied. "Why are you here? You should *not* be here."

"I n-need to speak with my dearest Yrsa." Emmerich's voice wavered.

"He's mortally wounded, Hammond," Warren whispered.

Emmerich shuffled forward a few more steps before his leg buckled and he fell hard to his knees. Although he groaned in pain, he kept his dagger gripped tightly in his fist, and once shakily on his feet, he took another step.

"Where is she?" Emmerich's voice grew louder with each word. "Where is my Yrsa?"

"He's no threat to us; he's dying," Hammond whispered back to his brother.

"No, listen to me, he's a bigger threat now than ever—" Warren began.

"Where is she?" Emmerich spit blood on the floor as he yelled. "Where is she?"

Unable to endure the tension, Helen answered, "She's here."

"Hammond, you must release me now." Warren's words came out fast. "This is your last chance. Release me before Emmerich kills us all."

"Do it," Helen pleaded.

Hammond shook as Helen walked toward the bandit leader.

"The key, Hammond," Warren urged.

Helen led Emmerich to Yrsa, scooping up her daughter, who had fallen asleep. Ensnared by her curiosity, Helen stood still as Emmerich knelt slowly by Yrsa, trembling and moaning in pain as he moved.

As he rested his forehead on Yrsa's belly, he began to cry.

"Please forgive me, Yrsa," he sobbed. "I never should've treated you so, my goddess. I never should've hurt you."

As Willa awoke, Helen dashed out of the alcove past Emmerich, over a trail of blood.

"Helen, do you have the key?" Hammond asked as she approached, but she only stared despondently in reply.

After she placed Willa at her father's side, Helen returned slowly to Emmerich, drawn in by his pain and her desire to help him. The man's condition—dying but in desperate need to see the woman he loved—touched her.

Helen watched him from the tunnel, she could see that the blood from his stomach stained his leather pants all the way down to his boots, and the fabric of his shirt was stretched, no doubt hung low with the heaviness of gore.

Helen turned to face Hammond; she wondered if he would be so romantic in his last moments.

"Where's the key, Helen?" Hammond whispered.

"Father?" Willa yawned.

"Yes, darling?"

"That key?" Helen saw Willa point to the floor next to where Yrsa rested.

"Helen," Hammond whispered. "The key."

While she looked at the key, Helen listened to Emmerich and once more became engrossed in the bandit leader's words to Yrsa. Emmerich was confessing a long list horrible acts, sexual, violent, and deviant. The more he spoke the less romantic the scene became. While Helen figured the man had treated Yrsa reprehensibly, she had no idea to what extent until now. All compassion drained from Helen and slowly her eyes focused on one of the man's long daggers hanging at his belt.

How easy it would be to snatch it from him and sink it into his back. I have slaughtered many pigs before; to plunge a blade in his flesh should be no different, she thought.

Helen crept forward ever so slightly, her eyes glued to the dagger. She imagined her fingers around its cold handle as she reached for it; she would have the weapon soon.

"Good. Grab the key."

Hammond's voice was so loud that it startled everyone. On his feet suddenly, Emmerich turned and buried the dagger he still held in his hand into Helen's stomach, twisting it as he forced the blade up into her chest cavity.

There was shock on her face but no pain. She felt her eyes go wide, her mouth open as if to speak, but she made no sound as she slid off the point of his dagger and stumbled backward.

His footing lost, Emmerich fell forward hard to the ground, hands first.

"Helen, no!" Warren yelled.

Helen stood still, as the red dot under her hands blossomed.

"Gods no!" Hammond screeched as he gripped his own stomach.

"I will kill you, bandit!" Warren shouted.

"I'm already dead." Emmerich stood again, now shoulder to shoulder with Helen. "The demons killed me."

Helen was somehow still on her feet and trapped in an unbreakable stare with her husband, who had covered their daughter's eyes. She heard everything, but the world seemed unreal, like a bad dream.

"She has amazing resolve, this one," Emmerich said before he unhurriedly sliced his dagger across her throat. "Too bad."

Helen felt nothing, but she knew Warren screamed. *Warren will save...*

Warren had seen death, but never had he witnessed such a cruel act upon his family.

Helen—so kind and pure. She's not a fighter; she's a mother.

Warren's love for Helen finally gave him the strength he needed. Arms forward, his muscles burning with fire borne from Muspelheim, Warren finally pulled the chains off the hook on the wall; he was free.

His scream filled the cellar as he charged down the tunnel toward Emmerich, the heavy chains drug behind him, but he paid them little mind. He would have pulled a cart full of stone down the tunnel if he had to; there was nothing that would stand between him and his enemy.

Emmerich attacked with his dagger, but the swing was loose and sloppy, and Warren swatted the weapon from his hand with ease as he tackled him. Emmerich was seemingly knocked senseless, but when Warren's rough hands wrapped around his neck, he returned to life.

"You can't bring her back," was all he said.

With large hands that had been strengthened by years of farming, Warren crushed Emmerich's throat.

"You bastard, you killed her! You killed her!" Warren growled in the dead man's face. "You killed her!"

At that moment, as if awakened from a long night's sleep, Yrsa opened her eyes and stretched her arms. "Where's my baby?"

CHAPTER 65

ASTRID COULD NOT RECALL SUCH an ache before in her body, such pain from exhaustion, and it resonated in a spot so foreign: her wings. With the last vestiges of strength, Astrid flew out of the hole to collapse at the edge, where the earth still poured loosely down. She sunk her tired hands into the dirt and debris, pulling herself away from the hole until she finally reached a broken plank of wood that looked to be stable enough to hold her weight. Eyes on the dark sky, she spied millions of tiny snowflakes. She knew it was a sign from the gods—they were present. It calmed her and filled her with vigor at the same time, but it did not ease the pain at her core. After a long, cleansing exhale, Astrid retracted her wings and shouted at the heavens to release the pain she felt in her back.

Jokul rushed across the debris field to her side. He looked well, much better than she felt. She gazed at the thick gore that painted her arms from fingertips to elbows. She had killed the large demon, but to do so she had had to burrow through its neck.

"Astrid, are you well?"

"My spear?" She looked around for it.

"Here." Jokul picked it up from where it lay near her. "Astrid, tell me, were you successful?"

"I destroyed the demon."

Still at the edge of the sinkhole, Jokul peered down, causing Astrid to do so too. The demon's head had been all but torn off its body, its rocky flesh chipped and sliced in a hundred or more cuts.

"How did you do this?"

"I…" Astrid moaned, lying back. "Is the battle finished?"

Where the trees had once moved in the forest was silent—there was no motion, no sign of trouble.

"I believe so." Jokul looked around as he answered.

"Something still feels very wrong."

"Wrong in being victorious?" Jokul shook his head. "What do you mean?"

"Birka," she said with a pained exhale. "I remember fires burning, bright lights…a deeper sense of dread."

He agreed, "Aye, me too."

"How could a gang of bandits defeat the demons, but not the skilled warriors of our homeland?"

"You are right."

Astrid sat up, slightly recovered, but knew the ache between her shoulder blades would not go away anytime soon. She reached out for Jokul's hand, and he lifted her from the ground.

"Where is Erna?"

"I do not know." Jokul shrugged.

"My heart tells me she possesses more information than she has shared."

"We best find her then."

The quakes from earlier suddenly returned, but stronger and faster. Astrid stumbled backward toward the sinkhole, which opened larger by the moment. She began to slide, but Jokul caught her before she was gulped down by the hole.

"We must get away from this area."

They ran toward Warren's home, but they could not seem to distance themselves from the source of the quake. Jokul looked over his shoulder as he ran, searching for something. His jaw fell open, and he shouted at Astrid; the sinkhole had grown and now swallowed up homes.

"Keep running!" Jokul tugged her arm when she slowed down.

"The town!"

They sprinted toward the farms, which were on slightly higher ground.

"Jokul!" Astrid stopped when she realized something sickening. "Stop, Jokul! Stop! I was wrong!"

"Wrong?"

"Gods, I told them all to flee to their supply cellars. I told them to hide underground, Jokul..."

Astrid stared at the center of Grømstad in disbelief. All those families—the sinkhole was consuming them alive. Just when her heart felt like it was going to tear in two, the ground bubbled up near the edge of town, near Hammond's home, and then exploded. The bodies of bandits and townsfolk alike were catapulted through the sky. Rock, wood, grass, and all sorts of goods from food to pottery and weapons showered down.

"We need to find refuge, Astrid." Jokul tugged Astrid to the side of a home that they stood near to take shelter from the dangerous rain.

"No, Jokul, look!"

There was movement through the dust cloud where the blast had come from. Something large was down there. Astrid knew it could only be one thing: the demon lord. He had taken Yrsa's baby and now destroyed Grømstad.

Astrid raced across the field, praying to her family for strength and to the gods for another blessing. Today, she would call upon all that she had seen, lived, and experienced to defeat a great adversary. As the dust cleared, she saw exactly what she would have to overcome.

Astrid stopped dead in her tracks and gasped. She could only see the demon lord's head and shoulders as it pulled itself from the ground, and that much was already larger than she ever could have imagined; it was three or four times the size of the one she had killed. *It's a giant—no a titan,* she thought. *It could eat me in one bite. I would be nothing more than a morsel.*

Astrid went cold and numb.

"Impossible!" Jokul exclaimed as he caught up to her.

"I am sorry, Brother."

"When this is over, remind me I need to pay dear Freyja a visit. For this, I imagine she will owe me greatly."

"You would seek treasure from Asgard's vaults?"

"Not Asgard's, Sister. I have my eyes set on a treasure only Freyja can provide."

Astrid chuckled.

"We will need a good plan to defeat this one."

The snow had increased, and now lightly coated the ground. Snow—it made Astrid feel more alive.

"I have seen that look on your face before, Sister. That one raid, where we turned the tide of—"

"The cold, Jokul," she interrupted him. "Freyja said the demons have trouble with the cold."

"She told me the same."

"And now it snows," she said, palm out.

"An excellent sign, indeed."

"Perhaps we could lead it away from town to a lake, drown it?"

As Astrid and Jokul spoke, she spotted something in the air above the emerging demon; it was Erna. She had readied her own attack. She spiraled down toward the demon lord, her speed increasing as she descended. With her mace in hand, she made herself a projectile. Astrid held her breath in anticipation.

"Did she land her strike?" Astrid squinted her eyes to get a better look, Erna was a blur of motion for the last few feet before she struck the demon lord's head, and it was difficult to make out the details, as the demon was so big it was like trying to watch an eagle land on a mountain top.

"Aye, she did," Jokul cheered.

Erna's mace had split the demon lord's rocky head, but no blood seeped from the wound, no gore was to be found inside it. Erna stood on its head and tried to free her mace, which appeared to be wedged so deeply it was trapped.

"She's in trouble now," Jokul stated.

Astrid exhaled with a puff, a moment before her wings flashed into existence and spread out from her back. "Gods, no."

"Sister, wait," he said.

Astrid flew as best as she could. Regardless of the pain that spiked with each extension, she sailed across the rubble of the town toward the demon lord and hooked two hands under Erna's armpits and lifted her out of danger just before the demon's hand would have reached her. Astrid could hardly bear the pain of flight, let alone with the increased weight of another body. Rising out of the demon's way, Astrid quickly hit her flight ceiling and together they began to drop.

Erna fought to get free of Astrid's arms, and when she came loose, both women were able to fly better, landing safely behind the wreckage of what used to be a home.

"Do you seek to get us both killed?" Erna wasted no time in reprimanding Astrid.

"You must be mad!" Astrid responded in shock. "Had I done nothing that thing would've grabbed you. It would be chewing your bones as we speak."

"Such assumptions—"

"Erna, if the gods were not depending on us, I would gladly sit here and watch you eaten. In fact, if you do not answer my questions, I might still."

A moment of silence passed as the ground shook.

"What is it you want to know, Astrid?"

"Why do the gods hide from these demons? Why don't they fight these things themselves? Destroying one should be child's play to them."

"So new are you to the world, young Astrid, that you have not had time to realize."

"Realize what?" Astrid yelled over a rumble.

"Our gods are the old ones now. They are worshiped less and less every day."

"So—"

"So without worship and adulation, a god loses their power and becomes, well, I presume they become mortal."

Astrid grabbed Erna by the shoulders and shook her. "You lie."

"Lie? Why would I?"

"The gods cannot simply lose their powers and stations."

"No? Then why would Odin bring an end to the Valkyrie?" Erna sneered.

"He did so because of our blood. With no Valkyrie, there would be no maiden's blood for the Ashvolk to consume."

"Why, Astrid? Why would he, father of the gods, fear a simple demon?"

"He—"

"Because he has grown weak. Even the Allfather sees the end of his reign. The time has come when a new deity will rule us. Odin, in his endless selfishness, tries to hold on to a crown that is no longer his. Odin's end is here."

Astrid shoved Erna away.

Erna has to be wrong. There's no way what she says is true, Astrid refused to believe it.

"The Ashvolk were once a weak demon clan, just seers and spies, but it was that ability to sense the coming tides that gave them the hint that an end was approaching. They acted on it years before any god in Asgard knew."

Astrid hated Erna's words, and more, she hated the woman who spoke them. *This is blasphemy.* As Astrid stared at Erna, she began to wonder just whose side she was on.

Another crash made both women jump. The demon lord was further out of the ground now, up to midtorso; the cold had only somewhat slowed its ascension. If possible, Astrid thought she spied a look of frustration on the thing's beastly, flat face when it slammed its fists into the soil.

"Yrsa," Astrid whispered. "I should have given her the armor."

Erna sneered again. "This armor, it is much better than my original. It has all the power and none of the ties to Asgard."

"What do you mean?"

"Odin severed Freyja's connection to the Valkyrie in the tomb. By doing so, Freyja could not recall her to Valhalla or Fólkvangr. The woman had her freedom but never had a chance to enjoy it." Erna shook her head. "The gods cannot manipulate me now."

A new, deeper rumble drew Astrid's eyes to the sky. It was thunder. The snow fell faster, and now the sky flashed. When a bright branch of lighting split the sky, Astrid got an idea.

"I know what to do."

Jokul jogged up to Astrid and Erna, his battle-axe in one hand, Astrid's spear in his other. With him were three men of Grømstad who had taken up arms and five additional bandits who had clearly already faced hard combat this day by the injuries they had.

"This place shakes so much it was difficult to circle round," Jokul stated.

"Did you see many other survivors?"

"There are at least a dozen or so bandits hiding back there." He pointed at a pair of houses that had collapsed into each other. "Could be more."

Boom.

The thunder was followed with a rumble from the direction of the demon lord.

"Listen to that, Astrid. Reminds me of the time you, me, and Hak got caught in the storm while fishing, you know, that one time the lightning struck Hak's sword where it sat against the trees."

"Aye, precisely what I was thinking, Jokul." Astrid beamed. "Where is Emmerich?"

"Dead by now, I wager," one of the bandits, a man who wore a fresh cut across his forehead, replied.

"Really?" Astrid thought the news would make her happy, but it did not. "Who is in charge then?"

"You?" the bandit answered hesitantly.

"Good. Gather your men tell them to collect every spear or polearm they can carry. Only the ones that are fully metal; leave anything that has wood. I want to see arms full. Start piling them at the Grömsala."

"What would you have me do, Astrid?" Jokul asked.

She had an important job left; she needed someone she could trust but did not want to waste Jokul's fighter's prowess on this task.

"I must admit, I am beginning to wish Warren were here."

"Why? So you could chain him to a grain silo, use him as bait for that...that thing?" Warren's voice was steeped in anger; he seemed less concerned about the colossal demon that crawled out of the earth than he was Astrid's response.

"Warren..."

He walked into the open, his chains dragging and rattling behind him.

"Get down, man!" Jokul motioned for him to take cover.

"No."

"Your foolishness threatens us all. Again I say, get down."

Jokul grasped Warren's shoulder as he stepped up to the group and tried to force him to take cover, but he resisted and a test of strength began. Speechless, Astrid watched, and when Warren finally swatted Jokul's hands off him, he turned his full attention to the large man who had stepped up to face off with him.

"He's yours?" Jokul asked his sister, chest to chest with Warren, who had stepped on some debris to make himself equal in height.

"Aye, he is," Astrid replied.

"Then I will spare his life...this one time."

"Spare my life? I have killed barbarians like you by the dozens," Warren boasted.

"Barbarians?"

The word reignited Jokul's willingness to brawl, and Astrid knew by the look on her brother's face, that if she did nothing, there would be bloodshed, so she separated them with a shove.

"Control your men, Astrid, or I will," Erna griped as she watched the demon lord continue to rise.

"Elder?" Warren said with a look of shock.

Erna peered over her shoulder and smiled at Warren, her black hair scattered across her face and speckled with snow.

"You are young and—"

"Beautiful?" Erna answered then returned her gaze at the demon. "No darkness to conceal me now, is there? After all these years...am I what you expected, Warren?"

"You're a Valkyrie."

"Enough," Astrid interrupted.

"Enough?" Warren looked at her crossly.

"Warren," Astrid snipped. "You are right, your elder is-was-is a Valkyrie. I will explain later. First, you must tell me, is Yrsa well?"

"No thanks to you she is." Warren crossed his arms and his chains rattled.

"What do you mean, little man?" Jokul grumbled, as he stretched and flexed his large arm muscles.

"What happened?" Astrid gagged, nearly sick to her stomach. "Did the cellar cave in?"

"No. The cellar held, but they are no longer there. They fled on one of Hammond's carts. I instructed them to hide at the old ruins north-west of here."

"Good."

Astrid took a breath of relief before Warren raised his voice and continued, "No, not good. Not at all, Astrid." Warren's voice grew angrier, and with his rage, the shackles rattled more.

"Would you remove those cursed chains? The demon lord looks this way each time they clatter. He can set fire to things with his eyes, you know," Erna complained. "I'm shocked he hasn't set you ablaze already."

"Warren, I know you are mad that I left you there—"

"Left me there!" he yelled as Jokul broke the chain attached to his right wrist. "You chained me to a wall after seducing me. You decided for me, a veteran of many wars, whether I would fight or not today."

"I had to." Astrid looked away.

"I should kill you!"

After he detached the second chain, Jokul placed his sword to the Warren's throat. "Watch your tongue," Jokul warned.

"You should know something, Astrid. Your decision—your selfish decision—it cost Helen her life."

The strength left her legs and she nearly fell over.

"Emmerich came looking for Yrsa." Warren was overwhelmed with emotion, and his voice rose. "He butchered Helen in front of us. I could not save her, and do you know why, Astrid?"

"Because I chained you to the wall." Astrid choked.

"Yes! Damn you!"

"Warren, had I not chained you...*you* too would be dead."

Warren's hands felt like a pair of arrows when they slammed into her chest and he shoved her. Any other time, Astrid would have overflowed with the need to fight back, but not now. She knew she deserved the brunt of his anger and more. Back on her feet, Astrid stepped to Warren and waved her brother's blade down.

"Go ahead, Warren, strike me again."

Warren pulled back a fist, but just held it there, where it shook with all his pent-up fury.

"Hit me."

Warren's fist tightened further as he spit, "Damn you."

Slowly, his fist loosened, his hand dropped, and his breathing slowed.

"I will not hit the woman I love."

"Good choice," Jokul interjected.

A loud clap of thunder chased another large branch of lightning; the storm was directly over head now.

"Done?" Erna asked.

With a long exhale, Warren answered, "Aye."

"Very well. We need to act. Now or never, friends," Erna said.

"Agreed," Astrid added, her eyes still locked with Warren's. "I need you to help me. Can you do that?"

Warren paused a moment; it seemed like forever before he agreed.

"I need you to save the families, get them out of their cellars, and move them far from town."

"I can fight."

"Then fight for these trapped people, Warren. They need someone to save them when all I have offered is—"

"Pain and suffering?" Erna finished for her. "The demons are here because of you, Astrid, do not forget that. To think, Freyja nagged that I made too many mistakes…"

"Jokul, find soldiers and bandits—any man willing to fight and send them to the Grömsala. Now go!"

"Here." Jokul handed Astrid her spear. "Stay safe."

Astrid nodded her thanks then watched as everyone ran off. She was alone with Erna again, who continued to watch the demon lord, her back to Astrid.

"No orders for me?" Erna asked.

"I need you to keep it distracted until we are ready to fight it. Together."

"Is that all?"

"As long as you keep out of its—"

Astrid's words stopped when the Ashvolk lord heaved a handful of rocks and debris at the remains of the home she and Erna hid behind. In the blink of an eye, the structure was leveled and the two women were knocked to the ground.

Buried under the detritus, Astrid pushed up to her hands and knees and scurried away to another wall to keep covered. Erna was already missing. Astrid looked to the sky, expecting to see the elder-turned-Valkyrie in flight again, but the heavens were empty of all but snow.

When she looked back down, she spotted movement. Erna was covered with dirt and wood, buried deeper than Astrid, and under a heavy support beam from the house; she needed help. Astrid dashed out to her, clasped her hands around both of Erna's wrists, and tugged hard. Erna was yanked free but covered in a thick layer of muck.

"Are you hurt?" Astrid asked.

"Had we been mortal that would have killed us."

"Nevertheless, I do not wish to have that happen again. We need to keep moving."

The two zigzagged around damaged homes until they were at a safer distance.

"Could it have heard us speaking, Erna?"

"I do not know."

Astrid watched the demon abruptly cease its efforts to haul itself out of the ground and, instead, drill its fists down at its sides: it looked like it wanted to loosen the earth surrounding its trapped body. Astrid had hoped not to face the monster at its fullest height, free to move about, but now that had become less likely.

"There's no time left."

At that moment, the giant demon surged up, breaking its confinement. The ground buckled under its force, sending out a shockwave. Astrid and Erna were both knocked over with such energy that they slid and rolled backward over their shoulders. Rock from the area near the demon blew high into the sky in chunks as large as boulders, some even the size of homes.

"Gods, it's free," Erna whispered as she stood. "We must move or be eaten."

"Move then!" Astrid screamed.

Astrid summoned her wings and began to fly away. At first, she found it easy to avoid the rock in the sky, as the larger boulders were simple to spot and did not go as high or far, but the smaller pieces showered down like hail, pelting her and Erna so hard they lost altitude and crashed into the grass near the forest's edge.

"I've had enough!" Astrid yelled as she faced the gigantic demon from across the field. "No more running."

Astrid pulled her sword and swung it into the closest tree. When it fell, she chopped at it again.

"Trim that end, make it flat."

"Why?"

"Battering rams. We strike together."

Erna did as she was told, and in no time the two Valkyrie had a twenty-foot long log of wood each.

Once more they each took flight, slowly at first, to readjust to the added weight. Flying as fast as they could, the two women circled as they climbed into the sky above the demon lord, and when Astrid shouted, the attack commenced.

With the cool air and the flakes of snow crashing into her face, Astrid tightened her grip on the tree and released a battle cry in preparation of the collision. Erna was right where she should be; although she had to dodge one of the demon lord's hands, it looked like she would strike at the same time, as planned.

The two trees collided with the demon's head simultaneously. The force, which was hard enough to demolish most things, only cracked its head slightly on both sides; pieces of brittle rock fell to the demon's shoulders and the ground. The impact sent both Erna and Astrid flying forward, where they slammed into the demon's skull along with the wood. Astrid felt as if she had been punched in the back and then thrown face first into the ground. Dazed, she folded over the thing's massive shoulders and back. As she fell, Astrid saw Erna also fall but forward, to the ground at the thing's feet.

Archers fired a volley as it bent over to pick up Erna, but their arrows did no damage. When the demon was nearly to Erna's motionless body, it staggered and fell to its hands.

Astrid and Erna had rattled its senses.

When Astrid stood, she was behind the demon lord, not far from its left foot. Although dazed, she saw an opportunity. Her family sword in hand, she swung at the demon's heel. To her surprise, she sliced it open and out spilled a putrid-smelling, thick, red ooze. The stench was so strong she had to cover her nose and gag.

Before Astrid could swing her sword again, the demon lord kicked out with its other foot, and shoveled her back several hundred feet.

A crash of thunder rang out as she climbed haggardly from the wreckage of a small home.

"Erna!" Astrid shouted. "Erna!"

Astrid's eyes fixed on Erna; she wasn't moving. The demon lord had quickly recovered and was lowering his head toward her. *Gods no.* Astrid could feel it in her heart, the demon was about to eat Erna, and there was nothing she could do to stop him.

CHAPTER 66

Spit, thick as amber honey, dripped from the demon lord's teeth; if Erna did not move soon, she would be dead. Astrid tried to fly but her wings would not flap. The sound of horse hooves approached, *is that Sleipnir, I hear? Would Odin himself come to save Erna?*

The demon lord turned its face, and Astrid saw what it did, Jokul drove a wagon pulled by two horses directly at the giant demon's head.

"Jokul!" Astrid cheered when her brother dove off the wagon a moment before it made impact.

The horses galloped directly into the demon lord's mouth, one straight down its throat while the other was shredded by its jagged teeth. The cart bounced up, crashing into its eyes, a perfect distraction.

Astrid watched her brother move quickly, picking Erna off the ground and fleeing. Above them, the demon lord reeled backward. From its mouth spilled chunks of bloody horsemeat, the lower half of a leg striking the side of Jokul's shoulder.

The demon lord's sudden movements had created a thick dust cloud of which the wind blew, obscuring Astrid's vision. She tracked Jokul's escape for as long as she could, but quickly lost him.

"Odin bless you, Brother."

"Where's your sister?" Erna asked when she awoke.

Jokul placed Erna on her feet before he answered. "She was kicked across town. *You* were almost eaten."

"Was I?"

"Aye." Jokul scanned the area. "No worries, I saved you."

"I figured as much," she said, wiping the dirt from her face.

"When this battle is over, I will tell you the tale so you might share it with—"

Enraged, the demon lord pounded his fists on the ground, and the jolt blew over the homes that remained and sent Jokul and Erna sailing through the air.

"Cover your eyes!" Erna screamed.

Jokul had already spotted the storm of dust that blew his way, and produced a hidden scarf from within his furs. He wrapped his face and ducked his head. When the cloud struck, it was filled with pebbles and smelled like ash.

"Where is it?" Jokul asked when two more thumps on the ground rattled the area.

"I don't see it." Erna's voice fell off when she began to cough.

Jokul heard Astrid calling to him from a distance. He moved, trying to look for her, but the dust was still too thick to see through.

"Astrid!" he yelled back.

"Here!"

She was close.

"Astrid!" Jokul called out again.

"I think I see her," Erna whispered.

A hand on his shoulder, turned him.

"I found you, Brother," Astrid said.

"We need to go now," Erna urged.

"Take my hands, both of you...now!"

Erna and Jokul joined hands with Astrid, and as they did, she lifted off. The trio was not five feet from the ground before they were struck back down. Crashing in a tangle of limbs, the three once more tried to flee as the dust cloud cleared and the demon's eyes became apparent.

Jokul watched Astrid straighten up, a look of determination in her eyes.

"Stand back," she said.

Astrid spread her wings, but her right wing was not moving—he could see it. It was broken and hung lifelessly at Astrid's side.

"I cannot feel my one wing."

"It's ruined," Erna said pointing.

"Then, Erna, you must fly us free," Jokul commanded.

Erna summoned her wings again, but as she spread them, one of the demon lord's tentacles sprung out of the ground and pierced the left like a spike. Before Erna could move, more tentacles were upon her, quickly grasping each wing.

"Off me, demon," Erna shouted.

"Erna! Odin, no!" Jokul gasped.

"Astrid! Jokul! Help me!"

CHAPTER 67

EVERYTHING SEEMED TO SLOW. ASTRID looked at Erna, then across town to where the demon lord knelt, his hand dug into the ground. Although his face was inhuman, at that moment, he bore an easily detected smile.

Astrid swung her sword at the nearest tentacle, and the thing easily severed in two. As she lifted her sword to swing again, Astrid watched the tentacles that grasped Erna's wings pull them in opposite directions until they came free with a stomach-churning pop.

Astrid knew they were losing.

To her left, Jokul was struggling to stand. To her right, Erna lay severely injured and shrieking in pain. Directly before her, the demon lord stared; Astrid had no options left.

Sword lifted high and steady, she pointed it forward. If this was the end, if she was to be consumed, it would be with weapon in hand. Astrid would cut her way down the demon lord's gullet if she had too; she was ready to die.

The screams of a hundred or more men packed her ears, as the demon lord lunged at her. Astrid first thought it was the cries of dying men, like she had heard on so many battlefields, all calling to her to be carried off to Valhalla. *What a fitting sound to hear at my own death*, she thought, but then the shouts became clearer. They were not cries for help; they were battle cries.

The survivors of Grømstad, bandits from Emmerich's army, and kingdom soldiers who had attended the bazaar, poured in from all directions.

The men flanked the demon lord, each carrying multiple spears. Astrid wished she could commend the bandits for their bravery—she would if any lived to the conclusion of the encounter—if she lived too.

The survivors charged the gigantic demon, spearing its rocky flesh. Astrid saw one bandit leap up in a pitiful attempt to pierce the demon lord's face, only to be snatched midair and eaten.

"They fight for you now, Astrid," Jokul grunted.

"Why would they?"

"Is it not clear?" Jokul asked, back on his feet though hunched. "What did Father tell us once, after a battle where he lost many men?"

"Never question the loyalty of men who are willing to die for you."

"Never question, only—" Jokul began.

"Command and respect them."

Astrid summoned her Valkyrie spear and raised it high. As a simple command formed in her mind, the demon lord swept its last elongated tentacle over them.

More men advanced from the rear of the demon, this time in ranks, three lines of twenty or more; she could not count them in the chaos. As she drug Erna away from the battle, Astrid watched the lines begin their attack, led by one man.

"Erna, where's your spear?"

Seated with her bloodied back to a wall of debris, Erna could hardly speak through the pain.

"Summon it now, I need it."

Erna collapsed onto her side and groaned in response.

"Do it!"

Erna closed her eyes and drew her legs up to her stomach.

"You wanted this, Erna, you wanted to become a Valkyrie again, and this was the risk you accepted. You may die today, but to die like this, huddled behind the wreckage of some poor farmer's home—do you really want that?"

"I know this person."

"What?"

"I know whose home this was. An honorable man with a sweet daughter."

"And where are they now?"

Erna winced in pain as she sat back up.

"I watched him die earlier, fighting the lesser Ashvolk."

Astrid stared down at Erna. She did not say another word; all she did was offer her hand—which Erna took.

"You may have my spear."

Erna summoned her holy spear and handed it over. Once Astrid had both spears, she placed them dull end to dull end and summoned a golden glow, encasing both spears with a shine so bright they were momentarily washed from sight. When the glow receded, the two spears were one. Now almost twice her height, the weapon had become something more—and Astrid had a plan for it.

"How did you know to do that?"

Astrid did not answer; she was unsure.

"Erna, my brother—"

"Go, Astrid, I'll help him. You fight. You win this."

While they talked, the demon lord had turned to face the ranks of spearmen who had cluttered his back with their long, metal spears. Looking across town, Astrid found the man who led the brave soldiers; it was Warren.

Astrid could not fathom how Warren knew her plan, or how his actions could have matched hers, but there was no time to waste. She raced toward a grain silo that had been tipped over and now rested precariously on an old damaged home, as she watched the demon lord kick and swat at the men, killing them three and four at a time. There would be no one left to fight soon; the force she saw rush in had already been reduced to a quarter of their number. Only Warren's men, in the three ranks, had yet to be scattered.

As Astrid ran up the side of the tipped over silo, she was careful not to lose her footing. The snow fell steadily, thunder rumbled in the distance, and the smell of death mixed with a robust winter dampness in the air. Grey clouds filled the dawning sky. From her height, Astrid could see the bodies, hundreds of them cluttered town. *Why aren't they glowing?* she paused to think. *Where are their souls?*

The Ashvolk lord launched his fingers out from his hand like four giant arrows, the tendril-like spikes crushing all in their path. The destruction swallowed Warren up; Astrid could no longer see him, or tell if he was alive or dead.

Had her wing not been broken, she would have flown. Now, all she could do was jump, so she launch herself toward the demon's shoulders. Astrid leapt from the end of the fallen grain silo at the demon's back, the double spear gripped tightly with both hands.

In that moment, one that she figured might be her last, she called to the Allfather.

"Odin, hear me, I give my life to save yours."

The end of the spear sunk into the thick, coal-colored skin of the demon lord like a finger into fresh bread. Astrid had hit her mark. Before she could release the shaft of the spear, the demon had reached around its back and snatched Astrid from where she hung. The rough skin of its palm scratched her armor, cutting groves so deep she thought her skin must be scored as well.

As the demon raised Astrid to its face, she did not feel fear. When she heard Warren's screams from below, she did not feel sadness. When she spotted Jokul, his battle-axe in hand, she did not feel pride. All Astrid felt was tranquility.

The sky darkened again and as the demon lord pulled her toward its mouth, Astrid's hair began to rise, strand by strand.

Thunder boomed and a massive bolt of lightning struck the doubled Valkyrie spear in the demon's back. Just as she had hoped, the bolt forked, and struck each spear down the thing's back and through its legs.

The flash of lightning blinded her. Gone was the demon lord's gaping maw, its ooze covered teeth, its brown writhing tongue; all Astrid saw was white.

CHAPTER 68

WARREN WATCHED FROM BELOW AS the lightning bolt struck the demon lord. The boom of thunder was unlike any he had heard before; born straight from the gods, it deafened his ears. But his eyes never left Astrid. Clutched in the demon's hand, her arms twitched lifelessly.

Please be alive. Please, Astrid, please be alive.

Hobbled and unsteady on its feet, thick, white vapors rose from the enormous demon as it began to sway like a drunkard. Not sure where it might fall, Warren shouted for the men to run, but he did not move. Even if it meant forfeiting his own life, Warren would stay until he knew Astrid's fate.

The force of the demon lord crashing to its knees shook the ground worse than the quakes had. Warren should have lost his footing, but resolve kept him on his feet.

Another bolt of lightning struck the demon lord, and this time, its eyes rolled back in its head, and a cloud of vaporous air blew out its mouth. Its hand opened as its arm shook, and Astrid fell free. Across the slippery snow and scattered debris, Warren raced to catch her, but she was out of his reach, and she crashed into a pile of broken stone.

Warren scooped her up into his arms and held her tight as he fled to the forest. Behind him, he heard the giant demon crumble to the ground.

Is it dead? No…that's a question for someone else. I am done, done with this place, this battle, and especially done with all this death.

"How did you know?" Astrid's voice was weak; she sounded like so many of the dying men whose hands he had held at the ends of battles.

"Know what?"

"My plan."

There had been a voice, soft and sure, inside his head. The voice told him of Astrid's plan, every detail, but it had not been her voice.

"I don't know, Astrid. It was just meant to be."

"The gods..." Astrid's voice grew fainter. "They favor us, Warren."

Astrid went lifeless in his arms. She bleed from cuts on her legs and arms and through various cracks in her armor. A bruise on her face had puffed out the corner of her lower lip and was caked with dirt, but she was alive.

"They favor us?" Warren asked aloud, as he gazed at her. "We shall see, my love."

EPILOGUE

Deep in a dark forest, Astrid awoke. She could smell snow and pine trees before her other senses returned; they were welcome scents, ones that always made her happy. Her eyes fluttered open and she focused on her brother Jokul as he leaned over her. He smiled. *Could we have actually won this battle?*

"What happened?" Her voice was weak, as if she had spent a day screaming, but it was loud enough for her brother to hear.

"You were injured. It's true, even the mighty Astrid the White can be felled in combat." Jokul playfully smirked as he spoke.

Astrid was wrapped in long furs, and lying atop a bed of leaves in the snow. She wrapped her arms around herself and spotted a glow pulsating in the distance.

"Fire?"

"The town. Destroyed," Jokul nodded. "You watch it burn."

"Then we failed, we lost it…" Astrid dropped her head back. "Where are the other survivors?"

"Few escaped with us."

"Yrsa, I was with her…"

Jokul looked confused.

"Does she live?" Astrid finally asked.

"She does."

Astrid sighed with relief. "And Father? Hak, Ulf, Vignor?"

"Sister, Birka is gone…" Jokul shook his head and scratched his thick blonde beard as he spoke.

She tried to sit up, but her stomach and chest ached. Finally propping herself up against the broken stone wall behind her, she looked around.

"Where are my arms and armor? My sword, Jokul?"

"I have them all."

Warren's voice came out of the darkness before he did. As soon as she saw him, Astrid remembered. That glow, those fires—that was not Birka that burned; that was Grømstad.

"I just completed my rounds. No sign of the demons."

"Very good." Jokul nodded.

More and more, the reality of what had occurred returned to her. Astrid remembered the lightning strikes, her body ablaze with ripping pain, and the bright white light that had warmly enveloped her. "Is it dead?"

"It is, Astrid. Odin's lightning killed it." Jokul patted Astrid on the leg as he spoke.

"Are you sure?" She looked at Warren as he steadily held her gaze.

"It's dead." His voice was void of emotion. "I went back. Some dozen or more of Grømstad's men had hacked its head off with pickaxes. I promise you, the thing is dead. You almost died too, Astrid."

She heard his words but did not respond; she was listening to the sound of running water and the hoot of a distant owl. Although sore from head to toe, Astrid felt content for the first time in days.

"Erna healed you and your brother before she left," Warren revealed.

"Where is Yrsa?" Astrid turned to her brother.

"Worry not. Our sister is here."

Jokul pointed off to the side where a campfire was burning. The outline of twenty or more people flickered before the fire. After she distinguished one of the seated outlines as that of her sister, she smiled and looked back at Warren.

"Erna healed me?"

"Yes," he replied.

Astrid slowly looked back at Jokul, and asked, "She left? You let her go?"

"She made us promise we would not stop her from leaving once she healed you. She's gone, Sister."

"Where did she say she was going?"

"After trying to convince many of us that the aid we received during the fight was not from Odin, but another...more powerful god, she alleged that there was unfinished business she needed to attend to."

Astrid sat up further, cleared her throat, and gathered her thoughts.

"Unfinished? Could Erna be searching for Yrsa's child? Could the baby still be alive?"

Warren and Jokul both looked surprised.

"Astrid, Erna clearly had her own concerns here. Why would she seek out our sister's baby?" Jokul asked.

"Freyja whispered words to me before I left her—a secret I was not meant to remember unless I defeated the demons." Astrid drew a deep breath before she continued. "The child is not only of Yrsa, but of something else, something...powerful."

THE END

The story continues.

THE WOLF WILL SWALLOW THE SUN will be released in 2018.

ABOUT THE AUTHOR

Kevin James Breaux is an award-winning author and artist. He has nearly ten years of professional writing credit, including short stories and novels and has completed seven books.

He is a member of the Horror Writers Association and the Science Fiction & Fantasy Writers of America.

Breaux has a growing fan base, including foreign markets in Great Britain and other parts of Europe, and has never stopped striving to better himself as an author as well as to encourage his fellow writers.

Write Makes Might!

Author website: www.kevinbreaux.com
Facebook: www.facebook.com/KevinJamesBreauxAuthor
Twitter: @kevinbreaux
Author Blog: kevinjamesbreaux.blogspot.com
Book Blog: www.lbifw.com
e-mail:kbreaux23@yahoo.com

Made in United States
Troutdale, OR
08/04/2023